ABOUT THIS BOOK

TAMING THE BEAST BY NADIRAH FOXX

Stealing from a mafia boss is the dumbest thing Izzie Itzae has ever done. Getting lost in the mountains is a close second. But both events pale compared to meeting the one male she's not ready for. As a nagual shifter waiting for her first transformation, Izzie's anger and frustration grow every day—bonding with her soul mate is the last thing she needs.

Hunter James knows bonding is exactly what Izzie needs, and he's more than ready for her. He's dreamed of her often, while his shaman grandfather's had visions of the female who can break the family curse. Hunter doesn't care that Izzie's a late bloomer—in fact, he's eager for the challenge. As long as Izzie can handle his brand of proclivities, he's sure he can tame her inner beast.

When they meet, the chemistry is instantaneous, no matter how much Izzie tries to deny it. But obstacles abound, including Hunter's ex-girlfriend, who will do anything to get Hunter back in her bed, including stooping to dark magic.

A threat to Izzie's life is the ultimate test for her. To save herself and Hunter, she must choose—cling to her stubbornness or give in to her heart's truth. But only one will tame her beast.

PLANS LAID BARE BY J.D. NELSON

Mavis LeGrand had always suspected her grandfather was a little off, and when he suddenly moved them to a remote town in Utah, her suspicions rose. Nevertheless, she lived a typical life—high school, friends, and eventually college in the small but safe town he'd chosen. But when she finds his journal after a life-altering accident, she learns the hard truth—her grandfather isn't human, and neither is she.

She also discovers his plans to use her power in the evil scheme he's been arranging since her infancy.

Knowing her very existence depends on him never finding her, Mavis makes her escape and hitches a ride with the devilishly handsome half incubus, Cameron DeSalle. Despite her initial trepidation, she instantly feels a connection with him and believes him when he says he'll do everything in his power to protect her.

Mavis finds herself falling for Cameron, the ice in her veins melting away with every heated look and stolen kiss. But whether Cameron feels the same desire for her or it's his incubus nature bringing them closer, Mavis isn't sure. The only thing she knows for certain is until they defeat her grandfather, they'll never have a happily ever after.

SHIFT OF FATE BY VICTORIA ESCOBAR

Audrey Smith has never had a place to call home, living as a nomad because of what she is and what she's not. A shifter without a shift, she doesn't belong with a pride, but she's too much "other" to blend in with humans. Her last attempt turned her into a science project. And finding a mate? Forget about it. She'd always been told she wasn't shifter enough for it to happen.

When Audrey totals her car and awakens in Havenwood Falls, she immediately makes plans to leave. But the sexier-than-sin paramedic who pulled her from the wreckage has other ideas, claiming her as his. But based on everything she knows, that's impossible.

Nicholas Jordan never expected to find his mate and settle down. If she lived in Havenwood Falls, he would have met her already. Then Audrey literally crashes into his life. Not only does he want her, but he *needs* her. She belongs to him, and he to her.

Accepting Nicholas's claim would betray everything Audrey's ever believed about herself. But the longer she denies the mating bond, the more dangerous it becomes for them both, putting their lives—and the pride's future—at risk.

HAVENWOOD FALLS SIN & SILK VOLUME ONE

A HAVENWOOD FALLS SIN & SILK COLLECTION

NADIRAH FOXX   JD NELSON   VICTORIA ESCOBAR

HAVENWOOD FALLS SIN & SILK BOOKS

Taming the Beast by Nadirah Foxx

Plans Laid Bare by J.D. Nelson

Shift of Fate by Victoria Escobar

Stolen Wishes by Victoria Flynn

Damned Allure by Justine Winter

Savage Salvation by Kristie Cook

Dark Seduction by Michele G. Miller & R.K. Ryals

Soul Laid Bare by J.D. Nelson

Stray With Me by E.J. Fechenda

Chase the Flames by Desiree Lafawn

Prison of Asria by Randi Cooley Wilson

More books releasing on a monthly basis

Also try the signature line, Havenwood Falls, and the historical paranormal line, Legends of Havenwood Falls

Stay up to date at www.HavenwoodFalls.com

TAMING THE BEAST

NADIRAH FOXX

~ A Havenwood Falls Sin & Silk Novella ~

HavEnwood Falls

sin & silk

Taming the Beast

SF BENSON WRITING AS
NADIRAH FOXX

Sometimes submission is a good thing.

CHAPTER 1

IZZIE

It's just my luck to end up in the middle of nowhere without a damn cell signal. For the last hour, I've been trying to make heads or tails of a map—how primitive. Leaning my palms against the SUV hood, I push my dark hair out of my face and think about how this was supposed to be an uncomplicated trip allowing me to check out the fall colors and escape.

The plan seemed simple enough. Catch a flight out of New York, rent a car (now with an empty gas tank, although it was full an hour ago), and hide away in my best friend Senora's cabin. In all fairness, she warned me the roads could be tricky, but I didn't listen. Thought I could rely on my phone's GPS. Staring down at the device, I realize my stupidity. I forgot mountains and signal strength don't mix.

I'm ready to pitch the damned thing when a distant rumbling grabs my attention. A huge pickup truck comes into sight. The shiny black vehicle stops inches from me, and a female jumps out of the cab. The tall redhead, dressed in jeans and a tank top, comes around the front of the truck.

"Everything okay?" she asks with a wide smile. Her sparkling gray-blue eyes appear friendly, but my guard, as always, is up.

"I'm good," I blurt, not wanting her to get too close for both our sakes. "Just need to figure out where I'm going."

"Really?" The stranger points to the car. "You're out of gas and lost."

"How the—" My words freeze when I notice the pendant around her neck—a green jade coyote. The familiar nagual pulse passes through me, and the tension rolls off my shoulders. She's a kindred spirit. Most likely she took one look at the map and figured out my problem.

"I'm sure you can take care of yourself, but it'll be dark soon," she offers. "Nights can be freezing, not to mention the other beasts roaming these parts."

Confrontations aren't ideal for me. At least until my transformation happens. Then I'll be able to go up against other creatures—even other naguals if needed. "I suppose I could use a ride."

"Where you headed?"

"Grand Junction."

The female laughs. "Sorry. You *are* lost. That's north of here and about two hours away. How about this? I'll take you to town, where you can stay overnight. In the morning, I'll point you in the right direction."

It's tempting to say no, but fate speeds up time, sending the sun into a quick descent. The choice is made for me. I open the back door, drag out my suitcase, and roll it over to the truck.

The redhead hops in and cranks the ignition. Over the interior noise, she introduces herself. "My name's Cheresse."

"Izzie."

"What brings you to Colorado?"

"Just a getaway." It's all I'm offering. Being on the run makes trust precarious.

"I get it." Cheresse gives me a sideways glance. "We all have secrets, but if you want to share . . . Just saying." She slips into silence.

After a few miles, Cheresse leaves the state highway and turns onto a two-lane county road lined on both sides by forest. The welcome sign for Havenwood Falls comes into sight. As the truck passes the layered stone and black metal lettering marker, my pendant—a jade quetzal—heats. The sensation startles me. Automatically, I touch my neck.

Common sense would have been to tuck the totem beneath my shirt —avoiding the possibility of any knowledgeable nagual discovering I'm powerless—but I don't always act with sagacity. I'm a would've-should've-could've type of female. Unfortunately, the gesture draws Cheresse's attention.

"Don't worry. That's normal. My totem heats up every time I enter town, too. It's just the magic here."

"Magic?" Whoa. A town with magic? So the tales I heard growing up were true. Although I grew up with shapeshifters and shamans, I had no experience with the mystical arts. I thought the stories of a magical town were as wacky as the "tobacco" the elders smoked.

"Havenwood Falls is a safe place for supernaturals. You'll need a visitor's tattoo to remain in town."

"Why? I don't do ink. Nothing against those who do. It's just not my thing."

"Whether it's your thing or not isn't the point. The tattoos let the leaders know who's in town. For some of us, there's an extra benefit to having one."

Somehow I seriously doubt if some ink is going to help my situation, but I'll play along. "Like?"

"Take the vampires, for instance. It allows them to go out in the sun." Cheresse looks over at me. "Before you ask, it won't help you."

My defenses immediately go up. This female nagual can't possibly know anything about me.

"I can't read your thoughts, but I sense your immaturity. If you don't mind my saying, you seem a little old not to have transformed yet. You're what, twenty-two? Twenty-three?" Cheresse's tone isn't condescending, just annoying.

"Almost twenty-five," I mutter, strumming my fuchsia-colored nails against the door.

Transformation usually happens for nagual females at twenty-one. So, yeah, I'm a little late. Before my grandmother died, she told me it wasn't unusual to mature later in life. I'm not worried. Just pissed. All the damned time. It's an unfortunate trait of an immature nagual—intense anger as my beast struggles to emerge. Mine has been trying for three years. Anger doesn't adequately describe my fury.

Nothing eradicates the intense negative feelings crawling beneath my skin. Mom also warned me, before she died, that there would be days like this. The closer the age of metamorphosis gets—puberty for naguals—the more erratic my emotions. Maybe my birthday, in a week, will end this constant roller coaster of emotions.

I bite my tongue and hang on to the comments I'd like to throw at Cheresse.

Sadly, she doesn't know how to keep her mouth shut. "Hey, I'm sorry. Some of us are late bloomers. I had mine three years ago."

Good for you.

Chatty females like Cheresse is why I'm best friends with an empusa. The creature of the night is more likely to chat up a male victim than spend time conversing with me. Senora and I tolerate each other, giving space when it's needed. My eyes slide toward the clock on the truck dashboard—nine o'clock. *Mental note: call Senora when I get settled.*

The darkening landscape changes as we crest the ridge up ahead. Inky black mountains—replacing the riot of oranges, reds, and browns—surround the town like an ominous silhouette. Cheresse drives past a housing development decorated with eerie orange lights and ornaments. Lots of jack-o'-lanterns, cut-out ghosts, spider webs, and even a few animatronic figures adorn the yards. In my haste to leave New York, I nearly forgot about Halloween.

Cheresse takes the right fork in the road, and I get a glimpse of what the small town has to offer—a townhouse-and-villa complex, a three-story high school, a shopping center, and an apartment complex. Every structure, including the closed shops in the town square, is decked out for the holiest of holidays for supes.

The car comes to a stop in front of a large Victorian manor with its own creepy, very realistic looking cemetery in the yard. Cheresse laughs. "It's just decoration. In Havenwood Falls, we take the holiday seriously."

Instead of her words imparting comfort, they piss me off further. I don't appreciate anyone finding humor in my discomfort. My fists clench, and I give a low growl.

Cheresse pays no attention to my anger—supes rarely do. Once another supernatural discovers that I'm an immature nagual, they disregard my fury, treating me like a petulant child.

"This is Whisper Falls Inn," she points out. "You should be able to get a room for the night. Michaela Petran is the owner. She's okay, if you don't mind vamps."

"I don't." Hey, my friend is a lot worse than a vampire.

Cheresse opens the door and freezes. "Shit."

"Problem?"

"My ex . . . my *boy*friend is here. That's his bike."

"Oh," I say, exiting the cab.

Headed in our direction is a handsome, slightly muscular male with wavy black hair and penetrating turquoise eyes. The sexy scent of sandalwood tickles my nose. Our eyes meet, and his lips curl up. Then he notices Cheresse, and a frown crosses his face.

She plasters on an obviously fake smile and says, "Hi, Hunter."

He keeps a considerable distance from the ginger-haired female. Odd if they're supposed to be a couple. In a low voice, he says, "Cheresse."

The palpable tension between them is thick, but it's none of my business. Instead, I grab my suitcase and try to ignore the warmth rising out of my totem. As I get closer to him, however, a sudden flash catches my eye. Hunter's pendant—a jade puma—glows. Cheresse's totem remains solid while mine scorches my skin.

Not good.

There's only one reason for totems to react like this.

My gut tells me to run for the hills, but I'm here now, and Hunter's blocking the path to the inn. Cheresse slips past me and grabs his hand, but he doesn't try to hold hers. His focus is on me.

"I don't think we've met," he says to me.

"No. We haven't." I leave it at that. The name stitched on his jacket —Trapper—is ironic. Getting tangled up with him would indeed have me trapped.

Might be nice.

"Silly me," Cheresse chimes in. "*Isis*, this is my boyfriend Hunter. Hunter, this is my friend Isis."

If we're friends, the bimbo would know my name. "Actually, it's Izzie."

"I'm just dropping her off," Cheresse continues. "And then I'll head home and make dinner for us."

Hunter shakes his head. "Cheresse, that's not happening. You know we're not . . ."

Things just got interesting. I let my hand slip off the luggage handle.

Cheresse's voice trembles a bit. "Never mind him. We had a nasty fight, but that's over." Cheresse slips her hands around Hunter's arm and tries to pull him closer, but he doesn't budge. "Let me make it up to you, sweetheart."

Hunter gives me a *don't believe it* stare.

The clueless female persists. "Okay. We'll meet up later. I'll prepare something for Izzie and me instead. Give us a chance to get caught up."

Marijuana may be legal here, but I think this female is smoking something a lot more potent. We have nothing to catch up on.

"That's enough, Cheresse." Hunter steps away from her before touching my forearm. "It was nice to meet you, Izzie. Don't be a stranger."

He saunters toward his bike, and I notice his jacket insignia—the words "Swords of the Infernal Night" with a picture of a sword sticking through a skull. A biker. Why did I have to attract *his* attention? Motorcycle clubs are notorious for treating women poorly. The males are players, and I don't have time for those games.

"Hunter!" Cheresse calls behind him. "Don't forget our agreement."

Hunter whirls around. His hooded gaze bounces from Cheresse to me and back again. "Consider it void."

He straddles his bike, cranks it up, and drives off.

I start to ask what he meant, but think better of it. "Thanks for the lift."

Cheresse loses her polite demeanor. Looking down her nose, she says, "Don't even think about it. He's mine."

Cutting my dark eyes at the statuesque female, I'm ready to deliver my own warning. *Unnecessary.* My plans don't include the shit unfolding between the couple. Emotions, however, churn like a storm brewing beneath my skin. I don't possess powers, but I still want to beat the crap out of Cheresse. Instead of ripping into the stupid female, I roll my suitcase toward the building.

The inn's interior is an enchanting marriage of the past and the present. I'm appreciative of the modern fixtures and the centuries old architecture. Behind the desk is an attractive female with brown hair and odd gray-green eyes. Moroi. Vampire.

"Can I help you?" she says.

"You must be Michaela. I was told I could get a room."

"Great." She reaches for a large book. "How long are you staying?"

Before I can speak, my phone buzzes with a message.

"Excuse me." I remove the device from my back pocket and peer at the screen.

Senora Graves: Izzie, you need to stay away. Chekhov was here looking for you. He said if he ever sees you again, you're dead.

I'm tempted to send Senora a reply, but I can't. Kazimir Chekhov undoubtedly has his goons out, tracking my whereabouts. The man has three million reasons to find me. Senora is powerful, but I won't knowingly compromise her.

Tomorrow, I'll purchase a burner phone. For now, I need to find a more permanent place to stay. Facing the owner, I ask, "Any possibility you have something for long-term stays?"

A cautious gaze rakes over me for a moment before she says, "I have a one-bedroom cottage available. We just need to get you signed in with the Registry."

"Registry?"

Michaela leans over the counter and lowers her voice. "The Court likes to know where the supes are in town."

"How did you know?"

She points to my neck. "I'll call Addie to come do your tattoo."

~

MINUTES LATER, I'm pacing the floor instead of unpacking, unable to focus on the task. I still can't wrap my mind around the whole course of events—getting my ass lost and then hopping into a truck with a stranger. *Fuck! I left the rental car! How the hell am I going to get that back?* No way am I spending my recent fortune on somebody's used vehicle.

A knock on the cottage door disrupts my mental scolding. On the other side is a girl around my age dressed in ripped jeans, a thick black sweater, and knee-high boots. Her light brown hair is in a ponytail, and her brown eyes blink at me from behind a pair of black-framed glasses. She's carrying an old leather satchel.

Shit. Guarantee she's the chick wanting to do the damned tattoo. What kind of town requires ink to live in it? Another reason for me to hit the road as soon as the sun comes up.

"Izzie?" she asks.

"Maybe." Contempt curls in my voice.

The girl's gaze narrows briefly. "My name is Addie, and I'm here to do your tattoo. Maybe we could talk first? I'll answer the questions you have."

Tilting my head to the side, I ask, "How did you know?"

"Part of my job is answering questions for all newcomers. I assumed you'd have some." She looks over my shoulder. "Can I come in?"

I take a deep breath. This girl isn't responsible for my misfortune. Stepping to one side, I say, "Sure."

Addie enters the living room, takes a seat on the sofa, and places her bag on the floor. "I realize all of this is overwhelming. Ask me anything. I'll do my best to fill you in."

Although I should feel relieved not to be doing the ink right away, I'm not. The events of the day have me so worked up. Usually when I get this bad, I find someone to fuck me hard—get me off. What do I do here?

"I can help you," Addie says quietly.

"Sorry, I'm not into females."

The girl smiles. "I'm not offering what you think. Sit down and close your eyes."

As soon as I take a seat beside her, I feel Addie's hand on my arm followed by a tingling. It mixes with the brewing storm beneath my skin. A sense of calm dissipates the fury. I open my eyes.

"What did you do?"

"It's a lot easier for us to talk without your anger. Your emotions surround you like a cloud." The pleasantness suddenly drops from her voice. "I'm here to help you, but don't mistake my kindness."

"Got it." Last thing I need is to get on the wrong side of a *bruja*.

Addie continues, "My family, the Beaumonts, is one of the founding families of the Luna Coven. That's the main coven of witches in town."

I sit back. "Witches, vampires, nagual . . . What else lives here?"

"Shifters, mages, fae, sirens, gargoyles . . . pretty much any species and subspecies you can think of."

Interesting. Back in New York, I never knew what was lurking around me until it was usually too late. Once, I made the mistake of pissing off a *bruja*. She threatened to send me back in time to the Maya. Thankfully, Senora saved me from spending the rest of eternity with the ancestors.

"So, only supernaturals live here?"

"No. The population here is split, with half being humans. For some reason, the town tends to attract nonhumans. We do our best to keep the town secret, but it hasn't stopped supes from finding us. According to legend, it's always been that way."

Sorry, I'm not convinced. Supernaturals stay hidden for a reason. There's no way that we can coexist openly with humans. Shit happens. "Next you'll tell me that everyone here gets along."

"That's what's *supposed* to happen." Addie doesn't say anything else, and I wonder what she's hiding.

"Tell me why getting this tattoo is so important?"

Addie reaches into her bag and pulls out a tattoo kit. "All supernaturals are marked when they come to Havenwood Falls. The design signs you into the Registry so the Court knows who's in town. Visitors get a temporary tattoo."

"Court?"

"The Court of the Sun and the Moon. They try to make sure we all get along." She places the kit on the coffee table.

"And when that doesn't happen?"

"It's not something you need to worry about." Addie's gaze darts away from me. "We have our rules, mostly don't kill the humans." She looks in my direction again. "Besides that, think of Havenwood Falls as a safe place. You'll find more naguals here. They'll be able to help you through your transformation."

"You can tell?"

Addie gives me a pointed look. "Have you been listening?"

"Witch. Right." How could I forget?

Removing a sketch pad, Addie says, "Let's talk about your design. From the look of your totem, I suspect you might want something permanent. I can make it invisible if you prefer."

Her words alert me. "What about my totem?"

Addie sighs deeply and gives me a thoughtful expression. "Your soul mate is here. Because of my job, I've had to learn about all the different supernaturals and magic. From what I remember about nagual tradition, when you discover the one meant for you, your totem glows."

And there it is. The main reason I need to leave this town—the sooner, the better.

"Any idea of what design you want?"

An invisible design sounds better than having ink splattered over my skin. I'm not totally convinced that this is in my best interest, but I ask, "Can you do anything Mayan?"

"What are you thinking?"

"Something with Ixchel, the moon goddess."

Addie laughs.

"What's so funny?"

"You just told me who your mate is."

My eyes narrow. "How?"

"Your choice in tattoo. Kinich Ahau is Hunter James's design."

Damn. That's the sun god Ixchel's husband. I am so screwed.

CHAPTER 2

*I*zzie. Exquisite. Sexy. Beautiful.

She jumbles my thoughts and makes my cock hard as fuck. No surprise. I was told when I met the right one, I'd feel like this. I was talking to Michaela when the first wave of intense emotions crashed into me. Each surge, full of fury, got stronger and stronger until I couldn't fight the pull and ran out of the inn.

When I reached the porch, tendrils of anger floated toward me along with ripe pheromones. My beast lurched and pitched, rattling within me like a dog inside a cage. The object of my disturbance stood at the curb beside the biggest mistake of my life—Cheresse Winters.

About a month ago, I quit the half-breed nagual. It was a long time coming. Cheresse is too needy for me. Hell, she's too clingy for any male. We had an understanding—I'd let everyone think she broke up with me. Cheresse acting like we just had a fight, however, smells like trouble. Her ability to easily ignore facts is another reason why we had to break up. She couldn't comprehend that what we had was simply scratching an itch. She wasn't my future, my destiny. It's a fact everyone in town knows. It's why Liam and the fellas questioned why I hooked up with Cheresse in the first place.

Honestly, I considered leaving Cheresse six months ago. That's when Baba, my grandfather, told me about his vision. My soul mate was a female matching Izzie's description. That's also when I started my monthly trips. I was desperate to find her, and now she's here. And I won't let Cheresse's dirty tricks and inane jealousy get in my way.

But first, I have to make sure Izzie is the female Baba spoke of before I claim her. That simple fact, along with dogged determination, is why I'm parked on my bike, watching the cottage door. As soon as Addie's done with Izzie, I'm going in. Good manners can take a damned hike when it comes to my future. Correction. *Our* future.

An eternity passes, but Addie is still inside. *Fuck it! I'm going home.* Confronting my potential mate will have to wait one more night. What's the expression? Good things come to those who wait. We'll see.

I'm about to take off when the door creeps open. The two females hug briefly, and Addie ambles away from the cottage. *It's now or never,* I tell myself as I inch toward the house.

"Wait!" I call out before Izzie shuts the door.

"Who's there?" Her gaze bounces around the area, but she can't make out my figure. Not yet.

Still clinging to the shadows, I edge closer. Irrational fear keeps me cautious. Untested, immature naguals can be a veritable challenge. Some are easy to tame, while others fight and claw, restricting the harnessing of their spirits.

Those like Izzie.

Taming her beast will come naturally with the first change. Her struggle against it only makes things worse. Fighting against the inevitable heightens her emotions. People get hurt as she refuses to surrender and let nature take its course. Izzie will have to let go or risk her beast revealing itself at an inopportune moment. But if she lets me, I can help her. Help her beast step forward.

Really?

Who the fuck am I kidding? Taming her is all about pleasure, not assisting nature.

"Show yourself or I'm closing the damn door," Izzie spits out.

Raising my palms, I step into the light spilling outside. "I just want to talk."

"About?"

Her sensual scent fills the air, distracting me. Reality dawns. Izzie's not *restricting* her beast. She has yet to experience her metamorphosis. *Fuck me sideways.* She's an immature nagual. Meant for me. *Fuck yeah.*

I touch my totem, and my fingers singe. "You feel it?"

She nods and leans against the doorframe. "But I'm not looking for a mate. I just want to be left alone."

Her hot-pink lips turn down, and all I can think about is feeling them wrapped around my cock—on her knees, hands tied behind her back . . .

Focus, Hunter.

"Are you serious?" My eyes rake over her curvy body. What type of beast is hiding within her? Please let it be a puma. True mates become the same creature, according to legend. "I could help you with your . . . uh . . . problem."

Anger wafts off Izzie like a heady fragrance. Intoxicating.

Watching her pushes the limits on my sanity. The light behind Izzie creates a halo around her midnight-brown hair. Tight jeans cling to her curves. Curves that trap and bend my mind. Making my beast want to claim her. Now. Thankfully, I'm more refined than that. I'll claim her soon enough. The right way. Well . . . with some caveats.

The first being whether she could stomach my . . . let's call them proclivities. When it comes to sex, I prefer certain kinks. My home, something I want to share with the right female, has its own dungeon —aka my playroom—complete with items I've purchased on my travels. A delightful shudder passes down my spine as I think about Izzie's body—beneath me, on top of me, restrained and panting . . .

Later. Much, much later.

An appreciative look in her hazel eyes screams yes, but she remains quiet. Her beast rumbles. It takes every fiber in me not to respond. To let her know I would never harm her.

"I promise you the only problem I have is your being here. We wouldn't want your *girlfriend* to get the wrong idea. Good night, Hunter." Izzie winks before stepping inside and closes the door.

"That's okay, Izzie. I'll be back," I shout out. This female might destroy the curse plaguing our family. I'm not giving up that easily.

My phone buzzes, the disruption like a fucking broken claw. Digging the device out of my jacket, I see Cheresse's name. What will it take for her to accept we're over? Refusing to venture down that path again, I decline the call and head to my bike. It's time for a beer.

~

IT's a sparse crowd at the Haven Saloon. A human with dirty-blond shoulder-length hair is behind the bar. Bent Brent, the owner. As usual, he has a joint to his lips. He stops talking to a female and waves me over.

"Quiet night?" I ask.

"Crowd thinned out after Hurricane Cheresse blew through." Brent takes another toke and offers me a hit.

"No, thanks."

He shrugs his slender shoulders. "What can I get for you?"

"Just a beer. So what happened?"

"You know Cheresse." Brent pops the cap on a longneck and slides it across the bar. "She came here looking for you. Got loud when I told her I hadn't seen you. Thankfully, Liam and the gang were in. They escorted her ass out."

Gripping the frosty bottle, I say, "What the hell am I going to—"

A heavy hand lands on my shoulder, cutting off my words. Then I hear the recognizable, hearty laugh.

"Monte, what brings you here?" Not bothering to look up, I just watch the towering male from the corner of my eye. I'm six foot two, but Monte has me beat by another three inches at least.

"Not your company, that's for sure." My best friend and fellow member of SIN straddles the stool beside me.

I glance over at him. He's dressed in his usual attire—ripped jeans, too-tight T-shirt, and leathers. "You come straight from work?"

"What makes you say that?"

I point at the grease beneath his fingernails. Monte, short for Montezuma, works with Josh over at the Havenwood Falls Garage.

When he's not at the shop, you'll find Monte tuning up the bikes for SIN members. It's how he earned the name Axle.

"Hell, I thought I got all of that. Had a last-minute tow. An SUV died out on 13. Towed it in and filled the gas tank."

"That was good of you." Brent slides another longneck across the counter. "What's going on with you tonight, Axle?"

Monte replies, "Been listening to chatter on the internet."

Other than servicing bikes for SIN, he's good at securing information. Monte's contacts outside Havenwood Falls keep us updated. If it weren't for my best friend's *research and recovery* skills, I doubt the club would keep Monte around. Hell, I know they only keep me around because of my ability to cook the books. Males that look like us—just short of cover models—aren't the usual biker types.

"What did you hear?" I ask as Brent hobbles away.

"A mob boss is missing some money. Apparently, a female robbed him blind. Three million dollars to be exact."

I whistle low before taking a pull from the bottle. "How is that important to us?"

"Last time she was seen was on a flight headed for Denver. I checked into it. The female rented an SUV just like the one I towed in."

Nearly choking on my beer, I spit it across the counter. "You sure?"

"Positive." Monte reaches for his bottle. "Biddie Half-Moon is spreading gossip around town about a newbie."

"How the hell . . . ?"

Then it comes back to me. While we were standing outside the inn, I noticed Biddie across the street. This time the human who wishes she were supernatural isn't blathering nonsense. My hope is that Izzie isn't behind the theft.

Monte gives me a curious look. "You know something?"

Feigning calm, I say, "Nope."

"Don't matter. In the morning, I'll check in with Addie. Find out who she's tattooed lately."

"Don't bother. I need to see her about something else. I'll get the 411." Maybe I can do some damage control if Izzie is responsible.

Taking another swig from the bottle, I say, "Changing the subject . . . does your grandfather still do his vision quests?"

"He stopped when my grandmother found his stash of sinsemilla."

I laugh. Both of our grandfathers claim the potent weed helps them find a higher ground when they need answers. I've always believed it was just an excuse to get blitzed.

"Why?"

"Never mind. I'll ask Baba. I need some confirmation."

Monte tosses back the rest of his brew. "Okay, bruh. I'm gonna head home, shower, and chill. It's been a long damned day. Want to run later?"

His inner beast is a jaguar. It might be fun to give chase up in the mountains. Get my mind off Izzie for a while. "Why the hell not? Call me when you're ready."

MANEUVERING my bike off Blackstone Road, I veer sharply onto the winding street leading toward Creekwood Estates, an upper middle-class development with a country club. As I speed toward my house, decadent images of the beautiful female I left behind consume my thoughts. I imagine coming home to her, enjoying her company over dinner and dessert, and eventually having my way with her in my playroom. Headstrong Izzie will be a challenge, and I accept it.

HOURS LATER, I'm relaxing with a brandy. Monte gave my ass a good run, and I'm worn out. I'm so deep in thought, I almost miss Baba slipping into the great room. Despite my grandfather's advanced age, the shaman moves with the grace of a younger nagual. He takes a seat in front of the fire.

"When did you get in, *noxhuiutze*?"

My head rocks up at Baba's use of the ancient word for beloved grandson. "An hour or so ago. I was running with Monte."

Baba leans forward. "Something is different about you." His head jerks back. "You found her."

"I did," I say, staring at my grandfather. Smiling to myself, I recall Izzie's stunning looks—silky dark hair that I want to run my fingers through and wrap around my hand, petulant sexy lips framing a mouth I can't wait to fuck, and a luscious ass . . . "She's beautiful, Baba. Absolutely exquisite."

He gives me a knowing grin. "Why isn't she here with you?"

Tipping the glass to my lips, I choose my words carefully. The last thing I want is for Baba to think I wasn't up to the task. "We need to be patient. Have a little faith. She needs a little time."

The old man chuckles. "You're sure of yourself."

"Perhaps." In all honesty, I'm not sure of anything other than my attraction to Izzie.

CHAPTER 3

IZZIE

*U*nwelcome sunlight sneaks past the blinds and drags me out of my sleep. It's not like I got any rest. The entire night I tossed and turned with X-rated dreams of a certain sexy nagual. I've never even seen the male naked, and suddenly I'm dreaming of his hard body pleasuring mine. Dream Hunter took his time with me, satisfying me over and over again—with his tongue and agile fingers. I wonder if the real nagual is as well-hung as the imaginary one? Could he truly appease my beast and make her happy?

Stop it!

The last thing I need in my life is another male, especially when one wants me dead.

Kazimir Chekhov—a man of nightmares.

That little fact slipped by me before I got involved with the mafia boss. All I saw was an attentive man who liked lavishing expensive gifts. Then he took things too far and pushed the boundaries of common decency. Someone should have told him females aren't possessions.

Rubbing my eyes, I swing my legs out of bed and pad toward the bathroom off the hall. My neck is on fire. Without thinking, I touch my throat and burn my fingers. A quick glance in the mirror, and I see the talisman glowing like a fucking beacon. Nobody can see this. Although humans can't see the object as anything but a piece of ugly jewelry, supes will want an explanation. Maybe I should get rid of it for now? Reaching behind me, I try to remove the necklace, but the chain is too hot. I double check my skin for any marks or redness. None. Odd. Oh well, I guess I'm stuck with the damned thing.

Why couldn't my transformation be uncomplicated?

Being a late bloomer isn't the real problem. The bigger issue happens after the totem changes. According to nagual legend, I have to bond with my soul mate within forty-eight hours. If the ceremony isn't performed, the universe reacts by taking him away. It'll be like he never existed. We'll both spend the rest of our lives alone. Unsatisfied and bitter. A punishment for not acting on the gods' benevolence. Totally unfair.

As important as the situation is, there are other matters to tend to —like a shower, buying a new phone, and contacting Senora. Getting an update on Kazimir's whereabouts is more crucial than a damned pendant. If I'm dead, cementing a bond with a mate won't even be a concern.

THIRTY MINUTES LATER, I'm clean, but turbulent emotions have surfaced again—worse than they've ever been so far. The agitating, crawling sensation makes me want to shed my skin and run. Scratching my flesh until it bleeds—as evidenced from the long gashes marring my arms—used to help. Now it's morphed into an overwhelming vibration that makes me want to lash out and hurt anyone in my path. Every step I take makes the totem glow brighter, and my fury grows stronger.

But the savage emotions are minor compared to the swelling agony between my thighs. Is there a stronger word than horny? It's another reason why I couldn't sleep last night. Right about now, I'd like to kick myself for leaving Mr. Fred—my vibrator (Yes, I named it. He stopped being a stranger a long time ago.)—at home. I dropped a fortune on the European device designed for supernaturals. Does this crossroads of a town even have an adult toy store?

I tug on my skinny jeans—probably not a good idea with the friction they're causing—slip into my high-heeled booties, and yank on a tank top. Remembering the chill in the air, I add a thick red sweater and twist my hair into a messy bun before storming out the door. Food can wait. Maybe a little information will tame my beast.

When I enter the lobby, I find Michaela behind the desk. "Good morning. Did you need something?"

With great effort, I fight past the snippy comments resting on my tongue. Michaela doesn't deserve my wrath. Besides, the vampire could probably take me down in a flash.

Inhale.

Exhale.

Inhale.

Exhale.

Feeling a little more in control, I say, "Yes. Two things. I need to replace my phone and get a ride back to my car."

"Try Miller's Plaza over on Main Street for a phone. It's on the west end of town." She glances behind me and nods toward the door. "*He* can tell you about your car."

Turning around, I see a very tall man—dark hair, slight muscular build, and scruffy beard—crossing the threshold. He's wearing a leather vest with the name Axle on one side, a wifebeater, and ripped jeans. My body tingles, and suddenly I want to climb him like a fucking tree.

"Hey, Monte," Michaela says.

"Hey, Michaela." His gaze lands on me, and his lips lift in a slight smile. "You must be Iris."

Shaking my head, I correct him. "My name is *Izzie*. Let me guess. You're a friend of Cheresse?"

"That would be a *no*," Monte says and hands me the car keys. "I gassed it up for you."

"How much do I owe you?" I say, reaching into my purse.

He waves his large hands and frowns. "Not needed. I was happy to do it." Monte glances at the floor before looking at me. "Got a minute?"

"Sure." I quickly thank Michaela for the information and follow Monte outside.

As soon as we step onto the porch, he says, "Just want to warn you 'bout Cheresse. She's not someone you want to tangle with."

I push back my shoulders and lift my chin. "I can handle myself."

He eyes my totem. "Not yet."

Automatically, my hand flies to the pendant, and it burns. "Ow!"

How many times am I going to do that before I learn?

"Interesting. How long has that been happening?" Monte asks as we descend the steps.

"Ever since I got to this place." I shove my stinging fingers into my jeans pocket. "So what's Cheresse's issue? We just met yesterday."

Stopping beside the rented SUV, Monte turns to me and says, "Hunter. I saw him last night, and his totem was glowing just like yours."

Looking up, I notice the jade jaguar around Monte's neck. "So you know what's going on?"

"I do. When it comes to Cheresse, it means trouble. She's a vindictive female. We were all glad when Hunter dumped her ass."

Fuck. I left a shit storm in New York just to encounter another one here.

"Thanks for the info," I say, unlocking the door. "I don't care what the totem means. I'm not looking for a mate."

Monte leans a hand against the vehicle, preventing me from getting in. "You may not be looking for one, but Hunter is looking for you. Keep that in mind while you're here. Cheresse knows what the totem means too. Puts you on her shit list."

NEW PHONE IN HAND, I call Senora. Resting my head against the seat back, I close my eyes and wait for her to answer.

"Hello?" Her groggy voice hits my ear.

Damn, I forgot. The empusa—a shape-shifting evil spirit—sleeps during the day. "Senora, it's me."

"Hey, girl. Don't tell me where you're at," she warns. "Are you okay?"

Thinking of the pendant and the jealous female, I say, "I'm not sure."

"Did you make it to the cabin?"

"No, I got lost."

"Lost!" Senora unleashes a tirade of swear words that could make a demon blink.

"Senora, that's not important," I interrupt. "What have you heard about Kazimir?"

My best friend breathes into the phone. "He called in his contacts with the Bratva. They know you took a plane to Colorado."

Not good if he's called in the Russian mafia. Kazimir only does that when it's something he can't handle on his own.

"Damn!" I slam my fist into the steering wheel. "Where are they?"

"I'm not sure, but connect the dots, girlfriend. Chekhov will search all over Colorado until he finds you." She pauses for a moment. "What about your totem? Any progress?"

"Understatement. It's glowing and burning the fuck out of my hand."

Senora shrieks. "That's good! It means your mate is nearby. He'll keep you safe from Chekhov."

"No."

"What do you mean by no? Honey, you're not letting your little mistake with Chekhov ruin your life?"

"Fucking Kazimir is more than a little mistake. If he finds me, it won't be pretty."

"I thought you just stole from him. Izzie, what the hell did you do?"

Memories of the first night I spent with Kazimir haunt my thoughts regularly. I've been trying so hard to forget the worst decision of my life, but the recollections refuse to budge. Dragging a hand

29

through my hair, I say, "I was horny and drunk. He approached me after work one night. I gave in."

"And?"

A low-pitched hum comes from my totem. Looking up, I see the tall, muscular nagual shifter striding toward the car. "Senora, I have to go."

"Not before you tell me."

Keeping my eyes focused on Hunter, I sigh and say, "Kazimir told me that if I ever left him, he'd kill me and whoever I hook up with."

"After one night?"

The shifter is nothing like the golden-haired Russian. Other than Hunter's dark hair and sea-colored eyes, he has this laid-back quality about him. Just look at him sauntering easily across the parking lot as if he hasn't a care in the world. Part of me wishes I could have met him much sooner. Before I made the biggest mistake of my life.

"It wasn't just one night," I admit and disconnect the call.

Stashing the phone in my purse, I prepare myself for a confrontation with the sensual supe—something I don't need—but when I glance up, thankfully, Hunter's gone. I do, however, notice the name of a shop worth investigating.

A CHIME SOUNDS as I open the door of Pleasurez. Unable to see past the red-curtained door and windows from the parking lot, I'm pleasantly surprised with a mecca of adult toys. On the left side of the store is a glass case and register. All sorts of toys are on display tables, and racks of racy lingerie and mannequins in skimpy outfits take up the center of the space. Just past the lingerie, on the right, are four fitting rooms.

I'm considering a leather bustier when I hear footsteps. "Hey, Ivy, I didn't expect you to come here." It's the clueless wonder, Cheresse. "Need anything?"

Yeah, for you to get my name right. Instead, I respond with, "It's Izzie, *Clara.*"

The red creeping onto Cheresse's face matches her fiery hair. "What can I help you with, *Izzie?*"

Unexpectedly, a vibrator that looks like Mr. Fred comes into view. The ache between my legs begs me to check it out, but I don't want Cheresse to know I'm looking for one. "Just curious about this place. You work here?"

"In a matter of speaking." She smiles brightly. "I own Pleasurez."

"Oh." That's fucking great. I bet she's always here.

"Is there anything in particular I can help you find? We have a great supply of masturbation devices for single gals like yourself," she points out in a mocking voice.

Rage, bottled up inside me, threatens to explode. I'd love to tell this spiteful female off. Two can play her fucked up game, though. "Really? Any recommendations? I'd love to get the one *you're* using." Tilting my head to the side, I say, "On second thought, maybe not. If yours did the trick, you'd be in a much better mood."

Cheresse glares at me, but there's still a twinkle in her gray-blue eyes. "You're mistaken. I've never had the need for a tool."

The tall bitch is working my nerves, but I'll play a little longer. "Is it okay for me to look around or do I need to have permission to check it out?"

Those words cause Cheresse to clench her jaw so tightly I'm waiting for it to snap. "You're free to check out whatever you like. I'd be happy to show you around, *Ina.*"

"Sure thing, *Claire.*"

The statuesque nagual turns on her heel. "Maybe you'd be interested in seeing the Very Private Pleasurez room? Follow me."

Good. I've grown tired of the game, anyway.

As I follow her to the rear of the store, the chime goes off over the door.

CHAPTER 4

HUNTER

There are days when I really love my job. My clients, some not-so-above-board, keep me intrigued with their different needs, like the motorcycle club and their various endeavors. Cooking the books for Cerberus Delivery is a challenge—hiding the extra money laundered without raising suspicion with the Feds, the IRS, or the Court.

The Swords of the Infernal Night gave an oath to keep our illegal dealings away from Havenwood Falls. It's my job to make sure it appears that way, and that's where the thrill comes into it. SIN operates just outside the law. Sometimes, it's downright intoxicating getting away with shit. Of course, I'm smart enough to keep all the club's files apart from Long & Associates, the CPA firm where I share office space. If Brian Long knew what I did, he'd kick my ass out so fast, I wouldn't have time to grab a pen, let alone a file.

But today isn't one of those days. Instead, I get to deal with the type of client that simply pisses me off. At the end of our transaction, there won't be any thrills, no excitement. Only a major headache, courtesy of the Pleasurez account.

It's the one client I've tried to give to other CPAs. No one else wants the agony, and Cheresse won't hear of it. When her father added the adult toy store to his investment portfolio, I was happy to work with him. Long hours were spent setting up his accounting. I even helped get the online store running. Then the man gave the shop to Cheresse. She figured I'd spend those same long hours locked in her arms instead of the office.

Now that my mate's in town, shit's gonna change. Continuing to see Cheresse, even for business, is a bad idea. No way will I witness two nagual females tear each other apart. My money's on Izzie giving Cheresse a good ass whipping.

Opening the covered door, I hear detached voices. The curtains over the entrance and the windows are intended to dissuade curious teens. Personally, I see them as a drawback for adults, giving the impression of an unsavory atmosphere. Yet, it hasn't hurt business. Hell, I've made my fair share of purchases from Pleasurez.

Not seeing anyone, but still hearing the murmuring, I venture past the racks of lingerie and display tables of paraphernalia. My goal is in the back of the store, the Very Private Pleasurez room—the VPP. Tucked in a corner of the first floor, the space is filled with a variety of bondage supplies and other items guaranteed to fulfill kinky needs.

The voices drift into the hallway, and I scuttle into the shadows.

"If you're looking for work, you could try over at Silk," Cheresse says flatly.

"What's Silk?" It's Izzie.

If it were anyone else, I'd have no problem with Cheresse recommending the nightclub, but she's talking about my mate. Any man, human or supe, ogling her like a car in a showroom bothers me.

"It's an entertainment spot. You said you've worked as a dancer. There's a gentleman's club inside it. I know for a fact that the owner, Melaina Savage, is auditioning new dancers. Use me as a reference."

"What's the address?"

"I have a business card up front." Cheresse pauses for a second. "Are you coming?"

Curiosity rings in Izzie's voice. "What's in this back room?"

"More exclusive toys," Cheresse says sharply. "I don't have all day."

"Well, I do. So, I'll grab the card before I leave. If that's a problem, I'll just ask Michaela about it."

"Suit yourself. Come up when you're ready."

Heels click across the floor, and then I feel her presence. Although I'm hidden, I'm sure she could find me. Nagual soul mates use a form of echolocation to find each other. Shaking my head, I remember Izzie hasn't transformed. This form of communication isn't available to her, so I position myself and watch like a damned voyeur.

Izzie picks up a package of drip candles, studies it for a moment, then puts it back on the shelf. As she makes her way around the room, I'm mesmerized by the side-to-side motion of her generous hips. Thoughts of seeing them naked makes my dick hard. I'm practically salivating as she looks at the bondage items with interest.

Finding a female who shares my same twisted appetite has always been a problem. Humans lack the stamina to keep up with me. I know it sounds like bragging, but it's the truth. Most of them fall asleep after only two rounds. Sadly, supes aren't any better. Every encounter I've had with even dominant ones has disappointed. As soon as I realize the creatures are easily broken, the thrill fades. Presenting a set of nipple clamps or even a simple riding crop, like the one in Izzie's hand, sends those partners cowering into a corner. Well . . . all except the one vampire who liked to feed off me as she climaxed. The memory still gives me chills.

Before my totem began glowing, I knew I wanted a dominant woman whom I couldn't frighten. I wanted a woman who could give as good as she got. A nagual whose beast beat strong and proud and fucking hot like Izzie. The idea of besting her excites me. Honestly, I haven't been aroused like this in a very long time. After a few more minutes of spying on Izzie, I adjust my crotch and step out of the dark just as she pauses at a display of spreader bars.

"I can show you how that's used," I say in a low voice.

Izzie jumps. "Are you following me?"

"Not quite. Just happen to be here at the same time." I pick up a cat-o'-nine-tails whip.

"So, it's a coincidence?" Her gaze follows my thumb rubbing the etched handle. "Your being here, that is?"

"Exactly, but I'm so glad we ran into each other." My eyes roam over Izzie as my craving for the immature nagual intensifies. The things I want to do to her . . . Running my fingers through her luxurious hair. Yanking it until she moans. Touching and licking her perfect breasts. And that ass . . . Sinking my dick into that taut, shapely ass. I want Izzie's long legs wrapped around me as her orgasm rocks her body.

Calm the fuck down before you come in your pants like a goddamned teenager!

I'm thankful for the dimly lit room. Leaning against the wall, I say, "Tell me which one of these items interests you."

Izzie's dark eyes widen as she casts a curious glance toward me. "You're serious?"

"When it comes to pleasure, I'm always serious."

When it comes to matters of the flesh, I'm always sincere too. I sense Izzie is earnest about her gratification as well. The way her eyes light up as she continues checking out the various items holds promise. I don't need our glowing totems to confirm it. This female is the one I've been waiting for.

Izzie picks up a studded paddle and then looks up through her long eyelashes. "Here's the thing, Hunter. I'm getting desperate. But it has to be a no-strings-attached deal."

Oh, this is interesting. Does she honestly think I'm going to settle for just a taste? But I'm willing to see what the female has in mind. "Okay."

"And it . . . Wait. Did you say okay?"

"I did. My question: your place or mine?"

I'll admit to being a tad disappointed when Izzie decides to go back to Whisper Falls Inn. Thankfully, she's staying in a cottage—no worries about how much noise we make.

I follow Izzie inside, and the first embers of lust burn in my brain. My imagination runs wild with thoughts of the tantalizing nagual—skin on skin, her sweat-slicked body beneath mine, Izzie writhing . . .

"Hunter?"

Her voice snaps me out of my musing. "What?"

Izzie gives me a lazy smile like a Sunday afternoon. "I asked if you wanted a drink. I—"

"No. I only want you."

"That is what we're here for," she says as she slides closer, pressing her breasts against me.

The simple gesture sends a delicious shiver down my spine. Before I can recover, Izzie's mouth moves dangerously over my cheek. Her breath fans my skin, making me moan. It almost takes more strength than I possess to keep from throwing this female down on the sofa, stripping her naked, and letting my dick find its home. But I want to savor her like a fine bourbon. Appreciate every fucking sip until I'm drunk on her taste.

A lust-filled grin crosses her beautiful face at the same time I growl, low and deep. "Maybe we should take this to the bedroom?"

"In a minute." Cupping her head, I slant my mouth over hers. I have every intention of taking my time, but as soon as I connect, I'm lost, ravaging Izzie with kisses.

I trace the seam of her lips with my tongue, and she eagerly opens her mouth, allowing me to bask in her wet heat. Kissing Izzie is a whole new experience. Every inch of me lights up with a burning, urgent need to possess her. Against her plump lips, I whisper, "Bed. Now."

"About damned time," she says, wrapping her legs around me as I lift her. "Straight down the hall. Past the bathroom."

WE FALL onto the bed and immediately undress. Slipping out of my jacket, I drop it on the floor before yanking my T-shirt over my head. Just enough time for Izzie to strip out of her clothes. I get a glimpse of her lacy underwear. Although it's sexy as hell, the garment covers too much. Reaching over, I grab the silky panties and rip them off.

"You're going to owe me another pair."

"I owe you something, but it's not a pair of damn undies," I growl. Taking a minute, I run my hand over her creamy thigh.

She shudders.

There's no need for pretense. We both know what this is about—taking care of needs, a proper introduction before our beasts get acquainted. My hand slides between her legs. She's so fucking wet. I'm salivating like one of Pavlov's dogs. As I work my fingers, Izzie writhes against me. I've waited long enough. Lowering my mouth, I take my first taste.

Heaven.

Fucking nirvana.

The female tastes like pure sunshine. Hell, I could drink from her depths for hours and never get enough. As my tongue finds that oh so sensitive bundle of nerves, Izzie's thighs tighten around my head.

"D-don't stop," she utters with her fingers twisting in my hair. Her hips lift off the bed as my tongue goes deeper.

I have no plans to stop until I'm drunk off her juices.

My phone rings. I guess I should have broadcast my fucking plans.

"Ignore it," she mumbles.

Lifting my head, I wipe my chin. "I can't. It might be club business."

Izzie rises up on her elbows. The scowl on her face lets me know those were the wrong words to say, but it's too late for apologies. Reluctantly, I get off the bed and find my phone on the floor. A look at the screen confirms I was right.

Accepting the call, I say, "Yeah."

"Took you long enough," Liam shouts. "We got an issue."

"Can it wait?" I glance up at the angry yet alluring nagual. "I'm busy."

"I don't give a shit who you're fucking at the moment. Get off the leg and get your ass over here. We got a three million dollar problem."

Shit. "Be there soon."

Izzie reaches for her shirt. "Don't even say it. I swear I should just buy a new vibrator."

I grab her ankle before she moves off the bed. "We're not done here. I'll come back once I see what this is about."

"Don't bother. I've got to see someone about a job."

Silk.

I still don't know how I feel about my future mate dancing there. If anyone puts his hands on Izzie, I'll lose my shit. Might as well be honest. "Listen, Izzie, I overheard you talking to Cheresse. I don't think you should work at the club."

Izzie crosses her arms under her breasts. "And why is that?"

"Are you gonna deny we belong together?" My totem is so hot I'm sure it's leaving scorch marks. "I'd prefer it if my mate didn't dance there."

She narrows her chestnut eyes. "First, we're not mates. We're not even fuck buddies. Second, you don't get to tell me what to do. The last fool that tried it . . . Let's just say his bank account is a little lighter."

A slight chill travels down my spine with Izzie's last words. For sanity's sake, I'm not going to focus on her possible confirmation. If I focus on it, then I'm obligated to do something about it.

Clearing my voice, I say, "Fine. Let me handle my business, and then I'll go with you."

"No."

"At least let me call ahead. Make sure the fellas working there keep an eye out for you."

"No. I can take care of myself."

That's what she thinks. I'll make the call on my way to the clubhouse.

CHAPTER 5

HUNTER

Twenty minutes later, I enter the Swords of the Infernal Night's clubhouse. No matter what time of day I come here, the place is rarely empty. At the moment, a few members along with scantily clad females sprawl over the furniture. One couple is sound asleep with their bodies wrapped around each other. Another pair makes out in a corner while members shoot pool, none of them looking in my direction. So this isn't a general meeting.

Not good.

Leaving the stench of snatch, stale cigarettes, and alcohol behind, I take purposeful steps down the long hallway to the back, steadying my mind as I go. Displays of weakness aren't allowed in this dwelling. Once I reach my destination, I suck in a deep breath before turning the knob and opening the office door. Liam Peters, founder of the motorcycle club, occupies a seat behind a pockmarked, mahogany desk wearing his usual sunglasses. He runs a hand through his sandy-colored hair and jerks his chin toward the empty chair.

My heart ricochets in my chest as I lower myself onto the ripped vinyl seat. My beast is strong, but he's no match for a hellhound. Clearing my throat, I ask, "What's going on, Liam?"

"You tell me." Fixing me with a gaze that penetrates his shades, he pushes a file across the table. "One of our suppliers is refusing to do business with us. They claim to have lost three million."

Why does that amount sound familiar?

My spine shifts while my muscles tense. Gritting my teeth, I fight to maintain control. This is not the time for my beast to make an appearance. Slamming my hand on top of the file, I say, "Are they saying we're responsible?"

"Indirectly." Liam pauses for a beat or two. "It's Chekhov Industries."

Damn. While Stone Falls Winery does a great job making sure the bars and restaurants have enough wine to satisfy humans and supes, Chekhov supplies liquor to the town. Cutting off booze to Havenwood Falls would cause an uprising that might rival the Vampire Massacre of 2005. The idea sends a shudder down my spine.

We've never had any issues with the company run by old Russian mafia. As long as we pay cash for all purchases, the Chekhovs deliver. Could this have anything to do with the chatter Monte overheard?

"I don't follow," I say innocently.

"Turns out Old Man Chekhov has a son who got involved with a stripper. They think she took the money and skipped town."

Images of the dark-haired beauty I left behind come to mind. Quickly, I push them aside and try to focus.

"Still . . ." Long-dead moths flutter to life and take off in my stomach. "How are *we* responsible?"

"Rumor has it she was headed to Denver."

"So?"

Liam gives me a stare so strong I feel its intensity through the shades. "Cheresse is talking about a new supe in town. Monte towed in a vehicle—one rented in Denver by this female." Liam opens a drawer, pulls out a photo, and shoves it across the desk. "You're the goddamned accountant, Hunter. Do the math."

Waist-length deep brown hair, captivating eyes, perfect breasts, and a permanent scowl on her plump lips—it's Izzie. My heart stops. If Cheresse had kept her ever-loving pie hole shut, Liam wouldn't have looked into this.

"Listen, Liam, I know nothing about any missing funds. Yeah, that's the new supe in town." I point toward my chest. "But she's here for me. As a matter of fact, you interrupted—"

Liam leans forward in his seat and lowers his glasses, revealing his dark eyes with reddish highlights. "I don't give a fuck what you do or with whom you do it. But if this is the female Chekhov is looking for, you need to turn her in. Let them handle their shit and keep us out of it. Understood?"

"Yeah," I say half-heartedly. Problem is no one's hurting my mate, especially if she can lift the curse on my family. Even if I considered turning her in, I'm not done with Izzie. I've had a fucking taste and plan to do a helluva lot more. "Anything else?"

"Naw." Liam reclines against the chair back. "Just be careful, Hunter. The Chekhovs can be dangerous. I'd prefer not having to put them in their place. Know what I mean?"

"Yeah." Going against the Chekhovs puts SIN at risk. Our agreement with the Court of the Sun and the Moon dictates we police ourselves. Pushing to my feet, I say, "Don't worry about it. Ain't nothing happening that shouldn't."

"Good to know." Liam grins up at me. "So, is she really your future mate?"

"How the hell—"

"Axle. I talked to him before I called you. He told me all about the new supe. At least what he knew."

Drawing in a breath, I exhale loudly. "Yeah, man. She's my mate."

"And you asked the fellas to look out for her?" He shakes his head. "You know Cheresse ain't gonna like that?"

"I do, but this doesn't concern her. Remember, I quit her weeks ago?" I make a mental note to have a confab with her. She can't keep shooting off her mouth to anyone who'll listen.

"All right then. Handle your business. You hanging out here tonight?"

"Nope. Going to Silk. Izzie's auditioning."

"Want me to call Melaina?"

A good word from Liam might help Izzie land the job. To be

honest, though, I'd prefer it if Melaina didn't hire my mate. Keeps me from losing my shit every time some fool looks at Izzie.

"Let my lady get this on her own."

"Whatever, man. Have a good night. Keep me posted if you hear anything about the money."

"Yeah." Something tells me that'll be sooner rather than later.

As I HEAD toward Miles Mountain, Liam's words keep turning in my head. What the fuck did Chekhov's son do to make Izzie steal from him—*if* she stole from him. Naguals aren't in the habit of stealing. Don't get me wrong. We do our share of dirt, but usually no one gets hurt. No one that doesn't deserve it, that is.

My phone buzzes as soon as I turn into the parking lot off Burdorf Pass. Killing the motor, I pull it from my pocket. It's a message from Oscar Vega, SIN's sergeant-at-arms and head of security for Silk.

Oscar Vega: trapper, your girl's here

Hunter James: I'm in the parking lot

Oscar Vega: FYI, Liam called Melaina. She's meeting with your girl before the audition

Shit. I don't need a fucking crystal ball to know what Liam told Melaina. Izzie will to have to come clean about whatever she's done.

Hunter James: I'm headed in. Do me a solid. When Izzie's done, send her to me. I'll be in my usual spot

Oscar Vega: might not be an option after Melaina's done

SILK IS HAVENWOOD FALLS' answer to adult entertainment. A little magic transformed the network of caves within an old mine into a hot spot. The main feature is the nightclub hosting lounge areas, a VIP section, tables, and two bars. The best part of Silk? It offers a little of everything, catering to humans and supes.

Down a corridor, there's a secure area just for us—exotic drinks and no glamour needed. It's okay if you don't mind a little edginess with your enjoyment. Deeper into the mine, on a level beneath the dance floor, are the exotic dancer rooms—one for the "gentlemen" and one for the "ladies." You'll also find similar, smaller rooms for supes only. I've spent considerable time in all four rooms, trolling for the right female to suit my various tastes.

I'm headed for Silk's true treasure—private rooms on the lowest level. In the largest room, auctions are held along with special shows. Members of SIN guard the entrances of all the rooms, making sure no one gets in who shouldn't. A tall, muscular male with dark hair waits outside mine. It took a lot of coercion—think pleading—with Melaina to get this space. I had to promise to tame down my penchant for kink, and restrict who I brought to it—no humans.

"What's up, Trapper?" says Kai Reynolds, a prospect who looks like he should be on the cover of GQ instead of joining a biker club. The vampire graduated from high school back in May.

"Hey. There's a female upstairs. Oscar's bringing her down soon. Let her in. No questions asked. Got it?"

"Sure thing."

I hold the key fob over the control panel beside the door and listen to the tumblers disengage. Seconds later, the metallic barrier slides open. As I step inside, recessed lighting flares up, casting a golden glow. I toss my keys on the side table next to the bondage sofa. Lifting my head, I catch a glimpse of myself in the mirrored wall behind the stage.

Deep pockets along with my promises to Melaina allowed me to outfit the suite to cater to my sexual inclination. Each room on this level is a little different, but I'm sure this is the only one with mirrored walls and a Saint Andrew's cross in the main area. A sturdy, four-poster bed is in the bedroom, along with a cabinet full of toys. The en-suite bathroom includes a shower big enough for a fucking orgy.

I flick a switch in the wall, and a song by Alina Baraz blares through hidden speakers. I'm able to indulge in my other predilection —voyeurism—via an eighty-inch TV in the bedroom. All the comforts of home.

Shrugging my shoulders and cracking my neck, I head to the bathroom. Turning on the rainforest shower head, I'm hoping a good deluge of water will relax and clear my mind. As I strip out of my leather cut and T-shirt, my thoughts return to Silk's supplier. If Izzie stole from Chekhov, will giving the money back be enough? If it's not, what will I have to do to get him to forget about her?

Steam fogs up the bathroom, interrupting my thoughts. As I step beneath the torrent of water, I grab the bottle of L'Occitane shower gel. The clean-smelling soap refreshes me and focuses my thoughts. Instead of worrying over what Izzie may or may not have done, I need to concern myself with what I plan to do with her—handcuffing her to the sofa, caressing her soft skin as I go down on her, and then fucking her senseless . . . *Aw, shit.* Now my dick is as hard as a rock. Wrapping my hand around my cock, I'm tempted to jack off, but don't. A little pain now is worth hours of pleasure later.

Turning off the shower, I reach for a towel. Time to make myself comfortable and wait for Izzie to come for me (pun intended).

CHAPTER 6

IZZIE

*R*iding up the side of a mountain in a gondola lift, no matter how plush, is not my idea of fun. Although Cheresse said no one can see outside the contraption when it's making its descent—keeps drunks from throwing up all over the inside—I'm not looking forward to that moment. It's the whole being suspended in mid-air that's bothering me.

The ride jolts to a stop, and a burly male is at the door, ready to help me out. He's wearing a leather jacket and sunglasses—another member of SIN. Apparently, the bikers and their significant others work at Silk.

"You must be Izzie."

His voice is so deep it reverberates through me (much better than Mr. Fred ever did). My eyes widen, and my mouth falls open. And his arms . . . Holy fucking hell. They look like graffitied tree branches—corded, massive biceps with tattoos of skulls impaled by swords. Someone must have carved his ass out of a rock wall. He can't possibly be human.

"I take it that's a yes. My name's Oscar." A slow smile spreads across his stubbled face. "Melaina wants to see you before the audition."

Picking my jaw up, I follow Oscar down a narrow pathway. A

larger-than-life neon sign with the name Silk hangs overhead. More twinkling lights line either side of the path leading to a massive door—are there giants in Havenwood Falls?—made of an odd metal. From a distance, the surface appears dull. It's not until we're closer that I notice the sheen. A slew of glyphs and symbols decorate the barrier.

Entering the club is like venturing into an excavated cavern. The sounds of "Hands on Me" by BURNS reach my ears. After crossing the empty dance floor, we head down a narrow, dimly lit hall. At the end of it is an elevator, with an Employees Only sign above the button.

"Employees enter the club here," says Oscar. "Go up one floor to the employee lounge. You'll find Melaina on the second floor."

"What if I get lost?"

"Her office takes up the entire floor. There are only two floors accessible to employees from this elevator."

Music surrounds me as the elevator doors slide closed. The pounding of my heart, however, nearly blocks it. Why the fuck am I so nervous? I've done this before. It's simple. Plaster a winning smile on my face and talk myself up to the boss. Convince her that I can bring in lots of money. Be prepared to flash my tits if she asks. No big deal. Right?

The doors open, and my heart stops. This is no ordinary office. All the walls and even the floor are made of glass. My future boss's desk is angled in a corner, giving an uncluttered view of the club below and even the employee lounge. Much better than any camera. My eyes bounce around the room before landing on a beautiful, tawny-colored female dressed in a purple bodycon dress with sky-high gold stilettos. Suddenly, my simple miniskirt and zip-front crop top feel inappropriate.

Standing with her back turned is a woman behind a desk. When she faces me, her golden hair swings like a satiny curtain. Nothing about her indicates she's not human, but I sense it. Then I remember Oscar saying she's a hellhound—a bearer of death and a being to never cross.

"It's Izzie, right?"

"Yes."

The female hellhound extends her hand, but instead of a handshake, she points to a chrome and leather chair in front of the desk. "My name is Melaina. Before we discuss possible employment, we need to go over some things."

"Like?" I ease myself onto the chair.

"A friend of mine called me before you arrived. It seems there's a problem with you being here."

My breath hitches a little as I grip the chair arms. "What type of problem?"

"Places like Silk can't exist without liquor. Our supplier has cut off future shipments until we deliver a special package to them."

My stomach twists, but I stay quiet. The sweat carving a path down my spine warns me where this is going, and it's not good.

Melaina places her hands on her desk and leans over it. "One phone call is all that's needed. You've met Oscar. He'll deliver you to Kazimir Chekhov, and I get my booze." Melaina stares hard at me for a moment. "Give me a reason why I shouldn't do it."

Twisting my fingers in my lap, I'm reluctant to tell this stranger the truth.

"Here's the thing you should know about me. I protect my girls. Every last one. If you want that protection, you need to work for me. In order for you to work for me, I need honesty." She pauses for a moment before standing taller. "It's up to you."

Yeah, right. I'm supposed to believe I have a choice in the matter? Make the wrong decision, and this female will send me to Hell before I draw in my next breath. But telling her . . . Shit, I haven't even told Senora the entire truth.

But you need the protection . . .

Exhaling, I say, "If I tell you, it has to stay between us."

"Tell me first, and then I'll decide."

"Not my deal." Pushing to my feet, I get ready to leave.

"Sit your ass down," Melaina snaps. "Leave and Oscar will escort you to Kazimir!"

My pulse speeds up as my beast claws at the surface. If I'm not careful, this hellhound might expedite my transformation. Sadly, I don't think my animal is a match for a protector from Hell. Forcing air through my cheeks, I try to calm down, but I won't sit.

Reluctantly, I confess, "I stole three million from Kazimir, and he wants it back."

Melaina folds her arms over her chest as she lowers herself on the chair. "Impressive, but why did you do it?"

"The ass thinks he owns me just because I let him fuck me," I admit.

"Now why the hell would you do that? Seriously? You couldn't do better than a human?"

"Call it the hazards of being a fledgling nagual. I'm not picky when I'm horny. Kazimir was one of my regulars. One night he was looking for more than a lap dance. It morphed into an exclusive arrangement —he'd come to the club, pay for a dance, and leave me a room key. We'd been together for a year."

Melaina nods. "What changed?"

"He put his hands on me in the wrong way. Granted, I don't mind a little rough sex, but Kazimir told me he owned me . . ."

It had been a long night and business was slow. I noticed a man lingering in the back of the room. My shift was over, and so I approached him.

"Got nowhere to go?" I asked.

"Only if you come with me," he drawled.

"I was exhausted and desperately needed sex," I tell Melaina.

"So you took him up on the offer?"

"Naturally."

We were walking to his car when suddenly a black sedan screeched to a halt in the middle of the street. The door swung open, and Kazimir jumped out.

"Where the hell are you going, Izzie?"

My new one-nighter snaked a hand around my waist. "Step off, man. The little lady is with me."

"That whore is no lady. Besides, she belongs to me." Kazimir stormed around the vehicle and yanked me toward him.

Unfortunately, the new guy proved to be a coward and quickly hightailed it out of there.

"Was that really necessary, Kaz?"

He responded by grabbing my neck with his free hand.

"I didn't want him to know I was scared, so I tried not to freak out. He squeezed until black dots floated in front of my eyes. I had no choice but to give him what he wanted."

"Which was?"

"Fear. I squirmed and tried to pry his fingers from my neck. He laughed in my face before letting go. Then he told me I belonged to him, bought and paid for."

"Why did you take the money? You could have easily walked away."

Shaking my head vehemently, I say, "Walking away from Kazimir Chekhov isn't possible. You have to pay him to get out. I don't have three million dollars saved to buy out my contract."

It wasn't something I'd entered into willingly. When I started seeing Kazimir outside of the club, he instituted the agreement. Since I didn't actually sign anything, I figured I could write my own rules. He let me know I was wrong the first time I attempted to end things.

"What did you hope to accomplish by taking it from him?"

"I'll give it back to him if he agrees to let me go. No strings attached."

Melaina's lip curls as if she's smelling something putrid. "Just give him his damned money."

My eyes widen. "No. He owes—"

"Forget the fucking contract. Put the money back in whatever account you lifted it from. I'll make sure you're protected."

"I can't. It's too risky."

"Your handling this on your own is too risky. I won't say it again. Give the money back, and you have a job with me. No audition needed. If you hooked Kazimir, you can dance."

"And you'll keep me safe?"

"Oscar is in charge of security. You'll be safe."

Kazimir doesn't deserve to get his money back, but if Melaina is guaranteeing protection . . . "Fine. I need a computer."

Melaina pushes a button on her desk. "Gloriana, I need you up here." Silk's owner glances at me. "Gloriana is a dancer and Oscar's girl. When she's finished with you, Oscar will help you with the computer. Word of advice?"

"Yes?"

Melaina points toward my neck. "Hook up with your mate and don't fuck around with any of the customers. I'll do my best to calm Kazimir down. Last thing we need is a damned war over a nagual who can't keep her fucking legs closed."

~

A PRETTY, pouty-lipped Latina leads me into the employee lounge. The room is comfortable with plenty of soft leather sofas and reclining chairs. She points to a closed door.

"You'll find changing rooms through there, along with showers and toilets. Each dancer has her own locker. Oscar will give you a code for yours." Gloriana's voice is tired, but with a bit of an edge.

"Is there a problem?"

She cocks her curly head to one side. "I'm still trying to decide. You were checking out my man earlier."

"Excuse you?" Is she claiming Hunter, too? "I wasn't."

"No? And why not? All the other bitches around here do." A laugh bursts from her. "Don't worry about it. I'm just testing you. Can't have some *chica* thinking she can move in here and take what's mine."

"No problem." I swear the females in this town have issues with their males. "Melaina's a hellhound. What are you and Oscar?"

"I'm a *bruja*—a Spanish witch. Oscar's a hellhound."

"That's an odd combo."

"We make it work. You'll find a few mixed couples here. It's not a big deal."

"Speaking of big deals . . ." Logic along with Melaina's warning tell me I need to know more about Hunter and Cheresse. "Mind if I ask you a question?"

Gloriana plops down on a sofa and pats the cushion. "Sit. You want to know about your potential mate and his ex."

"How did you know?"

"I read your thoughts. Naguals aren't the only ones who can read minds. I don't broadcast that information, though." The witch pauses for a moment. "Cheresse and Trapper were an item, but he quit her about a month ago. Trapper's grandfather didn't approve of the half-breed."

"So Hunter and his grandfather are prejudiced?" I ask, taking a seat.

"No. Their family has been looking for Trapper's true mate to break a curse. Only a full-bred nagual can do it."

My heart beat kicks up a notch. "Curse? What curse?"

"You don't know? Shit, I could kick Trapper's ass for not telling you." Gloriana shifts her position. "Okay, here's the short story. A witch fell in love with Trapper's father. When he turned her down, she cast a spell rendering future males infertile."

"What about Hunter?"

"He's the last of his line. The spell can only be broken if he finds his true mate—the one who shares his heartbeat."

"And Cheresse wasn't it."

"No. Besides, she's a clingy bitch who nobody likes. But be careful with her. Cheresse is jealous and vindictive. She thinks Hunter belongs to her and nobody else."

"Thanks for the information." Unfortunately, I'm not sure what to do with it.

"If there's nothing else, I need to get you downstairs. Oscar's waiting for you."

Fifteen minutes later, the three million is back in Kazimir's personal account. I hated seeing the money leave, but I think I'd hate losing my life more.

"That was all of it?" Oscar asks.

"Yes. I spent none of it."

"Good. Melaina will contact Chekhov. Hopefully, we'll be back in business soon."

"If not?"

The chair creaks beneath Oscar's huge frame. "Stop worrying. You gave Chekhov his money. If he threatens you, he answers to us. When do you start work?"

"Tomorrow. Right now, I plan to go back to the inn."

"Not happening. You're going downstairs to see Trapper."

My hands instantly fist. "I don't need a babysitter. Besides, Hunter and I aren't a couple. He has no reason to show up."

"I have my orders. Maybe you should take it up with him."

*A*fter transferring the money, Oscar gives me a tour of the club. The club doesn't open for another hour or so, but the DJ is playing music anyway. Bartenders fill the time stocking the bar while a few of the dancers hang out at the tables. Gloriana and another Latina with generous curves and flawless skin sit together.

"Yo, Oscar," says Gloriana, her Bronx accent seeping through her speech.

We approach the females, and Oscar places a chaste kiss on Gloriana's golden cheek. "Hey, babe. What's up, Liberty?"

"Another damn newbie," she says in a not-so-quiet whisper. The female purses her lips and gives me the once-over before leaving.

"What's her issue?" I ask, wondering how she can move in the exceedingly tight corseted dress.

"Never mind her." Gloriana waves her hand. "Honestly, you never know with a xana. Liberty can be moody, too."

I swear living amongst humans is easier—you can tell who's who with one glance. With supes, there are far too many species to keep straight. Xanas are Spanish fae. They can be benevolent or evil. I've never had a run-in with one, and I'd like to maintain my record. I make a mental note to keep my distance from Liberty.

"Where you headed, Oscar?" Gloriana asks.

"Showing Izzie the rest of the club."

"Including the private rooms?" Amusement glints in Gloriana's dark eyes as a slow grin quirks her mouth.

Glancing up at my beefy tour guide, I see his mouth twisting in a knowing smile. What the hell am I missing?

Gloriana scoots off the stool. "Then don't let me keep you. Come find me when you're done."

She sashays toward the bar with Oscar's gaze glued to her backside. I clear my throat, and the big guy's cheeks color.

"We'd better go." He points toward a hall leading away from the dance floor.

OSCAR DEPRESSES the button for the elevator—this one is in an alcove off the hallway. He leans against the rock wall, and his head slowly nods as if he's checking me out from behind his shades. In a lowered voice, Oscar says, "You'll do well here."

"You can tell that just by looking at me?"

"Yeah . . ." Oscar licks his lips. "I can."

"Does Gloriana know about your roving eye?"

The doors slide open, and we step inside the compartment. "Who said anything about roving eyes? Besides, her status doesn't keep me from appreciating a beautiful female. Just looking. No harm done."

My blood boils. His statement is why I want nothing to do with bikers. The assholes think they're doing females a favor by bedding us. Someone should really give them a clue—we could do without the sloppy sex and riding on the back of noisy machines. We prefer males loyal to us and not to a bunch of Neanderthals with horrendous manners.

A little judgmental?

Okay. I'll admit my knowledge of bikers is limited to the few bastards I've known in my lifetime.

"Simmer down, nagual. You're spoken for, and I don't plan on battling over a little pussy."

Agitated, I fold my arms over my chest and face him. "Let's get something straight. First off, I don't belong to anyone, and no one's fighting over my pussy." I let my eyes drift down to Oscar's crotch. "Besides, I'm not interested in little dicks."

"I promise you there's nothing little on me." Oscar chuckles and pushes a button. "Now I get it."

"Get what?"

"You're perfect for the bean counter. He deserves a spitfire like you."

~

MINUTES LATER, the grand tour ends outside a metal door guarded by a male who could easily be a model or maybe even work one of the rooms in the club. He exchanges a shrewd look with Oscar. The big guy waves a key fob over a control panel, audible clicks fill the space, and the door slides open.

"Enjoy yourself," Oscar says and ambles away.

My gaze drifts over to the muscular guy wearing a leather vest with a prospect patch. He simply shrugs. Great. He doesn't have the balls to tell me what's going on or what's inside the room.

Stepping across the threshold, I'm met with a golden glow. On first glance, the room resembles any other private thrills space, especially with the stripper pole on a stage. Then I notice the red oak coffee table with black hardware—perfect for bondage. Even the leather sofa has similar hardware in strategic spots. The saltire cross with its restraining points complete the tantalizing, scary atmosphere. Kinky sex and I aren't strangers, but I've never been in a dungeon.

A wave of apprehension suddenly washes over me. I know what's supposed to happen in a room like this, but does Melaina expect me to have sex to secure my job? Goosebumps pebble my skin as I turn back to the door. No knob. How the fuck do I get out of here?

Without preamble, the sensual sounds of Sabrina Claudio singing "All to You" fill the air. My eyes dart around the room, trying to find the source of the music. Then an intoxicating, sexy smell tickles my

55

nose. Hints of lavender, a little nutmeg, and the underlying scent of burnt wood surround me. There's only one male who belongs to the enticing aroma.

Pivoting on my heel, I come face to face with Hunter. First, I notice the Maya tattoos on his sculpted muscular chest. As my eyes travel I see that he's practically naked except for a towel. It barely covers his stiff dick jutting forward. Holy fucking hell.

"What took you so long?" he asks, lust filling his teal-colored eyes.

"I . . . um . . ."

Snap out of it! He's not the first naked man you've seen.

Hunter comes closer and brushes his hand over my cheek. Feelings take over, and my brain turns to mush. I forget my left from my right, and I'm seriously considering ripping that towel off with my teeth. Dropping to my knees . . . taking his cock between my lips . . .

Stop it! Focus! You're not looking for a mate!

"I asked you here," Hunter says. His hot breath fans over me. My brain burns with licentious images. "Because I want to finish what we started earlier." He nuzzles my neck. "I can't get you out of my mind."

Blood throbs in my veins as I think back to earlier. His tongue—oh . . . the things he does with it. My body trembles with need. The ache between my thighs becomes more intense as Hunter presses his thick length against me.

"We don't have to use any of my playthings now. Just come back to my bedroom."

"Yes," I pant too quickly. This is madness. We hardly know each other. For all I know, fucking him could be a colossal mistake.

Not fucking him could be a bigger one.

Our hands intertwine, and I allow this sexy man to lead me out of one room and into another. Hunter stops in front of me. His nimble fingers grasp my top's zipper.

Whoosh.

My bare breasts fall forward. His fingers circle one hardened nipple, pausing long enough to give it a tweak. My head falls back.

"Ahhh."

Hunter turns me around, and I lean against him. He fondles one breast while the other hand dips below my waistband. "You're overdressed, Izzie."

"Mmm . . ." I've lost all ability to think rationally. Dragging my thoughts together, I reach between us and release the snap on the skirt. With one tug it slips down, puddling around my feet.

"Much better." Hunter's hands trail down my body and over my bare ass. He slides his finger beneath the scrap of fabric keeping the G-string together.

Rip!

Hunter drops to his knees. When his tongue swipes across my butt cheeks, I forget all about my ruined, soaked underwear. As he explores my ass with his mouth, Hunter slides a finger between my legs. I gasp.

"I-I n-need to lie down."

Instead of acknowledging me, Hunter turns me so that my crotch is in his face. "Not yet."

His hands stroking my thighs feel like hot brands. My hips gyrate as Hunter's tongue plunges deeper. Lashing me. Working me open. Driving me fucking wild.

"Hun . . . ter!"

My body's on fire. It jerks forward and then . . . and then . . . I melt. I'm a pool of emotion. Flowing freely. Taking all the tension inside me with it.

Right before I fall over the edge, the floor drops, and Hunter catches me in his strong arms.

"It's my turn," he says near my ear.

Picking me up, he carries me to the bed and places me gently on it. Hunter covers my still-trembling body with his. Skin on skin.

What happened to that towel?

"You ready for me?" Hunter husks.

Unable to speak, I simply nod.

He teases me, rubbing his heavy, hard cock over me. My pussy throbs, and I spread my legs further. Hunter thrusts into me. I moan and suck in air as this male fills me like no one has ever done.

"That's it, babe," he says, before pressing further, deeper.

He's impossibly huge. I can't . . . It hurts . . . It . . . it . . . Just when the pressure seems too much, the discomfort gives over to pleasure, and it's so damned good. Hunter's hips move to the rhythm of the music. With each thrust, our fucking finds its own pulsing melody. The headboard bangs the wall as he drives into me. Over and over again.

"I'm . . . I'm coming." He grunts.

My pussy tightens around his dick, and we come together in one shuddering wave.

~

MINUTES LATER, Hunter is still semi-hard, lying beside me. My legs are like jelly, but the total calm I'm experiencing is strange. No anger. No lingering arousal. Just peace.

Hunter wraps his fingers around mine and pulls my hand to his mouth, planting a kiss on my knuckles. "Are you okay?"

"I think so."

"Think so?" He faces me with raised eyebrows. "That's a new one."

"Trust me, this is new for me too. I'm usually ready to go another round or punch the shit out of someone."

"And now?"

"I'm at peace for the first time in years," I admit with a little apprehension.

"That's because you've never been properly fucked," Hunter replies with a cocky grin on his lips.

Staring at him, I say, "Awfully sure of yourself. Maybe I was just relaxed."

"Yeah, right." He rolls on top of me. "I think you need more."

"You do?"

"It's the best way to tame your beast. Mates need to fuck as much as possible."

Mates.

Why can't we just enjoy the sex? Keep things uncomplicated?

Hunter's gaze meets mine. "Izzie, we're mates. Deal with it."

"We can't be. We don't even know each other," I whine.

"We can get to know each other after the ceremony." He pushes the hair away from my face. "It has taken me years to find you. I can wait a little longer."

Time won't erase my fears. What if I put all my faith in Hunter, and he turns out to be no better than my father?

Hunter cups my face with both hands and our eyes meet. His gaze deepens, and I sense what he's doing—reading my thoughts.

"Listen, don't compare me to your father," he says. "Family is everything to me. It's why my grandfather lives with me."

"Where are your parents?"

"They're here, in the same house I grew up in." He gives me a lopsided grin. "And they still love each other. Proof that naguals can love and stay committed to each other."

Dropping my gaze, I say, "Sorry, but there's no guarantee we'll have the same relationship."

"Life doesn't give guarantees. I *can* promise that if you give me a chance, I won't desert you. I want to learn all there is about you—in and out of the bedroom. Let me in, Izzie. Let me learn to love you." His lips brush mine in a brief kiss. "Stay with me tonight."

"I—"

"You don't start work until tomorrow night."

"I don't have a change of clothes," I argue.

"Stop making excuses. I'll get you whatever you need. Will you please stay with me?"

"Here?"

"Yes. It's a private room. No one's coming in here."

"Fine." Lifting my eyes, I say, "You don't snore, do you?"

"I promise that's one noise that won't be in this room tonight."

CHAPTER 8

HUNTER

Sensual music greets me, but the bed is empty and the shower isn't running. There's no chance my future mate slipped out. She can't without a code. Shortly after I had this room built, a female exited the room using my keys. After that fiasco, I added a control panel within the arm of the couch, only accessed with my fingerprint.

Call me paranoid, but I don't care. I was fortunate the one time. She could have gone to the authorities, claiming I tied her ass up, forced her to do things, and kept her hostage. It's better to err on the safe side. Last thing I need is Sheriff Ric Kasun raiding Silk and shutting shit down. I'd prefer not answering to Melaina and her brother. They've already warned me about my predilections—not everyone is into bondage play. If I cause problems for Melaina, she'll personally rip my room and my ass apart.

Tugging on my jeans, I reach for my T-shirt and head toward the living room, where the music is much louder. Izzie's dancing on stage. Her attention is totally fixed on the pole. I lean against the doorframe, mesmerized by her scintillating curves. Izzie spins around the brass before straddling it with her legs spread in a V. My dick twitches. The female continues with her erotic acrobatics, unaware that I'm watching. She's poetry in motion and all mine. We'll make beautiful cubs together. Honestly, we could start now.

I'd be lying if I said my interest was purely sexual. No, I'm tired of being single. The fuck-'em-and-leave-'em game has grown tedious. I want to wake up to someone who does more than simply whet my sexual appetite. Claiming Izzie as my mate, however, isn't just about loneliness. I'm ready to build a life, connect with a female who'll make me want to be better. My days of running around like a sex-starved teen are over.

Slowly, I clap my hands. "Beautiful."

She climbs down the pole and leans against it. "I'm sorry if I woke you. I just wanted to get a little practice in before tonight."

"No need to apologize. But *cariño*, you don't need practice." My gaze takes in the tiny red G-string—a waste of fabric. Then I notice her pert nipples, like tiny sharp peaks, poking through the thin, cropped T-shirt. The provocative ensemble is courtesy of Gloriana. The witch made sure the items were here this morning along with a pair of jeans for Izzie. "You're perfection, *dulzura*."

"Not hardly. Dancing for supernaturals isn't the same as doing it for humans." Izzie steps off the stage.

My gaze follows her across the room. "How so?"

She slips into the jeans. "For starters, supes like to see more tricks on the pole. To them, anyone can dance. They need stunts to arouse them and keep them interested. Humans are all into the visual and not so much the talent. Flash your crotch at humans, and they couldn't care less if you shimmy up and down or spin around the pole. They're mesmerized by the fantasy."

Coming closer, I slip my fingers into her belt loops and pull her to me. My mouth swoops in to steal a kiss. Memories of last night rush back. If I don't stop, we'll never leave this suite. I break off the kiss and bite her lip. Fuck. She tastes incredible. Restraining my desire, I stop and lean my forehead on hers.

"I'd prefer it if you only danced for me."

She grins at me. "Unfortunately, dancing for you won't make me any money."

"You don't need it," I say as I caress her cheek. "My house is big enough. I'll provide whatever you need."

Izzie places her hands on my chest and pushes me away. "Uh-uh. I'm not looking for someone to take care of me."

"You didn't ask me. I'm offering."

"Doesn't matter. The outcome is the same." She goes over to the sofa and picks up a discarded pump. "It's why I don't like the whole soul mate thing."

Plunking down beside her, I grab the other shoe and hold on to it. "Explain."

"My mom died when I was seventeen. Dad left years before that. So I had to figure out fast how to take care of myself and my brother and sister."

"Where are they now?"

"In college. My brother will be graduating in a year."

Lightly stroking her forearm, I say, "It had to be hard taking care of them by yourself."

"It was, but I got lucky. I met my best friend, Senora, and she helped me get a job at Captive Thrills. Not bragging, but I've done a hell of a job. I don't need any help." She reaches for her shoe.

I hold it out of reach while my eyes search hers for an answer. Some clue to why she's resisting what should be a natural thing for our kind. "What are you afraid of, Izzie? Granted, you've had a hard life. You're possibly stronger than a lot of females I've encountered, but it's not a sign of weakness to let someone take care of you."

She straddles my lap and takes the shoe from me. "Can you just drop it? I don't need a protector or a caretaker."

My hand trails up her thigh to her hip. "Tell me what you need. What can I do for you, *cariño*?"

Izzie's fingers run over my shoulders. "I don't do relationships. People always get hurt." She sighs. "I'll admit that we have great chemistry. Even so, letting you into my life has to be on my terms. Let's keep it fun, nothing serious."

My hands wrap around Izzie's waist, keeping her in place a moment longer. "That doesn't work for me. I've had my fill of meaningless trysts."

"Well, I'm sorry. I can't commit to anything more than that." She gives me a quick kiss. "Where is it written that soul mates have to be tied at the hip? I want to explore all this life has to offer. Besides, you have your house. I'd like to find my own place to live. I value my independence, Hunter."

"I'm not trying to take it away from you, but I need more than what you're offering." Drawing in a breath, I conclude I'll have to move slowly with Izzie. She has to want—no, *hunger*—for me before she'll give in. I exhale and say, "Let's do this. We'll take our time and get to know each other. Make no decisions yet."

Izzie holds her head to the side and purses her lips. "No expectations either?"

"If that's what you need."

A warm smile slowly spreads over her pretty face. "I think I can agree to that."

"Good." This female will be the death of me. Leaning in, I place a brief kiss on her full lips. "Spend the day with me."

"No, Hunter. I have things to do."

"I'll make sure we'll go by the cottage long before tonight. Hell, I'll buy you a new outfit, cosmetics . . . whatever you need for tonight, it's yours. Just stay with me."

She laughs, and it's melodious. It's a sound I want to hear from her constantly. "You're terrible. Do you plan on spending every minute with me?"

"As much as I can." My hands grip her ass. "Come shower with me. Then I want to take you to my place."

Izzie's gaze darts around the room. "This isn't it?"

"Hell naw. This is just my playroom. I want you to meet my grandfather."

"It's too—"

I place my finger on my mouth. "It isn't. He needs to meet you."

AN HOUR LATER, I unlock the front door of my house. Izzie stops beside me as I check the mail Baba left on the hall table. Smells of chorizo, potatoes, and eggs drift toward me, and I decide the bills can wait.

"Baba," I call out and reach for Izzie's hand. "We have company."

My grandfather, his waist-length white hair hanging in a braid over his shoulder, comes around the corner. "No need to shout. My hearing works just fine." His deep-set, bluish-green eyes take in Izzie, and his jaw drops. "You found her. *Bienvenida, bendecida.*"

"Blessed One?" Izzie's gaze rocks to mine. Her eyes narrow. "This is the shit Gloriana was talking about."

My stomach tenses as I imagine what the *bruja* might have said—what she might have gotten wrong. "What did she tell you?"

"I'm not here to break a curse," Izzie exclaims.

Thankfully, Baba intervenes, grasping Izzie's elbow and guiding toward her a chair. "Perhaps you should take a seat? Hunter, bring the coffee."

I'm surprised when Izzie goes into the great room with Baba. Maybe she's not as stubborn as I first thought.

BABA SET up brunch on the coffee table near the fireplace. I've barely eaten any of it as my attention is fully on him, filling Izzie in on our history.

"So I'm supposed to believe that you've had visions of me?" Izzie says.

Baba's eyes widen. "Has no one told you about shamans and our purpose?"

"I knew a few growing up," she admits. "Our family wasn't close. I didn't know my father's side of the family, and Mom was estranged from her parents."

"Everyone should know their heritage," Baba says sadly.

Izzie takes a sip of coffee. "Can I ask why you're having dreams of me? It's not like we've met or anything."

"On a different plane we have, and have had many conversations," Baba starts.

"About?"

"History." He glances at me before continuing. "Years ago, a witch fell in love with my son-in-law, Eadrich James Patee. He was in love with my daughter and showed no interest in the witch. So she cast a spell on him. The witch hoped that if my son-in-law couldn't produce children, my daughter would leave him."

My father gave up his given last name when he left the ancestral home with my mother. His family didn't want them together, and so they abandoned everything and everyone they knew for love. Dad met up with the witch after they came to Havenwood Falls.

Izzie looks over at me. "Gloriana told me part of the story. How was Hunter born after this curse?"

It's not the first time I've heard the story. No matter how many times it's told, I never tire of it. Knowing the reality behind my birth makes me appreciate my life more.

"We're fortunate to have Hunter, but he has no siblings. No matter how hard my daughter and son-in-law tried, they couldn't produce more children. They went to see a shaman outside the family. He told them only true love shared by soul mates would break the curse. Hunter is the hope for our family."

"That's a lot to burden one being with," she says.

Baba's head bobs up and down. "Understood, but there aren't any other options. We even forced Hunter's transformation early in life so he could have enough time to find the Blessed One."

The news flash agitates my beast. "Becoming a full nagual at sixteen was planned?"

"Yes." Baba rests his hand on my knee. "We did what had to be done."

Jumping to my feet, I run a hand through my hair and pace the floor, trying to maintain control. "Did you foresee the hell my life would become?"

"I did, but you survived." Calmly, Baba says, "Now that you've found your true mate, our family will continue."

Izzie interjects, "I hate to burst your bubble, Mr. . . . ."

"Babajide Chapula is my given name, but you may call me Baba."

My grandfather pauses for a beat or two. "I appreciate your reluctance to believe our tale, but all of it is true. You are my family's future."

Before I can stop her, Izzie rushes out to the patio.

"Go to her, Hunter. Change her mind."

Rubbing the back of my neck, I say, "I promised I wouldn't pressure her. We were going to take it slow."

"You don't have time. If this curse is to be broken, you must do it before Samhain."

Shit. I forgot about the deadlines. Once mates discover each other, they have to bond within forty-eight hours. Once the bond has been activated, we only have eight fucking days—no pun intended—to break the curse.

CHAPTER 9

IZZIE

*W*hen Gloriana told me about Hunter and that damned curse, I should have followed my first mind. Hooking up with him was a bad idea, and my life is full of enough stupid decisions. He should have been the one to tell me, instead of putting me in this precarious position. If I don't enter into the bond, I look like an ass. Giving in means starting a family. I raised my siblings. I'm not ready to be someone else's parent.

The glass patio door creaks open behind me. I hold my breath as heavy footsteps collide with the wooden deck.

"Izzie?"

Gripping the wrought iron banister, I refuse to turn around. "I'm not ready for this, Hunter. I told you I don't do relationships."

His hand goes to my waist, and he tucks me against him. "Izzie, I respect that. Really, I do. But this is about my future. What would you do in my shoes?"

My heart goes out to Hunter, but my beast isn't willing to play nice. She's back to her snarky self. "Be honest. Tell my so-called mate that this is more than a casual hookup."

"I believe I told you that." Hunter kisses my forehead. "Besides, if I led with that, you wouldn't be here now."

I glare at him.

"Here's the thing, *cariño*, like it or not, we're destined to be together." Hunter strokes a calloused thumb over my cheek. "Ignore the bond, and we're both doomed. My line dies out, and we live unhappy, separate lives. Is that what you want?"

Thank you, Captain Obvious! I didn't need to hear any of that. "No, but you lied to me."

"No, I didn't." Hunter grins. "I just left out a few details."

"Lie of omission. Same thing." I try to push him off me, but Hunter doesn't budge.

"Here's a truth for you. Baba just told me, and I'm not happy about it." He exhales before saying, "To save my family, the bond has to be in place before Samhain."

"No!" Summoning all the strength I can, I extricate myself from Hunter. "That's in eight damn days. Not fair, Hunter."

He tilts his head back and looks up at the sky. "What can I say? Life isn't fair. I don't like this any more than you do, but it's my reality." Hunter glances over at me. In two long strides, he crosses the deck and stops in front of me. Tentatively, he touches my upper arm. "Correction. It's *our* reality. Izzie, I'm not one to beg, but I'm doing it this time. Please commit to the bond. We can still take our time getting to know each other."

"How?"

Hunter drops his hand. "As much as I want you here with me, I'll agree to us living apart for a while. We can date, if that'll make you happy. Do whatever shit you require until you're ready to live with me as we're meant to be."

"What if it takes me months to be ready?" Honestly, it might take years. I don't want to simply live with a mate. Believe it or not, I want the engagement, the big-ass wedding, and the frou-frou dress. Yes, I want all the pomp and circumstance that goes along with the big event, but there's something more important—the only thing that should be important. "I require love."

He nods. "Understood. Whatever it takes, *cariño*. I'm yours, and I'll wait on you."

Hundreds of arguments could be made against Hunter's

suggestion, but honestly, I don't feel like battling. This male has done what no one else has done—tame my beast. Make her lie down and consider other options. Like marriage. If Hunter's willing to wait, I can at least meet him halfway.

"Fine. I'll think about it. Right now, I need to go shopping for tonight." I stride past Hunter, but he grabs my wrist.

"I said I'd take you. We're still spending the day together."

Of all things, he has to remember that. It's the total opposite of what I want—time to think. A long soak in a tub, a glass or two of wine, and a good meal are the things on my agenda today. "I'll agree to shopping, but Hunter, what I need to do is think, and I can't do that if we're hanging out."

"But if we don't spend time together," he grins, "how will you fall in love with me?"

Could my future mate be any more arrogant?

SHOPPING IS NORMALLY a great remedy when I'm in a foul mood—which is more often than I care to admit. A little indulgence always brightens my spirits. When Hunter parks his bike in front of Pleasurez, my temper darkens. It's the last place I want to be.

I'm still seated on the back of the bike as Hunter walks away. In a few steps, reality dawns, and he faces me with a curious look on his handsome face. "What's wrong, Izzie?"

Removing the helmet, I ask, "Is this the only store in town?"

"For what you need? Yes." His gaze bounces to the front door and back to me. "Is there something I should know?"

He can't be serious. The issue should be obvious to anyone who can add—and he calls himself an accountant. "Your ex."

Hunter saunters over to me, snakes his hand through my hair, and drops a kiss on my lips. If he thinks a kiss . . . if he believes his mouth can work magic . . . change my mind . . . make me feel things . . . Okay. He has my attention.

Breaking off the kiss, he strokes my cheek. "I realize Cheresse is a pain in the ass, but you're with me, *mi amor*. She'll get the message."

His touch makes me shudder. The message he's sending has me ready to give up whatever dignity I possess and make out with him in the middle of this plaza. What the hell is wrong with me? One night with him, and I turn to putty from a kiss? Well, it was a hot kiss with the promise of so much more.

Snap out of it!

Too bad Hunter isn't picking up on the right info. If he did, he'd get why this is a bad idea. But males, regardless of whether they're human or supe, can be seriously clueless. Flaunting your new interest —especially one that's a so-called soul mate—in front of a former girlfriend isn't smart. It's a downright stupid decision, asking for trouble.

And if you had packed for more than a quick getaway, you'd have your outfits and this excursion wouldn't be necessary.

"Are we doing this?" Hunter intertwines his fingers with mine and electricity sparks between us.

If *doing this* means finding an available bed, table, or back seat, I'm down for it. Shopping with Cheresse nearby? A resounding no.

"If it bothers you that much, we don't have to shop here. Come to think of it, I know that Brian Long is looking for an assistant. Interested?"

"No." I draw the line at answering phones for a living. "All I got to say is she'd better not start shit with me."

Hunter laughs as he drags me off the bike. He winks. "I think I'd love to see that fight."

~

OF COURSE, Cheresse has to be at the register when we enter the shop. She finishes up with a customer and greets us with a too cheery "Hey there. I'll be with you in a minute."

Hunter leans in. "Told you. No problem."

He's too blind to see it—the tight nod along with the carefully controlled voice and simmering stare. Evidence of a pissed off female. My gut tells me to get the hell out. Shit, I'll dance in my underwear or ask Gloriana to conjure up something.

"We should leave, Hunter."

"Nonsense." He tugs my hand and leads the way to a display of six-inch heels. Picking up a pair of clear, strappy sandals, he says, "What size do you need?"

"Seven," I mumble.

"I don't know if I have that one in *your* size," Cheresse says behind us.

Hunter turns and shoves the shoe at her. "Check. We'll keep looking."

Red seeps across the statuesque nagual's face before she storms off.

"You shouldn't make her mad," I warn him.

"And she needs to remember her place around here." Hunter frowns. "She runs a store that's supposed to cater to everyone."

"Still . . ."

Hunter ignores me and heads toward the outfits. "What else do you need?"

Hurrying behind him, I grab a hot-pink-sequined fishnet top along with a pair of silver booty shorts. "This will do."

"That's only good for one night. Get whatever else you need," Hunter urges.

"Look, I'll talk to Gloriana and get her to help me out. I can order some things online too."

Cheresse returns with a shoe box. "Is this what you wanted?"

Hunter opens it and pulls out the right shoes. He checks the size, inspecting them like the shoes are for him.

"Yeah. Add this outfit." He takes the stuff from me and shoves it toward Cheresse.

I cringe—why do anything else to piss off this nagual?

Moving away from us, Hunter goes through the racks. A shiny leopard-print, double-string bra and thong set gets added to the pile. He stops in front of a turquoise beaded bikini. "Nice?"

Stiffly, I nod.

The male completely disregards what I told him. He selects bra and thong sets, bikinis, strapless dresses, and even booty shorts. I'm surprised he gets the sizes right.

The whole time we're shopping, Cheresse fumes. Her nostrils flare, and every few minutes, she tosses a heated glance my way. After twenty minutes, she's carrying a large pile of clothing along with the shoe box.

"If you want to keep shopping, I need to put these at the register," she says through gritted teeth.

Gee. No offer of a fitting room? The only offer I suspect Cheresse wants to give us is one involving the front door.

Hunter looks over his shoulder. "Maybe that'll do for now. Come on, *cariño.*" He reaches into his wallet and pulls out a platinum card. "You pay for it. I'm going to call a prospect to collect it all."

Would not have been an issue if he'd stopped at the one outfit and shoes, I think as I trail behind Cheresse.

"You know you're not the first female to take advantage of Hunter's generosity," Cheresse says as she places the garments in a bright pink bag.

My head jerks back as my face tightens. "What are you blabbering about?"

She snatches the credit card from me. "Over the years, I've watched females take up with Hunter. He spends money on them. Beds them nightly. Gives them all his attention, and then every single skank bounces." Cheresse points at herself with the card before tossing it on the counter. "I'm the only one who has ever loved him. If you hurt him, your ass will be mine."

Flipping my hair off my shoulders, I glare back. "Is that so? Well, my ass is right here. Come get it."

Cheresse cracks her knuckles. "Glad to."

Before she can come from around the counter, however, Hunter intervenes. "Ladies, ladies, ladies . . . enough." He wraps his arm around my shoulders. "Cheresse, anger doesn't look good on you. Don't worry. We won't be returning."

She shoves the bag across the counter. "Make sure *she* doesn't."

This won't be the last confrontation between us. Females like

Cheresse don't like losing eligible males. They fight hard to get and keep what they want. Something tells me the angry nagual doesn't even know the meaning of the word stop. Too bad. I'm more than willing to teach her.

~

A SCRAWNY MALE with more tattoos than skin waits for us as we exit Pleasurez. Hunter hands him my purchases with the instruction to take the bags to Silk. The prospect and Hunter exchange a few words before he climbs into his pickup and drives off.

"Hunter . . ."

"No, *cariño*. I know what you're going to say, and I don't want to hear it. It makes no sense for that stuff to be at the cottage. Everything will be waiting for you in the employee lounge."

"The lounge? But I thought . . ."

"You thought I was moving you into my suite." Hunter turns and gives me a cocky masculine grin. "In time. For now, I'm here for you however you need me to be."

He leans in to kiss me, but before his lips connect, I notice a pale hand pushing aside the shop door's curtain.

CHAPTER 10

HUNTER

*W*hen it comes to Izzie, I'll take whatever victory I get, and our shopping trip definitely belongs in the win category. I was more than happy to lavish money on her.

Poor Izzie. I really should tell her that I can hear her thoughts. It's a benefit—or a drawback, depending upon your viewpoint—to being mates. Shame on me for taking advantage of her immaturity. Once she matures, she'll hear all my thoughts—good and bad.

Despite Izzie's opinion about clueless males, I noticed Cheresse's behavior. Hell, who could miss the attitude dripping off my ex? But I can handle her. Put Cheresse in check from time to time. Let her know who's boss and everything is right in the world. Honestly, the female is all growl and no claws. Nothing to worry about.

The second victory of the day comes when Izzie agrees to come back to my house instead of the inn. I had hoped to take her to the country club and dine at Allura's, but Izzie said she'd rather cook for me. Once I get home, though, food takes a back seat to desire. Watching her in the kitchen—her round ass gently swaying while her shoulders shimmy to J. Balvin playing over the speakers—arouses me. I'm yearning to touch her, taste her . . . fuck her.

As she seasons the steaks, I approach from behind and press my body into hers. Bracketing her waist, I rub the arcs of her hips with my thumbs. Every part of me is turned on. I simply can't get enough of this female. Nuzzling her neck, I whisper, "Skip the steaks. I'd rather eat you."

Izzie moves her hips from side to side, making my dick harder. She asks, "Where's your grandfather?"

"Out." Thankfully, Baba is at the Circle J pot dispensary, getting a fresh supply of sinsemilla. Afterward, he'll hang out with Monte's grandfather. "He won't be back for a few hours."

Izzie's head drops back against me while she gyrates her hips. "I need a shower."

"You'll love mine. But first . . ."

Lust blindsides me as I turn Izzie around. I slant my mouth over hers, capturing her lips with a possessive hunger. The aching need to be deep inside this female nearly obliterates my thoughts.

Although we're alone, I'd rather not chance Baba returning early. He disapproves of my lifestyle, but swore he'd look the other way as long as he never had to see or hear any of it. Upstairs? No. The playroom. It's closer. I just need a damn surface behind a door. Sweeping Izzie into my arms, I head for the stairs.

"Where are we going?" Izzie asks in a breathy voice.

"Someplace I can fuck you uninterrupted."

The door slams behind us as I descend the steps. Just like at Silk, recessed lights flicker on as I enter the room. To be honest, I'm not ready to introduce Izzie to this side of me. My playroom is more salacious than the suite at Silk. In the past, the space with its assortment of kinky paraphernalia scared away a few females.

All except Cheresse.

Focus.

Lowering Izzie onto the red and black bondage bed in the corner, I hope for the best.

"Hunter?" Worry and curiosity mix in Izzie's voice.

So much for hope. Yanking my T-shirt over my head, I say, "Can we talk about this later?"

Izzie lifts her hips and shrugs out of her jeans. The corners of her lips curl up as she reaches for my hand. "Definitely."

~

UNFORTUNATELY, *later* insists on announcing its presence before I'm ready for it. Izzie pulls on my T-shirt and gives me a narrowed stare. "Explain."

Reaching for my jeans, I mutter, "Welcome to my world."

Izzie touches my arm. "Hey, no judgment from me. I just want to know what all you're into. The room back at the club seems mild compared to this place."

For the first time, I see my basement through someone else's eyes —risqué bordering on the horrific. Over the years, I've only brought a few females to the space. Those who have been in my inner sanctum haven't revealed its contents to anyone.

Common sense would have been stopping at the bondage bed with a frame meant for hanging things (sometimes people), but I pushed the boundaries and added other treasures. A couples' swing dangles from a corner. There's even a spanking bench and a bondage chair. Cabinets, holding equipment meant to tempt and tantalize, occupy the other corners of the room. I've spent ridiculous amounts of money on adult toys—floggers, cock rings, butt plugs, spreader bars, and other such gear. In all honesty, it would take days to catalog it all. Thankfully, Izzie can't see the viewing area from here. It's too soon to share that proclivity with her.

"Hunter, talk to me," she urges.

"This is what happens when a nagual matures too early."

"Huh?" Izzie bites her lip.

Fuck me sideways.

"If you want me to tell you, don't do that with your mouth."

A mischievous smile spreads over her face.

"Stop it." She's killing me. All I can think of is what else that mouth is capable of, what it can do to me. Zipping my jeans, I say, "When a nagual male matures early, it's hard to satisfy him. It didn't matter how many females I had sex with. I just couldn't find a release. Then one night I met someone. She liked rough sex. She wanted me to tie her up, choke her while we—"

"I get it."

Speechless, I suck in a quick breath and settle back on the bed.

"It turned you on. You found your release." Izzie scoots closer to me. "I've tried the same thing. Problem is, bondage and all the toys haven't worked. My gratification lasts for minutes, but my partners never want a second go-round."

Tipping my head to the side, I ask, "None of these items turns you off?"

"No." Her eager gaze darts around the room. "I say we explore. Find out whether you can get me off with any of it."

My breathing slows, and my pulse steadies. This female astonishes me. Izzie is definitely the one. She grounds me, letting me be myself.

Izzie and I have spent the entire day together, mostly in bed, but it's getting late. As much as I don't want her to leave, I realize she has a job to do, and I've got a meeting with Liam. I'm not going back on my promise. Just knowing that she understood my needs and shared my same issues gives me peace.

Pulling her into my arms, I glide my fingers over her back and place my hand on her ass. "Thank you for spending the day with me."

She wraps her hands around my neck. "Believe it or not, I had fun."

"So when can we plan the ceremony?" I ask, only half joking.

"Don't push your luck. It hasn't even been a day since I said I'd think on it."

Can't blame a nagual for trying.

After Izzie leaves, I stay home. Seeing her dance might just send me over the edge. The last thing I need is to get into a fight with some creature ogling her. Sweet-smelling weed drifts through the great room's doors, and I find Baba in a chair, toking on a joint.

"Evening, *noxhuiutze*," my grandfather says and waves his free hand toward a chair. "Care to join me?"

"No, thanks." I'm still riding a high that's much sweeter than anything Baba could inhale.

"Where's Izzie?"

"At Silk." Baba cuts an eye toward me. "Don't. I promised her independence."

"You should be with her."

Shaking my head, I say, "No. It's in everyone's best interests if I'm not."

Baba puts out the blunt and lays it at the edge of the ashtray. "You should be with her for protection."

My heartbeat ratchets up a notch. My grandfather's words always mean something. "Why?"

"Trouble is coming."

Shit. "What type of trouble?"

"Izzie's past and her present will collide. Both of your futures are in jeopardy."

Raking a hand through my hair, my voice rises. "I don't mean to be rude, but give it to me in plain English."

Baba glares at me for a moment before saying, "This is plain English. Two forces want Izzie. They both intend harm. She will need your help. First, you must find the person holding the key to the puzzle."

"Can I get a clue?"

"Ada Daryn. Find her and you'll find the source of the trouble."

ALTHOUGH I'D RATHER BE at Silk keeping an eye on Izzie, I'm waiting to meet with Liam at the Fallview Tavern. Odette Alverson, the owner, waves at me as I sip my beer. I look around the homey atmosphere and wonder why Liam wanted to meet here.

Heavy footsteps echoing across the hardwood floor catch my

attention. It's not just Liam. He has his son, Jack, and Savage with him.

"What's up, Liam?"

He lowers his big frame onto one of the chairs near the fireplace. "Dinner and follow up."

"On?"

Liam stares at me. "Have you taken care of what we talked about?"

"It's handled."

"It better be," Liam warns.

Savage, sitting in the chair beside Liam, says, "It shouldn't have been a fucking problem to begin with, Trapper." He drags a hand through his shoulder-length messy locks. "I swear, one more goddamned issue, and we're kicking your ass out. It's enough that we put up with your shit at Silk. Now you're putting our fucking livelihood at risk because of a goddamned female."

The look on Jack's face mirrors my own sentiment—can I get the hell out of here?

The few people in the tavern look over. Liam jerks his head toward the onlookers, and Savage stands up and walks away, taking Jack with him.

In a lowered voice, I ask, "Liam, was that necessary? I told you it's been handled. Don't believe me? Check with Oscar."

"I will, but I agree with Savage. Either get your shit straight or you're out—that includes your kink den at Silk."

I SWEAR I could have done without that come-to-hell session with Liam and Savage. Frankly, I think the two hellhounds just wanted to fuck with my head. Someone probably complained that I stayed overnight at Silk—something I try to refrain from after the last female I had there. She puked her gut to anyone who would listen. Savage stepped in and got someone from the Luna Coven—I'm guessing Lyra Beaumont—to help out with a little memory spell.

I hope that's the only interruption tonight. Going to Silk and looking into this threat Baba mentioned is my plan. Perhaps Crusher—if he's on the door tonight—might be able to give me some info. I should talk to Monte. He may have heard something through his network.

I'm on my way to Cerberus Delivery Inc.'s warehouse. As I pull up to the light near Miller's Plaza, I see an unusual pairing outside Pleasurez—Cheresse and none other than Ada Daryn. I watch the two females talk. The light turns green, and a car horn sounds behind me. Curiosity nags me, but then I see the bright pink bag in the hand of the Green Coven's leader. I guess she's getting her freak on tonight. I'm not one to judge.

◦

MINUTES LATER, I'm at CDI. I park alongside Monte as he straps on his half helmet. He looks over at me. "I didn't expect to see you tonight."

Removing my full-face helmet, I announce, "We need to talk. Baba had a vision."

"About?"

"Izzie. Some shit about her past and present colliding." I glance down at the dark visor, realizing my grandfather's image is just as obscure as the face shield. Unfortunately, it's all I have to go on. "Baba also mentioned Ada Daryn."

"I thought shit calmed down when Chekhov got his money back."

"Same here. Look, I need your help." A slight tremor courses through my arms. I take a deep breath and force my beast to stay still. Going off half-cocked won't do anyone any good. "Have you heard anything? Is anyone from Chekhov's camp looking for Izzie?"

Monte's jaw works back and forth.

My hand grips the bike handle so tight, the steel dents. "God damn it, Monte! Tell me!"

He looks around the area. Lowering his voice, he says, "Bratva. The Chekhovs and the Russian mafia are associates. I checked in with

Oscar. His connections spotted teams in Grand Junction and Durango."

"When the fuck were you going to tell me?" My best friend since high school stays quiet, confirming what I suspect. "You didn't plan on telling me. What the hell happened to brotherhood?"

Monte places a fist over his heart. "It's because of brotherhood that we kept it from you. Oscar said to let him handle it. Liam doesn't—"

My free hand fists. I'm ready to toss my helmet at the wall, but I just bought the damned thing. Instead, I breathe in and out, trying to find some semblance of peace. "This ain't Liam's call."

"I know, but let us handle it. Nobody wants to see you get your ass killed."

"I'm not the one you should worry about," I shoot back.

"Well, now you know. What are you gonna do?"

"Go to Grand—"

"Wrong," Monte interjects. "We're going to the clubhouse. Kai Reynolds and a few other prospects are keeping an eye on Izzie."

"I'm not sure about that." The idea of a bunch of recruits watching over Izzie irritates the shit out of me.

"Stop worrying. Crusher's working the door tonight. They report to him."

Better.

Monte continues, "We need to meet with Oscar. Go over the plan. We don't do shit without Liam's approval."

Not saying a word, I put my helmet on, crank up my bike, and follow Monte out of the parking lot. This will be one long-ass night.

CHAPTER 11

IZZIE

Silk's dressing room is nothing like I expected. It's more like an office space with private cubicles. Nothing like the one at Captive Thrills. The New York club's changing space resembled a high school locker room. Lockers lined one side of the space. Wooden benches occupied the floor in front of a long mirror attached to a wall. Outlets were beneath the mirror.

Although Silk's facility is a step up, the cattiness is still present. Half-naked females, steadily bitching and moaning about customers, parade through the area. Frankly, I could do without their whining. When you choose this line of work, you have to be prepared to take the good—flexible hours and easy work—along with the bad. No need griping about the crappy tips, customers with grabby hands, and managers who don't give a shit about you.

Dropping my bag on top of the counter in my assigned space, I glance in the mirror. The pink fishnet halter top with sequins was a good choice, while the booty shorts emphasize my ass. Keeping myself in shape has its rewards.

"Hey, girl." Gloriana leans against the short pink wall.

"Hey, yourself." I jerk my head toward the two females arguing across the room. "Are they always like that?"

"Yeah. Happens every single night. They get to arguing over tips and who made eyes at a customer." Gloriana leans close. "Would you believe they're a couple?"

My mouth drops. "Really? Why are they dancing here then?"

"Fuck if I know. If I rolled that way, I sure wouldn't want to see my partner dancing for strangers." She taps my arm. "Hey, you're on center stage tonight. After you dance, you work the floor. Oh, and you're dancing for humans tonight."

"Why?" Captive Thrills didn't segment the customers. I was looking forward to dancing for supes only.

"It's an easier gig. The humans who visit Havenwood Falls tend to have deep pockets and pay better. Besides, it keeps Trapper calm. Last thing he needs is for you to draw another supe's attention."

I don't know whether to be thankful for being placed in the larger room or pissed that Hunter's wishes outweigh my own.

DANCING FOR HUMANS IS EASIER, but so exceedingly boring. Listening to "Back That Thang Up" doesn't inspire creativity either. Just doing a few spins and twists on the pole excites this crowd. When I flip upside down and perform a perfect Scorpio—hanging from one leg while gripping an ankle, the men hoot and holler. Grabbing both heels, I slowly slide down the pole. Before I reach the ground, I flip around and dismount with a cartwheel. Big bills land at my feet—mostly twenties and fifties with a few Benjis thrown in for good measure. My quick assessment? Close to three hundred dollars. Not bad. Time to work the floor.

I SASHAY toward a table with a man dressed in jeans and a T-shirt. His wavy hair and blue eyes stand out. Even with wire-rimmed glasses, the man is unbelievably hot for a human.

"Hi," I say.

"Hi, yourself. You're very talented."

"Thank you."

He jerks his head toward the vacant seat beside him. "Name's Stephen Zander."

Before I can sit down, a force hits me. I look over my shoulder and see Gloriana. "Sorry. She's busy."

He smiles and says, "Maybe another time."

Gloriana pulls me to the side. "Girl, your phone is blowing up back in the dressing room. Go shut that shit up, but make it quick. Melaina doesn't like us handling personal business while we're working."

"Thanks," I say and rush toward the lounge.

My mind is so focused on who might be calling me, I collide with someone in the hall. Looking up, I see Cheresse. Damn.

"Watch where you're—oh, it's *you*," she screams. Whatever was in her glass drips off her skimpy blouse.

"Hey, I'm sorry, Cheresse," I say sincerely. "I'm in a hurry. Let me pay for another drink."

Her lips flatten, and she rolls her eyes. "I'm headed back to the dance floor. Tell a waitress to bring me a Midnight Cooler made with Patron."

Patron—preferred drink of high-maintenance bitches.

"I'll make sure the bartender gets you another one." Heading toward the elevator, I put the incident behind me.

Or not.

Before I can find sanctity within the elevator, a pale hand sneaks in and the doors stop. It's Cheresse. Her eyes are blazing. "Here's the thing. I don't appreciate smelling like a distillery all night."

Oh hell. She's messing with my time, and I don't appreciate *that.* My arms remain at my side while my fists tighten. "Then go home. Nobody's forcing you to stay here."

"But that's where you're wrong." Stepping farther into the elevator, she pushes a finger into my chest as the doors close behind her. "*You're* forcing me to stay here. Somebody has to make sure your ass stays away from Hunter."

"Not this shit again."

Her nostrils flare. "Yes, this shit again."

The crazy bitch gets in my face. My hands come up between us, preventing her from getting closer. One good shove, and her back hits the elevator door. Cheresse's face turns red. She lunges for me, but I'm prepared. Lifting my right fist, I clock her in the jaw. She stumbles backward before sliding to the floor. Claws rip through her hands.

No way am I fighting her beast in close quarters. I mash the button repeatedly. The doors part, and I rush toward them. As I move past Cheresse, she swipes at my ankle, drawing blood. That shit hurts. Raising my free foot, I kick her in the chest. Her breath whooshes, and her beast stays put.

Leaning over Cheresse, in a deliberate voice, I say, "This is over. Hunter's with me. Keep the hell away from the both of us."

Cheresse, still on the floor, growls, "This isn't over, bitch."

Normally after knocking someone out, I feel good. Not this time. Instead, I get the sense that this skirmish was only the tipping point. Announcing I'm with Hunter probably wasn't the wisest choice.

You're with Hunter? Since when? What changed your mind?

Maybe it was the threat to my source of peace. Maybe it was how I truly felt at the moment. Either way, I can't dwell on it. Finding out who's calling me matters more. The elevator doors close behind me, leaving Cheresse to nurse her hurt feelings. My focus shifts from the club to the man who wants me dead. What if Kazimir found me and hacked my number? It wouldn't be the first time.

"Hey, Izzie."

My heart stops, then my head rocks up. It's Gloriana.

"Did you take care of your phone?" She stops in front of me. "You're needed on the floor."

Honestly, I despise lying. It always leads to a bad situation, but desperate times call for little white lies. My beast scratching the surface lets me know I don't have options. Grasping Gloriana's slim arm, I turn her away from the elevator. "About that—the elevator seems to be out. If you know what I mean."

"Oh, hell. Sometimes customers get their freak on inside it. I'll get Oscar." Gloriana walks down the hall with me. We stop in front of a door. "Use the service elevator." She points to the control panel. "Just punch in your code. If anyone asks, tell them I told you to use it."

"Thanks, girl. I'll only be a few minutes."

~

LUCKILY, the lounge is empty. I rush to my locker, find my phone, and discover ten texts from Senora. I scroll to the last one.

Senora Graves: Check your voice mail.

My hand shakes as I press the icon. Senora's panicky voice greets me.

"Why the fuck aren't you answering your phone? You need to get the hell out of there. Kazimir's jet landed in Colorado Springs a few hours ago. My sources say he's on his way to Grand Junction. Go south. Now. Give me a location, and I'll meet you. You can't handle him alone."

Shit, shit, shit. Tossing the phone in my bag, I slam the locker. Someone is behind me. I whirl around and see Cheresse.

"You need to move out of my way!" I yell and attempt to pass her.

"Not before I give you something you deserve," she says with a smile on her face, and her hand raises.

"I don't have time for—"

She blows on her hand, and a blue mist impedes my vision. The lingering haze chokes me. I drop to the floor. A solid kick to my ribs is the last thing I feel before darkness surrounds me.

~

CRACKING OPEN MY EYES, I squint at my poorly lit surroundings. Faint images—equipment or maybe supplies—fill the space. I blink a few times. My vision clears, but leaves me confused as hell. Why am I in one of the back rooms of Pleasurez?

Time to get the fuck out of here. I can't move. My arms, slightly numb, are over my head, while my feet won't budge. Something cold is around my neck. When I find the person who hung me on this fucking saltire cross, I'm going to gut them.

Something's wrong. I'm angry, but I don't feel like I could rip shit apart.

The sound of high heels click across the floor, coming closer. They stop in front of me. My eyes follow the long limbs until I'm locked in a stare with Cheresse. In her hand is my totem.

"Looking for this, bitch?"

Rage courses through me, but it's not from the beast. Fuck. Without my totem, I can't even try to summon her. "Give it back, Cheresse!"

She inches forward and swings the pendant in my face. "You'll get it back after Samhain."

"Why—" Hunter's words float back to me. The curse. If we don't commit to each other before Samhain, the curse remains and our mating is only a memory. "You're fucking crazy," I spit out. "You can't keep me here that long."

Cheresse tucks my totem into her jeans pocket. "Oh, but I can." She ambles around the room, turning over items as she goes. "Funny thing about a town with supernaturals? There's always a witch willing to do favors. It's amazing what one will do with the right incentive."

I stay quiet.

"Here in Havenwood Falls we have good witches and those not so good. Guess which ones I'm friendly with?"

My fists ball up.

"Beast got your tongue?" Mocking laughter fills the room. Cheresse props herself on top of a spanking bench. "No one knows you're here. Ada glamoured the room. Customers will only see a room full of boxes and a sign saying closed for inventory. Scream, shout . . . hell, sing if you like, but no one will hear you."

"Hunter will find me."

"I don't think so. He's at the SIN clubhouse following a false lead. It'll be too late when he finds you."

My heart beats wildly, but I have to stay calm. I refuse to let Cheresse see my fear. "What's the point? This won't reunite you and Hunter."

Cheresse's lips flatten. "You're right. It won't, but that's not my goal. This is payback. He should have stayed with me. I could have made him happy. Now he won't ever find happiness. His family line will die out, and he'll never have his so-called soul mate."

This female is batshit crazy. "You really are delusional. Hunter doesn't love you."

"That may be so, but . . ." Her lips curl up. "I don't believe in soul mates. If Hunter had only loved me . . ." Sadness resides in her voice for only a minute before bitterness takes its place. "Be nice, and I'll make sure you're fed each day."

"What if I need to use the bathroom?"

"Piss on yourself. I don't fucking care. And to think I was only doing a good deed when I brought you to town. I should have left your ass on the highway." Cheresse rises and trots across the floor. "Bringing you here helped Hunter forget about me. Well, he won't remember you when this is all done."

"I want my totem."

"And supes in the Infernum want freedom. Neither one is happening." She turns off the only light in the room. "Good night."

Her angry footsteps blaze a trail to the front door. The chime sounds, the lock twists, and the bitch is gone. Senora once told me counting would help calm me. Frankly, I've never believed it, but escaping this room requires a clear head.

One.

Cheresse is the first one I kill when I'm free.

Two.

Kazimir is the next one.

Three.

Four.

Five.

On a long exhale, my thoughts settle down, and I think about the one thing that'll save me. Cheresse may not believe in soul mates, but they exist. As much as I hate being bound to one soul forever, it has to rescue me. Hunter and I haven't said the words, but we've fucked. More than once. All he has to do is get Gloriana involved. She can do a locator spell with his totem.

I just need to be patient.

CHAPTER 12

HUNTER

*S*narling, angry faces gather around the clubhouse table, trying to figure out where things went wrong. Correction—how *I* got things so fucked up. The Chekhov debacle rests on my shoulders. Some members think I'm the one responsible for the canceled liquor shipments, while others accuse me of theft. The fools have the audacity to accuse me of stealing from SIN and Cerberus as well as Chekhov Industries. All of it's bullshit, and they know it. I cook the fucking books for *them*, not me.

Oscar slams his hand onto the marred mahogany table. "Enough! Arguing about shit ain't gonna get us anywhere."

Truth, but this group of bastards doesn't get it. We don't meet without Liam. Although I'm a little pissed at him, his presence keeps the peace. With Oscar, somebody's head will roll before they calm the fuck down.

Touching my totem, a calming gesture, fills me with unexpected dread. The pendant is stone cold—it hasn't felt this way since Izzie's arrival. We may not have officially bonded, but we've mated. It's enough of a connection to let me know there's something wrong. Fear courses through me while anxious words form in my mouth. Incessant buzzing interrupts my thoughts. I peer down at my phone and see a text message from an unfamiliar number.

Have you seen Izzie?

What kind of question is that? My jaw clenches while blood rushes through my head. Automatically, I assume something's happened to Izzie. My gaze rocks toward Oscar. "Not to cut you off, but does anybody know where Izzie is?"

The big male blows air through his cheeks. "My men are watching her."

"Check on her, Oscar." Growling, I hold up my phone and wave it around. "I just got a message from somebody asking if I've seen Izzie."

"Fuck," he grumbles and pulls out his own phone.

While I wait for an update, I send a response to the anonymous person.

Hunter James: No. Not for a few hours. Who is this?

The answer comes in seconds.

My name is Senora Graves. I'm Izzie's friend. I've been texting her all night, but haven't heard from her.

Not good. The puzzled look on Oscar's face confirms it.

"What's going on, Oscar?" I ask.

Dissatisfaction twists his brow. "Gloriana found a note in the dressing room. Some motherfucking gibberish about Izzie feeling sick. According to the note, she was going home, but her rental car is still at the club. No one saw her leave."

Jumping to my feet, I talk as I hurry to the door. "We need to find her. Now."

Monte grabs my shoulder. "Not so fast, bruh. Got a message saying Chekhov's outside town, and he has your lady."

"Fuck!" I bellow as I push folks out of my way, running for the exit. "How the hell does Chekhov even know where we are?"

There are wards in place. If he got close to them, we'd know. The only way Chekhov could find us is if someone helped him. Who the hell is that?

Cheresse.

How the fuck she knows about the connection between Izzie and the mafia boss beats the hell out of me.

"Hunter?"

"Don't bother." I shake off Monte's hand and storm out of the room. Shouts hit my back like bullets, but I keep moving. The constant ringing of my phone, however, brings me to a stop. Someone collides into me.

"Hello?"

"This is Senora," the stranger's voice purrs. "What's going on with Izzie?"

Monte steps in front of me. Holding up a finger, I continue, "I'm not sure. Do you know Kazimir Chekhov?"

"Bad news in a handsome package," Senora says. "He's after Izzie."

Not a news flash. It's risky, but I'll take the gamble. "Then you know about the money?"

"Hell, yeah. Izzie stole three million from him. She would have returned it after he set her free."

"Set her free?" A sour taste settles in my throat. Leaning against the wall, I try to prep myself for the worst.

"Izzie wouldn't be straight with me, so I checked into it. Kazimir buys females. All it takes is one date with him. He lavishes them with gifts and then informs the victims they belong to him. Apparently, he pulled that shit with Izzie," Senora admits.

I'm seeing red as my beast threatens to take control. Through gritted teeth, I say, "According to our sources, Kazimir has her."

"Where are you? I can be there in minutes." When I don't speak, Senora adds, "I'm an empusa. All I need is a mental image, and I can be there."

Against my better judgment, I prattle off a location outside the city limits. Ending the call, I pocket my phone and glance up at Monte.

"Was that wise?" His face tightens. "You know, giving a stranger that information?"

Monte has always been a worrier. Not a good thing for someone who keeps company with those living slightly outside the law. I guarantee he's concerned about the Court. After we find Izzie, I'll smooth things out with them.

"She's a friend who knows about Chekhov. She might come in handy."

Monte falls in step with me.

"How many of us are heading out?" I ask.

"You, me, and Oscar," says Monte. "A few of the fellas are headed toward Silk. A small army will meet us outside town."

"Good. Let's do this shit." Nobody takes what's mine.

~

NIGHT RIDES ARE ALWAYS enjoyable and, dare I say, peaceful. Maybe it's the crisp, clean air that does it. Sadly, I can't capture serenity tonight. I'm doing my best to stay in control, but every second Izzie's not with me makes it harder. Makes my beast want to pounce. For Chekhov's sake, he'd better not have Izzie. I won't be responsible for the shit that happens to that motherfucker.

A half mile past the border of the wards, someone stands in the road. Slowly, I bring my bike to a halt. Oscar and Monte stop and bracket me like a couple of bookends. The figure, decked out in black leather pants and a jacket, comes closer. She's a beautiful female with shoulder-length, wavy hair, full red lips, and flawless bronze skin.

"Are you the empusa?" Oscar asks.

"I am," she drawls in a captivating voice. Her dark gaze darts from Oscar to Monte and then me. "I'm guessing you're Izzie's mate."

Removing my helmet, I say, "I am. So tell us how to find Chekhov?"

There's no time for small talk. A prolonged visit with Senora is ill-advised since empusai work their charms to attract men before killing them.

"Here's the thing." Senora saunters over to me. She drags a finger down my sleeve. "I don't believe Kazimir has her."

"Why do you say that?" Monte asks. "I got a message saying otherwise."

"May I see it?" She holds her hand out, keeping her eyes locked on me. Once she has the phone, she breaks her gaze and peers at the screen. "Whoever claimed to see Kazimir with Izzie lied. This message isn't genuine."

My nose wrinkles as I shake my head. "Sorry. I don't believe you can tell that from a text."

"Is there someplace we can talk?" She looks around for a moment. "The forest has ears."

I gesture for her to hop on the back of my bike.

~

To be on the safe side, we bring the empusa back to the clubhouse, but from the way the members and their old ladies glare at Senora, it might be a bad idea staying out in the open. Quickly, we usher her to the meeting room and shut the door.

Senora perches on the edge of the table. "Let me drop a little knowledge on you. Something Izzie doesn't know about me is that I also work as a hired gun and . . ." Her gaze bounces around the room. "I collect things—information and artifacts, mostly."

Oscar's and Monte's eyes widen. I don't react. Not showing any type of response in a tense predicament comes in handy. An accountant who can keep a straight face under interrogation is an asset to any company or outlaw affiliation.

"It's my job," the empusa continues, "to find discrepancies. Sometimes the lie is easy to detect. Other times, I use a little magic to ferret out the details."

"That's what you did with the message to Monte?" I ask.

"Yes." She extends her hand, and a phone appears. "I'll call Kazimir and get his location."

Something tells me not to trust this female, but I don't see how we have much choice in the matter. "Go ahead."

Senora puts the phone on speaker and ringing fills the room. A few seconds pass before someone picks up.

"Hello?" A rich, accented voice flows through the speaker.

"Kazimir, it's Senora."

He breathes deeply. "Where's Isadora?"

"I only know she's not in New York," Senora says sweetly. "But for the right price, I'll help you find her."

94

"How much?"

Senora hops up and swaggers around the table. "Twice your exit fee."

"Six million! Are you fucking kidding me?"

"Do you want her found or not?"

"Fine. How long?"

"A day or two." Senora stops in front of me. "Where do you want me to deliver her?"

More heavy breathing. "Good damned question." He speaks to someone with him, "Where the hell are we?"

The person with him says, "We're about thirty miles away from the next town, boss. We left Montrose, and we're headed south."

Damn. If Cheresse really helped this fool, he might be on his way to Havenwood Falls.

Senora purses her lips. "You're not driving so wire me my money, and I'll get to work." She types on the screen. "There. I sent you the details. I expect the funds deposited within the hour."

"Just find my goddamned merchandise," he growls and disconnects.

The phone disappears as Senora faces us. "See? I told you he didn't have Izzie."

"Yeah, but now we have a bigger problem," announces Oscar. "We can't let him find this place."

Senora produces a business card and places it on the table before Oscar. "I'll make sure you'll never have to worry about Kazimir or his men."

"How much?" I ask.

The empusa tilts her head to the side. "Keeping this town secret is very important to all of you." She points at me. "Plus, you'd do anything for Izzie. Since Kazimir is sending me a nice chunk of change, I'll do it for . . ." Senora taps her chin like it requires a lot of thought. "One million."

Monte swallows hard. "Dollars?"

"I'll pay it," I say. Senora makes a loan shark seem like a saint. "I need a few hours to transfer funds."

"Pleasure doing business with you," Senora says, before strolling to the door. "I'm sure we'll see each other again."

After she's gone, Oscar says, "That was my first encounter with an empusa, and I sure hope to hell it's my last one."

"You and me both."

Despite what just transpired, Monte says, "You know, it wouldn't hurt to have her on retainer."

"Fuck no," Oscar exclaims. "The last thing this town needs is a flesh-eating scavenger collecting shit."

"Think about it." Monte props his butt on the table. "When we have trouble and need to get rid of someone, an empusa is the best supe for the job. Did you know empusai eat their victims? No bodies to dispose of."

A shudder goes down my spine while my skin crawls. "That's fucking disgusting."

Monte grins. "Yeah, but damned efficient. Make sure you don't lose her number."

I want to ask him if he's serious, but I already know the answer. My friend just gave credence to popular opinion—he's a sick motherfucker.

And people talk about me.

CHAPTER 13

HUNTER

*W*ith Senora handling the Chekhov problem, we focus our efforts on finding Izzie. We check the cottage at Whisper Falls Inn, but she isn't there. We do a discreet search of Silk too. Sadly, we don't know where else to look. Oscar contacts Gloriana, and she comes to the clubhouse.

"*Nena, hola,*" Oscar says. His arm snakes around her waist as he pulls her close. The sergeant-at-arms has no shame as he delivers a too intimate kiss.

Monte clears his throat, and the decadent show stops. Gloriana wipes the smeared lipstick from Oscar's mouth before taking a seat at the table. "Have you heard anything from Izzie?"

"No," I say, shifting on my chair. The movement causes the cold totem to slide over my skin, sending a shiver through me. I can only interpret an unresponsive pendant as meaning one thing—a possibility I don't want to face. "We don't have a clue where to look either."

"Seriously?" Gloriana rolls her eyes. "I swear males can be useless pricks." Oscar growls, but Gloriana doesn't apologize. "Your totem is supposed to help you find Izzie."

My fingers grasp the chilly medallion. "How?"

"I'm assuming you've slept with her."

Personal information, but I nod.

"Good." Gloriana sinks into the chair and crosses her legs. "Doing so activated the totem. As long as she's wearing it, the trinket acts like a tracker. I'll cast a locator spell to find Izzie's general location. Then the totem will lead us to her."

"Why can't we just let the totem do its job?"

Gloriana gives me a pointed look. "Has it told you anything yet?"

"No," I mutter.

"Then there's a strong possibility that she's not wearing it. Personally, I like covering all avenues first. This way I don't have to backtrack, which is a major waste of time."

"Fine." Honestly, I'm good with anything that gets me to her quicker. "Tell me what you need."

"A map of the town, four green candles, and pure soil."

What the hell is pure soil?

Oscar jumps up before I can say anything. "Any soil and matches, right?"

She nods, and he rushes out. "Basically, I need to purify a small amount of soil. Purification frees the energy in the earth. I'll do an incantation and spread the pure soil on the map. If Izzie is still in town, a trail will form and point out her location."

Gloriana snaps her fingers, and four dark green candles appear on the table. Oscar returns with a small metal bowl holding some dirt. He strikes a match and drops it on the pile. A small flame ignites, and a smell like feces fills the air.

Wrapping her hands around the container, Gloriana chants, *"Et rénova solo in hac tum praetoria nave."*

A bright blue light sparks from the flames. The glow remains for a second or two before the fire dies, leaving behind a rich, black soil. Gloriana motions to Oscar. Quickly, he spreads a map of Havenwood Falls on the table. Gloriana dumps the soil in the south-east corner, and then circles the table, placing a candle in the compass points on the map—east, north, west, and south. She shoves the box of matches in my direction. "Light the candles. Start at the east following the same pattern I made. Don't deviate from it."

Wasting no time, I light the match and touch it to each wick.

After I've done my part, Gloriana holds her palms over the table. "Let the earth locate Izzie Itzae. Let the earth locate Izzie Itzae." Gloriana repeats the words two more times in Latin, and then we wait.

Sweat trickles down my back while my beast claws beneath the surface. His answer to every difficult situation is to use force— sometimes deadly. It takes everything within me not to let him out. Part of me welcomes swift retribution. Something tells me, however, it's the wrong course of action. It might get Izzie killed—something I couldn't bear.

It's more than the curse or our destiny. I can't attach a label to my feelings. It's enough knowing my heart beats stronger when she's near. It's enough that my beast is a helluva lot calmer when I'm with Izzie.

Returning my focus to Gloriana's ritual, I witness the dirt slowly pick up motion like a tiny tornado cloud. It curves and then spreads in four directions before fusing into a distinct trail. The path weaves around the town square, pauses, and continues down Main Street. It persists until it stops at Miller Plaza.

"Is that it?" I ask, glancing at Oscar's old lady.

"Yes, but . . ." Gloriana's words trail off, and her mouth drops open. "What the hell?"

The trail of dirt moves again. It circles around the plaza, heads back to Main Street, pauses, and bolts toward Cooley Creek. The soil skips the creek and shoots toward Creekwood Estates. It stops at a point on the north side of the development, ruling out Izzie being at my house. My gut twists when I realize who lives in that area. The possibility of her involvement sets my beast on edge.

Without making eye contact, I say, "Oscar, send a team to the plaza. Don't involve Sheriff Kasun, though. He's the last thing we need."

"On it." Annoying staccato clicks hit my ear as Oscar texts the fellas. "I'm guessing you're going to Creekwood. Who do you want with you?"

Facing Gloriana, I ask, "Will you come with me?"

"I can." Her eyes narrow. "Maybe Oscar should come, too?"

Pushing my shoulders back, I shake my head. "If this is Cheresse's doing, we can handle it."

Gloriana's dark eyes dig into me as she searches for an elusive answer. "The operative word is *if*. Remember, Cheresse is only half nagual. Her powers aren't strong enough to do anything of consequence. She'd need help to get Izzie out of Silk without being seen. Whoever's behind this has full use of black magic. I could taste it when I entered the dressing room."

"Taste?"

"Magic changes the air. It leaves behind traces of itself. Black magic, particularly, leaves a foul taste. It's something other elemental witches are going to notice. I should check in with Lilith Blackstone and the Luna Coven. Might be a job for the Blackstones, since they're witch hunters."

"Maybe." Cocking my head to the side, I drag a hand through my hair. "So you know who helped her?"

"Not exactly, but I have a hunch." Gloriana scrutinizes me for a moment. "I think Ada Daryn is responsible."

"Why—" Before I can complete the sentence, the memory hits me like a punch to the gut. Ada and Cheresse in the parking lot at Pleasurez. And I thought it was just a business transaction. *Fuck!*

Gloriana and Oscar exchange a knowing glance, but it's the latter who speaks. "Hunter, what aren't you telling us?"

Exhaling loudly, I say, "I saw Ada and Cheresse together earlier tonight at the plaza."

Monte, quiet all this time, chimes in. "Here's the plan. Oscar will take a team to Miller's. I'm going with Hunter and Gloriana." My eyes cut to him. "You're not going without me, bruh. You need all the backup you can get."

For once, I'm not arguing with him.

MINUTES LATER, the three of us wind our bikes through the twisted roads of Creekwood Estates. I want to kick myself for believing Ada was on an innocent shopping spree. Nothing that witch does is blameless. If I had figured this out earlier, Izzie wouldn't be in danger.

As my mind forms possible, devastating outcomes, my totem wakes up. The humming is so strong that the trinket begins tapping a rhythm against my sternum. The closer we get to our destination, the more incessant the cadence. If I didn't know better, I'd swear it was a code. Raising my hand, I signal to Gloriana and Monte to pull over.

"What's wrong?" he asks.

I remove my helmet. "Kill your engines. I need you to listen to something."

Monte puts down the kickstand and comes over to me. "What is it?"

"My totem. I think it's receiving a message." If it's code, Monte can decipher it. He learned the skill as a teenager. His frequent knocking used to drive our parents crazy. They could never figure out where it was coming from or what it meant.

Monte holds his head closer. My heart races as time passes too damned slowly. Finally, he steps back. "It's acting like a beacon. Izzie's totem is with Cheresse."

Rage, bottled inside me, threatens to spill out. Through gritted teeth, I ask, "And Izzie?"

Monte shakes his head. "Not sure."

"We need to move. Now."

CHERESSE'S HOUSE is lit up like a department store Christmas tree, but she's not answering the damned door. I continue to lie on the doorbell. When I'm ready to kick the fucking door down, she throws it open.

"What the hell is the matter with you?" she yells.

Pushing past her, I storm through the entry and mudroom. Cheresse rushes behind me, but I don't stop. I check every room on the ground floor before taking the stairs, two at a time.

"Hunter! Hunter!" She grabs my arm as I enter the open kitchen. "You can't come tearing into my home uninvited!"

Wrong words. Whirling around, my hand goes around her slim neck, and I push her into the stainless steel fridge. "Where the hell is she?"

Although I could easily snap Cheresse's neck, she plays stupid. "I have no idea what you're talking about."

"Don't do it," Gloriana warns me. "She's not worth it. Think of Izzie."

I let my hand slide down.

A cynical smile twists Cheresse's lips. Amusement glints in her steely eyes as she says, "Hunter, *she's* not worth it. That nagual will be like all the others—only out for what you can give them."

My fist balls, but Monte grabs it before I can do any damage. "Walk away, man."

Gloriana struts over to my ex. "I have nothing to lose."

"You're no match for me." Cheresse looks down her nose at the witch. "I eat bigger things for breakfast."

"I'm sure you do," Gloriana says. "But I have no interest in your strange appetites. I'm here for what's in your pocket."

Cheresse tries to step past Gloriana. Suddenly the nagual's back is sucked against the fridge like a giant magnet. Gloriana holds her right palm in the air. Cheresse struggles, and Gloriana lifts her other palm.

"Monte," Gloriana calls out. "The totem is in Cheresse's back pocket."

When I try to go after it, Monte stops me. "You need to keep your hands off that *puta*."

I nod and watch my friend retrieve Izzie's pendant. Keeping my hands to myself doesn't include keeping my mouth shut, though. "Where the fuck is Izzie?"

"In the last place you'd expect. She'll be right in front of you, but you won't see her," Cheresse says with a grin on her face.

Gloriana says, "She has Izzie someplace that's glamoured. I'd guess Pleasurez."

"What do we do with Cheresse?" Monte asks.

"Let the Court deal with her. Gloriana and I need to go to the shop." There's no way, however, I'm leaving Cheresse alone or unrestrained.

Remembering a set of handcuffs I left behind, I hurry from the kitchen to the master bedroom off the hall. Last time I was in the all-white space, I used the restraints near the bed. Sure enough, the genuine Smith & Wesson cuffs are in the nightstand. I pocket the key and take the restraints to the kitchen.

Monte lifts an eyebrow when I hold up the cuffs. "Something you want to tell me, bruh?"

"Nope," I say.

Gloriana lowers a palm, allowing Monte to apply the restraints on Cheresse.

I'm about to leave when I remember Chekhov. Facing my ex, I ask, "Why involve outsiders, Cheresse? You realize how much trouble you're in?"

She holds her chin high. "I don't care. As far as I'm concerned, Izzie is an outsider. You shouldn't have hooked up with her. Whatever trouble is coming to town, blame yourself for it."

My gut twists into a massive knot, and my beast claws beneath my skin. Something bad is coming to Havenwood Falls. I just hope it's not too late to stop it.

Monte clears his throat. "Hunter?"

"Make sure to tell the Court about Chekhov, and stay with this trash until someone arrives. I got to get my lady."

CHAPTER 14

HUNTER

*M*y mind races as we speed toward Miller's Plaza. Pulling apart the events since Izzie's arrival, I can't find a warning. Is this my punishment for being involved with Cheresse?

We've known each other all our lives. We were friends for years before becoming lovers. Desperation drove me into Cheresse's arms, and she was willing and eager. I took full advantage of her offer—fucking her frequently while ignoring her epic jealousy. Eventually, I became her future.

But no matter how hard I tried, we weren't good together. Our vociferous arguments were often the talk of Havenwood Falls, especially among Irene Beckett and the other blue-hairs. We fought everywhere. Restaurants and shops, occasionally, threw us out because of our antics. Sex was the only good thing between us, and even that was too damned noisy. We made sounds that would make a porn star blush. It was always one extreme or the other with us.

On some level, I'm sure my ex would claim love is the reason for her actions. Total lie. Cheresse only loves herself. She craves attention like a fiend, thanks to her overindulgent father. He throws money at Cheresse to keep her happy. Hell, he even tried to buy me, but I can't be bought. The realization pissed him off.

Sadly, his daughter shares the same fury. The female could be vindictive, but her claws aren't deadly. She'll launch into a tirade, but eventually she runs out of things to say. Kidnapping? Partnering with a Green Coven witch? So not the nagual I know.

Time spent with Cheresse, however, can't compare to the moments I've shared with Izzie. Our inner beasts find calm in each other. With Izzie, I want to be honest and loving. It's the foundation for the relationship I want and need in my life. I'll fight anyone who tries to take it away from me. No one will ruin what's taken me years to learn —finding the right someone is better for me than anything I could ever buy.

Pulling into the plaza parking lot, I see SIN members standing around. Confusion dances on their faces. Gloriana parks her bike beside mine as Oscar approaches.

"Anything, *bebé*?" Oscar reaches for Gloriana's helmet.

She hands it to him and says flatly, "Izzie's somewhere inside Pleasurez."

Oscar shakes his head. "We've searched—"

Gloriana holds her hand up. "You'll never find her. Cheresse Winters has her in a spot that's been glamoured. I'm certain I can find it, though. Come with me."

We follow the petite witch through the throng of males and enter the shop. Gloriana stops in the center of the floor. She tilts her head to the side as if she's listening to something we can't hear. Lifting her hand, she moves her fingers like she's caressing the air.

"Anything?" I ask.

"One moment," she says over her shoulder. She switches hands and repeats the same gesture, reaching out to the space on the right of the store. "Yes, there's a glamoured area. The left side of the store has a unique energy. It's dense and menacing." Gloriana drops her hand. "I've never shopped here. Either of you know what's in the back of the building?"

It's hard to believe Gloriana hasn't been in Pleasurez before tonight, but it's common knowledge she doesn't get along with Cheresse.

"Yeah. A place a lot of residents wouldn't admit they've been in."

I'm including myself in the statement. I stalk past Gloriana and head to the bondage room.

When I get there, however, all I see are boxes and a sign about inventory. Unless Cheresse has a group of faeries working for her overnight, it's not possible to pack the entire room so fast. Besides, I've seen what it looks like when Cheresse is taking stock—tags hang from the shelves, but all the merchandise is still on display. "This has to be it, Gloriana."

I reach for the light switch, but the witch touches my arm as she stops at my side. "Hold up the totem, Hunter. Lights contain manmade energy and will block the totem. Once it finds her, the glamour will drop."

I hold up Izzie's necklace, and it tugs toward the door.

"Cross the threshold. Izzie's inside."

Pushing aside the thought of what else might lurk in the shadows, I creep closer to the door. I pause before passing through the simulated appearance.

"Trust me," Gloriana says. "I sense nothing else inside."

Nodding, I turn back to the room. My shoulders move against an invisible force. The air crackles around me, but it's too dark to see anything. Instead of dwelling on the inconvenience, I call upon my beast and let his night vision guide me. Glancing down at the pendant, the blue-green jade glows bright red before it starts humming. It vibrates when I reach the center of the floor.

"Hunter?" Izzie's voice reaches me through the bluish shadows.

"Izzie?" My gaze bounces around the room, desperately trying to find her. "Where are you?"

"Against the wall." She breathes in and out. "On the saltire cross," she rasps.

I'm going to fucking kill Cheresse. Over my shoulder, I call out, "She's in here. Hey, can you turn on a motherfucking light?"

Suddenly the room illuminates, and I see a worn-out Izzie. No bruises. No cuts. Just exhaustion and possibly a little dehydration. Izzie will be fine.

"Get me off this damned thing," she begs.

Now that I know Izzie hasn't been harmed, I allow a moment to enjoy the image. My dick twitches while my mind thinks of all I could do with her. A mischievous, cocky smile settles on my face. I need to make one more purchase for my playroom.

Monte walks up, looks at me, and drops his gaze toward the floor as he shakes his head. "You're one sick bastard."

He goes to unbuckle the restraints holding Izzie's wrists.

"Don't knock what you've never tried, my friend." Forgetting my desire for the moment, I go over to the saltire and undo the cuffs on her ankles.

Someone clears her throat. Our heads rock up. Gloriana, standing with her arms folded over her chest, says, "Could you stop thinking with your dicks for a minute?" She comes over and rests a palm on the collar around Izzie's neck. It releases with an audible pop. "You okay?"

Izzie rubs her throat as she steps away from the piece of bondage furniture. "I'm not sure."

"What was that on her neck?" I ask, gazing at the smooth silver metal.

Gloriana turns the item in her hands. "It was meant to speed up Izzie's transformation. She'll change soon. When? I'm not sure."

Izzie looks at me. "Did you get my totem from Cheresse?"

"Yeah." I step closer and place the glowing pendant around her neck. Within seconds, Izzie's demeanor changes from uncertain and relatively calm to irritated. The jade quetzal now sports pointed ears and a brownish color. The faint image of a puma takes shape. Izzie's mouth opens, but she doesn't speak. Her eyes cloud over, and her knees wobble. I catch her before she hits the floor.

"Damn," Gloriana says. "Get her out of here. Her transformation began when you put on the necklace."

Sweeping Izzie into my arms, I rush for the front door. It's only after I get outside do I realize I can't transport her to safety on the back of a bike. Oscar waves me over to a pickup truck belonging to a prospect. He opens the door and helps me get Izzie inside.

"Use it for as long as you need. We'll take your bike back to the clubhouse," he says.

"Thanks, man."

~

ONCE AGAIN, I'm frantic. I should have prepared for the possibility, but I thought we'd have time. My family's cabin is near Mount Alexa. The seclusion and the nearby woods will be perfect. As I drive past Sun and Moon Academy, Izzie opens her eyes. "Where am I?"

"In a truck, *cariño*."

She pushes the hair out of her face and sits up in the seat. "Going where?"

"Someplace safe." I glance over at her. "Not to alarm you, but your transformation is happening."

Automatically, her hand flies to the necklace. "Ow. Hunter? What the fuck?"

The first convulsions buffet Izzie's body, rendering her speechless. Moaning, she grips the door handle so tightly, I can hear it loosen.

Blowing air through my cheeks, I gather my thoughts.

You've got this. You've done it before.

The first time changing is always painful. How can it not be? Every bone and muscle distorts and reforms into a new shape. Cells rearrange. Skin recedes. Fur and nails push forth. Many have died going through transformation. Those who are lucky must endure the agony, no matter how long it takes.

The process is like childbirth—a necessary evil with a joyous outcome. Letting my beast emerge always refreshes me and clears my mind. After this first change, Izzie will yearn for those moments of complete freedom.

"Just hang with me, Izzie. You're not going through this alone."

She pulls her bottom lip between her teeth. Fucking sexy. *Not the time for it.* Unfortunately, she's not doing it for appeal. Her eyes bulge with fright. "I'm scared."

"I know." When I reach for her hand, claws dig into my skin, and I jam the pedal to the floor.

As SOON AS I kill the engine, Izzie's roar shakes the truck. Jumping out, I run around to the passenger side and throw open the door. She practically leaps from the front seat. The skimpy outfit she's wearing shreds, and her shoes fall from her feet. An orange glow, like a tiny fire, emits from her eyes. Izzie drops to her knees as a loud cracking fills the air. Watching her beast emerge arouses my own. Quickly, I undress, not wanting to be left behind.

CHAPTER 15

IZZIE

A chill caresses my shoulders as my eyelids flutter open. An amazing sense of calm fills me. It's like floating on a cloud. Then I realize I'm lying naked with only a blanket covering me. An intense fear erodes my peace as I notice the plank wood ceiling and exposed beams overhead. Sitting up on the king-size bed, my gaze takes in the stone wall and the roaring fire.

A cabin.

What kind of sick game is Cheresse playing?

Heavy footsteps approach, and the hardwood floor creaks. Looking toward the door, I see Hunter entering the room, carrying a tray. I let out a breath.

"What happened? How did I get here?"

Hunter sets the tray on a table near the bed. "You had your first transformation."

Glancing down, I get a glimpse of the myriad of scratches and cuts on my hands. "Why don't I remember?"

"That's normal." Hunter picks up a cotton ball, drenches it with a liquid from a dark bottle, and strokes it over my skin.

"Ow. That shit stings!" I yank my hand away.

"Sorry, but you don't want those getting infected." He returns the ball to the tray and faces me. "We'll finish it later. Tell me the last thing you remember."

"Seeing you." Reaching out, I cup his stubbled cheek. "I thought I'd never see you again."

Turning his head, he places a kiss on my palm. "Same here, *cariño*. It's over, though. No more worries about Cheresse."

Not that I care what happens to her. After all, if her plan had worked, I would have spent the rest of my life alone and angry. I hope never to cross paths with her again. "Is she in jail?"

"Not quite." Hunter reaches behind him and yanks his T-shirt over his head. "She went before the Court."

"What did they do?" I lift my eyes as Hunter stands and unbuckles his belt.

He unzips his jeans, letting them slide to the floor. "They banned Cheresse and her family from town."

"A little harsh, don't you think? How could they hold her family responsible?"

"Cheresse's father indulges her, and her mother refused to stay in a town that wouldn't accept her daughter."

Oh, well . . . it doesn't matter as long as there's another threat out there. The mattress dips as Hunter kneels beside me. Looking up, I say, "There's something I haven't told you."

He plants a trail of kisses on my skin, starting with my cheek, working his way down my neck, and stopping at my collarbone. His hand dips beneath the blanket. "What's that, *cariño*?"

"Back in New York . . ." It's really hard to think with Hunter's hand skimming over my thigh. My eyes close as a delicious shudder snakes through me. "There's a man. I stole from him."

"Kazimir Chekhov," Hunter says as he gently pushes me onto my back.

My eyes pop open. "How did you know?"

Hunter's rough thumb rubs my clit, and I suck in a breath. "Do you really want to discuss this now?"

Not really, but part of me—the part not ignited by Hunter's

111

fingers sliding into me—wants to know. Needs to know. I pant. "Promise to tell me after?"

He ignores my request, lowers his head, and I come apart. Replacing his fingers with his clever tongue sets off a blinding heat inside me. I fist the sheets as my back arches. Hunter's tongue circles my clit.

"Hunter!" My body vibrates.

Before he pushes me over the edge, the torture stops. Hunter moves and covers my trembling body with his. "I'll tell you whatever you need to know," he says as he hovers over me. "But first, tell me what I want to hear."

Searching his turquoise gaze, I find no trace of the self-assured, sometimes cocky male. Only desire flares in his eyes. Not too long ago, the possibility of not seeing that look again scared me. I learned one thing tonight. I don't want to be away from him ever again. Reality dawns. Only true mates can find each other when lost. If this male weren't my destiny, I'd still be in the back room at Pleasurez.

"Izzie?"

Coming to my senses, I say the words I should have said sooner. Words that could have prevented the nonsense with Cheresse. "I'm yours, Hunter. The gods put us together. May the god Tepeyolohtli bless our union forever."

Hunter's lips curl up as he repeats, "Izzie, I am yours. All of me." He thrusts deeply, and his fangs shine in the light. "Yes, the gods brought us together. May Tepeyolohtli bless us and keep us that way."

Simple words I've known my entire life, but was too reluctant to say to anyone. It took a threat to my beast's happiness to change my mind. But my beast needs to wait. There's something more pressing I plan on taking care of.

~

TONIGHT IS ABOUT MORE than simply taking care of a need. If I only desired time alone with Hunter, we could have easily gone back to the cottage. This is about curiosity and getting familiar on a different—albeit twisted—level.

"You're sure about this?" Hunter asks, leading me down the stairs to his dungeon. "We don't—"

"If you ask me one more time, we won't." I soften my tone and gaze up into his sapphire eyes. "I want this."

Hunter simply nods and closes the door behind us. The lights flicker on as we cross the floor. His head moves from side to side as if he's searching for something. "What first?"

"I'm game for whatever."

"*Cariño.*" His lips curl around the word. "That's a dangerous thing to say around me."

Cupping his face, I capture his mouth with mine, savoring the taste of him—a sweet muskiness. "And I don't mind a little danger."

"I know exactly what I want, though," he admits and tugs me toward the spanking bench.

"Here?" I ask, feigning innocence. Little does this male know that I enjoy a well-delivered paddling. My skin tingles just thinking of a crop reddening my backside.

"Wait." Hunter grasps the sides of my shorts and rips them off, leaving me in a skimpy top and a thong. "Down."

Eagerly, I lean over the padded bench, placing my hands and knees in the proper spots. Wiggling my bare ass, I look over my shoulder. "Now what?"

Hunter goes to a black lacquered cabinet tucked in a corner. He flips a switch, and the sounds of "Dancing with the Devil" by Niki fill the air. Next, Hunter opens and closes drawers, sighs, and comes back over to me with a tawse—a belt of stiff leather with one end split into two tails.

My heart rate kicks up a notch while my nipples stiffen.

"Safe word?"

"Unnecessary. I'm completely yours," I mutter and brace myself. I've never been a lightweight when it comes to BDSM.

Please don't let him be gentle. It's been a long time.

Hunter groans, rubbing his hand over my behind. His fingers

linger on my cheeks before he slips one down the crease. He mutters, "So perfect."

The tawse whistles in the air before striking my flesh. Gripping the edge of the padded hand rest, I shout, "Fuck yeah!"

"Like that?" Hunter asks, his voice deep and sexy.

The space between my legs throbs with anticipation. Panting, I say, "More."

Another flick of his wrist, and the leather brands my ass again. I gasp against the pure pain—punishing but good at the same time. Gritting my teeth, I'm waiting for my beast to rear up, but she stays silent. Actually, she's purring her approval.

Thank the gods.

Fidgeting, I sway my butt from side to side, begging for another one. The expected lash doesn't come. Instead, Hunter pinches my ass and then caresses it—not with his hand, but with his tongue. So soft, so gentle. Whispering across my burning flesh, he says, "You turn me on so much. I need to fuck you. Now."

I start to lift up, but he forces me to lie still.

Hunter rubs his finger between my ass cheeks again and then presses against the puckered opening. "Ever been fucked here?"

Swallowing hard, I admit, "No."

Anal sex has never held any interest or pleasure for me.

He drops a kiss on my lower back. "Aw, too bad. Another time perhaps," he says and steps away.

Have I disappointed him?

"Get up," he says, standing in front of me with a length of red nylon rope stretched between his hands. "You realize you've been bad?"

A delicious shudder shoots through me. I've never turned down a little bondage. "Very bad," I mumble.

Hunter walks behind me. He nuzzles my neck and kisses it. Grasping my wrist, he wraps the rope around it. "The other one."

Willingly, I do as he asks. Once I'm restrained, I say, "What now?"

"On your knees." I kick off my heels and slide to the floor as Hunter unzips his jeans.

Holy shit! The male is commando. Somehow, from this angle, he seems so much larger than before.

He runs his fingers through my hair, slowly twining it around his hand, and then tugs. "Sorry, *cariño*, I like it rough."

"Not a problem."

"Good." Hunter teases my lips with his thick cock, urging me to accept him.

Now my beast speaks up, but she needs to keep her butt quiet. This act is about me submitting to Hunter. Although my beast accepted and surrendered to his beast, now it's time for my human side to capitulate—prove that I'm willing to be his mate in every way. Later, I'll make sure he reciprocates, repeatedly.

I open my mouth, and Hunter slides his tautness in. Honestly, I've never sucked dick this way—hands tied up—but he guides my head. I take a second to calm my racing heart, then I flatten my tongue against his sensitive tip. Hunter moans. His hips jerk forward, burying himself even deeper and bumping the back of my throat. Glancing up, I watch as his eyes flutter closed.

"Fuck, you feel so damned good. Oh . . ." It's the last thing he says before his cock pulses in my mouth.

Hunter's grip on my hair tightens to the point of pain, and I'm forced to swallow every drop shooting down my throat. Seconds later, he pulls out—his dick still hard. "Your turn."

Not removing the rope, he places a pillow in front of me. Hunter comes up behind me, tips me forward, and thrusts into me. His girth stretches and fills me. Hunter's hands slip beneath my halter top, and he moves hard and fast while my body vibrates in response. The basement room fills with a new sound—the rhythmic slapping of skin on skin, my ass against his groin. With each frenetic thrust, Hunter pushes me closer to the edge. Unable to touch him, all I can do is focus on the sensation.

Sucking in air, I gasp for a release that seems prolonged.

Finally, Hunter's breath hisses—a scintillating sound of pain mixed with pleasure. "Oh, shit. I'm going to come."

Our bodies shudder together in a wave of shared bliss.

Afterward, Hunter carries me to the bed and cleans me up with a warm towel. My legs, still feeling like jelly, keep me rooted to the spot.

"Are you okay?"

I nod.

He plants a chaste kiss on my mouth. "You make me happy, *cariño*. I promise to always be by your side."

"Oh, I have a much better position for you."

"What's that?"

"It involves a butt plug and hanging you from a bar."

"Sounds positively sinful. I'll get the lube."

"In a minute." I rest my head on his chest, finally able to rest without any worries.

EPILOGUE

IZZIE

A month later . . .

The disaster known as Cheresse is finally behind us. Days after Hunter rescued me, I had a conversation with Michaela, and she confirmed what Hunter told me. The Court of the Sun and the Moon elected to ban Cheresse and her parents. Good riddance!

I got a shock when Senora petitioned the Court for residency. I was so sure she would return to New York. Turns out my friend has been a regular visitor to Havenwood Falls. When she disappeared back in February, I had no idea she came here. She said something about doing a job, but she wouldn't tell me what it entailed. Now I'm curious about the briefcase she brought back with her to New York. Right before Senora went to the Court, she had the case, but now it's gone again.

Even more shocking than Senora's request, her questionable employment was the fact Monte vouched for her. He told the Court she was invaluable to SIN, and her skill could even help the members of the Court, should the need arise. Despite all that, Senora has yet to be granted permission. When I asked her about it, she simply said there were some details that needed to be worked out.

These days I'm breathing easier, thanks to the odd disappearance of Kazimir. Hunter told me SIN took care of the situation. When I asked

Senora about it, she swore she knew nothing about it. I believe her about as much as I believe Baba when he says he doesn't enjoy the high from a good joint.

All these events left a real void in town. Without Cheresse, Pleasurez closed down. Honestly, I had no interest in being the person to resurrect the shop, but my dancing days are over. Not because I don't want to do it. More like I can't deal with Hunter's mood swings. When I'm not working the pole, he's sweet and loving, but as soon as I say I'm going to Silk, he becomes downright unpleasant to be around. So I took over the store.

Do I miss dancing? Yes and no. I miss the money, but I don't miss the lecherous stares. I surely don't miss the piss-poor working conditions, although Melaina runs a clean club. Nevertheless, I'm determined to make a success with Pleasurez, starting with upgrading the merchandise —no more cheap stuff. I've found a European supplier for adult toys. They cost a little more, but last longer than their American counterparts. Monte's computer knowledge helped me open a web store catering to Havenwood Falls residents too shy to come inside the shop.

As new management, I hired more help. Now the staff of Pleasurez includes more than dancers from Silk. The number of people applying for jobs surprised me, including stay-at-home moms with too much time on their hands. The biggest shock was Alina Roca. Her brother, Xandru (a very hot moroi vampire and Michaela's fiancé) said she'd be interested. I hired the morose female on the spot. She's one of my most trustworthy and dependable workers.

The door chime sounds and snags my attention. Hunter, dressed in a stylish flight jacket and jeans, strolls over to the display rack of vibrators I'm restocking. He plants a kiss on my cheek. "Hey, *cariño*. Are you ready to go?"

With everything that happened, I completely forgot about my birthday. I'm leaving early tonight so that Hunter can take me out for a belated birthday dinner.

"I think so." I wave at my assistant manager, who's working with a customer, and close up the box. "Let me drop this in the back."

Hunter takes it from me. "I got it. Meet you in the truck."

~

ANOTHER BIG CHANGE in my life is the connection I have with Hunter. Although I accepted the bond, my heart hasn't been completely in the relationship. Part of the problem is my parents' shoddy history. I can't forget how my father was the coward who slinked away like a thief in the night instead of facing his problems. I've always had trouble wrapping my mind around my mother's stoic behavior after he left us. She used the excuse that his departure was the nagual way. I don't want to be a mirror image of Mom—bless her soul. I want more from Hunter. I deserve more.

Thankfully, Hunter's determined. He continues to look past my flaws and cares for me regardless. Shortly after my rescue, he admitted he had fallen in love with me. I doubted it. After all, it was too soon. He, however, pushed aside my uncertainties. He swore he'd wait for me, no matter how long it took.

Snow clings to the exterior of the cabin. Although I'm from New York, I'm not looking forward to several feet of the white stuff. Winter has never been my favorite time of year. Hunter opens my passenger door, and our eyes meet. There's so much love shining in his. Joy wells up in my heart. I'm ready to tell him.

"Can we take a walk?" I ask.

Hunter gives me a grin and closes the truck door. "Sure."

Tucking my hands into my parka pockets, a little rush of butterflies takes off in my stomach. Before I lose my nerve, I start down the trail away from the building.

"What's going on?" Hunter, his voice full of concern, falls into step beside me.

At the edge of the woods surrounding the cabin, I turn to him. Panic claws at my throat. "It's really beautiful up here."

Why are you talking about the view?

"Not as beautiful as you, *cariño*." Hunter caresses my cheek with a chilly hand. His brows knit together. "Izzie, is there something you need to tell me?"

Nodding, I say, "Yes. I should have told you before today." My heart pounds so hard I'm sure he can hear it. I swallow the lump in my throat and glance into his worried eyes. "Hunter . . ."

Just say it. No preamble needed.

Leaning in, I brush my lips to his. A simple gesture meant to convey my feelings without saying a word. Maybe he'll get the message. Hunter is the first to break the kiss.

He watches me curiously and lifts an eyebrow. "Izzie?"

I shift from one foot to another. Despite the cold, sweat trickles down my spine. The words he's been waiting to hear come out in a whisper. "I love you, Hunter."

"What?" His eyes widen. "Did I hear you correctly?"

"You did."

The corners of his mouth turn up as he cups my face between his hands. "Say it again."

The joy in Hunter's voice is contagious. "I love you, I love you, I love you."

Unexpectedly, he holds his head back and shouts, "She loves me! Izzie Itzae loves Hunter James!"

A burst of giggles stirs my belly and mixes with the butterflies residing in it. "You're being silly."

"No. I'm a nagual in love and overjoyed that my better half loves me back. You, Izzie Itzae, have made me truly happy." He kisses me, slow and tender.

It's a moment I want to capture and hold close to my heart forever.

~

ABOUT THE AUTHOR

Nadirah Foxx, the alter ego for SF Benson, has a fondness for dark, twisted romance featuring suspense and adventure. Her characters are flawed, but they always find a way around their obstacles and demons.

Connect with Author Nadirah Foxx
Facebook: https://www.facebook.com/NadirahFoxx/
Twitter: @nadirahfoxx
Blog: https://nadirahfoxx.wordpress.com/blog/

ACKNOWLEDGMENTS

Thank you so much for reading Izzie and Hunter's story. Theirs is a tale inspired by Aztec and Maya mythologies. It was a lot of fun researching the ideology and finding ways to twist to fit my characters.

A special thank you goes out to all the Havenwood Falls authors! Your input and ideas were helpful. I appreciate your support.

I thank my editor/publisher, Kristie Cook. Being part of a project of this nature taught me a lot. You also showed me the value of being flexible—thank you for that!

Thanks go out to my cover designer, Regina Wamba/Mae I Design. It was great to work with you again.

Last but not least, I thank my parents—for without them none of this is possible.

PLANS LAID BARE

J.D. NELSON

~ A Havenwood Falls Sin & Silk Novella ~

Havenwood Falls

sin & silk

Plans Laid Bare

J.D. Nelson

To Nels, always Nels

PROLOGUE

"Shit! Shit! Shit!" I muttered, frantically shoving the clothes from the laundry basket into my backpack. I had to do this faster. "Think! Think, Mavis! You can do this!"

I blew out a breath, trying to calm myself enough to concentrate on what I needed to do next. Everything was moving so fast. I couldn't grab hold of the thoughts racing through my head. How could this be happening to me?

Stopping, I closed my eyes and took a deep, cleansing breath. I needed clarity, focus. And I needed it yesterday.

I opened my eyes. Money. I was going to need lots of money.

Straightening the room as I went, I stopped at the door to look for anything out of place. The room was messy, as usual, but not I-packed-my-whole-world-in-three-minutes messy. He was used to seeing this level of clutter.

This will work, I thought. *It has to work.*

Throwing my backpack over my shoulder, I set out at a brisk pace, making a beeline to the jar of mad money he kept on top of the refrigerator. As tempted as I was to take it all, I didn't. I had to make sure nothing was amiss. If anything was different, if anything caught his eye, he would know, and he would come for me. That couldn't happen. Having a decent head start would mean the difference between life and death.

CHAPTER 1

I ran until I couldn't run anymore. My feet ached. My mouth was as dry as the Sahara Desert. My clothes were dirty and torn from ducking behind trees and diving into ditches in blind, terrified panic. And I was tired. We're talking the weary-to-the-bone kind of tired. The kind of exhaustion you feel when you've been down with the flu for three days and try to do something normal . . . like breathe.

I smiled bitterly as I kicked a rock, listening to it skitter down the pavement into the darkness beyond. I knew I would never have to worry about something as mundane as the flu again. Because, as of two hours earlier, I had learned the truth about myself. I'd never been normal. I was as far away from ordinary as I could be. I was an ice demon.

Yes, an ice demon. Me, Mavis LeGrand, college graduate, ex-cheerleader, and high school debate club president, a demonic entity.

Of all the absurd things I thought could happen to me, finding out I was a creature of Hell hadn't even been on the list. The mere idea was ludicrous. Before this afternoon, my life had been boring. There'd been no excitement, no surprises. And no one could have had a more idyllic upbringing than I had. Sure, the thing pretending to be my grandfather had been a little cold and creepy, but a demon with a propensity for evil? Not in a million years would I have suspected him of that.

I snorted to myself, almost delirious in my exhaustion. As if any of that stuff still mattered. That fake life was over. It didn't exist anymore. And it never would again.

The faint glow of headlights in the distance pulled me out of my misery and set my heart racing. Darting to my right, I dove headfirst into a deep and, thankfully, grassy ditch and prayed that the vehicle wouldn't stop. I'd come so far. I couldn't let my grandfather find me after everything I'd been through tonight.

I tried to hold my breath as the sound of the tires grew closer, but a sharp sob tore out of me on its own volition when I heard the telltale squeak of the brakes and a door opening. All the effort, all the ridiculous abuse I'd put my body through—it was for nothing. He'd found me. My grandfather had found me.

"I'm not one to pry into someone else's business," an unfamiliar voice drawled, "but I've got to tell you, when I saw you take that Olympic dive into the drainage ditch, I had questions. Mainly, what the hell is that little blond woman doing?"

With tears streaming down my face, I sat up to see a pair of black boots come to a stop in the gravel in front of me. Though I couldn't make out his features with his truck's headlights shining so brightly behind him, I knew he was smiling down at me. I could hear humor in his deep, gruff voice.

"Aw, coach, I'm just practicing for the next meet," I told him, damn close to hyperventilating. "We're going to bring home the gold this year!"

The man's sharp bark of a laugh made me jump.

"You do that now," he said.

I grinned. "I'll give it my best shot."

"I never had a doubt. But before you do that, why don't I give you a ride somewhere. Where're you headed?"

"It doesn't matter," I said truthfully. "Anywhere that's out of town."

"Well, then, you're in luck. I happen to be heading in that direction."

I pursed my lips, weighing my options. Hitchhiking with a stranger was crazy. I knew it. He knew it. Everyone knew it. But the urge to take him up on his offer was overwhelming. The man did seem genuinely concerned by my ditch antics.

But still, my grandfather didn't raise a fool.

"How do I know I can trust you?" I asked him, narrowing my eyes.

"You don't. But riding with me is better than risking a rattlesnake bite every time a truck comes down the road, right? And I promise to behave myself, so what do you have to lose?"

I had to admit, even in early October, he had a point about those snakes. I didn't know how many more times I could repeat my swan-dive-into-questionable-ditches routine without suffering serious injury.

"Okay," I said finally. "Thanks."

Crouching down, he reached out a hand to help me up. "Here, let me give you a . . . shit." He stood up quickly. "Get down. Someone's coming."

Lying flat, I watched the man step closer to the edge and move his hands to his fly.

"What are you doing?" I hissed.

"Saving your ass," he whispered. "Now lie still. They won't stop if they think I'm taking a piss."

Closing my eyes, I concentrated on the crunch of crisp leaves as the vehicle slowly approached.

"Evening," I heard my would-be savior call. "Do you want to hold it for me or something?"

I trembled uncontrollably as a scolding, laced with obscenities, erupted from the driver. It was him. My grandfather had found me.

"Don't let him see me," I whispered as the car sped off. "Please."

"Come on, then," he said, squatting down to reach for me. "Hurry up."

I took the hand he offered and shouted, "Oh!" when a warm jolt of electricity traveled up the length of my arm.

"Sorry," he said apologetically. "I wasn't expecting you to be an immortal," he explained. "Humans can't feel that. I was trying to put you at ease."

"Put me at ease? What just happened?"

"I'm a cambion," he said simply, as if that would explain everything.

"A what?"

"I'll tell you in the truck." He opened the passenger side door. "We need to get going, in case he doubles back."

I nodded and quickly brushed the debris from my clothes, not knowing what to think about his revelation. Was a cambion a demon like myself or something different? Was he dangerous? Did that even matter? Whether he killed me or my impostor grandfather did, I was still one dead demon chick.

Finally, I decided to throw caution to the wind and climbed into the truck. Buckling my seatbelt, I waited for him to get in on the driver's side before I blurted out, "I'm an ice demon."

"Those are rare," he replied, nonplussed.

"Are they? Do you know anything about them?"

He chuckled and cranked his truck. "Don't you?"

I shook my head. "No. I just found out I was a demon, oh . . ." I checked my nonexistent watch. "About two hours ago. I'm hoping the learning curve isn't steep."

"What's your name?" he asked, whipping the truck around to head for the interstate.

"Mavis LeGrand."

He nodded, leaning over to switch on the interior light. "I'm Cam, Cameron DeSalle. Pleased to meet you."

I blinked a few times, letting my eyes adjust to the sudden brightness. Then I lost my power of speech. My Good Samaritan was a dark angel in tight blue jeans.

A furrow appeared between his brows. "Are you okay, Mavis?"

"Y-yeah, I just didn't expect . . ." I threw my hands up. "Cameron, you're like, crazy hot. You know that, right?"

He laughed. "Yes, but I don't think anyone has ever told me quite so bluntly."

"I'm sorry." I groaned, covering my face and lamenting my idiocy for a moment until I remembered how filthy my hands were and jerked them away from my face so fast, I accidentally hit one against the dash. When I looked up, nursing my aching hand to my chest, Cameron was staring at me with surprised amusement.

"You are a very entertaining ice demon," he told me.

"Thank you. And I'm sorry." I laughed. "It has been a day, and after everything else, I wasn't expecting someone so . . ."

"Attractive?" he asked. "Sexy? Irresistible?"

I gestured at his square jaw, thick black hair, and kind honey-brown eyes that would make any woman's panties melt right off. "Well, yeah. I mean, look at you, Cameron."

"Call me Cam," he reminded me.

"Okay. Cam the cambion, you're a regulation hottie. What's up with that?"

He groaned. "Come on, Mavis. A *Mean Girls* reference? I thought you were better than that."

"Then you thought wrong, because I'm really not," I told him, feeling almost hopeful for the first time since my world fell apart. "Now spill. What's it like to walk around with a mug like that twenty-four seven?"

"What's it like to walk around looking as pretty as you do?" he shot back.

"First off, don't even; I'm not the same caliber as you," I said. "And second, quit deflecting. I want an answer. Do women follow you around like the Pied Piper or what?"

He blew out a very put-upon sigh and leaned back in his seat. "Women are often attracted to me, yes."

"Knew it," I said smugly.

"It's not as if I want them to," he said, suddenly sitting upright. "I don't have a choice. My father is an incubus."

I blanched. "An incubus? Like, the steal-souls-by-having-sex kind of incubus I've read about in books?"

He gave me a winsome smile. "Yes. And that is a very accurate description."

"Do you do that? Steal souls, I mean."

He answered without the slightest bit of guilt. "Yes, but don't worry. You have nothing to fear from me."

"And why is that?" I asked, more than a little wary after his frank admission.

Cameron's dark eyes scanned my face for a moment before he turned his attention back to the road. "Because you don't have a soul, Mavis."

"I don't have a soul?" I asked in disbelief.

He shook his head. "Not that I can detect, no."

I sat back against the seat in stunned silence, wondering how this could be my life. Everything had been so boringly normal the day before. It was like I woke up in the twilight zone.

"I'm sorry," he said sheepishly. "That must have been a shock for you. I wasn't thinking."

"It's okay," I told him, my eyes welling up with tears again. "There's nothing to be done about it. It is what it is."

"There's a bottle of water in the glove compartment," he offered, looking at me as if he didn't know what to do about the dirty, tear-stained mess next to him.

Numb, I nodded and woodenly reached for the latch. I didn't know what to do about me, either.

"You're going to be okay," he said gently. "You're still the same demon you were yesterday. You just didn't know it yet."

I closed my eyes and inhaled deeply through my nose, holding it in a few seconds before exhaling. "Thank you, Cameron."

His expression turned serious as he clicked off the light. "It's no problem, but you do realize you're going to have to tell me what's going on, don't you? Obviously, you're in some trouble."

I pressed my lips together. As important as this was, it was hard to say something when you didn't want to hear it out loud. Hearing it out loud made it real. I wasn't ready for real yet.

"Come on," he urged. "I'm invested in this thing now. I want to help you. And that means I have to know who you're running from, so I can keep both of us safe."

"Okay," I said, straightening in my seat to face him. "I'll tell you, but only because I need help. And Cameron, if you're offering it to me, I'm going to take it. I don't have a choice. I don't think I can do this on my own." I blew out a shaky breath. "So, are you sure you want to help me?"

"I am," he said without hesitation. Then he pulled to the side of the road and shifted the truck into park. "Tell me how to help you, Mavis."

Wrapping my arms around myself, I sank back into my seat, staring at the road stretching out in front of us. "I'm running from my grandfather."

"Your grandfather?" Cameron asked incredulously. "Why on Earth would you do that?"

I met his gaze. "Because he's not my grandparent. He's not even related to me. He's an ice demon, and he's planning on killing me."

CHAPTER 2

J thought Cam would insist I get out of his truck—that he'd leave me in his dust. But he didn't. Instead, he asked, "Did you just say your pretend grandfather is planning to kill you?"

I nodded, trying hard to keep eye contact. "Apparently, I'm the Exitium Daemonium."

His eyes widened. "The Exitium Daemonium? Like *the* Exitium Daemonium? Are you serious?"

"One hundred percent serious," I told him glumly.

"So the prophecy is true," he said, more to himself than me.

"I guess. I know less than nothing about the whole thing. What do you know about it?" I asked.

"Same as any demon knows. The Exitium Daemonium will bring death and destruction to demonkind."

I rolled my eyes. "Look at me, Cam. Do I look like I'm going to bring death and destruction to demonkind?"

"No, you look like an extremely filthy librarian."

"I rest my case."

"How did you find out?"

"I had an accident today."

"Like a car accident or an I-killed-a-demon type of accident?"

As his words sank in, my heart began to thump wildly. "Do you really think I can kill a demon?"

He laid a hand on top of mine to stop my fidgeting with the cap on the water bottle. "Mavis, if what you're saying is true, you're the ultimate in demon destruction."

"That's the thing," I said, ignoring the zing of energy that shot through me when he touched my skin. "I don't feel like hurting any demons. I feel stronger and keep having cold flashes since the accident, but I'm not having homicidal urges or anything."

"I think you'd better start at the beginning."

"Okay." I took a deep breath. "Late this afternoon, I fell down a huge flight of stairs at the public library, and when I was rushed to the hospital and x-rayed for suspected broken ribs, they found this weird anomaly that looked like it was encasing my heart, so they did an MRI."

"What did they find?"

"Nothing from the MRI. The machine blew up the second they turned it on. The explosion should have killed me, or at the least, burned me, but nothing happened. During all the confusion, smoke, and sirens, I ran."

"And since then you've felt stronger and have been feeling cold?"

I nodded. "I ran all the way from just south of Provo and never broke a sweat."

His mouth dropped open. "But that's forty miles from here. You've been jumping into ditches for forty miles?"

"Or ducking behind trees, or mailboxes, or cars. Whatever kept me from being seen."

He shook his head in wonder. "So, this anomaly, it had to be a throttle of some sort, right?"

"A throttle? Do you think that's what it was?"

"I do. There's no other way you wouldn't have noticed by now your ability to manipulate the cold. Did you get a chance to see the anomaly on the x-rays?"

"Unfortunately, yes. I'm pretty sure it's going to haunt my dreams."

"What did it look like?"

"Something diamond-shaped with runes engraved into it," I answered. "I couldn't tell what it was made of, though."

"Do you know anything about the runes that were on there?"

"See, that's where this whole thing got even more freaky. When I was little, I stumbled across a set of journals that had the same runes on them in my grandfather's study. He was pissed when he saw me playing with them, so the memory sort of sticks out to me. As soon as I saw the x-ray, I knew there had to be a connection, and I knew I needed to find those journals."

Cam looked suitably impressed. "And did you find them?"

I stared down at his big hand still covering my small ones. It was warm, comforting, and sending a flow of energy through me so filled with slow-burning desire, I almost hoped he'd never move it.

"Mavis?" he prompted.

"I did sneak into his library to read them," I said, finally meeting his eyes. "But I wasn't able to get past the first one before I knew I had to get out of the house. I had to get as far away from him as possible. Whoever he is, he isn't my real grandfather. He stole me from the underworld when I was an infant. He has plans to . . . He plans to . . ." I broke off, not able to finish the sentence. The horror of what I'd read was too fresh to talk about just yet.

He squeezed my hand briefly, then turned his attention back to the road. "There's a cheap motel up ahead," he said, throwing the truck into gear. "We can figure out what to do next once we're there."

I sighed in relief. "Thanks, Cam."

"Trust me. I'm doing this for me as much as I'm doing it for you. We can't let you fall into the wrong hands."

I frowned. "You say that like I'm some sort of weapon."

He caught my gaze as we passed under a streetlamp. "Not some weapon, Mavis, *the* weapon. I have to protect you in any way I can. There's no choice here. My own immortal life could depend on your safety."

I swallowed hard and nodded my acquiescence. Cam was right. I just hoped like hell my new friend would be up for the task.

~

CAMERON PARKED his truck behind the Starlight Motel after making a pit stop at an all-night burger place. He left me eating a large order of fries and slamming a thirty-two-ounce soda while he checked us in. Five minutes later, we were inside room seventeen, staring awkwardly at each other.

The room was clean and tastefully decorated with the latest in hotel chic. And me? I was incredibly dirty and feeling filthier by the second.

"I'm going to shower," I told him, grabbing my backpack. "I'll be right back."

"Take your time," he said through a mouthful of bacon cheeseburger. "Do you need clothes? They might be a little big, but I think I have a pair of sweats and a T-shirt that will do."

I had a few moments of pure yearning as I looked over to the overnight bag he was pointing to. What would it be like to be warm and wrapped up safe with his manly scent all over my body?

"Mavis?"

My cheeks heated up with a blush, and I sputtered, "Thank you. But I packed extra clothes in my backpack. I'm all right."

He nodded and helped himself to a handful of my uneaten fries. "Have a nice swim, then."

Once inside the bathroom with the door locked behind me, I twisted on the shower taps and braced my arms on the vanity.

"You will not think about how hot he is," I told the wistful, gray-eyed girl in the mirror. "You will ignore the unbelievable hotness."

And I did. For the next half hour, I didn't think about anything but the methodical process of washing the dirt from my body. When I was squeaky clean and feeling a hundred pounds lighter, I toweled off, brushed my teeth and hair, and dressed in clean yoga pants and a V-neck sleepshirt. I stepped out of the steamy bathroom looking and feeling like a new demoness.

Cameron had made himself at home while I showered. Lounging on the bed in gray sweatpants and a Smashing Pumpkins T-shirt, he was just putting down his cell phone and picking up the remote to flip through the channels on the ancient TV when I walked into the bedroom.

"Feel better?" he asked, barely glancing up.

I sat cross-legged on the opposite bed, facing him. "A whole lot better. Thank you."

He muted the TV and faced me, propping his head up on an elbow. "Well, well, well . . . you clean up nicely."

"Thanks," I said, looking away from his raised shirt and the tanned, lightly haired expanse of his stomach that was on full and glorious display.

"Very nicely," he mused. "I think you might be wrong about us not being the same caliber."

I didn't look away from the tacky hotel bedspread, but I could feel the weight of his scrutiny on me. And it did . . . things to me—bad things, naughty things.

He chuckled darkly, knowing precisely what I was thinking. "So, tell me about yourself, Mavis LeGrand, ice demon and Exitium Daemonium."

Shrugging, I met his lazy gaze. "There's not that much to tell. I got my MBA from the University of Utah and have—*had*—a good paying job. I was living a totally normal human life. Three hours later, here we are."

"That would make you, what, twenty-two or twenty-three, right?"

"I'm twenty-six. How old are you?"

"Older than twenty-six," he evaded.

I shook my head, smiling at him. "That means you're really old and don't want to tell me, doesn't it?"

He returned my smile. "Something like that."

"Do you plan on being this evasive all night?"

"Not at all," he said. "I plan to sleep at some point."

"Funny."

He clicked off the TV, leaving us in the dim light of the lamp between our beds. "So, what does a twenty-six-year-old college graduate do for money these days?"

"Well, this one was given an accounting job with her grandfather's firm in New York. I telecommute Monday through Friday. The job is a waste of my degree, but he didn't like me leaving the house. Sometimes, it was easier to do what he said than argue with him and his stranger-danger logic."

"Telecommute, eh? Why do I get the feeling your fake grandfather has made you somewhat of a recluse?

I frowned. "I'm not a recluse."

"You also don't have much of a life, from the sound of it."

"I have friends that I see occasionally, and I go to the library pretty frequently. I'm not a shut-in."

He coughed out, "Recluse."

I glared at him. "Well, what do you do, Cam the solitude-hating cambion?"

"I'm self-employed."

"What kind of work?" I asked.

He clenched his jaw, looking like he'd rather talk about anything else.

"Come on. It can't be that bad."

"I'm an escort," he said finally. "Women pay me to 'take them out.'"

"Take them out? Wait a minute. You steal souls and get paid for it? That's a little diabolical, isn't it?"

He waved his hand back and forth. "Yes and no."

"Yes and no, it's diabolical? Or yes, you steal souls, and no, you don't get paid for it?"

"I could deplete a human's soul over a few visits if I chose to be that big of a douchebag," he explained. "But I can't take all of it in one go. Not like my father can. And yes, I do get paid for sex, if that's what my clients want."

"Do any of your clients ever not want to have sex with you?"

He raised an eyebrow. "What do you think?"

Hugging one of the thin, but thankfully clean, bed pillows to my chest, I answered, "Honestly, I think you probably fuck a lot, Cam."

His smile was pure, unadulterated sex. "You're not wrong."

I laughed nervously. "I guess you really are your father's son."

"That I am," he said, regarding me with a look of interest.

I ignored the close examination and asked, "But you're not all incubus, right? What's your mom's half?"

"Human. Cambions are the sons and daughters of an incubus father and a human mother."

"Really? Is she in your life?"

"She died when I was six years old."

"I'm so sorry."

He waved away my concern. "It was many, many years ago, and truthfully, I was lucky to have the time I did have with her. Human women rarely survive mating with an incubus in their true form. The insemination can be violent, and the pregnancy fatal. My father was stupid to try for more offspring with her."

The angry vehemence in his voice made me flinch away from him. Noticing the movement, he said, "My father is not a topic I enjoy discussing. He is the biggest asshole I know."

"Only because you haven't spent much time with my 'grandfather,'" I grumbled.

He chuckled. "I'd say it's a demon thing, but then we'd be included in this demons-are-douchebags theory."

I unfolded my legs and scooted to the edge of the bed. "Speaking of being a demon, do you have a different form? You know, something more demon-y, or do you always look like this?"

Cam swung his legs off the bed and mimicked my position. "For a girl that was only a human yesterday, I would have thought you'd be afraid to see what a demon looks like."

"That was yesterday," I said. "Today, I'm the Exitium Daemonium, and I'm running for my life. Things have changed a bit."

He nodded. "I guess they have."

"So, let's see it. Demon out or whatever."

"Demon out?" he asked, a slight smile playing on his lips. "Sorry to disappoint, but this is my only form. If I were a true, full-blooded incubus, I could be anything you desire, male or female."

My mouth dropped open. "Anything?"

"Anything. An incubus can sense what you want and shape-shift accordingly. They'll do anything they have to, to take a soul."

"Then I'm kind of glad I don't have a soul."

"No, but you have other things an incubus, or even I, could take from you."

My breath quickened as I stared into his eyes. The shade of brown was so mesmerizing; I immediately lost myself in the flecks of dark chocolate and warm amber. "Cam, you're . . ."

"I'm what?" he asked, his gruff voice so close to my ear, I jumped.

Blinking fast, I pulled away from Cam with no memory of how I'd left my bed to join him on his.

"What just . . ." I trailed off again, staring at Cameron. His full lips looked so soft, yielding but firm at the same time. I wondered, if he kissed me, if I would feel the warm jolt I'd felt before when he touched me. I wondered if I'd feel it everywhere he touched me.

"Mavis!" he said sharply.

Coming back to myself, I shook my head to clear it. "What did you do to me?"

"I let you feel me in my natural state."

With my heart pounding, I scrambled back to my bed. "That was your natural state?"

He shot me a rueful smile. "You're still being throttled by the magic device around your heart. My charm shouldn't affect an ice demon, or any demon for that matter. Whatever that device around your heart is, it's cracked, but clearly still doing its job. The only question is if your power will be limited by the throttle permanently or if the break will slowly trickle magic into you until you're whole again."

"So, the more magic I develop, the less I'll be affected by your . . . um, charm?"

"I'm sorry, yes. You don't know how much I wish I could turn it completely off—the want, the desire. I'm holding it back as much as I can."

"I don't want you to turn it off," I said, surprising myself.

His brows lifted. "No?"

I smiled, thinking of how my body felt when I looked into his eyes. "No way. Giving myself over to your hypnotism, or whatever it is, feels decadent, delicious, like sliding into a hot bath at the end of the day. I like it. A lot."

"Yeah?" he asked.

"Yeah," I purred, matching his tone. "And that warm lick of sexual electricity you send through my body when you touch me? It's heaven."

"I like the way you describe that," he said, in a voice that could be considered foreplay. "It has a lot of my favorite words in it."

"Oh?" I asked. "Like what?"

"It has warm, and lick, and . . ."

"And what?" I asked, hanging on to every word.

"And sexual electricity."

The sound of him growling out the word *sexual* made me grab the edge of the mattress with both hands to brace myself. I swallowed hard. "Holy shit, Cam. You're really good at this seduction thing."

Cameron groaned and shifted his hips, drawing my attention downward. I gasped. He was hard—and massive. My eyes snapped back up to his.

Panic crossed his beautiful face for a split second. "Don't, Mavis."

"Don't what?" I asked, my voice barely above a whisper.

"Give in to the desire. You must resist this."

Nearly breathless with a need that was as unfamiliar as it was overwhelming, I asked, "Why?"

"Because I don't know if I can tell you no."

CHAPTER 3

I awoke to the dim orange light of the afternoon sun shining through the sheer curtains with no memory of going to bed. Worse than that, I woke up with my face smashed into a man's muscular chest. I froze, trying to get my bearings before I drew attention to myself.

A rumble of laughter sounded in my ear. "Hey there, sleepyhead. I've been wondering when you'd finally wake up."

"Cam?"

"Were you expecting it to be someone else?" he asked, amusement coloring his voice.

I peeked up at his handsome face through my crazy bed head. "No, but . . . um . . . do you mind telling me how I got here?"

"Well, let's see," he said, smoothing my hair away from my face. "If I remember correctly, I drove you here after I picked you up out of a ditch last night. You were such a dirty girl."

I rolled my eyes. "You know what I mean. Why am I half on top of your naked chest?"

He chuckled at my annoyance. "Oh, that."

"Did you . . . uh . . ."

"Did I give you the ride of your life?" he suggested, his golden-brown eyes twinkling with merriment.

"You're enjoying this far too much," I grumbled.

"I'll have you know I have a very blue pair of balls that say otherwise."

"Yeah, about that. You do realize you have a fairly large fun stick wedged against my hip, don't you?"

"As a matter of fact, I do. I also notice you haven't exactly extracted yourself from the precarious position with said 'fun stick.'"

I smiled against his smooth chest and closed my eyes, getting lost in the clean scent of his soft skin. "I'm just going to enjoy your charm for one more second. Then I'm getting up."

"Be my guest. Hell, get naked. We can continue from where we left off last night. I hear sex with me is pretty good."

"Okay," I said, springing up. "I'm done enjoying it."

Cam relaxed the arm I'd been laying on and moaned. "Oh, thank the sweet Virgin Mary. My arm has been asleep for over two hours now."

Laughing, I settled back on my knees and watched him rub the circulation back into his shoulder. Then I made the mistake of letting my gaze follow the trail of dark hair from his chest down to his stomach, and even further still, to the hard erection nearly lifting the band of his sweatpants.

"Like what you see?" he asked, catching me in the act.

"I'm not feeding your ego," I told him, shaking my head. "Your confidence is already through the roof."

A slow smile slid onto his face. "I think I'm going to like you, Mavis."

"Oh?" I asked, unable to keep the skeptical tone from my voice.

"You're all no-nonsense. It's kind of a turn-on."

"Then we're a perfect match, because you're almost all nonsense and ridiculousness. We'll probably cancel each other out."

He clutched his chest. "You wound me, demon."

"And you're a perv," I added for good measure.

"To be fair, I am a half incubus. It does kind of come with the territory."

"Yeah, about that territory . . . what happened last night? How did you end up in my bed?"

"Darling, I think you'll find we're in my bed."

I looked over at my unused double bed in horror. "What did I do?"

"You tackled me."

My eyes shot back to his. "I what?"

Cam's grin lit up his face. "You tackled me, Mavis. You tackled me, got me all hot and bothered, and then you fainted."

I stared at him, aghast. "You're making this up."

"No!" he exclaimed. "You did! One second, you had your tongue in my mouth, and the next, you were keeling over. I think after yesterday's ordeal, and the . . . what was it again?" He grinned. "Sexual electricity? I think all that excitement and you gaining some of your demon power may have overwhelmed your system."

I groaned, remembering how I'd acted while I was under his spell. I'd wanted him more than I'd ever wanted anything in my life.

"And if I hadn't passed out?" I asked. "You were just going to let me . . . um, have my way with you?"

He shook his head. "No, of course not. We didn't get to the whole consent thing before you leaped off your bed like a sexed-up cheetah."

"Noooooo," I moaned, burying my face in my hands. "I'm really sorry, Cam."

"For what? You knew I was willing."

"But still. I don't know what came over me."

He pulled my hands away from my face. "I'm a cambion, Mavis. It was me that made you do that."

"Yeah, but . . ."

"No buts," he interrupted. "You couldn't fight it if you wanted to. My gift amplifies your lust."

"So, if I weren't attracted to you, I wouldn't have . . ."

"Straddled me like you were going to ride a stallion?" he suggested, wiggling his eyebrows.

I looked skyward for help or sanity—something that would get me out of this awkward conversation.

"If there is anything good or just in this world, I will wake up, and this will all have been a stress-induced nightmare," I griped.

Cam settled back against the pillows, looking put out. "I think I might be offended."

"No! I didn't mean it that way!"

"Really?" he asked, sounding a little petulant.

"Really."

"I knew it," he teased. "You're hot for my fun stick."

Snaking my hand forward, I snatched the pillow out from under his head and smacked him with it. "You're going to drive me crazy!"

His grin was positively sinful. "Crazy with desire?"

"Don't flatter yourself too much. I haven't had sex in two years. I could get turned on watching a metronome tick."

"Harsh, Miss LeGrand, very harsh."

"No, it's truthful, Mr. DeSalle."

Cam studied me for a long moment before saying, "I want you to come to Colorado with me."

My brows shot up. "What's in Colorado?"

"My apartment. You'd like it there. It's freezing, just like you. Do you realize you were hovering around twenty degrees last night? It was like sleeping with an extremely hot ice block."

"Wait a minute. If you live in Colorado, what are you doing in Utah?"

"I met with a client in Provo."

"You were on your way back from a booty call?" I asked, gaping at him.

He glared at me. "No. I was on my way back from a trip to obtain a middle-aged housewife's soul in return for mind-blowing sex that she'll never forget."

I blanched. Cam's flippant charm and handsome face made it easy to forget what was underneath all that sex appeal. He wasn't an ordinary man. He was a demon, a demon that stole souls from humans. And the way he spoke so nonchalantly about it told me he didn't have any qualms about taking something so precious.

"So," he said, nudging me with his foot. "Do you want to go to Colorado with me?"

I considered him for a moment, taking in his beautiful face and seemingly sincere smile. I didn't know if I trusted him enough to go out of state with him, but honestly, what choice did I have? No one else was offering me safety and the promise of a sexual encounter, the likes of which I would never experience again. Cameron DeSalle was. And Cameron DeSalle looked to me like he'd be worth the risk.

"Mavis?" he prompted, his smile faltering when I remained quiet.

"Yes, I'll go. The farther I'm away from Leon, the better."

"Is that his name? Leon?"

"Yeah, Leon LeGrand."

He nodded. "You'll be safe from him in Havenwood Falls, Mavis. I promise."

"Safe sounds outstanding, Cam. Thank you."

"It's the least I can do. Besides, I'm looking forward to spending more time with you. You've put a little excitement into an old demon's very mundane life."

"How old?" I asked, my interest piqued.

"I was born in nineteen sixteen."

I did a little quick math in my head. "Wow. You are old."

"And you were raised by an evil demon, so I'll ignore your rudeness."

"Sorry. I wasn't expecting you to be quite that . . . experienced."

He huffed. "That's better."

"Uh-oh. Is someone sensitive about his age?"

"No, but someone is going to be riding in the truck bed to Colorado if she keeps it up."

"Duly noted," I said, laughing at his sour expression. "The teasing stops now."

Relaxing back into the pillows, he sighed in exaggerated relief. "Good. Because I can dish it out, but I can't take it."

*C*am pulled into a random diner's parking lot a few hours after we left the hotel. I grinned at him and jumped out of the truck with exuberance.

"A diner!" I squealed.

"Wait until I put the truck in park," he yelled, jumping out after me.

"I've never been anywhere like this before," I explained happily. "It looks just like the diners do on TV."

"And how's that?"

"You know, small and clean with red leather booths and fifties décor. That kind of thing."

"Well, then, I'm glad I picked the only restaurant open this time of night," he said, winking as he opened the door for me.

"Sit anywhere you like," a waitress called out to us. "What can I get you two to drink?"

"I'll have coffee," Cam said, giving her a friendly grin that made her nearly drop the plate she was delivering to the single patron sitting at the bar. "Black, no sugar, please."

"And for your sister?" she asked, apparently dazed by Cam's siren song.

"A soda is fine," I muttered, feeling irrationally irritated with the mile-long-legged curvy blonde that was practically having eye foreplay with my favorite new demon friend.

Trying to hide his bemused smile, Cam told the waitress, "My wife will have a Coke," and led me to the back booth.

The blonde's come-hither smile fell, but she recovered fairly quickly for the sake of her tip. "Coming right up."

"I think you have a fan," I teased, once we were seated.

"She can't help herself, Mavis. I'm irresistible."

"And so modest, too," I complained, picking up a menu.

"Jealous, little ice demon?"

I ignored the bait in favor of scanning the extensive menu. "Oh, look! They have biscuits! I've always wanted to try a biscuit."

Cam stared at me. "Are you telling me you've never been to a diner and you've never had a biscuit? Never . . . in twenty-six years?"

"I'm telling you we had a personal chef that prepared all our meals, none of which included biscuits. My grandfather would never eat something so common. He has his tastes and ways and isn't a huge fan of people. I guess that makes more sense now that I know he's a demon."

"Tell me more about this snobby, reclusive demon with the colorful language. How dangerous is he? Should I be calling for backup?"

"Do you have backup?"

"No, but I could probably scrounge together a small crew of supernatural misfits if I need to."

"That's good to know. Because my grandfather is something of a monster, from what I read in his journal."

"Here's your coffee, handsome," the waitress purred as she made her way to our table and leaned across Cameron to set down the white ceramic mug on his other side. She took her time straightening before she lightly slammed my soda on the table next to me. "And your wife's Coke," she said, nearly sneering at me.

When she sashayed back behind the counter to fill salt shakers, I asked, "You don't think she poisoned me, do you?" and sniffed the contents of the plastic tumbler.

He chuckled. "No, I watched her fill the cup. Know what you want?"

"Right now? Personal safety. On so, so many levels."

"And?" he pressed.

I shrugged. "World peace?"

Cam narrowed his eyes. "From the menu, smarty-pants."

"Oh," I said, my eyes wide and innocent. "The Biscuit Supreme, please."

"Thank you," he said, taking my menu with exaggerated exasperation.

He motioned to the waitress, who snapped to attention the moment she saw his hand. "What'll you have, handsome?"

"We'll have the Apple Walnut French Toast and Biscuit Supreme, please."

She beamed at Cam like he'd asked for her hand in marriage instead of our breakfast. "Coming right up."

"Thank you, Breanne," he said, making a show of reading the nametag on her chest while handing her our menus.

She giggled and straightened her top, pushing her breasts closer to Cam's face. "You're welcome, lover."

Finally fed up with her blatant flirting, I cleared my throat loudly.

Breanne shot a nasty look my way for interrupting whatever she thought she had going on with Cam, but the action had the desired effect. She stormed away to turn in the order, shooting daggers my way every few seconds.

"Am I going to have to break up a cat fight between you two?" Cam asked, looking more than pleased with himself.

"I'm not going to say it's off the table," I seethed.

"Mavis, you're not my real wife. Don't worry about the waitress."

I huffed in frustration. "It's the principle of the thing, Cam. She's disrespecting me." I glared over my shoulder at the waitress. "And I may just have to kick her ass for it."

He sat back and studied me thoughtfully with his arms crossed. "I think I enjoy seeing you riled up. You're all demonic claws and teeth underneath that librarian spinster façade. It's sexy."

"Librarian spinster?" I spat. "Am I going to have to kick your ass, too?"

Cam raised his hands defensively. "Hey, now. I was paying you a compliment."

"Some compliment," I muttered.

He smirked. "Do you want a better one, wifey?"

I squinted at him, knowing he was up to something but decided to indulge him anyway. "You know what, hubby? I think I might."

Cam took a sip of his coffee and moved the cup to the far side of the table so that he could lean toward me.

I met him halfway. "Well?"

"There's nothing about you I couldn't compliment. You're smart and pretty, and you've got these perfect hand-sized breasts and this luscious ass that makes me want to—"

"That'll do," I said, interrupting him.

"But I'm not done."

"Oh, you're done," I assured him.

He flashed a panty-dropping smile at me and stage-whispered, "I like how hard you make me."

"Shh!" I hissed.

"What?" he said, in a much louder voice. "I can't tell the whole room how much I want my sexy, beautiful wife? Why not? It's not a lie." He grinned at the customer at the bar and the waitress, who had just come out of the kitchen with our plates. "I'd be tempted to get her naked right here on this table if it wasn't illegal."

The waitress reacted to this information by stomping her way to our table to drop off our food, then fuming all the way back to the kitchen. The customer just laughed and asked, "Newlyweds?"

Cam grinned. "Yes, sir. We met in Vegas, and I just knew she would change my life. I'm taking her home to North Dakota with me."

"Well, I wish you both the best," the old man said, getting up and throwing a twenty-dollar bill on the counter. "Take care, now."

"Thanks," we said in unison.

When I heard the tinkle of the doorbell and knew we were alone, I turned on Cam. "What are you doing?"

Switching our plates, he cut a maple-syrup-drenched bite of French toast and chewed it before he answered. "Trying to make you smile. I like it when you smile. The frowning thing, not so much."

"You don't think that way was a bit extreme?"

"It had a dual purpose."

"And what could that possibly be?"

"It's so people remember us as a newlywed couple on their way from Las Vegas to North Dakota. Even if you are recognized, they'll be looking for you a few states away."

I stared at him. "You are something else, Cameron DeSalle."

"I meant what I said. I do think you're smart and pretty, and I do think you're going to change my life."

"Really?"

"Really," he assured me.

I sighed. "Well, now I'm disappointed that you didn't mention my perfect, hand-sized breasts and luscious—"

"That'll do," he said, mocking my earlier words.

"But I'm not done."

"Oh, you're done," he said, grinning at me. "Eat your biscuit, little demon."

WITH FULL STOMACHS, Cam and I piled back into the truck and set out for Colorado. I couldn't wait to get there. Going somewhere I would never have to worry about Leon again sounded like heaven. I just hoped living with me wouldn't be hell for Cam. With his lifestyle, I was bound to get in his way.

"What are you thinking about?" Cam asked.

"About the future."

"I think we'd better focus on the short term. We have to get you somewhere safe before we start worrying about the future."

Dejected, I sat back in my seat. "I feel so helpless, Cam."

"Which is why I'm helping you."

"Distracting me is more like it."

"That, too," he agreed. "As I said, I like it when you smile."

"Is it because you like to see me happy or because you want to make sure I don't start killing demons with some ridiculous power I know nothing about?"

He laughed. "When you put it that way, I'd have to say both."

I groaned. "What am I going to do?"

"Turn on the heat? You've got it freezing in here."

"Sorry," I said, trying to stop whatever I was doing.

"Close your eyes, Mavis. I'll help you."

I obeyed. "Now what?"

"Calm yourself. Center yourself. All those worries you have, just let them drift away. Now I want you to take a breath in through your nose for four seconds. After that, hold that breath for seven seconds. Then I want you to slowly blow it out your mouth for eight seconds and tell me how you feel."

I opened my eyes. "Do what now?"

"Inhale through your nose for four seconds, hold it for seven, and let it go for eight seconds. Here, I'll do it with you."

We both took in a slow breath as Cam counted to four with his fingers, then held it for seven seconds. Closing my eyes, I slowly let go of my breath for the eight seconds and let my head roll to the side.

Smiling over at him, I asked, "Where did you learn that?"

"One of my clients suffers from anxiety attacks after sex sometimes. I help her calm down before I leave."

"That's sweet of you."

He shrugged. "I don't mind. She's paying me a small fortune to steal her soul. It's the least I can do."

"Do you like the sex you have with your clients, or is it like any other job after a while?"

"Honestly, I can't imagine anyone enjoying prostitution."

"Then why do you do it?"

"Because I don't want to hurt innocent women. The women I escort aren't faithful. I make sure of it. If I have to collect souls from

159

women, I want to take them from those who might be going south already."

"Do all cambions and incubuses have your stellar moral fiber?"

"Not any that I've ever met. They only have one goal—collecting souls."

"What makes you so different?"

He hesitated before answering. "When I was a kid, I had every possibility in front of me. I could be or do anything. Then my mom died, and I was left to be raised by an incubus. This is not the life my mother would have wanted for me, Mavis. Every demon knows right from wrong. It's what you do with that knowledge that matters."

I stayed silent, just processing for a moment. "Do you have to do this? Is it mandatory for your kind?"

"My father told me, in no uncertain terms, that if I do not collect souls for him, he will take the soul my mother gave me himself."

I gritted my teeth. "He would do that to his child?"

"He would do that to his one and only child," he assured me. "I'm nothing but an embarrassment to him. He has no use for a son who doesn't want to hurt humans and won't obey his every command. He says my mother spoiled me by not teaching me to think and act like a demon."

"That makes no sense. How would she even know how to do that? She was human."

"Yes, and so am I, and apparently, that is unforgivable in his eyes."

"But he was the one who . . . uh . . . mated with her, right? It's not like he didn't know you'd be half human."

"Of course he knew. There is no other choice for us. Incubuses can't procreate naturally. They don't have souls. The only way to impregnate a human is to acquire sperm from a succubus's victim and transfer it to the host while in their true form."

I wrinkled my nose. "Ew."

"Yeah," he agreed.

"Being a demon isn't all it's cracked up to be, is it?" I asked.

He chuckled and shook his head. "I don't think anyone hears 'demon' and thinks it's the greatest thing ever."

"No, but damn, Cam. You fuck people pretty much against your will, and I was born to be some ice-loving demon killer. What the shit is that? There's got to be something good about it."

"You forget that you're immortal."

"Oh, yeah. Great. We can have these horrible lives for an eternity."

Cam came to a stop at a red light and met my eyes. "Even the most horrible life has its good moments, Mavis."

CHAPTER 5

Cam and I talked almost the entire drive to Havenwood Falls. I learned that he loved horror movies (the bloodier, the better), hiking, and strawberry rhubarb pie. He discovered that I hated all those things and that I didn't appreciate his critique of my favorite movies and books. But to be fair, there are only so many times a demoness can hear the word *overrated* before she snaps.

Our bickering about Colin Firth's acting abilities aside, it was nice to get to know more about Cam. From what we'd discussed, I could tell he was planning to keep me around for a while. Knowing his likes and dislikes would make it easier for me to keep my new roommate happy and be less of a nuisance to him. Plus, underneath all that sexy brooding, he was an interesting demon—an opinionated, sex-driven trickster of a demon, but an interesting demon, nonetheless.

On the last stretch of our trip, Cam was quiet, so I kept myself entertained by watching the scenery fly by the window. The trees were beautiful here, majestic and magical in the bright moonlight. I took a deep breath, feeling a liberating sort of freedom flow through me. I was almost to safety.

Cam gestured up ahead. "We're nearly there."

Looking to where he pointed, I saw the black metal-and-stone sign welcoming us to Havenwood Falls.

"What's it like?" I asked excitedly.

He shrugged. "It's Havenwood Falls. It's home."

I laughed. "Care to elaborate on that?"

He sighed. "I might as well. You'll have to know soon enough."

"Know what?"

"Well, first, there are supernatural beings of every sort there."

I stared at him, mouth agape.

He smiled at my reaction. "Mavis, Havenwood Falls is not like other towns. It has safeguards in place that make it nearly impossible to find. You won't even find it on Google Maps. That alone makes it a refuge for supernatural creatures and humans alike. There's nowhere in the world you could be more protected than here."

"How is it protected? Dragons?"

"By magic and strict rules. The dragons pretty much keep to themselves."

I shook my head, dumbfounded by what I was hearing. "How strict are the rules?"

"They're nothing crazy. It's basically just don't be a dick and don't reveal yourself to the humans."

"Does that ever happen?"

"Very, very rarely. All supernaturals, including demons, whether visitors or residents, have to register with the Court of the Sun and the Moon. They'll give you a tattoo that will hide your true nature from the rest of the population."

"A tattoo?" I screeched. "No way. I'm not getting a tattoo."

"If you intend on staying, you will. It's required. You can pick whatever you want, and it can even be invisible. It's not a big deal. Plus, we don't know what you'll look like if your power decides to make an appearance. The tattoo will keep the humans from seeing what you look like in your demon form."

I paled in shock. "W-what do you mean?"

"Mavis, ice demons differ from almost all of the other demons. They do not naturally look human unless you have one as a parent. The beautiful woman in front of me is some sort of glamour, no doubt included in that throttle of yours."

I stared at him in horror. "What?"

"Don't tell me you didn't already think of this. You asked me to see my true form last night."

"But I didn't think of it," I told him. "I can't believe I didn't, but I didn't. Is it terrible?"

"Beauty is in the eye of the beholder, of course, but I will tell you that the few ice demons I've seen look pretty similar to each other. They have very, very pale skin, white-blond hair, and silver eyes. The males have these huge intimidating horns and large patches of ice crystals spread out over their body. The females have smaller, daintier horns and tiny patches of ice along their temples and shoulders."

I shuddered. "That sounds hideous."

"Honestly, the females are pretty hot as far as demons go. You'll still look the same, just with paler features. And those horns really are adorable."

"Is that supposed to reassure me?"

"Not in the slightest. If anything, it's supposed to let you know I'm game for sex with you no matter what you look like."

I shook my head. "You're incorrigible."

"And you're home," he said, as the streetlamp-lit town appeared before us.

"Wow," I exclaimed, surprised at how charming and picturesque the town was, even from here. "It's beautiful."

"It's one of my favorite sights on the planet."

"It's easy to see why," I said, smiling at the proud expression on his face.

Cam drove slowly in the darkness, allowing me to take in everything I could. Soon after entering the town, I saw the grand entrance of Creekwood Estates and Country Club, Havenwood Falls High School, and a shopping center, Miller's Plaza. All the businesses and food shops in the plaza looked closed for the night, but I could imagine them lively and full of people during the day.

I grinned at Cam. "We're so far into the mountains, I thought it would be a one-horse town, but this is amazing!"

He returned my excited smile. "I am rather fond of it."

"How long have you lived here?"

"Since I was very small. There are some types of demons that will kill a cambion if they can get close enough. Havenwood Falls was the safest place for us."

My jaw dropped. "Well, that's not terrifying or anything. I'm glad your parents put you somewhere safe."

"Trust me. My father only wanted to protect his investment. Wouldn't you, if you got credit with the bigwigs downstairs for every piece of soul I steal?"

"And the town is okay with you stealing souls? That doesn't fall under the don't-be-a-dick edict?"

"The Court has never approved of stealing souls, which you would've seen firsthand had you shown up a few months ago when some of the mammon demons got banished."

"Then why do they let you do it?" I asked.

"Because my case is different than theirs. I don't do it because I want to hurt humans; I do it because my soul literally depends on me keeping my father happy, so they're a little sympathetic to my plight. Not to mention, I'm a long-time resident who has never caused one iota of trouble. The only caveat they've given me is that I'm not allowed to sleep with anyone in the town limits."

I shook my head in disgust. "Your father is a piece of work. He really doesn't have any redeeming qualities, does he?"

"Not even one," he answered darkly. "Which is the reason he's only allowed to visit Havenwood Falls every few weeks. And really, that's only because I've lobbied the Court on his behalf and assured them that I can keep him on the straight and narrow."

"Why would you do that for him, after everything he's done to you?"

"Because the alternative is a cranky, pissed off demon who will make my life a nightmare," he said simply. "It's true what they say about keeping your enemies closer, you know."

"Demons," I said, sighing and clucking my tongue.

Cam laughed and pulled into a driveway, parking next to a

building labeled *C*. He turned off the engine and aimed a mischievous smile at me. "Welcome to Havenwood Village."

I smiled back, but couldn't seem to get myself to move from the warmth of the truck.

"Is it weird that I'm suddenly super nervous to see your apartment?" I asked.

He drew a halo around his head with a finger. "I promise to keep my hands to myself."

"I'll believe that when I see it," I told him, reaching for my door.

He stopped me with a gentle hand on my arm. "I'm serious. Until you can resist my charm, I don't think that it's a good idea for us to have sex. I wouldn't feel right about it."

"I don't think it's a good idea for us to have sex under any circumstances, Cam, but that doesn't keep me from wanting it," I told him.

His eyes roamed from my face to my body, then he sighed. "Me neither, Mavis. Me neither."

"So we're agreed on no sex until my magic shows up all the way?"

He nodded.

"What if it never does?"

He shrugged and sat back in his seat. "I reserve the right to make addendums after an appropriate amount of time."

"Then I accept your terms," I told him, offering a handshake. "Any more ground rules?"

He accepted my hand but didn't shake it. He only held it in both of his own, examining the lines on my palm for who knew what. "Just the usual. No smoking, no pets, no illicit drugs, and no demon-killing inside the town limits. The Court will give you the freedom to figure this out on your own, but one big slipup, and they'll swoop in on us like a SWAT team."

"Anything else?" I asked, surprised by the sensual sound of my voice.

He grinned and let go of my hand. "Try not to walk around naked in front of me."

"Trust me. You have nothing to worry about there. You're the one with the positive body image, remember?"

Cam scoffed. "Of course it's positive. Have you seen my body?"

I rolled my eyes. "As usual, your modesty astounds me."

"You'd think you'd have lowered your expectations by now," he said, opening the door.

MY FIRST IMPRESSION of Cam's apartment was that it was sparkling clean, but it had the sparsely decorated, sad look of a place that was only used for a place to sleep. It made me wonder how often Cam went out of town on his "business trips."

"Your bedroom is at the end of the hall on the right," Cam said, directing me to the hallway off the right of the living room. "Your bathroom is on the left."

I peered down the darkened hallway. "Where's your room?"

He turned in the opposite direction and pointed to an identical setup at the other end of the apartment. "Right down there. The kitchen and laundry are through the doorway before the hallway."

"Okay," I said, fidgeting with a loose thread on the hem of my shirt. I couldn't think of anything to say now that we were here and alone.

"It's awkward now, right?" he asked.

I laughed. "So awkward. But we'll figure it out."

He smiled that devastatingly handsome smile of his and nodded. "That we will. I still want to get in your pants. I'm willing to play nice as long as it takes."

"You are a terrible demon," I said, shaking my head.

"I know. It's both a blessing and a curse." He grinned and opened my bedroom door. Flipping on the light switch, he said, "The sheets should be relatively fresh, and there are extra blankets in your closet if you get cold. It can get a little chilly at night."

"I doubt I'll have to worry about that," I said, rolling my eyes. "Cold is sort of my thing."

"Well, it's not mine. I sleep in the nude. I want to keep my shrinkage to a minimum."

I snorted. "Understood. I'll try my best to keep myself at room temperature."

"See that you do," he said, smiling down at me. "So, see you in the morning?"

"I'll see you then. If you have trouble recognizing me, I'll be the burden you picked up in Utah."

"You're not a burden, Mavis. I told you I'd help you, and I will. I keep my promises."

"I know," I said, letting out a heavy sigh. "I just feel like I'm going to get in your way."

"You won't," he assured me. Then he grinned mischievously and poked my shoulder with a finger. "And if you do, I'll just give you a little shove."

"As long as you realize that I'll shove you back," I retorted, putting both palms on his rock-hard chest and giving him a little push.

He slid his fingers into the hair at my temples and pressed a soft, lingering kiss to my forehead.

"Sleep well, Mavis." His voice was low and husky, and his brow was creased with concentration as if he was struggling to keep his actions chaste.

I slid my palms down to the waistband of his jeans, never taking my eyes off his. "Sweet dreams, Cam."

"You move your hands any lower, and they're going to be sex dreams instead of sweet dreams," he warned, backing me up against the wall.

"You mean, like this?" I asked, tracing the hard outline of his erection through the denim.

Cam hissed and spoke with clenched teeth. "What about our agreement, Mavis?"

I popped the button on his jeans. "Fuck the agreement."

His eyes flared with desire. "Tempting, but how about I fuck you instead?" he asked, sending shockwave after shockwave of power through me when he moved his hands to cup my ass.

Instead of answering, I kept my gaze locked on his, slowly and deliberately lowering his zipper.

"Mavis," he growled, his tone pleading.

"Shh," I whispered, taking his hard length into my palms and stroking him from base to tip.

"Fuck, Mavis!" he shouted, bucking in my hands.

"I think that's what we're doing," I teased.

He groaned with restrained pleasure and pulled away, gasping for air. "My bedroom, little demon. Now."

Without a word, I walked away, shedding my clothes as I went.

Cam trailed slowly behind me, taking in my strip show in silence. When he reached me, he looked at me from head to toe, hunger darkening his brown eyes to nearly black. His erection was as hard as a rock as he pulled off his shirt and pushed his jeans down his muscular thighs.

"I'll try to be as gentle as I can," he said, though his face told me the exact opposite.

"Don't you dare," I told him bravely. "I want all of you."

"Don't forget you said that," he said, his smile downright devious as he joined me on the bed and tugged me up to his body.

I went willingly. I was aching to touch him, to taste him, but as much as I desired him, I was hesitant to make the first move. I wanted this to be perfect. Cam wasn't some frat boy in the back of a Camaro. He was a professional.

Cam raised his brows. "Are you okay?"

I chuckled. "You're not going to believe this, but I'm a little nervous."

He smiled. "Good."

"Why is that good?" I asked.

He threaded his fingers in my hair, his lips so close to mine, I could practically taste him. "You know why."

And when Cam pressed his lips against mine, I did know why. It was in the way he laid out his need for me in his kiss, the way he seemed desperate to relay what he couldn't say in words. He didn't want this to be another job for him. He wanted something real.

And so did I. As much as I enjoyed the way his charm made me feel, it didn't compare with the genuine lust and affection I felt for him when he touched me like he was doing now.

Cam lifted his head to gauge my reaction, then retook my mouth, licking it open to deepen the kiss.

I groaned and sagged against him. "Please," I whispered against his lips.

Nodding slightly, he kissed me again, urgently this time. Then he settled on his knees between my legs.

I arched against his heavy erection. "Please, Cameron."

Without preamble, he positioned himself at my core and started to push inside slowly. His eyes were closed, and his teeth gritted in concentration.

I whimpered at the pleasured pain.

He stilled, his eyes searching my face. "Mavis?"

"Don't stop," I panted. "I want you."

Resigned, Cam bent his head to take my mouth, swallowing my cries until he was finally fully seated within me. Then, with aching slowness, he withdrew and pushed back in, making me moan into his mouth.

"Please," I begged, wanting him to fuck me until I couldn't think anymore.

Groaning, he hitched up my legs and pumped hard and fast, eliciting a pleasured scream from me as the delicious pressure I craved ratcheted up.

I clung to his shoulders, letting him set the furious pace that was bringing me closer and closer to orgasm. "Harder!" I cried out.

Cam obliged, moving into me so fast and hard, he lifted me off the mattress with every thrust. "Come for me, Mavis."

As soon as the words came from his lips, I had no choice. I seized up all at once, screaming out his name.

He followed right after, roaring as he spilled deep inside of me.

I laughed as he rested his forehead against mine then sighed. "Well, that was long overdue . . . for both of us."

He grinned. "I was honestly worried about waking up stuck to the bed in the morning."

"That is way hotter than it should be," I told him.

"You're way hotter than you should be," he shot back.

I rolled my hips. "Is that why you're still hard?"

He groaned. "It's not like I have a lot of choice in the matter. Mavis, you were so hot and wet for me, I can't help but want more of you."

"Were?" I asked wickedly. "Cam, if you haven't noticed, I'm still hot and wet for you."

"Fancy a ride, then?" he asked, rolling us over so that I was on top of him.

"I thought you'd never ask," I said, starting a cadence that had him digging his fingers into my hips and meeting my thrusts.

He chuckled. "Believe me. It hasn't been easy."

I leaned down and nipped at his lips. "Well, if I would've known it would be this good, I might've given in the night we met.

"So you're saying you like?"

I offered him a sultry smile. "Oh, I like a lot."

"What else do you like?"

"I like the feel of you inside of me. I like that look of restraint on your face. I think it's hot as fuck that you're holding back what you want to do to me."

His brows lifted in surprise. "What do you think I want to do?"

"I don't think," I purred. "I know. You want to dominate me, make me beg for your cock, fuck me so hard and good, it makes me wet every time I think about your dick."

His eyes were as black as coal as he asked, "And if I said that was all true? How would you feel about that?"

"If I didn't want that, I wouldn't be here right now, Cam. You're half incubus. I know what that entails."

"And if I say I want more than that from you?"

"I'll give it to you. I'll give you anything you want. I want you to ruin me for every other demon."

"Anything I want?"

"Name it."

"I want you to get a particular tattoo tomorrow, one that marks you as being under my protection."

"Done. Anything else?"

"Yes," he said, slipping his hand between us. "I want you to come, because I'm not going to last much longer."

CHAPTER 6

*C*am was still sleeping when I finally slipped out from under his arm and padded to the bathroom the next afternoon. I had been loath to do it. I loved being tangled up with him in our cozy little nest of sheets and blankets. It had been so warm and comfortable, and his dick had been so very accessible.

I shook my head and laughed to myself. The night before had been . . . I didn't think there were words for what the night before had been. Cameron was a fantastic lover. His dedication to pleasing me had been something to behold.

And I hoped to behold it at least ten more times before the day was over.

The only thing I was unsure about was what the sex had meant to Cam. It was true that he was half incubus, so it was possible that he just wanted to fuck, but somehow, what we'd done didn't feel like casual sex. What I was starting to feel for him didn't feel casual at all. It felt right. I just hoped he felt the same for me.

Ridiculously giddy at the thought of rejoining Cam and his nakedness, I closed the bathroom door and found the light switch. And then I screamed bloody murder.

Cam burst through the door seconds later. His eyes were wild with worry. "Mavis! What is it?"

Holding up a shaky finger, I pointed to myself in the mirror, but I couldn't seem to make words come out of my mouth.

"Oh, that." He gave me a warm smile. "You're beautiful."

I glared at him. "I'm hideous, Cam!"

"You're an ice demon. Ice demons aren't hideous."

"What the fuck is going on in here?" asked a feminine voice from outside the bathroom.

Cam and I both jerked our gazes to the owner of the voice. She was a tall, pretty woman with long brown hair and laughing chocolate-colored eyes. And I'd never seen her before in my life.

"Hi. I'm Penelope," she said, her smile fading as she looked down. "Wow. You guys are really super naked."

I looked over to Cam, who was holding a hand towel over his crotch and trying not to laugh. He didn't seem to be surprised by the strange woman in his apartment or worried that she was witnessing his demon friend have a nervous breakdown.

"Mavis," he said, trying to regain his composure. "This is my neighbor from next door, Penelope Osbourne. Penelope, this is my girlfriend, Mavis. She just moved in last night.

"I get the feeling that a lot of things happened last night," she said, motioning to me and my brand spanking new demon face.

I threw my hands up. "Thank you! Can we get back to the crisis at hand? Look at me!" I cried, pointing at the demon with the unnaturally pale face and hair in the mirror. "Wait! Did you say I was your girlfriend?"

Cam chuckled at my one-eighty and wrapped his free arm around my waist. "Yes, I said girlfriend. And I am looking at you, darling. Trust me. If this towel weren't here, I would show you just how much I like the view."

"Gross," Penelope groaned dramatically. "I think I just threw up in my mouth."

"And I think I just heard the washer stop," Cam told her pointedly.

"Subtle, Cam," she said, going back the way she'd come. "Very subtle."

I grabbed a towel to wrap around myself and ran after her. "Wait! Are you a demon, too?"

Penelope laughed. "Nope, just an ordinary human."

"But you're so calm about . . ." I gestured to everything that was going on in the bathroom. "All of this."

She shrugged. "I've known Cam is a demon since I was in high school. The walls are thin, and I'm super nosy. I know plenty of things most of the humans here are oblivious to."

"But how are you not affected by his charm? I thought all humans were affected."

"I told you that the local monsters get a tattoo," Cam reminded me. "This is a prime example of why."

"It's a good thing it works, too," Penelope said, humor coloring her voice. "Otherwise, I'd be humping his leg or something."

My jaw dropped. Did Cam have that kind of power over humans?

"She's just kidding," Cam said, rolling his eyes.

Penelope shook her head from the doorway and mouthed, "No, I'm not," behind his back.

"This day took a bizarre turn," I said, suddenly too exhausted to stand.

Cam led me back to the bedroom and sat me down on the foot of the bed. "You need to calm down. You'll go back to normal soon."

I sighed in relief. "Good."

Penelope looked to Cam in confusion. "But isn't this her natural state?"

Cam shot her a warning look.

"Right," she said, taking the hint. "You know, I think you're right. The washer is done. I'll just put my stuff in the dryer and see myself out. It was nice meeting you, Mavis."

"You, too, Penelope," I said. Then I turned on Cam. "Is she right?"

He cringed under my stare. "Technically, yes. She's right. But as I said, you can go back to the Mavis you've known your entire life if you just calm down. Do the breathing exercise I taught you."

"I can't be like this forever," I whined, falling back onto the bed.

"You can, and more importantly, you will." He smiled as he

absentmindedly stroked my ankle. "You're so beautiful like this. You don't even realize how much."

"I look like a creature of Hell."

"You are a creature of Hell. We both are. Now put your big-girl panties on and deal with it."

I sighed. "I don't even know where my panties are."

Cam stifled a smile and held out a hand to me. "Come here."

"Why? Where are we going?" I asked, warily putting my hand into his.

He opened the closet door to show me a full-length mirror hung inside. "I want to show you something."

"What?" I asked, barely able to look at what I'd become.

"Do you know what I see when I look at you?"

"A demon?"

"A beautiful demon," he corrected. "Everything about the way you look makes my cock hard . . . everything." He ran his palms down my shoulders. "Your luminescent skin, the otherworldly look to your eyes and hair, those ridiculously adorable horns . . . all of it makes me want to fuck you."

"Cam . . ."

He cut me off with a finger to my lips. "No arguments, Mavis. And no more degrading yourself. You were stunning before, and you still are. Maybe even more so."

"But . . ."

"Don't make me spank you, little miss demoness," he whispered in my ear. "Because I will."

My brows shot up as I felt him press his hardness into the small of my back. "Are you threatening me, Mr. DeSalle?"

"That depends on you," he told me, nuzzling my neck.

I relaxed against his bare chest and tilted my head to the side to give him better access. "Oh?"

"Yeah," he said, loosening the towel from my breasts and letting it fall to the floor. "It depends on whether you'll take a damn compliment or if you'll continue to be stubborn."

"I'm a little tempted to be stubborn when you make it sound all sexy like that."

He barked out a laugh. "And I'm the incorrigible one?"

I scoffed. "Without a doubt."

"Not even one?" he asked.

Cam's dubious face made me laugh. "Stop trying to cheer me up and commiserate with me."

"Would but I could," he said. "I can't have sympathy for you if I don't think there's anything wrong."

"I bet your tune will change once you have to have sex with me like this."

He smiled at me in the mirror and kissed my neck. "I had sex with you like this for hours last night."

I snaked my hand behind me and smacked what I could reach, which turned out to be his naked hip. "Why didn't you tell me?"

"Because I knew you'd freak out, and I didn't want it to ruin our first night together. Plus, it was sexy as fuck seeing you like this for the first time." He lifted a finger to one of my horns and ran it from the tip, down my cheek, into my cleavage, and finally across my waist, before plunging into my heated flesh. "You don't know how beautiful you were last night."

I moaned loudly, my hips bucking forward against his hand, chasing his hard and fast rhythm.

Cam's smile was wicked as he watched me writhe around his talented fingers. "Open your eyes. I want you to see what I do when you come."

I did as he asked, but I couldn't look at myself, not when I could see Cam as he was right now. His face was wild, animalistic in its intensity. He was barely in control.

"I want you inside me," I said, locking eyes with him.

Without hesitation, Cam grabbed me by the waist and lifted me onto his rigid sex. Instinctively, I wrapped my legs around his thighs and fell forward, bracing my hands on either side of the mirror. He slid his hands under my knees to support my weight and groaned as he watched my breasts bounce with every pump of his cock between my legs.

"Come, Mavis," he demanded.

I was helpless to disobey, screaming out my climax so loud, I thought I might shatter the mirror. Cam followed right after with a sharp yell and sank to his knees, taking me down with him.

When we'd calmed down, and we were no longer breathing like we'd run a marathon, I started laughing and continued to laugh until big fat tears were leaking down my cheeks.

Cam looked at me like he was concerned for my sanity. "What's so funny?"

Wiping tears from my eyes, I said, "All this time, and I didn't even notice."

"Notice what?"

"The sexual electricity, it's gone."

He laughed and stood to help me to my feet. "You didn't notice?"

I slid my arms around his waist and kissed his chest, careful not to poke him with my horns. "I don't notice a lot of things when you have your cock in me," I said. "It's very distracting."

"A good distraction?" he asked, tugging me forward to kiss my lips.

I grinned and pecked him on the lips. "The best kind of distraction."

HOURS LATER, when we finally made it out of the bedroom to shower and rejoin civilization, Cam answered the doorbell and let in a pretty woman with long, light brown hair, brown eyes, and a sparkling diamond stud in her nose, to tattoo my upper arm. Adelaide Beaumont, or Addie for short, was a witch and a member of what Cam called the Luna Coven, and she was in a big hurry, which was evident by the way she went to work after only a cursory introduction. I tried not to watch while she did her work, concentrating on the soft sound of her many bracelets and bangles to distract myself. When she'd finished, she nodded at the strange symbol she'd drawn at Cam's direction, packed her things, and asked Cam to walk her outside. With a wave and a grin, she said goodbye to me and was gone as quickly as she'd come.

After a minute or so, Cam returned, looking resolute. I watched him close the door, then said, "Well, that was anticlimactic."

He gave me an indulgent smile. "I told you it was no big deal, didn't I?"

"You did," I said, gingerly touching my arm. I was surprised there was no pain or tenderness. "But you know, it was needles, so . . ."

He laughed. "So, how about dinner? What are you thinking?"

"Pizza?" I suggested.

"Sounds good. Napoli's has the best pizza this side of the Mississippi. You just wait. You'll love it. Do you know what kind you want to order?"

I squinted at him. He didn't realize it, but this was a pivotal moment in our budding relationship. His pizza choice might be the deal breaker I'd been anticipating since he tossed out the girlfriend card.

"What?" he asked, looking at my skeptical face with nervousness.

"What kind of pizza do you like?"

"Anything. As long as it doesn't have pineapple on it."

I blew out a breath. "Oh, thank God! If you would've been one of those awful pineapple lovers, I would have had to find some other demon to take me to his hometown and make me his love slave."

He rolled his eyes as he grabbed his phone, but I could tell he was amused. "So, pepperoni is good?"

"More than good, but be warned. If you pick the toppings, I get to pick the movie."

Cam eyed me suspiciously. "I think it might be better if you pick the pizza."

"Why?"

"Librarian spinster," he said, waving an arm in my direction.

"And what is that supposed to mean?"

"It means that my TV has a No Jane feature. No Jane Austen. No Jane Eyre."

"Who said I even watch those movies?"

"Uh, you did, on the car ride here, remember?"

I grinned. "Oh, yeah."

"So?"

"Half cheese, half pepperoni."

"Perfect. Just don't ask me for any of my side."

I plopped down on his cushy beige couch and sighed petulantly. "Aren't you supposed to be wooing me?"

"Do you need wooing?" he asked, kneeling in front of me with a smirk that made him look like a cat that had eaten several canaries.

"Maybe."

"Then let me get right on that," he growled, seconds before the doorbell rang.

Cam jumped to his feet. "Fuck."

Alarmed, I sat up straight. "What? What's happening?"

He glowered at the door. "It's my father."

CHAPTER 7

$\mathcal{T}$he moment I saw Severin DeSalle, I knew I would hate him. A tall dark-haired and dark-eyed male, he was dressed in a black suit that hugged his muscled frame beautifully, but his face was snarled in a sneer that spoke volumes of his disdain for his only spawn.

"Father," Cameron said in greeting, nodding his head in respect.

Instead of responding, the demon ignored him and walked across the room to the couch I sat on. His eyes traveled the length of my body before he bestowed me with a smile that promised sexual delights the likes of which I'd never experienced. "Cameron, introduce me to your lady friend. She is positively delicious."

I cringed inwardly but managed to slap a friendly smile on my face and ask, "Was that a compliment, Mr. DeSalle, or do you want to eat me for dessert?"

His dazzling smile widened. "As tempting as eating you would be, it was only meant as a compliment, Miss . . . ?"

Cameron's jaw twitched as he exhaled through his nose. "Father, this is Mavis. She's staying with me for a few days. Mavis, this is my father, Severin DeSalle."

"Is she now?" Severin asked, clearly affronted that Cameron hadn't cleared my stay with him first. "And for what reason are you staying with my son, Mavis?"

I lifted a brow at his presumption. Cam may have been afraid to stand up to his father, but I sure wasn't.

"Do you normally give out your personal information to a new acquaintance the first minute you meet them?" I asked him cheekily.

Severin's brown eyes flashed to black. "I am very old and very powerful, Mavis. My age, along with my stature in the demonic community, should secure a little respect from underlings such as yourself. You would do well to remember that."

His haughty tone made my cheeks flush hot with anger. "And you'd do well to remember that you have no idea who you're dealing with," I seethed. "You have no idea what I'm capable of. Maybe you should examine your own shitty behavior."

Cam's eyes widened in fear as his father took a step toward me and hissed, "Mind your tongue, you little wench, or I shall teach you manners myself!"

I narrowed my eyes at the insult and took a step closer to him, feeling calmer than I had in days as I boldly squared up with him. "Bring it, jackass."

Roaring in anger, Severin screamed, "You will respect me, demon!"

"If I do, you will have earned it, you fucking asshole!" I shot back, feeling a cold draft circle around us.

He clenched his fists to his sides as if he was struggling not to throttle me with his bare hands, and then he whirled on Cameron. "I'd like a word outside. Now."

Cameron pressed his lips together and followed his father, looking back at me with a *what the fuck* expression before he closed the door behind them.

I dropped to the couch, feeling numb. What had I just done? I was so angry over the high-handed way he'd treated me, I didn't stop to think how Severin might be tempted to take out his frustrations on his son.

After a few minutes, Cameron came back in wearing a shell-shocked expression. "You're not going to believe this," he said, "but my father liked you."

"You're kidding?" I asked, feeling a little shocked myself.

"When he asked me to go outside, I thought he was going to go apeshit, but he just laughed and said he'd like to shut you up by shoving his cock down your throat. There was a load of other graphic sexual threats, but I'll spare you those."

I screwed up my face in disgust. "Ew. Did he say anything else?"

"He asked if we were fucking."

My eyebrows shot up. "What did you tell him?"

"I told him we were. I may be able to get away with some important omissions, but my father can always tell when I'm lying. It's a skill he's perfected over his many years of manipulating humans."

"Exactly how many years has he been a douche?"

"Six hundred and something. I forget the exact number."

"Holy shit," I exclaimed. "No wonder he was pissed at me."

Cam sat down on the couch and pulled me into his lap. "I think he might have been more intrigued than pissed. I doubt anyone has talked to him like that since my mother was alive."

"I don't know. He didn't seem too intrigued to me."

"Trust me. He was."

"How could you tell?" I asked, relaxing into the warmth of his body.

"He told me."

"He told you he was intrigued. Like, he literally said he was intrigued by me?"

"He did . . . in so many words," he hedged.

I squinted at him. "What words?"

"He asked me to tell you to give him a call when you want to fuck a demon that can make his cock as big as you want it. Oh, and he said he'd be happy to teach you some discipline and respect in the most painful way possible."

"I think I'm going to puke," I said, feeling queasy.

"I think I'm a little scared to leave you here alone while I'm gone tomorrow."

"You're leaving?" I asked. "Where are you going?"

Cam leveled me with a stare. "Mavis, you know what I am and what I have to do."

"I do. But do you have to do it so soon?"

"If I want to keep my soul and pay my rent, yes."

I sighed and tried to keep the pout from my face. I didn't want to admit it, but I didn't feel any empathy for the women Cameron would bed; I only felt jealousy. As selfish as it was, I wanted him for myself and despised the thought of someone else enjoying what I considered mine and mine alone.

"You know I wouldn't go if I had another choice," he said, noticing my disquiet.

"I know," I admitted.

He kissed my forehead. "I know things are moving fast for us right now, but everything will settle soon. You'll be bored with me and my unchangeable dick in a month."

Reluctantly, I grinned at him. "It'll never happen."

AFTER A DELICIOUS DINNER from Napoli's, Cam and I decided to stretch our legs by taking a walk to the square to see the decorations being put up for the holiday. But though I was anxious to see the town while it had actual people milling about, I was concerned that we'd run into Cameron's father. I didn't think I was ready to see him so soon after hearing what his idea of a good time with me would be like.

I explained this fear to Cam as we started walking down Main Street, but he brushed off my concern with a laugh. "You have nothing to worry about. My father hasn't stayed for any real length of time in Havenwood Falls since the 1940s."

"Too many burnt bridges?" I asked, taking notice of a bar called the Haven Saloon on the corner and a store named Shelf Indulgence next door to it as we walked.

"Exactly."

"Why do you think he's such an asshat? What made him like this?"

Cam eyed the crowd of giggling teenagers walking toward us and slung an arm around me, pulling me closer to his side. "My father is a demon, Mavis. Being an asshat pretty much comes with the territory."

"But you aren't a jerk," I argued.

"I'm also half human," he pointed out. "Those of us lucky enough to have grown up outside of Hell, even the ones that aren't part human, are surprisingly tolerant. My father, on the other hand, has spent most of his time with demons."

"So, if demons raised me, I'd probably be the same."

"More than likely. Demons are not pleasant folk. They're rather like vampires who live in a nest. They feed off each other's angsty emotions."

"Vampires are real?" I asked, trying to keep my shocked voice low enough that none of the passersby would hear.

Cam pointed to a quaint gazebo covered with autumn décor on the far end of the square and laced his fingers with mine as we walked across the street to the opposite sidewalk. "You don't blink an eye at hearing there are other supernaturals, but you freak out about vampires?" he asked quietly.

"Yes!" I hissed. "I can't believe you thought this was the safest place for me! The town is full of monsters!"

"I *know* this is the safest place for you, Mavis. The resident monsters won't bother you. They probably won't even know you're a demon. That's the beauty of the tattoo you were given. It keeps our identities and our powers secret."

"So, there could be more demons in Havenwood Falls that you don't know about?"

"No. Remember, I've been in Havenwood Falls a very long time."

I let Cam lead me up the steps of the gazebo and leaned against a railing. "It's so easy to forget that you're a senior citizen."

He scoffed. "Senior citizen, indeed."

"Okay, maybe you're not that old, but there's no doubt you've seen a lot of things I couldn't imagine."

"It is true that I have seen my fair share of happenings in the town, but I mostly keep to myself. Penelope is one of the only residents I routinely spend time with."

"She seems nice."

"She is nice. She's been a great comfort to me for the past few years she's lived next door."

I eyed him speculatively. "How much of a comfort?"

He smiled, clearly enjoying seeing me jealous. "I haven't had sex with her, if that's what you're asking. Though my father does regularly ask me to steal her soul."

I gritted my teeth. "Severin is a dick."

Cam shrugged. "As I said, he's a demon. They all hunger for more of what they want—more power, more money, more souls, more sex—it's always something."

"I'm starting to realize how lucky I was to have found you on that road."

Wrapping his arms around me, he nuzzled his face into my hair. "I'm the lucky one, darling."

My eyes closed, and I breathed in his clean male scent. "I'm going to miss you, Cam. I wish you didn't have to go."

Pulling away to meet my eyes, he said, "You have no idea how much I want to stay."

"Then stay. Stay here with me."

"My father may change his mind about liking you if I stay."

"That is a chance I'm willing to take," I said, growing angry. I wasn't about to let some prick demon keep me from being with Cameron, father or not.

He tucked a lock of hair behind my ear. "It's not one I'm willing to take. I can't lose you, Mavis. I've grown rather fond of you."

My smile might have lit up the entire town when I heard those words come out of his mouth. He liked me. Cameron DeSalle liked me. And no matter what his occupation was or how controlling his father was, I knew I liked him back.

"Are you sure it's not the sex you're fond of?" I asked teasingly.

He narrowed his eyes at me. "That's not the response I expected."

I laughed and kissed his soft lips. "I'm rather fond of you, too, Cam. Never forget it."

He picked me up, and I squealed as he swung me around the gazebo. When he settled me back on my feet, he kissed me until I was breathless then leaned his forehead against mine. "I will never forget."

*A*n hour after our walk around the square, Cam and I lay curled up in his bed, our arms wound around each other as we talked. Both of us had happy, silly smiles plastered to our faces as we still reeled from our admissions of fondness.

It was hard to imagine anyone liking me the way he'd admitted to. Yes, I had had relationships before, but none of them were ever serious enough that I'd considered bringing them home to meet Leon, as antisocial as he was. But Cam—I would have been proud to take him back to meet my family. It was ironic that I felt that way now that I had no home to go to anymore.

I smiled at a goofy grin he was wearing as he stared at me and felt a sharp pain in my chest when I thought of him leaving the next day.

"Stop thinking about it," Cam said, pulling up the blankets and wrapping them tightly around us.

"Thinking about what?" I asked, trying to smooth out the telltale furrows on my forehead.

He returned to our cuddling position and ran a thumb across my worried face. "Me leaving tomorrow."

I sighed heavily. "How did you know?"

"It's forty below under these covers," he said, rolling on top of me to lick my cheek.

"Ew! Why did you do that?" I screeched, wiping his saliva from my skin.

"I wanted to see if my tongue would stick to you," he explained.

I shook my head. "You are a ridiculous demon."

"And you are a beautiful demon," he said, pressing his lips to mine.

I groaned and arched my body up to his. I could feel his searching hardness as I opened to him. He wanted me.

"You have far too many clothes on," I griped.

"I could say the same to you, you know."

"You're welcome to take them off," I said, sliding my hands up his shirt to explore the firm muscles of his back.

"I could," he said, smiling down at me.

I lifted a brow. "Well?"

He sighed and rolled off me, sitting up. "I can't right now. I have to make arrangements for that thing you keep thinking about, but don't want to talk about."

I sat up, my disappointment clear in my expression. "What kind of arrangements?"

"Some for me and some for you. I need to call the grocery store before they close to make sure you're able to add things to my tab, and I need to call Penelope and ask her to keep an eye on you."

"And for you?" I prompted.

"Hotel arrangements," he admitted, grudgingly. "And I need to confirm the appointment time with the client."

I pressed my lips together and stared down at my lap. I couldn't seem to make myself look at him.

"Don't worry about her, Mavis. These women mean nothing to me."

"They mean something to me," I retorted. "They're real people with souls I'm sure they'd like to keep."

He sighed and grabbed his laptop. Opening it, he powered it up and called me over to look at it. "This is Francesca Menish, Mavis. She's the woman I'm going to see tomorrow."

My eyes widened at the middle-aged woman with the soccer mom haircut. "She's not what I was expecting."

"You were expecting someone younger and more attractive?" he asked. "Someone more like yourself?"

I nodded.

"Darling, you have to understand that who I get for clients is beyond my control. I can't cherry-pick the young, attractive ones. And honestly, I rarely get anyone like that anyway. The women I fuck are usually middle-aged, and they're always married. They get bored with their husbands and go looking for someone who appears young and virile. Yes, I steal their souls, but they aren't shy young women being taken advantage of, Mavis. They pay me to be a whore, as they so often like to remind me, and I'm expected to do what I'm told."

I blanched. "That's . . . awful, Cam."

"It is, but this is my lot in life. And I've been living this life for a long, long time. I've grown accustomed to what my father expects, and in the whole scheme of things, it isn't so bad. I consider myself to be very fortunate. Some cambions have it much worse than I do. Some are slaves to their fathers. Some have never stepped foot out of the underworld. As evil as my father is, and as much as I despise him, he has never taken away my all of my independence, and I cannot be anything but thankful for that blessing."

"When you put it like that, your dad doesn't seem like such a dick."

"Oh, make no mistake. He's definitely a dick, but I'm worth more to him out here doing his bidding than I am in the underworld doing whatever the other cambions are tasked with."

"Have you ever been to the underworld?" I asked. "What's it like?"

"No, I haven't, and I hope never to have to go."

"I take it it's not a place I want to see."

"Absolutely not." He cupped my face. "I would die before I saw you go to the underworld, Mavis."

I circled his wrists with my hands and closed my eyes, just enjoying the feel of him touching me. "Let's hope it never comes to that, then."

I felt the bed dip down as he leaned in to kiss me. "Even if it does, Mavis, it would be worth it."

189

~

CAM LEFT EARLY the next morning, leaving me sad but completely spent and sore in his bed. I'd idly wondered aloud as he was getting dressed if he would be able to perform to his best ability after the hours we'd spent tangled up in each other's bodies the night before, but he'd just laughed and said that an infinitely hard cock was one of the incubus perks. I could certainly agree with that observation. He had rocked my world so hard, I'd passed out cold without even remembering it.

I languished in bed for a few hours, alternatively feeling happy and then regressing and crying bitter tears of hate. It made me so angry that Severin would make his son do this for him. And what made it so much worse was that there was no end date on this situation. Cam was saddled with this curse forever.

When I couldn't take lying in bed and doing nothing anymore, I showered, got dressed, and talked myself into going next door to visit with Penelope. Cam had mentioned more than a few times that he wanted me to become friendly with her, but I wasn't great at making friends and wasn't sure how to approach her. Would she even want to be friends with me?

By the way Penelope snatched the door open the second I knocked and exclaimed, "Finally!" I had to guess she did. Squealing, she grabbed my hand and dragged me into the apartment before I could explain that I was the demon she'd met before.

"Wow!" she said excitedly, showing me to the sofa. "You look so different without the horns!"

I had to laugh. "Those horns are hard to get used to, believe me."

"I'll bet. So what brings you by? I know you couldn't tell by my reaction at the door, but I really didn't expect you until later, especially after the grand send-off I overheard last night."

"I'm so sorry about that," I said, my cheeks growing hot. "I guess we need to look into some soundproofing?"

She waved away my embarrassment with a hand. "No way. I'm

living vicariously through you guys. I can't find anyone around here to touch my vagina with a ten-foot pole."

I guffawed. "That . . . sounds painful."

"I'm just telling you how it is. All these hot guys in this town and no one wants the boring human. It's either that, or they don't like the smell of Chinese."

"Huh?"

She giggled. "Sorry, that sounded weird. What I meant was that I work over at Sakura Buffet in Miller's Plaza. I come home smelling like sweet and sour pork five days a week."

"Do you like working there?"

She shrugged. "I have no complaints, other than the food smells embedded in my clothes. It pays the bills, and it could be worse."

"Yeah, you could have Cam's job," I said with more than a little vitriol in my voice.

"Yes!" she shouted, throwing up a fist. "I was hoping we were going to talk about this."

I sighed and relaxed back onto some of the fluffy colorful throw pillows she had scattered around the sofa and chairs. "I hate it, Penelope. Thinking about him out there with some other woman, it makes me irrationally angry."

"I don't think it's too irrational. You like him, right?"

"It seems weird to say that so soon, but yeah, I do like him, and he says he's fond of me."

"I don't doubt it. Do you know how many times he's asked me to watch over one of his lovers?"

"No. How many?"

"None."

"None?"

"None," she assured me. "I have never once seen Cameron bring any female home, demon or otherwise. He always said he was fine being alone, that he didn't want to subject anyone to his father or his lifestyle of prostitution."

"Prostitution . . ." I shook my head and stared at my hands. "I never thought I'd be dating someone involved in the oldest profession."

"And I never thought I'd be best friends with a prostitute, but here we are."

"Do you think he hates the sex with those women?"

She blew out a raspberry. "No. Well, maybe he will now. But before you, that was the only sex he was getting, so he looked forward to fucking something other than his hand."

We stared at each other, then burst into helpless giggles.

"I'm sorry," I said, trying to pull myself together. "I just have a hard time believing that someone as good-looking as Cam would only be having sex with himself."

"It is rather unbelievable, and honestly, if I didn't have to listen to him whine about it for the past few years, I wouldn't believe it. He is gorgeous, isn't he?"

I smiled, thinking of Cam's handsome face. "He really is, but he must look like his mom. Severin didn't look much like him."

"I'd be scared to see what his father really looks like. Severin isn't human, remember? That form he takes when he comes into town is just a manifestation of what he thinks is most pleasing to the eye of a human woman."

I frowned. I couldn't believe I'd forgotten that so quickly. "I guess I'm not used to this whole demon thing yet."

"Yeah, about that," she said, getting up to join me on the sofa. "How is it possible that you hadn't seen your demon form until yesterday?"

I started to answer, but then wondered if that was a smart course to take. Cam said Penelope could be trusted, but could I tell her something as big as the truth about myself? What if she wasn't as trustworthy as he believed? What if she somehow knew Leon LeGrand and would alert him to my whereabouts?

I sighed, mentally slapping myself. I was being silly. Penelope was a human. What would she know about the whole Exitium Daemonium thing?

Finally, I summoned up my nerve and said, "It's a long story."

"I have leftover Kung Pao Chicken. Want to heat some up and talk demon shit?"

I laughed at her composure with the "demon shit" and nodded. "Sounds good."

Penelope clapped her hands and danced to the kitchen door, her waist-length brown hair swinging behind her. I stood and followed her into the kitchen, taking a seat on a barstool at the counter.

"So," she began, measuring out equal scoops of fragrant chicken and vegetables onto two plates. "Let's hear your story."

I took a deep breath. "I found out I was an ice demon three days ago."

She stopped spooning. "Three days?"

"Yeah, I fell down a flight of concrete steps at the library and had to go to the hospital."

"Ouch."

"That was only half as painful as what I found out later."

She put the first plate in the microwave and set it for two minutes. "What did you find out?"

"That I'm some demon-killing machine called the Exitium Daemonium."

"You're a demon killer? And Cam, a demon, brought you home to stay with him?" She laughed. "Well, he's an idiot."

"I didn't give him a lot of choices. He found me hiding from my fake grandfather in a ditch."

"This story gets weirder and weirder," she commented, opening the microwave to switch the plates. "But go on."

"Basically, when I went in for x-rays at the hospital, there was this diamond-shaped thing in my chest covered with runes—runes that I had seen on journals in my grandfather's study."

"Creepy!" she blurted out, handing me a plate and a fork.

"Creepier than you know," I agreed, forking a bite and attempting to cool it without freezing it to the spoon.

She leaned on the counter. "So, what do the runes mean?"

I shrugged. "From what Cam and I can figure out, they were some spell to keep my power throttled. Obviously, the demon masquerading as my grandfather wanted to keep me from knowing I was anything but one hundred percent human."

"Obviously," she agreed. "What did the journals say? I assume that's how you found out your grandfather was fake."

I nodded, chewing thoughtfully. "I only read one all the way through, but it basically was an account of how this demon, Leon LeGrand, was tasked with stealing me from the underworld and raising me as a human until he would use me to kill every demon that stood in the way of his master."

Enthralled by the story, Penelope ignored the beeping microwave. "Who's his master?"

"I don't know. I ran out of the house as soon as I could grab a few changes of clothes and money."

"Wow."

I nodded, "When you saw me yesterday, that was when I realized the throttle wasn't working anymore. I've been practicing a little with the ice thing since then, but the demon killing, not so much."

"Yeah, that you might want to keep under wraps, especially when Cam is home."

"Trust me. Cam is the last demon I want to kill."

She smirked at me knowingly. "I wouldn't want to kill the demon giving me all those orgasms either."

CHAPTER 9

Though I warned her I didn't have much cash, Penelope insisted we go to Miller's Plaza to shop for what she called "Netflix supplies" after our meal. I didn't argue. Going to the store with her would give me a chance to check out more of the town. Plus, I was learning a lot about Cam and his habits, likes, and dislikes as she chatted good-naturedly. It was clear they'd been friends a very long time.

But once we pulled into the parking lot, I knew Penelope had more up her sleeve than grocery shopping.

"What are you to?" I asked, staring at the windows draped in red curtains and the telltale sign proclaiming the business in front of us was called Pleasurez.

A slow smile spread across her face as she realized I was on to her. "Whatever do you mean, Mavis?"

"You know exactly what I mean, Penelope. Pleasurez? Really?"

"Yes, really! Don't you want to get something sexy to show Cam what he's been missing while he's been gone? You don't think those women are wearing something sexy for him?"

"If there's anything decent and good in this world, they're all wearing bloomers," I told her, grimacing at the thought.

"Come on," she said, opening her door. "Just humor me. Remember, I'm living vicariously through you. I *need* this."

I rolled my eyes and met her in front of the car. "We have to find you a man before this gets any weirder."

"Preaching to the choir, sister," she said, throwing a hand up to the heavens. "From your mouth to God's ears."

"Let's just do this," I said, gritting my teeth and opening the door for Penelope, who was wearing a supremely patronizing smirk as she sauntered past me.

Upon entering the store, I stopped still, immediately daunted by the sheer number of things to look at. It was all tastefully done, of course, but to a girl who had never been in this kind of place, it was just north of overwhelming and just south of "what the hell am I doing here?"

"Oh my gosh!" Penelope squealed, running up to a mannequin wearing an open-crotched, see-through lace bodysuit that left absolutely nothing to the imagination. "This would be gorgeous on you!"

I checked the price tag. "Wouldn't it be cheaper if I just showed up naked? I'm pretty sure things will still go in the right direction."

"Mavis!" she whined. "Let me enjoy this!"

"If you need something to enjoy, might I suggest one of those glass dildos on the table over there and some of this garishly pink strawberry lube?"

She glared at me and grabbed a size small from the rack. "Take this to the nice lady and tell her to wrap it up. I'm buying it."

"Fine," I said, sighing at her insistence. "But just so you know, I'm going to be really quiet next time and you'll never even know that we're doing it."

She pouted. "You suck."

"And you need a boyfriend . . . badly."

ONCE WE WERE BACK at her apartment with the lingerie and enough

Twizzlers and Sour Patch Kids to sugar up all the kids in town, we watched most of season four of *Supernatural.* Penelope said it wasn't worth watching until Castiel's character joined the show, and I couldn't disagree. I didn't think she'd let me. She was a colossal Castiel fan.

Around ten o'clock, Cam texted Penelope, worried when he couldn't get me on the home phone. She berated him for interrupting her bingeing and passed the phone to me with a loud, "IT'S YOUR LOVERBOY!"

I rolled my eyes and put the phone up to my ear. "Hello?"

"Hey, baby."

I melted a little bit when I heard his smooth, sexy voice. "Hey, yourself. How's it going?"

"I was going to ask the same. What are you and Penelope up to?"

"Watching *Supernatural.*"

He chuckled. "Of course you are. She's been pissed at me for months for saying Crowley was the best character. She refuses to watch the show with me now."

"That sounds . . . accurate," I told him, grinning at the way Penelope was kissing her fingers and pressing them to Misha Collins's lips when he was on the screen.

"You have no idea."

I laughed. "So where are you calling from?"

"Cheyenne."

"Wyoming?"

He sighed. "Yes, and it's every bit as exciting as it sounds."

"I don't want to hear how exciting it is," I muttered.

"Darling, you won't ever hear about that."

"Thank God for small favors. So, when can I expect you back?"

"Sometime around midday tomorrow, or sooner, if I can get away."

"Good," I told him.

"You're sulking. I can hear it in your voice."

"Do you blame me? You just traveled to Cheyenne to fuck some middle-aged married lady who probably drives a minivan."

"Oh, damn!" Penelope yelled, laughing her ass off. "I like her, Cam!"

"And I'm second-guessing introducing you two," he responded. "I don't think I thought it through."

"Hey, you brought this on yourself," I told him. "I can't help it if you have good taste in friends."

"You'd better not be saying anything disparaging about me, asshole," Penelope yelled. "Not you, Castiel," she added, blowing a kiss to her favorite TV angel.

As if he could hear my train of thought, he said, "She's obsessed."

"If only you could find an angel for her here on Earth."

He didn't answer.

"Cam, please don't tell me there are angels here in Havenwood Falls."

"Okay, I won't."

"I can't tell if you're kidding when you're not here."

"I don't think you can tell when I *am* there."

"Yes, I can. You blink a lot when you lie."

"Are you teasing me?" he asked, his voice suspicious.

"Maybe," I sing-songed.

Cam laughed. "I really do miss you, you sassy thing."

"I miss you, too, ridiculous demon."

"Then I'll see you tomorrow?" he asked.

"If you plan on coming home, you will," I answered.

He groaned. "Go home soon. You're already starting to pick up Penelope's snark."

"Yes, sir."

"Bye, darling."

I handed the phone back to Penelope and tried to wipe the silly smile off my face before she saw it.

"You guys are adorable," she said, grinning at me from the floor. "I'm glad he picked you up from that ditch."

"Girl, you and me both."

~

I EXCUSED myself to go home at daybreak, which coincided with the time Penelope started to nod off into a bowl of Skittles, and walked back to the apartment feeling excited about seeing Cameron soon. At first, I thought it would upset me, knowing what he'd been out doing with another woman, but now I had a feeling I would just be glad to see him come home safe . . . if he showered for a couple of hours after.

When I unlocked the door to the apartment, I almost turned around and went back to Penelope's when I caught a whiff of unfamiliar aftershave, but I convinced myself that I was imagining things. The door was locked with a deadbolt, and there were no windows accessible from the outside. Cam had assured me I'd be perfectly safe by pointing that out before he left.

Brushing off my fears, I showered, shaved my legs, and spent extra time blow drying my hair, so I wouldn't appear as if I stuck my finger in every light socket in the apartment while he was gone. Dressing in the cute panties and bra set I'd bought at Pleasurez, I wiped down the foggy mirror on the back of the bathroom door and looked at myself at every angle. Risqué lingerie wasn't really my thing, but I had to admit, I looked damn good in this getup. Yawning, I smiled at myself and opened the door, ready to climb in bed for a few hours of sleep before Cam got home.

The moment I opened the door, I heard a low whistle. Twirling around, I came face to face with a tall blond man I'd never seen before.

"Who are you?" I asked, covering myself with my hands as best as I could.

"Leon LeGrand sent me to get you," he said, his cold blue eyes lewdly raking up and down my barely covered body. "But I don't think he'd mind if I were a little late getting you back to Utah. He didn't mention what a tasty little tart you are."

I backed away a few steps. "I don't know who you're talking about," I lied. "I don't know any Leon LeGrand."

"Oh," he asked, pulling my backpack from behind him. "This isn't your wallet in here with a Utah ID that has your picture on it? I have to say, the picture does not do you justice."

"You need to leave before I call the police," I said, my voice trembling.

"How are you going to call them? With the phone in the kitchen? You know, Cameron DeSalle called for you earlier on that phone. I traced the number to Wyoming. Is your half-human lover in Wyoming, sweet thing? Did he leave you here by yourself?"

I didn't answer. I couldn't explain. I was using every bit of my brainpower to try to maneuver myself out of this situation. I was not getting raped today or ever.

"Look," I said finally. "I'm not going back to Leon. You've come all this way for nothing."

His lascivious, nauseating smile ratcheted up as he stared at the breasts spilling out of my demicup bra. "I wouldn't say it was for nothing."

Taking another step back, I concentrated as hard as I could on making my power come to life. I needed a weapon, something I could throw or attack him with, but there was nothing.

He took a step closer. "Come on, baby. Let's have a little fun before I take you back to Utah."

"Get away from me!" I screamed, throwing my arms out in front of me.

"Hey!" he yelled, ducking under the icicles I unknowingly slung at him. He straightened. "That wasn't very nice, Mavis."

"I said, get away from me!" I yelled back. I was done with this guy causing me trouble. I was in my demon form now. I could feel the weight of my horns on top of my head and the ice ready to go at my fingertips.

The man stepped back a few steps and held up his hands in a defensive motion. "Whoa, now. Just calm down."

"Get the fuck out!" I bellowed at him, swallowing hard when a pain shot through my chest.

"I will," he said, inching his way closer to the front door.

I took a menacing step toward him. "Then go!"

Just then, the door swung open, and Penelope stormed in with an aluminum baseball bat. She took in the man facing me with his hands up and me in in my demon form and lingerie. "What the fuck is going on in here?"

The stranger didn't wait a beat. He lunged for the bat, wrestling it from Penelope's hands and shoving her into the corner all in one movement before slamming the front door shut.

"Well, well, well," he said, looking positively giddy at the turn of events. "Looks like it's my lucky day." He examined the baseball bat and continued. "Now ladies, I think we should all calm down, and then you can figure it out amongst yourselves which of you will be sucking my dick first."

Penelope let loose with a tirade like I'd never heard before when he finished his revolting speech, standing up tall in the corner and looking like she'd rip him apart with her bare hands. I just stared at the action playing out in front of me, a wave of calm flowing over me, seconds before I walked up to the surprised man and laid my frozen pale hands on his arm. I had no idea what I was doing. I just instinctively knew that was what I needed to do.

The man screamed as a glowing white light engulfed his arm and spread out like wildfire across his body. His screams grew louder and louder until he seemed to come to a breaking point. Like, a literal breaking point. As soon as his screams cut off, the white light expanded into every nook and cranny of the apartment, and he exploded into a million minuscule pieces of demon.

When the light of my magic had faded, and every bit of what was left of the stranger had settled onto the carpet, I sank to my knees. I had killed someone. It was true that he might've hurt Penelope or me, but did he really deserve a fate as awful as what I'd done to him?

"I know what you're thinking, Mavis," Penelope said softly. "You did what you had to. He could have raped and killed both of us. His death was justified."

I looked up at her with tears streaming down my cheeks. "I don't know what I did."

She crouched down next to me and threw her arms around me, hugging me tightly. "You did what you had to."

I held onto her, utterly adrift. I felt like I was riding the line between dreaming and wakefulness. None of this could be real. Would I wake up tomorrow safely tucked into my childhood bed, all of this a dream?

Looking around me, I knew that wouldn't be the case. There was no way my brain came up with something as real and vivid as this.

"Oh my God," I said, breaking away from her. "We have to clean this up. Cam can't come home to this."

"I'm on it," she said, jumping to her feet. "Give me two seconds."

I nodded stiffly and stayed put as she ran out the front door.

Seconds after she left, I heard her say, "Hi, Mrs. Woods!" then she laughed. "Nope, there's no one getting murdered in there. We had a blender explosion with our raspberry smoothies. I keep telling Cam to let me use the appliances, but you know he never listens." Another laugh. "Yes, ma'am. See you later. Say hi to Jordan for me."

Sighing with relief, I got to my feet and surveyed the mess. It wasn't as bad as I'd thought it was going to be. The worst of it was the blood stain, but the rest of the organs and bones seemed to have disintegrated in the explosion.

Penelope came back in the door a moment later with a wet-dry vacuum and two huge bottles of hydrogen peroxide.

"You're lucky I buy in bulk," she said, handing me the bottle tucked under her arm.

"I'm lucky you showed up. I don't know what would've happened if you didn't."

She stared down at what was left of the man and laughed. "You don't?"

My lips twitched. "Don't make me laugh. This is serious."

"Yeah, seriously awesome. Dude, can you do this to my ex-boyfriend?"

"I'm not even sure what I did." I jerked my gaze to her. "What if you had been a demon? I could have killed you with that light thing, too."

"I don't think so," she said. "I couldn't even feel it when the light covered me."

"But that could have been because you're a human. What if it just works on demons? Oh, fuck! What if I accidentally do this to Cameron? What am I going to do, Penelope? I can't hurt him."

She put down the vacuum and slapped me. "You're hysterical, Mavis. Calm down."

"Hey!" I said, holding my cheek.

She threw her hands up. "Sorry, I'm a little hysterical, too. This is crazy pants territory, you know?"

Leaning down with my hands on my knees, I closed my eyes and took in a slow breath, counting down and holding it in like Cam showed me. Slowly, I opened my eyes as I blew out the breath and was relieved to find I was calmer.

"Better?" Penelope asked, her lips quirked up in a half smile.

I straightened. "Much."

"Good, go fill this reservoir with hot water for me. I'll vacuum up the . . . bits."

I took the plastic basin to the kitchen and turned on the tap, waiting for it to warm. Sighing heavily, I held my hand under the water and let my mind wander. I couldn't believe what was happening. An hour ago, I was happily watching Sam and Dean Winchester figure out where all the reapers had run off to, and now I was meting out death like I was one of them.

When the tank was full, I carefully took it back out to a severely disgusted Penelope.

"This is so gross," she told me. "We need to figure out how you can do this without the mess."

"I'm not doing this again," I said sternly. "Ever."

"Never?" she asked skeptically, holding up a bloody cell phone and a wallet. "What if I told you this guy had the number of one Mr. Leon LeGrand in his contacts?"

"I knew Leon sent him," I admitted. "He told me."

"What in the name of Hell is going on in here?" Cam asked, striding into the apartment. His face was thunderous and terrible in its beauty as he took in my state of undress, the baseball bat, and the bloodstain in the middle of the living room carpet. "Someone tell me why the Court is blowing up my phone. Now."

"I think that's my cue to leave," Penelope said, handing me the vacuum handle. "Call me, Mavis."

"Wait," Cam demanded.

She stopped just short of the door and whispered, "So close."

"I did it," I told him. "It was me."

He looked to the floor then back to me. "What is this?"

Penelope piped up. "Franco Ross is what his license says."

"And why is Franco Ross now a stain on my freshly shampooed carpet?"

"Because I'm the Exitium Daemonium?" I asked.

The shock on his face was understandable as he looked me over for injuries. "You did this with your power?"

I nodded. "I threw an icicle at him first, but he ducked out of the way."

He pinched the bridge of his nose, sighed, and then pulled me into his arms to bury his face in my hair. "Was it Leon who sent him?" he asked.

"Yes."

His grip tightened. "I'm sorry I left you. If I had known, I would have never left you. I thought you'd be safe here."

"It's not your fault, Cam," I said, stroking his dark hair with shaky hands. "You couldn't have known. And it's not like you can babysit me forever. At some point, we were going to have to continue living our lives."

When he pulled back, his eyes were black. "I will not rest until Leon LeGrand is dead. Fuck my father and this job. I have money saved. I can take off as long as it takes to finish him."

"You don't even know where he is."

"Utah is a pretty good guess."

"Stop being stubborn and listen to me, Cam. You're not going to risk your soul to sit around and wait for nothing to happen. That's your emotions talking. Once you're calm and we have Mr. Ross out of the carpet, maybe then cooler heads will prevail, and we can move on responsibly."

"Maybe," he agreed, grudgingly. "But first, can you tell me why you're wearing sexy lingerie to commit your first murder?"

CAM KICKED Penelope out and sent me to shower after we told him everything that had happened. I went willingly and without argument.

Though I felt bad that he insisted on cleaning up what was essentially a crime scene of my own making, his face told me he would brook no opposition. Secretly, I was relieved. I desperately wanted to get the sticky lingerie off my body, and maybe to burn it at the first opportunity.

Cam joined me in the bathroom twenty minutes after I got in the shower. I was still washing my hair. I'd washed it five times already, but I didn't feel clean. I wasn't sure I'd ever feel clean again.

"Are you okay?" he asked me through the clear shower door.

I nodded. "I think so. Are you?"

He pulled his shirt over his head and threw it in the hamper along with his pants and boxer briefs. "No, and I'm going to have to buy Penelope a new vacuum cleaner."

"I'm really sorry," I told him, sniffling a little. "It just happened."

He slid back the shower door and joined me under the spray. "Don't worry about it. I've taken care of it with the Court."

"How?" I asked, a little dubious. Cam might be a demon, but as far as demons went, he was on the weaker side. Even if he wasn't half human, incubuses had one type of magic and could only really hurt someone who had a soul.

"I do have some tricks up my sleeve, darling. I'm not as feeble as you think I am."

I frowned at him. "I do not think you're feeble. I just don't know how you could go up against Leon without some sort of demon-killing weapon."

He stilled my hand when I reached for the shampoo bottle again. "I do have a demon-killing weapon."

"You do?"

He nodded. "Mavis, you don't survive being a half human demon for a century without some survival skills and a weapon. I try to live an uncomplicated life here, but I am prepared."

"So what do you think we should do? We could leave town for a while," I suggested. "He can't find me if he doesn't know where to look."

"We're not leaving town. We're not going to run away from this.

We're immortal, Mavis. Do you want to be on the run for an eternity?"

"No, of course not. I just meant for a couple of weeks. Surely, Leon will come in the next few days if he knows where we are. If he sees we're not here, he'll begin searching somewhere else, and we can come home."

He pondered what I'd said as he soaped up his chest and rinsed off. "I'll consider it, but I don't like the idea of running. The Court is protecting you here. We don't know what we're up against outside the town limits."

I leaned my cheek against his smooth, clean chest and hugged him. "I'm glad you're home."

He wrapped his arms around me and squeezed. "I don't know what I would've done if Mr. Ross would've managed to steal you away from me, Mavis. I can't lose you."

CAM USHERED me into his bed after we'd toweled off. I didn't have the strength to fight his wishes. Without getting any sleep the night before and all the excitement the morning had brought with it, I was exhausted. Apparently, eating a pound of gummy worms, watching mindless TV, and killing a stranger took a lot out of a demoness.

I snuggled right up to Cam when he joined me and sighed contentedly. He was warm and safe, and I knew, without a doubt, that I could trust him to protect me to the best of his ability.

"Did I mention how much I missed you?" I asked, kissing his chest.

He kissed the top of my head. "You couldn't have missed me half as much as I missed you. Every second away from you was torture."

I lifted my head to look at him. His chocolate brown eyes were full of an emotion I'd never seen in them before. "Are you positive about that? I have been nothing but trouble for you since the moment you found me in that ditch."

"That moment was the best moment of my life. I didn't realize it at the time, but my life had become monotonous and mundane. Finding you made me feel like I had a purpose, a reason to get out of bed in the morning."

"Ditto," I told him, pressing my lips to his. "You're the best thing that's ever happened to me."

He grinned, a little of his personality shining through the gloom of the situation. "You just like my fun stick."

I shook my head. "Nah."

Eyes narrowing, he rolled me onto my back and hovered over me, his cock heavy against my most intimate part.

"You want to try that again?" he asked. "This time you might want to say it in a more believable voice."

I laughed, then hissed as the movement pushed his hard sex against me. "You'd better be careful with that thing."

"How careful do you want it?" he asked, a telling smirk on his face.

"Very careful," I answered, opening my legs to him. "I like . . ."

"Shh," he interrupted, moving down on the bed and kissing each thigh before catching my eye with his smoldering ones and grinning like the devil incarnate. His hot breath made me shiver in anticipation.

"Please," I begged, aching to feel that first sweet sensation. "Please, touch me."

Nodding, he slipped his muscled arm across my stomach and took a firm grip on my hip, letting me know exactly who was in control.

And me? I could only pant, my anticipation sending every nerve in my body on high alert. "Fuck, Cam," I breathed out. "If you don't touch me soon, I'm going to start hyperventilating."

He chuckled and lowered his head, rasping his tongue slow and steady against my clit. It was a testing, teasing stroke, one that made me cry out with embarrassing relief, and when he repeated the motion, I couldn't stop myself from convulsing and arching up to press myself to his mouth. There was no grace, no shyness. At that moment, there was nothing but pure need.

"Please," I begged again, twisting my fingers into his hair.

Cam slid his body up, settling between my legs, and kissed me, thrusting his tongue into my mouth. I groaned as I tasted myself and matched his movements, abandoning all pretense of restraint. Every bit of my focus was on that kiss, every bit of my hunger. I wanted him, wanted what he could give me. And I wanted it badly. He growled, breaking away and sitting up on his knees. I stared at his massive erection longingly, wanting so much to feel him inside me.

"See something you want, darling?" he asked teasingly.

I poked my bottom lip out in a pout. "You know what I want."

"Careful, darling. I'll bite that lip while I'm showing you how fun this cock can be."

I met his nearly black eyes with my own. "Bring it, big boy."

Cam dove for my mouth, biting, licking, sucking until my lips felt bruised and swollen. I didn't care. Nor did I care when he pushed into me hard and without warning. I dug my nails into his back and cried out for more. The action only seemed to spur him on. Lifting my legs over his shoulders, he cupped my breasts, pinching the nipples hard as he unmercifully pounded into me. He filled me over and over until I screamed out his name and a few other things that were certain to make even an incubus blush. Moments later, he roared with his release, pulling out of me and pumping his slick cock with his hand until he spilled all over my breasts.

Breathing hard, he collapsed next to me and handed me a discarded T-shirt to clean up. "Holy fuck," he said.

I laughed as I sat up and wiped myself dry. Dropping the shirt off the side of the bed, I rolled over to him and nestled in his arms. "I take it back. I do like your fun stick."

He chuckled and yawned. "I knew it."

CHAPTER 11

*C*am and I spent the next couple of days putting security measures in place and generally readying the apartment for anything crazy that might happen. For the moment, there was nothing else to be done. We could only wait for Leon to show up so that we or the Court could take care of him as quietly as possible and move on with our lives.

But as much as I was ready to do just that, Cam was dead set against me getting involved in the fight. And as much as I appreciated his overprotectiveness, I knew in my heart the only way to defeat Leon was to serve him the same justice I'd served Mr. Ross. He had to die to secure my safety. It was nonnegotiable, and that wasn't something I was sure a half incubus could accomplish on his own.

"What are you thinking about?" Cam asked me late one afternoon. He sat next to me on his couch and pulled me into his lap. "Your face is all scrunched up in concentration."

"Nothing you want to hear about," I assured him, thinking about his father. I'd been thinking about him a lot lately. Now that the demons searching for me had somehow infiltrated the town, I knew some of them could possibly talk to demons that were still loyal to Severin. Cam had said he had burnt his bridges in town, but I wasn't so sure. If Severin found out Cam had been hiding a prize like the

Exitium Daemonium under his nose, he might take me away, and possibly take Cam's soul in the process. I couldn't let that happen.

He sighed and curled a lock of my blond hair around his finger. "You need a break from all this."

"I do?"

"Yes, and I think I know just the thing."

"What's that?"

"It's been snowing all night."

I furrowed my brow. "And that should excite me because . . . ?"

"Because you're an ice demon? I thought it might be fun to take a walk in your element."

I grimaced and slipped off my sneakers in favor of a pair of boots. "Do you think it's safe for me out there?"

"Safer than it is in here. No one is going to look for you in the mountains."

"We're going up the mountain?"

"Just a short way up Mt. Sousa. You can't practice your power in town, Mavis. The tattoo doesn't protect humans from seeing that."

"But won't someone see us out there?" I asked, lacing up my boots.

"It's not very likely. I'm taking you to a spot that's usually pretty isolated."

I smiled at Cam, determined to not ruin this for both of us. We'd been using sex to fight off cabin fever for days. It was time to get out of our cell for a breath of fresh air. "Sounds good. Do you think Penelope will have a coat I can borrow?"

Cam grinned at my forgetfulness. "How many ice demons need a coat?"

"Oh," I said, blushing. "Then I guess I'm ready when you are."

He slipped on a black formfitting coat and turned back to me, looking so mouthwatering, it made me weak at the knees. "I'm ready."

"We'd better go or else I'll be dragging you into the bedroom. I've never seen anyone look as good in a coat as you do."

"That's because you've never seen anyone as good-looking as me," he said. "Damn these magnificent incubus genes. I'm just too irresistible for words."

"I know, I know," I said, blowing out a very put-upon sigh. "Hotness comes with the territory."

He bent down and laid a not-so-chaste kiss on my lips. "If we don't leave now, I'm the one that's not going to be able to keep myself from taking you to the bedroom."

"Don't think I'll tell you no," I countered.

"Some days I'm not sure which of us has the incubus parentage," he said, retaking my mouth, this time in an all-out assault as he kissed me deeply, thrusting his tongue inside.

I gasped in surprise at his urgency and groaned into his mouth as he palmed my breasts and pinched the nipples just hard enough to make me moan.

Cam pulled away. "Let's go, darling. I can't be alone in this apartment with you without wanting to sink my cock into that hot, wet pussy of yours."

I lifted my eyebrows in surprise. "That sure doesn't sound like you want to go."

He groaned and put more distance between us. "Come on. We need to get the hell out of here."

CAM and I left his apartment, walking briskly down Eighth Street in the late morning sun and paying attention to nothing but one another until we reached the other side of the town square. I had meant to take in more of the town that I hadn't seen on trips out before, but I couldn't seem to keep my eyes off him. He appeared to be suffering from the same problem. Every time I looked at him, he was staring back at me, his eyes alight with lust and something I couldn't place. Pride, maybe?

"Come here," he said, pulling me toward a small coffee shop on the corner of Stuart and Eighth Street. "It's freezing out here. I need something to warm me up."

"I may know a way to warm you up," I purred. "As a matter of fact, I think it could make you hot."

His eyes flared at my blatantly sexual remark. "Do you, little demon?"

"Once I get you away from the town, I just might have to show you."

He groaned as he discreetly adjusted his erection under his coat. "Come on, darling, let's go in before you get us both in trouble."

Smirking, I allowed Cam to usher me into the coffee shop, knowing it was just prolonging the inevitable sexual encounter we'd be having on Mt. Sousa. I couldn't keep my hands off his body, just like he couldn't stay away from mine. Honestly, I thought the town was lucky we hadn't christened every surface in the square with our escapades.

Broastful Brew was darker and quieter than I'd expected it to be, but it was cozy and warm as we stepped inside and wiped our feet on the door mat. An older woman Cam quickly identified as Mabel welcomed us with an energetic "HELLO!" that seemed out of place with the hushed tones of the rest of the patrons, who looked up to see who the newcomers were, then ducked their heads back into their conversations.

"Hello, Miss Mabel," Cam said, smiling pleasantly. "Two coffees to go, please."

"Coming right up!" She buzzed around the counter and pulled out two cups, filling them quickly and expertly.

Bemused, Cam said, "Miss Mabel, I don't think I've introduced you to my girlfriend, Mavis."

She grinned up at Cameron. "I should say not! I think I'd remember you bringing a girl in here." Turning to me, she added, "Nice to meet you, Mavis! How are you liking our quaint little town?"

"I'm liking it just fine," I told her. "It's so beautiful here with all the festive fall decorations."

"That it is," she agreed, happily putting the lids on the cups. "You should see this place around Christmas, when it's all snowy and lit up. It's really something then."

Handing over a ten-dollar bill, Cam told Mabel to keep the change and handed me one of the cups. "Well, we'd better get going. I'm taking her up Mt. Sousa to see the sights this morning."

Mabel clapped her hands together. "Oh, you'll love it, Mavis! The fresh fallen snow on the mountain is one of the best sights in the world! But you be sure to borrow this young man's coat if it gets too cold. I don't know what he's thinking, letting you traipse around town without one."

I grinned at her. "I will, Miss Mabel."

"Have a great day, you two!"

"She was really nice," I commented, once we were back on the sidewalk.

He nodded. "You know what else is nice?"

"What's that?"

"Thinking about the ways you'll warm me up on that mountain."

I shivered, my body heating up with desire. "You keep that talk up, and I'm going to be hot enough for the both of us."

His smile was pure sex. "I like the sound of that."

We continued our eye-fucking all the way to the base of the mountain and down a lengthy trail that led to a clearing so small, I would have missed it if Cam didn't point it out. Looking at the dense, snow-covered trees around us, I smiled. "It looks like a Christmas card. It's beautiful."

"You're beautiful," he said, cupping my face and kissing me softly.

Ignoring the compliment, I grinned and walked him back to the nearest tree. Sinking to my knees in front of him, I unbuckled his belt and unbuttoned his jeans, my breath catching as his cock sprang out hard and huge in my hands. "Oh, I am going to enjoy this."

Teeth clenched, he growled and stilled my hands.

"Not right now, you won't," he said, disbelief peppering his voice.

"Are you sure?" I asked, my heart thumping loudly in my ears.

He shook his head. "I'm not sure of anything right now."

"Good," I said, taking that as a yes and licking his cock from base to tip before taking it into my mouth as far as it would go.

Cam gripped my short ponytail and pumped himself into my mouth, taking control. "Fuck, Mavis," he groaned. "Suck my cock."

I happily obliged, alternating between letting him fuck my mouth and sucking him hard, using my teeth and hands to heighten the sensations.

I was so thoroughly engrossed in the task at hand, using Cam's grunts and moans as a guide, I didn't hear anyone approaching until a tree branch cracked and a voice asked, "Mavis, my love, do you mind telling me why you have that filthy human's cock in your mouth and what has become of my associate, Mr. Ross?"

CHAPTER 12

The second I heard Leon LeGrand's voice, my demon form shot to the surface. Freezing stock still, I knew what I'd find when I turned to the sound, and I was right. Standing before us was the same black-suited, gray-haired man I'd come to know so well over the years.

Cam took one look at my transformation, and his handsome features ran the gamut from confusion to understanding and, finally, to murderous. Turning to face Leon, he zipped up his pants, stepped in front of me protectively, and growled, "He's mine."

Leon laughed heartily. "What are you going to do, cambion? Fuck me to death? You have no power over me."

I laid a hand on Cam's shoulder to calm him. "He may be a weaker demon than you, Leon, but I'm not. You'd do well to say your goodbyes now."

"Oh, so you've figured out what you are, have you?" His condescending tone made me want to stake him in the chest with an icicle. "Congratulations, granddaughter."

"Don't you fucking call me that," I spat. "You're less than nothing to me."

"Well, I can't say I'm disappointed that charade is over. I was sick of you by the time you were twelve years old. I never saw what was so special about you."

"Good. Then you won't be surprised when I end you. What do you think, Cam? I'm thinking icicles through his eyes and heart might be the most poetic."

"You little idiot. Ice will not affect me. I, myself, am an ice demon."

"No?" I asked. "Then let's see how you fare with my little secret."

Leon's eyes widened. "What do you mean, Mavis?"

My grin was sharp. "What do you think I mean, *grandfather*?"

"Is that what you did to Franco? You used your other power?"

I laughed. "I'm not some evil overlord who will tell all of her plans and devious deeds before you're miraculously saved by a hero, Leon. You won't be saved tonight. And I do not need to tell you what happened to your associate or to prolong your death."

I stepped forward, and Cam jerked me back to his side. "No, Mavis. I don't think he's alone."

The grin spread across Leon's face told me Cam was right. He wasn't alone.

"Who's here with you?" I demanded. "Or maybe a better question would be, do they know what I can do. Because I can promise you, Leon, if they are aligned with your cause, I will have no qualms about killing them, too."

"Mavis, Mavis, Mavis," he began. "I don't want to have to hurt you or your incubus lover. Come quietly with me, and I will let both of you live."

My shrill laugh echoed around the quiet clearing. "You don't get it, Leon. You're not walking away from this. You will die here."

Finally fed up, anger burned bright in his brown eyes as he stared us down. "You don't get it, Mavis. You will do what I say, or I will kill Mr. DeSalle."

"You and what fucking army?" I asked.

Instead of answering, Leon held up his hands and shot two of the biggest icicles I'd ever seen toward us.

With a yell of warning, Cam pushed me off balance, and I landed face first in a snowbank. Lifting myself as fast as I could, I turned to find Cam on the ground, bleeding from his upper arm.

"Cam!" I screamed, scrambling to him on my hands and knees.

"I'm okay, darling. It's just a flesh wound." He grinned cheekily at me. "Shame about the coat, though."

Leon walked over to stand over us. "You see, Mavis, I will kill him. Don't make this any worse for him. You want your lover to survive this, don't you?"

"Can I finish this asshole now?" I asked Cam.

His eyes drilled into mine. "Only if you can live with yourself afterward, my love."

I slowly turned toward Leon as I stood, a wicked smile on my face. "Oh, you're fucked."

Leon's smile faltered. "Mavis, wait."

But I didn't wait. The moment I felt that telltale pain in my chest, I ran for him and pushed him to the ground by his face. He seemed to fall for ages, almost as if my magic had him suspended off the field as his body quickly deteriorated before us. With a soft thump, he finally landed a split second before he was nothing more than a blood spot on the snow.

I started when I felt a hand on my shoulder. Turning to Cam, I buried my face in his uninjured shoulder. "It's over."

Familiar laughter erupted from the trees beside us, and Severin DeSalle walked into sight. My mouth dropped open as he tsked at the bloody circle in front of us. "That was completely unnecessary, ice demon. Leon was an old acquaintance of mine, a very loyal one, I might add. Now I'll have to find another idiotic demon to do my dirty work." He sighed and kicked snow over the blood before he looked up at Cam and said, "Son."

Cam didn't say a word, but I felt his grip around me tighten.

"You have nothing to say to me, Cameron?" The handsome demon chuckled to himself. "After all this madness you put me through?"

"What madness are you referring to, father?" Cam asked, his teeth clenched in rage.

He waved a hand in my direction. "The hot piece of ass you can't seem to pull your dick out of, of course. When Leon told me that he had seen you near where he thought the Exitium Daemonium had run to, I thought, how fortuitous it is that the one asset I will always have at my disposal found my missing treasure, because I knew you would turn her over to me. I had no doubt. You've always been a sniveling little suck-up to keep what little soul you had." He snarled in Cam's direction, his anger palpable. "But then I visited you, and you lied to me. To me! You lied to me just like that whore mother of yours, and I knew then, the tenuous relationship we'd forged was gone. I couldn't trust you anymore. I knew I'd have to do something, something I've always been loath to do."

Cam's face was a mixture of horror, hate, and fear as he asked, "And what is that, father?"

Severin smiled. "Get my hands dirty."

Hysterical laughter bubbled up from my throat. "Fuck you, Severin. You've done nothing but shit on your son for a century. And from the sound of it, you're planning on dragging me along with this big bag of crazy, too. But let me tell you something, fucker. It's not going to happen. I'm done being someone's secret weapon. I'm a demon, and I make my own decisions. You can either respect that, or you can meet the same fate as your underling here."

Severin stared at me for a long moment, then adjusted the ridiculously sized dick in his pants. "I will so enjoy teaching you manners, Mavis. My son may let you get away with that smart mouth, but I will find other, more creative, ways to shut you up."

"Get that thing anywhere near my mouth, and I will bite it off," I promised.

"Bite all you'd like," he said, staring openly at my breasts. "I like to play rough. And what's more, you'll like it, too."

I shuddered. "You're disgusting."

"And you, my dear, are out of time." He looked to Cam. "Say goodbye to your lover, son. She'll be fucking a real incubus from here on out."

Cameron's grip on me tightened painfully. "No."

Severin's lip curled. "What did you say to me?"

"I said no," Cam said firmly. "Leave now before you end up like Leon."

His father's laughter rang out, thick and menacing. "Was that a threat?" He laughed again. "From you?"

"You fucking heard him," I piped up. "Leave or be a spot on the snow. It's your choice."

Severin wiped tears of laughter from his eyes. "It's my choice then, is it, Mavis?"

I stood my ground, not moving. "You heard me."

With a sudden movement almost too fast to see, Severin snaked his hand around my wrist and pulled me from Cam's grasp. Wrapping his arm around my chest, he pulled me flush against his body, digging his erection painfully in my lower back.

"How is this for a choice?" he asked, tightening his hold when I fought to free myself.

"Let her go!" Cam yelled.

"No."

Panic-stricken, Cam implored me with his eyes to do what I did to Leon. His father or not, killing him was the only way I could free myself.

Nodding, I let the power engulf my hands and laid them on the arm holding me. Nothing happened.

Severin laughed again. "Fools. Who do you think had the runed device put in your chest? Do you think I'm stupid enough to come here without protection?"

Cam fell to his knees, sorrow exuding from him. "Father, please. I will do anything, anything to keep her at my side."

"Anything?" Severin asked.

"Whatever it takes," Cam said hopefully.

"Will you give me your soul?"

"No!" I screamed, fighting harder than ever. "No, Cam. You can't!"

"I have to," Cam said, unable to look at me. "I can't lose you, Mavis."

Severin's cruel voice was harsh when he spoke next. "Stand up and face me like a male of worth, Cameron. You are the son of a powerful demon. We do not cower and prostrate ourselves on the ground. And to do it over a female? There are enough females in this world to fuck a different one every night. What does one demon matter? You'll find another soon enough."

"Father, please," Cam begged, desperation tinging every word as he stood.

"Fine," Severin growled. "In return for your soul, I will give you six months to use her as you will." His grip loosened, and I stumbled forward into Cam's waiting arms. "After that, she is mine to use." He aimed an indecent smile at me. "And use her I will."

"Cam, no—" I started, but he squeezed my arm and gave me an imperceptible shake of the head to stop me.

"I'll agree to it, father."

"Very well. But know this—if you try to hide her from me, I will kill you, whether you are my only son or not. She will be mine to command."

"Yes, sir."

Severin stepped forward. "Come here, son."

Cam pushed me behind him and walked to his father, a look of absolute hatred on his face as he accepted the kiss that would mean the loss of everything that made him human. When Severin pulled back, his face was expressionless as he glanced from me to his son, then disappeared in a puff of sulfurous smoke.

EPILOGUE

*A*lone in the clearing, I stared at Cameron, horrified at what had happened.

"Why?" I asked him. "Why did you let him take it?"

"There wasn't a choice, Mavis," he said, his tone exhausted.

"Of course there was!" I shouted. "You could have chosen to keep your soul. I could've taken care of myself."

"There wasn't," he argued. "Not for me. How could I not risk everything for what we have and what you are? Do you really think I could let him take you? He's taken everything else—my freedom, my mother. I won't let him take you."

"But at what cost, Cam? Now that jackass has your soul."

He gathered me in his arms, resting his chin on top of my head. "Darling, I'm a demon. That soul wasn't going to be a ticket into some glorious afterlife. It was just holding me back."

I pulled away and met his eyes. "How?"

He grinned. "Full incubus, full powers."

"Meaning?"

"Meaning, it'll be really hard for him to find me when he doesn't know what I look like."

My jaw dropped as Cam's beautiful face and body morphed into what must be an incubus's true demonic form, complete with horns, fangs, and even wings. I staggered back. "What the hell?"

In an instant, he returned to himself and grinned. "I don't think Severin realized what a gift he was handing us when he took my soul."

"No, I'm positive he didn't. Does this mean you can look like anyone?"

"Yes, I believe so. The magic is there. I can feel it."

"And we have six months to come up with a plan to defeat him."

"That's right."

I squinted at the smug, elated smile he was wearing, suspicious of what was running through his mind. "What's that grin all about?"

"I was just thinking we could continue what we were doing before we were so rudely interrupted."

I shook my head and laughed at his hopeful expression. "You are such a degenerate."

He shrugged. "I'm an incubus. It comes with the territory."

Read the conclusion to Mavis and Cam's story coming March 2019.

JD Nelson is a bestselling author of fantasy romance and adult paranormal romance. An avid time-waster, JD enjoys watching TV and listening to audiobooks when she really should be writing.

JD loves to hear from her readers. You can contact her through her website, AuthorJDNelson.com, or on Facebook, where she spends an alarming amount of time chatting with her many author and reader friends, much to the dismay of her continually neglected manuscripts.

www.AuthorJDNelson.com

ACKNOWLEDGMENTS

Thank you to Susan Burdorf for talking me into sending in a proposal for Sin & Silk. I would have never been able to summon the courage to do it without your gentle nudge. To Danielle Bannister, I'd like to send my gratitude and a big bottle of wine for being a sounding board and listening to my petulant whining when I got discouraged. To Kristie Cook and the rest of the Havenwood Falls authors, thank you for your helpful advice and general awesomeness. You guys rock!

SHIFT OF FATE

VICTORIA ESCOBAR

~ A Havenwood Falls Sin & Silk Novella ~

Havenwood Falls

sin & silk

Shift of Fate

VICTORIA ESCOBAR

CHAPTER 1

AUDREY

The Challenger roared down the winding highway of Colorado. The gas light wasn't on yet, but the time of reckoning would soon be at hand. Skipping a break in the last town proved to be a worse idea with each dark, sign-less mile.

"Audrey, you're a fucking idiot." If I had more sense, I'd turn the car around before there was no chance of making it back. Something visceral possessed me to keep going farther, faster, without stopping. All roads went somewhere, after all—even the dark, empty ones.

When the night terrors returned two days ago, I packed everything I owned—which wasn't much—and left Iowa. The longer the delay, the more the terrors would seep into daily life, and paranoia would eat at my sanity. Been there, done that, and it wasn't pretty or pleasant to think I was crazy.

So I left and drove. Hopefully far enough to leave the terrors behind. For a time. The cycle would eventually start anew, but for a while, I hoped for a pretense of peace.

Stopping would be required soon, though. A body, even one with perks like mine, needed rest and real food to survive. If I went another twenty-four hours without sleep, I might drive my junkyard rescue right off the edge of one of these winding roads. A few years ago, that wouldn't have sounded as scary as it did now.

I leaned over the steering wheel and squinted into the distance. The moonless sky made the dark wilderness somehow darker. The clouds covering the starlight added depth to the darkness, making it appear more like the pit of some abyss than a night-shrouded forest.

There had to be something out here. A homestead, or a cabin. A ski lodge even. I could pay for a room, and maybe talk to someone about gasoline. Even pay to use someone's spare gas can. Anything was better than ending up empty on the side of the road in the middle of nowhere. Especially since I wasn't sure where the road went.

Trees vanished into the horizon all around without showing any promise of civilization. Not even a dirt road that could lead to some recluse's cabin. I loved the wild, but the civilized part of me needed indoor plumbing and hot water heaters. The very thought of a warm bath made my tired eyes flutter closed.

The sudden blast of a new song on the radio jolted me upright. I shook my head and reached for the window to let in some of the cold air. Maybe the icy November chill would keep me awake long enough to reach some kind of destination.

Movement drew my attention back to the road.

"Fuck." I had enough time to register the ghostly looking deer in the road before I hit it and the car spun crazily out of control.

Metal ground against metal, and the noise terrified me. The air bag didn't go off as I threw my hands up to protect my face from the flying glass of the shattered windshield. When the vehicle pinged off the guard rail, my head smashed into the steering wheel. I saw stars in a very literal sense. In seconds, the car came to a sudden, neck-breaking halt in the middle of the road.

My normally crisp vision blurred and spotted; no amount of blinking cleared it. I could smell blood, oil, and gasoline. I tried moving, only to bite my lip against a scream when pain flared throughout my body. Until rescue came, I was stuck. I prayed the car wasn't on fire somewhere.

Would someone come by and see, or would I die on the unnamed road? I closed my eyes and hoped for rescue but waited for death.

~

NICHOLAS

I WAS ONLY in bed for twenty minutes when the message came through about a car accident on the very edge of the town's border. Instead of bitching about the ungodly hour, I climbed out of bed, dressed, and went out to do my job, calling Liam Peters on the way.

The city was either too cheap or too poor to hire on additional EMTs, but I never questioned it. Job security and all. Liam was a volunteer firefighter with an EMT certification, which made him more valuable than most of the others that took shifts with me. He met me at the ambulance bay of the fire station, wearing his usual sunglasses and carrying coffee.

My jaw cracked as I stifled a yawn. Since getting the paramedic certification a couple of months ago, I'd been busier. There was something nice about being the only certified paramedic in town, but at the same time, it fucked with sleep and anything else normal. I hoped a couple of the graduating high school kids would take the request for EMTs seriously, but I wasn't holding my breath.

If I was lucky, there wouldn't be much to do, the car's occupants would be dead, and I'd get another few hours of sleep before heading to the gym. Since my best friend Braden McCabe died, I made sure to hit the gym at least once a day. I wasn't an alpha, but I'd be damned if I would ever be too weak to save a friend's life again.

"That doesn't look pretty." Liam leaned forward in the seat.

I shifted the ambulance a little so I could see around the slowing tow truck. A whistle cut the air as I got a glimpse of the mangled car. "Elk, you think?"

Liam cocked his head. "Possibly. Only other thing I can think of that damn big is a bear."

My hand ran through my long fringe of hair, which reminded me —I needed a cut. Another thing to add to my list of shit to do when I found time. "Let's see if anyone's alive."

I pulled the ambulance off to the shoulder and climbed out, zipping up my blue work jacket with the bright silver reflective EMS on the back and "JORDAN" written across the left breast. I grabbed the medic box before slamming the door and heading over to the crash.

Shame about the car. The classic, while needing a paint job, was still a dream car for most. Probably some crazy-ass wannabe street racer. Stupid too, to be racing down the county road in the middle of the damn night.

Deputy Conall stood next to the driver's side—what was left of it —while Sheriff Ric Kasun leaned in through the crushed windshield. Conall directed a flashlight in through the mangled windshield. Even with the poor light of not quite dawn, both shifter men should have been able to see fine, but as a cat shifter, I didn't question them and risk a pissing match.

"Liam, Nicholas." Ric pulled his broad body out of the crash. "The girl's breathing, but I can't tell you the extent of the injuries. Joshua." Ric moved away from the crash to have a few words with the mechanic, who already had the tow truck in place.

"Should have brought a metalworker," I muttered, as Liam tried to find a delicate way of reaching the driver. I stepped up to the driver's window, but thanks to the collapsed pillar, I could barely get a hand in. I glanced across and then stood up to look at the other side. "Passenger side looks relatively undamaged."

Liam went around to the other side. He glanced at me as he tried the handle. "Door's locked."

I lifted a brow.

He shrugged and stuck his elbow through the window. "Door's open."

Liam slid into the passenger seat, not even bothered by the newly broken glass. He placed a hand on the girl's head and looked down at the pedals. "Wheel well is collapsed. Looks like her leg could be stuck. She's flirting with death."

"Let's see about getting her out and to the med center."

Liam climbed out of the car. "You're smaller than I am. You get in there and pull her out."

I snorted. "By what, two inches?"

"Wide, ass wipe. Despite your gym hours, you're still scrawny."

"Like fucking hell I am." But I moved into position and slid into the car. "Get the damn stretcher."

Her seatbelt was still firmly in place and the first thing I had to deal with. At least the girl was smart enough to be wearing it. Too often I got called out and the seatbelt hadn't been able to do its job.

I angled her so she would fall against my chest when I cut the strap. My safety tool sliced the belt like cutting butter. Her weight didn't even register when she tipped, and it brought a frown to my face. For her height—she was nearly as tall as me—she was too light.

With her face tilted toward the light, I could see sharp angles in her cheeks and a pallor to her skin that shouted malnutrition. My fingers ghosted over her cheek, careful of the bruises. Her lashes fluttered, and for a frozen moment in time, her molten gold gaze stared into my eyes.

Mine.

The unexpected claim slammed into me as hard as the elk had her car. All my muscles tensed. I fought a small battle with myself to stay calm and not lose my damn mind. She was injured, for fuck's sake.

The damn cat inside me took notice, and I forced my gaze away, closing my eyes. There was a time and a place—and this sure as hell wasn't it.

"Jordan, what's taking so long?" Liam tapped the hood next to my head. His head tipped just enough to let me know he noticed. The hellhound was perceptive as fuck.

"Yeah, yeah." I shifted under his scrutiny and returned my attention to where the woman's feet should be. She whimpered a bit when I tried to pull her free, but didn't regain consciousness. "Her left foot is stuck, and she's bleeding from her right leg. By the bruising, she's likely concussed as well."

"Let me get some help over here." Liam stepped away and flagged down Ric and Joshua.

I took a chance and glanced down at the woman again, but this time her eyes were closed. Dried blood crusted along her golden hairline and marred her temple. Her shoulder looked out of place . . . but she did otherwise look in one piece. My major concern now was getting her—my mate—out of the vehicle. Fate had a fucking twisted sense of humor.

CHAPTER 2

AUDREY

*P*ain entered my consciousness before anything else. Everything hurt. No amount of subtle shifting relieved it.

When I forced my eyes open, the ceiling above my head didn't have the familiar pattern of water stains in my room. I flailed into an upright position, with my heart pounding in my ears before the memory of the accident came back. I wasn't in Iowa anymore.

I rolled a shoulder and winced at the pain that radiated down to my fingertips. Motion from the left caught my eye. I froze.

An old man sat in a chair positioned in front of a curtain, with a book in hand. His eyes reminded me of ice storms in Montana, and I waited as their frosty blue gaze studied me. "Finally awake."

"How long have I been out?" I noted my back and neck hurt almost as much as my shoulder when I shifted in his direction. I racked my memory, trying to put the pieces back together.

I was nearly sure he wasn't the man who pulled me out of my car. He was too old to be doing rescue work, even though the intensity of his stare spoke volumes of his authority. The cane leaning against his chair added to the elderly visage.

"If you passed out immediately after the accident, then around sixteen hours. With the bump on your head, no one was sure if or when you would wake up." He stood, sliding the book into his pocket and grabbing his cane. "I'm Elsmed Fairchild. Welcome to Havenwood Falls."

"Havenwood Falls? I'm still in Colorado, right?" I rolled my pained shoulder a second time and grimaced as the bite went deep.

"You are. Where are you from?" He stepped up to the side of the bed, and I did my best to avoid his deep, soul-burning gaze.

"I'm driving from Iowa. Or I was." I grimaced as I attempted to find a comfortable sitting position. "I haven't hurt this bad in a while."

"You're lucky you're alive, really. Mule deer wouldn't have caused that kind of damage. The sheriff is assuming it's an elk, though no one has come forward with the kill. What was in Iowa, if I may ask?"

"Nothing important enough to keep me there." Giving up, I flopped back in the bed and closed my eyes. I wish I had something to deal with the deep aching.

"I'll call the nurse in and get you something for the pain in a moment."

I didn't voice how creepy it was he seemed to have read my mind. "Do you sit in on all accident patients who are unconscious?"

"Only the supernatural ones."

My eyes shot open and darted to his face. "Mr. Fairchild, I'm not supernatural."

The denial was automatic. I didn't pretend to not know what he talked about. There was something preternatural about his demeanor that said he wouldn't take bullshit. Even as old as he was.

"Yet you're not denying they exist, as most normal humans would. Your shift is there in your mind, but her presence is faint, almost as if she is covered, or blocked somehow." Mr. Fairchild shook his head. "It's not something that needs immediate attention."

I shifted, uncomfortable with the topic, as I always was when someone asked about it. "When can I leave?"

"Dr. Underwood mentioned something about a concussion. Now that you're awake, they'll likely be able to address that. Probably some kind of observation."

"Oh."

"I haven't left Havenwood Falls in some years. Tell me, do they talk about the Collector outside our little canyon?"

"Collector of what? There are all sorts of collectors in Denver. I met a dragon in Chicago that liked to collect shifter pelts. I didn't stay there long. Do you know what happened to my car?"

Mr. Fairchild pursed his lips a moment before speaking. "Joshua runs the tow company for Havenwood Falls. You'll want to talk to him, most likely."

"Oh, okay." I closed my eyes again, suddenly swamped by a wave of fatigue.

"I must inform you, there are rules for supernaturals here. I'm sure you'll understand in time. Due to current events in town, you'll need to be registered before you can leave the medical center. For your safety as much as the town's. Adelaide will come and discuss all that with you tomorrow."

Registered? I fought to stay awake enough to process the words. "But I don't have a shift."

"Knowledge is power, Ms. Smith. Never forget that. I'll fetch a nurse for you."

"Thank you." I clenched my jaw to keep from yawning. The voices outside the curtain faded into a dull murmur that reminded me of a stream's trickle as I drifted between wakefulness and sleep.

My mind lingered on Elsmed Fairchild a moment. What a strange individual. He felt powerful without looking it. As I drifted off to sleep, I realized he had said my name without me giving it to him. What kind of town was Havenwood Falls?

NICHOLAS

My parents have always been the rock in the storm of my life. Whenever I needed help—whether it be physical, like replacing the roof on my cabin, or emotional, dealing with the grief of Braden's passing—they were there. They made it clear when I was a child they would always have my back, and they had never let me down.

The drive through Creekwood wasn't long enough to put my thoughts in order. Tension followed me from the day before, and I hoped they'd provide a solution. My parents had always hoped I'd settle down with a nice local girl, regardless of supernatural status. A stranger from out of town, whose name I didn't even know, wasn't what I'd been expecting. Not that I really had been expecting anything at all. I enjoyed my bachelor life, and at thirty, still had plenty of years ahead of me to settle down.

I didn't knock on the door of my childhood home. If my parents weren't home, I'd have to say something to them about the fact I didn't have to use my key to get in. Despite crime being relatively low, there was no point in encouraging the temptation.

The familiarity of the house washed over me when I stepped in, but did nothing to relieve my tension. "Mom? Dad?"

"In the office, honey."

I followed Mom's shout to the office, where I found both my parents. Dad sat behind the desk, and Mom sat in the lounge chair thing by the bookcase. A book lay in Mom's lap; she liked Dad's company even if they didn't say a word to each other.

I pulled out the leather chair and sat down in it, but immediately stood and paced. There was no way I could sit at a time like this.

"Shouldn't my favorite son be at work?" Mom grinned and winked.

"I could say the same of my mother. My reports are caught up, and the station is clean." I rolled my shoulders, suddenly uncomfortable with the topic I wanted to bring up. "I didn't come to talk about work."

Mom canted her head. "Hoping for an easy meal? You're welcome to come for dinner tonight."

"It's not that either, though I appreciate the offer."

Dad looked away from his monitor and at me. "What do you need, Nicholas?"

My hand ran over my still-too-long hair. I'd stop at the barber after this. "I've met my mate—I think."

Mom sat up. "You think?"

Dad folded his hands in the *don't bullshit a bullshitter* pose of my youth. "Mates either are or aren't, son. There's no in between."

"I know that. You don't think I know that?" I walked over to the liquor cabinet in the corner and looked for something to pour.

"It's a little early—" Dad cut off.

"What happened, Nicholas?" Mom's voice was soft as I poured a scotch.

I tossed it back before answering her. "I had a rescue yesterday morning. Car accident. And don't start about the falling in love with the rescued shit. I took the classes. I know the deal. Why do you think I waited a day?" I poured another drink. The scotch wouldn't get me drunk—at least, not for long. Now if I tapped into Dad's bottle of Fey Spirits . . .

"So you went on a rescue?" Dad leaned back in his chair.

"Ten seconds, maybe. I had ten seconds of eye contact." The second drink went down as smoothly as the first. I faced my parents. "How did you know? That you belonged to each other?"

"It's visceral, Nicholas. Tell us how you feel." Mom set her book aside.

"Tense. There's an energy I can't burn off, and I've tried. Restless, anxious, unsettled." I began pacing again. "There's no reason to be this way. I don't even know the girl's name."

"What's stopping you from finding out?" Dad's eyes followed my movement.

"She's unconscious. Or was, when I took her in. I lingered when Dr. Underwood went in to look at her. Concussion. Dislocated shoulder. Fractured two ribs—where the seatbelt held her in place. Sprained ankle that would heal faster if it was actually broken instead. Honestly, she's damn lucky to be alive."

"Is she a shifter?" Mom asked.

I shrugged. "Smelled like a cat. Couldn't tell you what kind." I shoved both my hands in my hair and pulled. "I feel like I should be doing something, but don't know what that is. There's this . . . thing. It feels like it's pushing, but I have no fucking idea where or why."

"Start small." Dad gestured to the door. "You know she's unconscious, but was in a car accident. Do the things she can't do for herself at the moment. Where are her things? Has the insurance been contacted?"

"Does she have toiletries and items to clean up with when she wakes up?" Mom added.

"What's that supposed to do?" I stared at them both. They'd lost their minds. How were menial tasks supposed to identify this girl as a mate?

"It gives you time to figure out what you feel, and gives you vague insight to her life before the accident." Mom gave me a pointed look. "Only you can determine if this girl is your mate or not. If she is, you'll know."

"How? That's what I came to you for. How will I know? How did you know?" I glared from one to the other. "You're not going to help at all?"

Dad sighed. "We are helping, but we're not going to hold your hand through it. You're a grown, respectable man, and I couldn't ask for a finer son. However, if you can't figure out the basics of a mate, then somewhere along the line, I failed as a father."

"You haven't failed, Dad. I just . . ."

"It's scary and new." Mom stood and wrapped me in a hug. "You've always been so sure, and then when Braden died, you used your grief to become the best man you can be. But you never questioned the path you walked. Now you're uncertain. Flailing in the unknown. Take our advice. Go, do for her what she can't do for herself. And go visit Rose at Howe's. Ask her for the soaps and such that I get from her. A shifter woman would appreciate the gently scented items."

I sighed and hugged Mom back. "I don't want to go about this the wrong way."

"You can only be who you are, Nicholas. Trust in fate." She kissed my cheek and pulled away. "Shoo. Your father has paperwork to finish."

"Thanks." The dismissal stung, especially when it felt like they hadn't provided any information at all, but I did as asked. They wouldn't provide anything else even if I camped in the office with them.

The only thing I could do was follow instructions. Joshua towed the car; he likely had all her things. As far as starting points went, it was better than anything else I could think of. Since Howe's was around the corner from the garage, it wouldn't hurt to stop there too.

CHAPTER 3

AUDREY

A big man in comfortable-looking flannel and kind silvery eyes was the first to appear in the morning. Well, after the nurses woke me for the millionth time to ask my name and date of birth. He dragged the chair over to the side of the bed and sat. This close to me, I could smell his wolf.

"I'm Sheriff Ric Kasun. How are you feeling?" He pulled out a tiny notebook from the front pocket of his flannel, along with an equally tiny pen.

"I'd be better if they'd have let me sleep through the night." I stretched my arms over my head and winced when my shoulder pulled. The damn thing was going to take forever to heal.

"I've begun to write out the police report." Ric flipped open his notebook. "You were out of it when we arrived on the scene, but it's clear you hit an elk. I still need your statement for the report."

I chewed on my lip and debated a lie. In the end, his supernatural attributes decided for me. I skirted around the fact I might have fallen asleep behind the wheel, but kept the story mostly intact.

"Ghostly?" Ric scribbled on his police pad. "Magical is a possibility then, but you did say you were extremely tired. Though it does explain why no one in the community has found the elk yet. An animal that size isn't easily hidden."

Before I could reply, a woman colorfully dressed somewhere between boho and rocker chic entered the little room. An old leather messenger bag threatened to fall off her shoulder. "Oh, good, you're still awake. Taylor said you might be back asleep. Healing takes a toll on the body. I'm Addie. I'll be your tattoo artist today."

"Audrey." I frowned. "Tattoo?"

"For the Registry. We track supernaturals to monitor misuse of power and to assist in preventing the laws from being broken. Visitors get a temporary one, and residents have a permanent one." Addie sat on the edge of the bed. She rifled through her bag and pulled out a small notepad. "So what do you want for your design?"

"But I don't have a shift." I looked between the two.

The sheriff crossed his arms. "Being a shifter is a . . . complicated thing. You *could* be diluted too far to shift or you could have suffered a trauma that prevents you from shifting or . . . there are a lot of other reasons, and there's no point going over all of them. The point is, you do have shifter in you, and enough supernatural qualities to warrant being in the Registry."

"I agree." Addie tapped her pencil against the notebook. "It'll be temporary, anyway, since you'll need to get your car situated and you don't even know if you like Havenwood Falls yet. We can reevaluate after you figure out what you want to do."

"I've never thought about a tattoo." I chewed on my lower lip.

"Think about the things you like. Your personality or beliefs." Addie stared, waiting.

I sighed and stared out past Addie and Ric. "I have really bad nightmares sometimes. It's the only consistent part of my life. Unless you count the traveling. I move around quite a bit. I don't have any real beliefs. I loved bartending in Vegas. Los Angeles was beautiful."

Addie's pencil hurried over her paper. In a few minutes, she turned it around for me to see—a simple dream catcher, with a few extra lines and an arrow to create a compass out of the same circle. A skeleton key hung on the southeast side of the compass, and a horseshoe hung on the southwest side.

"It's beautiful." I looked beyond the image to Addie. "You're very talented."

"Thank you. Where do you want it, and we'll get it transferred?" Addie stood up from the chair.

I looked down at myself and shifted muscles gently to find the least painful place. I held out my right arm and tapped the spot right below the inside of my elbow. "I think this is the only unbruised part of me."

"Fair enough." Addie pulled a small tattoo machine from the bag.

I frowned. "I didn't know they made portable tattoo machines."

Addie winked. "We have our ways in Havenwood Falls."

Ric tapped his pen against the notebook. "Addie, have you heard anything about dark spells a couple nights ago?"

Addie shook her head as she took my arm and began the tattooing process. "No, why?"

"Audrey mentioned the elk looked ghostly. I thought a spell may have gone awry, or the wards."

I closed my eyes as the tattoo machine began to buzz. There was a reason I never thought about a tattoo. My stomach clenched a little, and I forced some calm, even breaths out.

Addie snorted. "That's not how the wards are built to work. They don't manifest into physical forms."

"Still, it's worth having someone look at the car. Maybe it's that curse you mentioned reacting with the wards. Bishop would be able to pick up any magic residue on her car, right? Roman said he wanted to be informed of unusual activity." Ric scribbled some more notes.

"Roman's been harder to deal with than normal recently. If you give me some time to check on my appointments, I'll go with you instead of bothering him." Addie set the tattoo machine aside and pulled out some other supplies from her bag with one hand.

"I have what I need for the report. I'll get that to you as soon as I can. Where will you be staying, Audrey?" The sheriff slipped his notebook away.

I flinched a little as the numbness from the constant sting faded away to actual pain. "I don't know where I'll be staying yet. I have to talk to whoever towed my car, and get my things."

"I can talk to Michaela, and we can reserve you a room at the inn. I can run you down to the garage when you're released, then take you to the inn. It's the best place until you can figure out your next step. I'll leave my card with my number, so you can call when you know when you can leave." Addie unfolded a cloth and dabbed lightly at the tattoo.

"Thank you." I didn't have the energy to question why she was being so helpful and just took it as part of her nature. Some people were like that, and had to help.

"You're welcome." Addie nodded, but her eyes were on my arm, where she wiped over the tattoo.

I followed her gaze and watched as the ink wiped away as if she'd drawn the tattoo with a ballpoint. "Is that supposed to happen?"

The other woman shook her head. "No. It's never happened before."

"What is it?" Ric stepped forward and watched Addie clean away the rest of the ink.

Addie's fingers probed the spot she'd tried to ink. Something intangible rippled in the air and made the hairs on my neck stand up. "There's something blocking the Registry. It feels malevolent. It wouldn't be wise to poke at it further without a full circle."

I tried to wrap my head around what Addie was saying. "I'm . . . cursed?"

"In layman's terms . . . yes, I suppose calling it a curse is the best term. It could be a geis or seal as well, but curse works. At a guess, based on what you've told us and the energy it throws out, I'd say it prevents your shift, and might have something to do with your nightmares, too. There's no way to know for certain without taking it apart, though, and that's never a good idea without knowing the who and why."

"Is she a danger to Havenwood Falls?" Ric squared up his shoulders and looked ready to haul me out of bed and drag me outside.

"No." Addie took my cold hand in hers. "We'll have to come up with something else for the Registry. If I'm right, I can charm a bracelet or necklace, and you can wear that. The curse—let's call it that for now—might apply to anything attempting to touch you directly. I wish I could examine it more, but it's not safe to mess with it without a circle and quite possibly a full moon. The moon was full at Thanksgiving. We'll have to wait for December's moon to poke at it."

"That's . . . You've given me more than anyone else has. I've never considered I might be magically cursed. I mean, as a child growing up in the foster system, I considered myself unlucky or cursed, but never like this. It's ironic in a way."

Addie cleaned up her supplies. "Foster care?"

I lay back down in the bed and closed my eyes. "Yes. A couple of boaters found me floating in the Rappahannock River in Virginia when I was eleven. I have no memory of anything before waking in the hospital. No one came to claim me."

"I'm sorry. That had to be hard." She patted my arm. "Well, you're here now, and Havenwood Falls has a way of making everyone feel at home."

Ric stood and moved to the entry. "I think I heard something about keeping you overnight again to monitor your concussion. They'll likely let you go in the morning, when they've determined you're okay enough to not need watching."

"Give me a call when they tell you if they're going to discharge you." Addie stood and followed the sheriff. "Welcome to Havenwood Falls, Audrey."

"See you in the morning." I clenched my jaw to keep from yawning, but could do nothing to keep fatigue from dropping me into unconsciousness. For the first time in days, I rested peacefully.

CHAPTER 4

AUDREY

The nurse's lecture went in one ear and out the other as I carefully changed into the simple button-down shirt and jeans Addie brought. My body still hurt—the shirt was a bitch to get on with my shoulder—and there was a deep ache in my soul I didn't understand, but overall, I was in one piece and didn't need to remain in the medical center.

"Thanks." I took the offered paperwork from the nurse and skimmed it. The instructions were basic common sense, and the billing information was listed at the bottom. I hoped the car insurance would cover most of it—if not all. I'd have to stay in Havenwood Falls a lot longer if there was a medical bill to pay as well as buy a new car. I didn't like to leave a place with debt to chase me.

"You really should allow the doctor to splint or boot your foot. It will heal faster with less stress." The nurse shifted to stay in my line of vision as I turned to Addie.

I shook my head at her. "I've allowed the doctor the compression sleeve, and I've promised to rest often and follow the instructions. It's good enough."

She wrung her hands together, but stepped aside. "At least the cane or crutches for assistance with rest?"

With a wave of my hand, I said my goodbye and hurried behind Addie.

"Oh. Before I forget." Addie dug around in her pocket as she led the way out of the medical center. She pulled out a pendant and tossed it.

I caught the necklace with one hand, the green striped stone pendant swinging like a pendulum. I frowned at it, then at Addie.

"It's for the Registry." Addie stopped outside the door and waited for me to follow. "Let's see if this works."

I pulled the long chain up over my head. The teardrop stone felt warm against my skin, but nothing happened that I could tell.

Addie's smile proved something different. "It works. Come on. The stone is malachite, in case you're wondering. Don't take it off for any reason. It's waterproof."

"What's malachite?" I limped after Addie, wishing I had accepted the cane, to a well-kept Jeep.

"A protection stone, for the most part. Helps with creativity and intuition, and wards against nightmares." Addie nodded at my surprise. "Seemed like something you would appreciate."

"Thanks. Does it actually work?" I climbed up and buckled in as Addie started the engine.

Her grin held mischief. "Let me know."

Addie pointed out some of the landmarks as she drove. The town looked like Christmastown relocated to Havenwood Falls for the holidays. Miller's Plaza held a bunch of interesting shops, and their decorations looked like they were trying to one-up each other.

Addie turned onto Eighth Street and then pulled into a lot behind a garage. "I'm going to have to leave you here. I have some errands to run, but the inn is right on Main Street. Just go back up and walk down past the shops. You can't miss it."

"Thanks, Addie. For all your help." I hopped out of the Jeep and winced as I came down too hard on my ankle. As I approached the garage, Addie tooted the horn, making me jump, and my ankle screamed its protest when I pivoted to look back.

Addie's head was out her window. "Ask for Joshua."

I gave her a thumbs up and tried not to limp walking into the little office. No one sat at the reception desk, and no one sat in any of the plastic waiting chairs. I hesitated, unsure of what to do, when a door leading to the garage's bays swung open and a man stepped through.

He cocked his head while he wiped his hands on a towel. His gray hair nearly matched his eyes. "Help you?"

"I'm here to speak to Joshua about my car." My hands white-knuckled around my purse strap. The car was my everything, and now . . .

"I'm Joshua. You'd be the Challenger girl, then." He stuffed the cloth in a back pocket before holding open the garage door. "Shall we take a look?"

Tears blurred my vision when I got a good look at what remained of my car. I should have been grateful I was alive and the car took the brunt of the damage, but I loved that car. I took a deep breath and put a choke hold on my emotions. It was only a car, and it was decades old. It could probably be fixed. Most anything could nowadays.

"You're a lucky one." Joshua tapped on the crumpled driver's side with a fist. "It's going to cost more time and money to fix than you probably originally paid for it."

I could only nod as his words sunk in. By the sound of it, I couldn't afford to fix it even if I wanted to. "The sheriff said he was writing the report, and I've got to get this reported to the insurance company."

"Nick was in here yesterday, and pulled your insurance information from the glove box. I let him use my office to get that started for you."

"Oh." I didn't know a Nick, but felt it wasn't polite to say so. "I have stuff in the trunk."

"He insisted we pull it out for you. It's locked in the office. He's probably right—it's not wise to let it sit in the garage. Not that I don't trust my boys, but there's less temptation that way. The devil's a cagey bastard."

"Thank you. Is there a junkyard around that I can sell the car to, or do you take care of that? I've never wrecked a car before." I followed Joshua back through the reception and into his office.

My things were stacked in a neat pile in the corner. The old-fashioned trunk held clothes, while the actual suitcase held shoes. A messenger bag sat on top with all of my electronics, and my book bag with overnight necessities rested against the suitcase. Overall, it was a pitiful number of items to sum up my life.

"Have a seat, dear. Can I get you anything? A drink?" Joshua sighed as he lowered himself into his office chair when I shook my head. "There's not much you can do about the car just yet. An insurance adjuster will likely want to come and take a look, though I can tell you right off, there's no way they're going to do anything more than call it totaled."

"Okay." My knees gave out, and I sank into the guest chair. The small hope of getting it fixed went out the window.

"You'll want to talk to Nick, and see how far he's gotten with reporting it to your insurance, and check their timeline. Havenwood Falls is off the beaten path, so getting any kind of payout is going to take time."

I nodded again. I was losing the battle with my emotions, and a traitorous tear trickled out of my left eye.

Joshua pushed a box of tissues in my direction. "You're allowed to cry. If I totaled a car like yours, I'd cry too. If you'd like, I can estimate its worth—what the insurance will likely pay—and we can discuss what you'd like to do about transportation."

"Okay." I sniffled into a tissue and wiped at my eyes. Taking a steadying breath, I met Joshua's patient gaze. "I'm sorry. I really appreciate your help."

He waved off the apology. "I have an auction coming up. What are you looking for in a car? I doubt we can get the same one."

"I picked that one because it's safe, and easy enough for me to maintain myself." My hand fisted around the tissue, and he nudged the wastebasket over with his foot.

"You know cars?" Joshua's brows rose.

My left shoulder rose and fell. "Enough to change the oil, rotate the tires, top off the fluids, change the brake pads, spark plugs . . . easy simple stuff really, but it all costs money to do if I took it to a garage."

"Sure does." Joshua leaned back in his chair and scribbled some notes on a nearby pad. "Anything else? Color, preferred make or model?"

"Cheaper parts would be nice. Parts for the Challenger aren't cheap."

"No. They're not." Joshua's pencil scratched across the paper. "I think Honda. They've got a good inexpensive line. And they run forever with the right care. I noticed the Challenger was a clutch. Still want a manual?"

"I don't know how much the insurance will pay out." I chewed on my lip. "Whatever's affordable, I guess."

"Don't worry about that right now. You tend to those bruises and sores. Health comes first. We can make arrangements if you don't get a fair deal."

"All right." I took a breath. "Okay. What do I have to do?"

~

NICHOLAS

I JOGGED up the short flight of steps to the medical center with a plain white gift bag in one hand. After spending the day before at the garage with Audrey's totaled car and her scent fogging my brain, I figured the best course of action—for both of us—was to be straightforward. Tell her what I thought; ask her how she felt. Kiss her stupid and go from there.

With the mountain lion population split between two families in Havenwood Falls, I thought I had more time to find "the one" and settle down. I thought it would happen when I was in Denver certifying, or renewing, but fate decided to play her hand. I either went with it or died from it. I wasn't really ready for either, but the choices were limited.

I nodded to the nurse at the desk. She smiled, and with my focus on Audrey, I couldn't remember her name.

"Hey, handsome. Whatcha up to?" The interest in her gaze might have drawn my attention once, but not any longer.

My cat bristled, wanting to ignore her and go find our mate. I quelled the cat and kept my smile friendly. The human wouldn't understand the blowoff, and I had to work with her. "Figured the car wreck girl would like some provisions. We didn't exactly grab anything from her car but her."

The nurse fluttered over her station. "Aren't you sweet? She discharged about an hour ago, though. Left with Addie. Refused the boot or splint. She's only going to injure herself further. I can take that bag off your hands if you want. I'm sure some other injured soul would appreciate it just as much."

I stepped back as my mind spun. Checked out? Where would she go? And why did she refuse medical care? "I didn't think she'd be leaving so soon, with her injuries, but I'm not a doctor."

"Dr. Underwood gave the okay." The nurse cocked her head, still smiling. As a predator, I recognized that smile, and stepped back a couple more paces as she came around the desk.

"Thanks. I appreciate it." I hurried out the way I came in before the nurse got any closer, and tossed the gift bag across the truck in frustration when I climbed back in. Where would a girl from nowhere go, if she had no vehicle to get her there? To the garage. To check on said vehicle, and likely gather her things.

I threw the truck in gear and pulled out onto Main Street in a hurry. Despite Havenwood Falls being a small town, there were times I didn't cross paths with my own family unless I wanted to. If I missed her at the garage, there was no telling when I'd find her again.

The light at Eighth forced me to stop—the driver in front of me didn't give me enough room to turn—and I idly noted that Leda had changed the jewelry display again at Summit Jewelers. The Christmas display highlighted several very classy and expensive-looking pieces. Would Audrey want a pretty ring to show off, as most women did? Was my mate more human than shifter, or vice versa? I'd have to ask.

As I drummed my fingers on my steering wheel with impatience, my eyes landed on a figure walking up the block. I narrowed my eyes and cursed. I may have only seen and held her once, but I knew in my gut the figure limping up the street was Audrey.

She shouldn't even be out of the med center, let alone dragging a trunk and loaded down with her baggage. I'd have to have a word with Underwood. A concussion along with all the other slew of damages—especially the ribs—warranted more than one day of medical attention.

Why the hell hadn't anyone offered to help her?

When the light turned green, I launched the truck up the street, squealing the tires, and pulled into the closest spot to my mate. I remembered to shut the truck off as I jumped out. Ric would have my head for unreasonable idling—our mountain air was pristine and we liked to keep it that way. I marched up to her with no clear idea of what to say.

My anger grew as I noticed she had a suitcase bungee-corded to the antique trunk, and wore a backpack and messenger bag. The words flew out before I considered them. "What the fuck do you think you're doing?"

She jolted, and when her golden eyes landed on my face, the force of the bond stole the air from my lungs. She sucked in a sharp breath, her eyes widening. I watched what little color she had drain from her face.

"It's not possible." Her words were almost lost to the noise of the traffic, but I caught them.

What wasn't possible? Didn't matter. We could have that conversation later.

"Get in the truck." I yanked the trunk handle out of her hand and walked toward my vehicle, expecting her to follow.

"I don't even know who the hell you are. Why would I get into a vehicle with you?" She grabbed for her case, but I pulled it out of reach.

The fact she wasn't a mouse amused and impressed me. When she glared, clearly ready for a fight, I struggled not to laugh. I liked a woman with spunk, and she appeared to have plenty.

"Nicholas Jordan. The guy who pulled you out of your mangled vehicle." I resisted the urge to touch her, stroke a finger down her cheek or wrap an arm around her. I *needed* to touch her, the way a starving man needed food, but if I did so, I wouldn't stop, and there were laws about allowable public activities.

She didn't seem the least bit impressed as she crossed her arms, drawing my attention to the puckered tips of her breasts. I wasn't the only horny one on the sidewalk. "Thanks, I guess. Give me my trunk."

I tossed the trunk and suitcase into the truck bed behind me with an easy fling. "Listen, kitten. I'm not having this conversation out on the street."

She snarled, but it only excited my cat. "I have nothing I want to talk to you about. The med center has my insurance. You'll get paid."

I leaned toward her and watched with fascination as her pupils dilated. Her breaths quickened, and I craved to close the remaining distance and seal my mouth over hers. I'd give her a real reason to gasp . . . but not in front of Coffee Haven. Not where all the old biddies could see, and gossip about it.

"No." Her breath tickled my mouth when I closed the distance to less than a hair's breadth, with the implication of a kiss. She smelled like the med center, and it wasn't as much of a turnoff as I thought it would be.

"Not here," I corrected. There were a lot more things I wanted besides a kiss, and that wouldn't be appropriate on the street. "Get in the truck, or I put you in the truck."

Tension coursed through the air for a heartbeat before she broke eye contact. "Fine."

She pivoted, and cried out as she crumpled. Before I could think about moving, I held her in my arms, mindful of the broken ribs. If I were any slower, she would have hit the concrete on her bad side. I watched her carefully as I helped her back up.

My fingers moved of their own accord, caressing small patterns on her soft skin, unable to let her go. I nuzzled her hair, unable to resist her allure. "I'm pretty sure the med center gave you a list of things not to do on a sprained ankle, and I think pivoting like you're in the military is on that list."

"Fuck off." She shoved me away and limped toward the passenger door. She pulled her bags off as she approached the door and tossed the book bag in the bed with her trunk.

I wondered if she was just as fiery in bed. The thought made my dick hard, and I couldn't wait to test the theory. Would she scratch and bite? I hoped so.

After counting to ten and taking several deep breaths, I walked around the truck and joined her. With every prolonged moment, my control slipped a little more. The mate bond wasn't meant to be fought, but embraced. Figuratively and literally. How the fuck she was so calm?

"So," I buckled up, mindful of my painful erection, "where to?"

"Whisper Falls Inn. Addie said the rooms would be reasonable even with the season about to start." She didn't look at me, but stared out the window at the shops.

"Do you like coffee? I could run in and get you some?" I suddenly felt awkward and didn't know why.

"Not right now."

I nudged the white bag she'd moved to the center seat. "It's a gift for you."

She eyed the bag with suspicion. "What is it?"

"Take a look." I angled in the seat to watch her study the bag before pulling out a bottle.

Audrey studied the handwritten label before opening the bottle and sniffing. "Soap?"

The light citrus and herb wafted through the truck cab. Mom's floral was too old lady esk in my mind, so I hoped Audrey was okay with the fruity aroma. For a moment, I imagined kissing her skin after bathing and wondered if she'd taste as good as she smelled. "There's shampoo, conditioner, lotion, too. My mother gets them from Rose at Howe's. They're gentler on the senses than the human stuff."

"Thanks, I guess." She dropped the bottle back into the bag.

A low growl rumbled in my chest. My job was easier than dealing with Audrey's prickliness. Maybe it was a perverse form of caution. Though I couldn't figure out why. "I have a guest room in my cabin. I wouldn't charge you for its use."

"I don't take handouts." She finally looked at me. "Are you going to drive or should I get out and start walking again?"

"It may take a while to get a replacement for your car." To prolong moving, I checked all the mirrors twice before pulling out into traffic.

"So Joshua told me." She leaned against the door, as far away from me as possible, and it pissed me off.

"Listen." I reached out for her hand, and she slapped me away. "There's no running from this."

She straightened in her seat. "I don't know what you're talking about."

"Bullshit. You're so scared of the bond, you won't even look me in the face." I side-eyed her without taking my attention from the road.

"You're driving, asshole. Your eyes should be on the road, not my face." Her matter-of-fact tone—with not even a hint of anger—made me angrier.

I took a deep breath and tried again. We were stuck, fates chosen, and there was no way around it. If I let her piss me off at every turn, I was going to spend a lot of time angry. "Let's start over. Hi. I'm Nicholas Jordan."

The perverse creature didn't even turn from the window. "Audrey Smith."

"Nice to meet you."

"Sure."

The muscles in my jaw twitched. The tension in the truck was almost suffocating. When I pulled into the inn's lot, Audrey jumped out almost before we completely stopped. I wasn't going to let her ghost me. No way in hell. It wouldn't end well for either of us.

CHAPTER 5

NICHOLAS

I beat Audrey to her bags in the truck bed. Instead of submitting to her silent demand for her bags—like holding her hand out was really going to work—I walked toward the front of the inn.

"Michaela could tell you more, but the inn has been here since the founding of the town." I waited for her at the door and grinned when she tilted her head, as if trying to imagine the old Victorian manor back in the day.

"Why is it Whisper Falls Inn then, instead of Havenwood Falls Inn?"

I tipped my head and focused my hearing. On busy days it was hard, especially now with the ski resort open for the winter season, and people enjoying the brisk fall air, but I could still hear them. I wondered if she could. "Close your eyes and listen."

Skepticism crossed her face before she did as I asked. My stomach twisted when a genuine smile lit her face. I fought the urge to gather her close and kiss her stupid. There would be time for that. I needed to be patient.

"Is that a waterfall?"

"Yes." I couldn't help the gruffness in my voice and was glad my hands were full, or I'd have been all over her when her eyes locked onto mine.

Her smile faded, and the wall between us returned. "I should check in."

I followed her into the inn and waited with her until Sindi came out to the lobby, wiping her hands on a towel. She tucked the edge of it into the back pocket of her impossibly tight pants.

"Hey. Welcome to Whisper Falls Inn." The pretty redheaded vampire tipped her chin at us as she took her place behind the front desk.

"Hi. I'm Audrey. I'm sorry. I don't have a reservation—" Audrey began, but Sindi smiled.

"It's okay. Addie was here yesterday and told Michaela and me all about it. I'm Sindi, by the way. You've had some pretty bad luck the last couple of days. However, Michaela did put one of the rooms upstairs on reserve for you. You have to share a bathroom, but it's a fair price until you get situated."

"Thanks." Audrey set her purse on the desk and rifled around.

"How long will you be staying?" Sindi tapped away at a keyboard.

"Oh, um." Audrey froze. She ticked off something on her fingers and sighed. "Honestly, I don't know."

"Let's start with a week, then. We can always adjust it after you get things figured out."

"That sounds wonderful. Thank you." Audrey pulled out a wallet the size of a small purse. How she couldn't find it in her purse I couldn't figure.

I shifted and drew Sindi's attention. I shook my head and mouthed the word "mate," hoping she'd understand my silent plea. Even without sound to the word, standing this close, her vampire hearing should pick it up—and hopefully not the prickly kitten in front of me. Sindi continued to smile, but I saw a sparkle of curiosity in her gaze that wasn't there before. Whether or not she'd help me out was another matter.

Audrey flipped open the wallet and hesitated over the line of cards before pulling out a gold one. "Use this one."

Sindi tapped away and swiped the card. Frowned and swiped again. "I'm sorry, but it's declining."

I forced my face to remain uninterested when Audrey cut a suspicious look over at me. I smiled at her. "Need some help? I have a guest room, as I mentioned before."

She hissed out a breath and turned her attention back to Sindi. "The card is brand new. It can't have declined. I've never used it."

"Maybe you forgot to activate it." I stepped up before Sindi would have to make up a lie. "Happens, you know. Here." I fished out my wallet and held out my AMEX Platinum card. I never used the damn thing, and since my life was relatively low key, I had decent savings and credit. Jobless and homeless Audrey wouldn't be able to attest to the same. "Put it on mine."

"No." Audrey turned and jabbed a finger into my chest. "You're not paying for my room."

"Two choices, kitten. I pay for your room, so you have a room, since your card declined, or you come stay in my guest room at no cost." I covered her mouth with a hand when she opened it to spew more distaste at me. I shivered when her tongue darted out and licked my palm. It took all my control not to groan. "And I will add these are nonnegotiable choices."

"You can always switch the card later, after you get it straightened out." Sindi shrugged when both of us glared at her. "We don't charge the full price until after checkout anyway."

Audrey shoved me back. "Fine. I'll call the card company later."

Sindi set a key on the desk along with a paper printout. "Last room on the right, closest to the bathroom. Fair warning, it's the noisiest room, but the least expensive."

Audrey grabbed the key and tossed the paper at me. "I've had worse."

Without a word, I followed her up the stairs, wondering what was worse than water pipes and flushing toilets even as my eyes took in her curves from behind.

"Stop looking at my ass." Audrey didn't turn.

"What makes you think I am?" I wondered if I should bring up the fact my guest room had its own bathroom and less noise than the inn would have.

"Because you have a dick in your pants."

I bit my tongue instead of responding. My mother didn't raise a fool. Anything I said or did would be used against me in the future.

At the room, she held the door for me, and I nodded thanks as I set her bags next to the small dresser.

"Thanks for carrying my bags up."

I didn't give her a chance to say more. I knew a dismissal when I heard one. She wasn't getting rid of me that easily.

In less than a heartbeat, I was in her personal space with my mouth on hers. I gave her no chance to escape.

Her small gasp was all I needed for invitation to dive further. My tongue coaxed hers to dance. She tasted like chocolate and cinnamon, and smelled like need and promise.

I dropped a hand to her waist, pulling her closer even as my free hand fisted in her hair. I wanted more. I needed to feel her against me. Kissing her wasn't enough.

She shivered when I rubbed my body against hers and moaned in my mouth at the press of my cock against her stomach. My blood raced, and any thoughts outside of her were gone.

I wanted to cover her in my seed, fill her with it. Bury myself in her. Claim her as mine in ways that only a shifter would understand.

Her violent shove surprised me enough to throw me back several steps. I tried to clear my head as we stared at each other, both chests heaving. I reached out a hand, and she stepped back, raising her arms in a defensive position.

"I want you to leave." Her voice shook.

I wasn't sure I understood her words. The mountain lion roared his displeasure. Closing my eyes, I tried to focus beyond the cat and the pounding in my blood. My tongue was thick, and I sounded drunk. "You can't be serious."

"I'm not a whore."

The cat wanted to leap forward and pin her down. Actions meant more than words to the cat, but this wasn't the time or place for force.

I ignored the not-so-silent nudging and held her gaze. "I never thought you were."

"Please leave."

I shook my head. "You're insane. The bond has started. Do you know what kind of pain we'll be in if I just leave?"

"I don't know what you're talking about." Her arms wrapped around her torso in a self-hug.

"The mate bond. I know you feel it." I stepped forward, and she stepped back.

"I don't have a mate. I would need a shift for that, and I can't shift. Never could. So you're mistaken." Her tone hardened.

"You don't need a shift. That's snobbery and purity talking. You exist. That's all you need to draw a mate bond." I wanted to press her into admitting it. In another two steps, she'd be against the bed, but it wasn't just desire I smelled. She feared me, and her fear effectively killed my desire.

Her eyes shifted away. "Nicholas, please leave."

I tried to soften my tone, suddenly unsure of where I stood or why she feared me. "We can't ignore this, Audrey. That's not how the bond works."

"You're wrong!" She threw a hand toward the door. "Get out."

Actions meant more than words. I braced myself. This wasn't going to be kind to either of us.

I made it to the door before the pounding in my temples started. This was an all-around bad idea, but I couldn't force her to accept me. I wouldn't; it wasn't in my nature.

The door clicked quietly behind me. The sensation was like a rubber band being pulled too far. Eventually it would snap.

At the top of the stairs, my vision blurred and grayed as pain exploded through my body. I missed the step and tumbled down the flight. I barely felt the pain of the fall.

Someone rushed to help, but I couldn't clearly see who.

"Outside," I managed through racking spasms. I needed to get farther away before the bond tried to relink.

"You can't drive like this." Michaela's voice pierced the pain.

"Outside." I attempted to crawl toward where the door might be. I couldn't see a damn thing, not even the rays of sunshine that should be warming the floor.

She sighed, and I was hefted up from both sides—Sindi helped, too, by the smell.

In the bright light of day, the pain receded enough for me to regain some of my senses. I stumbled over to the truck and leaned against the cool metal. My head cleared a little more but the pain in my chest remained strong. It hurt to breathe—likely would until Audrey accepted or we died from denial.

"Thanks. I'm better." I turned to look at the women who followed me out. "Let her charge whatever to the room. Make sure she eats. Can you write a note for me? She's going to be looking for work."

Michaela crossed her arms. "What was that, Jordan?"

I rubbed my sore chest. "Nothing you need to worry about. It's . . . personal."

Michaela didn't look convinced, but Sindi sniffed. "You smell like sex."

"Sindi." Michaela slapped her arm.

Sindi shrugged. "What's the message?"

I sighed and hoped Audrey would accept a helping hand, as it was intended, and not consider it a handout. "Thanks. I appreciate it."

~

AUDREY

MY MORNING WAS SPENT in agonized spasms. I curled up on the bed silently crying and waiting for pain worse than any injuries from my accident to pass. Even my broken ribs didn't hurt like this. My soul felt like it was being forcefully ripped from my body.

Despite Nicholas's words, despite the slap of truth, I still couldn't believe I had a mate. Everyone I encountered in the past was adamant it wouldn't happen. Snobbery and purity he had called it. I didn't want to believe him, but there was nothing else that explained the racking pain, not even the car accident.

When I could move without tears, I began the mission of finding a job. I slipped out of the inn without being seen by Michaela or Sindi. For now, I didn't want to face any personal questions. I'd have enough of them while applying for work.

The shops on the square would be a good place to start. After a frustrating two hours of nothing—even with the season starting, no one was looking for help—I returned to the inn. Michaela smiled and waved me over to the desk when she saw me.

"Here. Nicholas left you a note. And you've been granted permission to charge food to the room if you need to."

"I don't need his fucking charity." I studied the sticky note Nicholas wrote. The handwriting looked suspiciously feminine, but I doubted Michaela would lie about its origin. The directions were clear, and yet vague at the same time. I wondered what kind of person Melaina Savage was to open a club in an old mine. It certainly took a whole lot of innovation.

Michaela shrugged when I asked her what she knew about Silk, and provided alternatives—the Haven Saloon and the Dirty Knuckle —for employment. With nothing else to do with my afternoon, I went and scouted them out; options were always a good thing. I felt good about those applications and chances for employment, though the pay worried me a bit.

When night fell, I headed out once more, following Nicholas's instructions. As I walked down Main Street toward where I was assured the parking lot for the club was, I checked out the shops on the street again, and in Miller's Plaza. For such a small town, there was a surprising variety of businesses and places I could see myself using when I got back on my feet.

Despite being a strange small town, it didn't feel unsafe to walk along the road in the dark. Perhaps that was naïve of me, or maybe it was some kind of magic. I could definitely understand why people chose to live here, though. Simple night sounds filled the air, and the ski trails were lit up on the side of the mountain. The town was beautiful. Havenwood Falls felt safer than a lot of the cities I had lived in, and the air was just as crisp and beautiful as in Glacier in Montana.

Although closed for the day, the nail salon—my guilty pleasure—caught my attention, and I glanced down at the eighteen-day-old polish on my fingers. It wasn't chipped, but it was growing out. I'd have to see about that soon or take it off to remain professional looking.

The couple mile walk was over faster than I expected. Next time, I'd bring a flashlight; some of the streetlamps along the road weren't lit, and I couldn't afford to trip and add to my injuries. Until I mapped out a running path, the walk would be good to stay in shape.

I studied the gondola lift from the edges of the decently lit parking lot. My brain expected a hole in the ground, not several stories up the side of the mountain. I'd never been on a gondola before, and the idea of it gave me a bit of apprehension. I never tried roller coasters or Ferris wheels either.

I considered my options. I could wait to hear from one of Michaela's suggested places or . . . stand still. Do nothing. And those options weren't acceptable.

If I wanted to pay my debts off, I needed a good job, and in a town this size, I didn't have a lot of choices. There was no way a business would be open in the mountain if the way to get there wasn't completely safe. I released a deep breath and muttered a prayer under my breath as I approached the gondola.

A big man in a suit stood in front of the entrance, screening the people. I noticed some flashed their cell phones at him and others showed bright red business cards. The big man turned out to be one of average size when I was close to him—the benefits of being a tall woman.

He was still taller than I, though not enough that I had to tilt my head back to look in his eyes.

"Hi." I smiled at him before he could speak. "I'm here to see Melaina Savage about a job."

I couldn't see his eyes behind his sunglasses—who wore sunglasses at ten at night?—but I watched his brow furrow. "Name?"

"Audrey Smith." I chewed my lip. "I don't have an appointment or anything. I wrecked my car a couple of days ago . . ."

The wrinkle between his brows smoothed out. "Oh. You're the Challenger girl. Shame about the car. Sweet ride."

I canted my head and studied him a little closer. I didn't remember seeing him in the last few days. "How did you know that?"

"Liam was on duty. Gimme a sec." He pulled a walkie-talkie from his belt. "Ms. Savage, there's a lady down here looking for a job. The elk girl."

Static crackled on the radio before a woman responded. "Send her up."

The man put the radio back on his belt and gestured to the gondola. "Ride on up."

"Thanks."

He jerked his chin. "Hurry, before you miss this one. She doesn't like to be kept waiting."

I nodded and hurried over to the almost empty gondola. As it lurched from the ground, I reminded myself they wouldn't use it if it was a hazard. When it lifted up barely below the treetops, I found myself pressed to the glass, staring out in wonder.

The town was even prettier from above. How did anyone not ride the gondola a hundred times just to see the town from this angle? Maybe that's why Melaina built so high—to show off her town?

I wiped my damp palms over my clean black pants. There was nothing to be nervous about. My clothes were clean and professional and my hair pulled back. The ache left in the wake of Nicholas's absence was ignorable, and I knew how to do the job I wanted.

The ride was too short, and I stepped off last behind the others, not sure what to do or where to go. I realized after a moment there was only one way to go, unless I got back on the gondola. I followed the crowd down a short hall and tried not to gawk at the big beautiful doors and gorgeous front room area, or the perfectly stunning woman standing at the hostess podium.

I felt frumpy and overdressed in comparison to her tight dress and stiletto heels, but reminded myself what I wore was standard for most bartenders. Dress for the job you wanted, right? And the all-black look was flattering to a degree. Still, the woman's perfect curls and to-die-for curves didn't boost my self-esteem any.

"Excuse me." I waited for the hostess to turn her attention from the touch screen and tried to not look down on the woman. She smelled unlike anything I'd ever encountered before, so I was cautious. There were more supernaturals in the world than animal shifters, and many of them a lot more dangerous. "I'm here to see Melaina Savage."

The woman's blood red lips curved. I didn't fidget as her eyes traveled down and back up again. When she spoke, her voice came out with a sultry rasp. "I am Melaina Savage. You must be Audrey."

"Yes, ma'am." I folded my hands at my waist. "I was hoping to speak to you about a bartending job, but I can waitress, too."

She eyed me once more, her tongue sliding over her lips. "Follow me. I'm a busy woman, and I don't give handouts. You're lucky I'm short-staffed or I'd be forced to question your common sense, coming at this time of night. You want a job, I'm willing to give you a chance, but you have to earn it." Melaina turned from the podium and headed into the main space. "Our main area has several bars, lounge spaces, some tables. You see the dance floor. This main area is open to the public—as long as they pay the hefty cover charge. Invitations for private events are coveted by the rich. We're in season right now, so hours of operation are nine to three. Every day. You'll get two days off a week, depending on business needs. At the moment, those days will be Tuesday and Sunday. Those are subject to change."

Melaina smiled and nodded at patrons as we walked through the main space and up a short four steps, past two bouncers and into another smaller bar area that looked out over the main space—everyone's eyes following her. I forced myself to keep pace with Melaina instead of staring. The transformation was incredible. No one would ever guess the club wasn't the intended purpose of the cavern. Silk could rival any club on the Las Vegas Strip.

"This is VIP." Melaina held open the bar swing. "Consider this a working resume. Impress me and we'll get your paperwork done at the end of the shift. Disappoint and I'll pay you in cash, and tonight never happened."

I nodded and stepped through to the bar. Melaina pointed to the bouncers. "If you get into shit, just whistle. The guys will come to your rescue."

"Yes, ma'am."

"Good. I'll be back at the end of the night. Help should show up around mid-shift to give you a break." Melaina sauntered away without any further directive.

I glanced around, noting that while VIP wasn't busy, it wasn't dead either. I took notice of drinks on tables and the two men at the bar as I made myself at home behind it. This was my comfort zone, and I had no problem with Melaina's test.

CHAPTER 6

NICHOLAS

The bright bouquet of flowers on the passenger seat mocked me. Reagan, owner at Fairy Tale Florists, insisted the irises and carnations were a perfect mix for a first date. Shifters didn't need the flounce and preamble of courtship, a mate was a mate, and yet . . . I found myself about to propose just that. My mate—I refused to call her anything else—had better appreciate the effort I put in. I didn't want to go through another restless night.

She had no shift, though I wondered why, since the cat was on the surface of her scent.

The thought didn't bother me. As I picked up the flowers and slammed out of the truck, I wondered why it bothered her. Then again, the outside world didn't have the safety of Havenwood Falls' rules. Rules could be broken, of course, but the consequences were dire. I lost a friend to broken rules, and Dad's best friend lost three children.

I pulled myself out of past memories as I entered the inn. Sindi gave me a once-over and smirked at the flowers. "You're seriously going this route at eight o'clock in the morning?"

I ignored her and headed up the stairs. Yes, this wasn't the greatest of ideas. However, I didn't have to explain my lack of reasoning to anyone but Audrey. And if I couldn't sleep, why should she be able to?

After a deep breath, I knocked on Audrey's door. When no noise came from the other side, I knocked a little harder. As I knocked for the third time, rattling the door in its frame, my mind went over our possible future once she accepted facts.

Would she like the cabin? I didn't live fancy, but it was a nice cabin. My ancestor built it when he arrived in the valley some hundred years ago. Would it be big enough?

How many kids did she want? What if she didn't want kids? All shifters wanted kids; it was part of our nature . . . but she wasn't raised like other shifters. I pushed the worrisome thought away to address later. I had to win the girl first—a ridiculous thought for a mountain lion shifter, but it was what it was.

Maybe she slept as heavily as I did? Our poor cubs would have a hell of a time getting to school if that was the case. Mr. Brauner didn't stand for tardiness, and was even more of a stickler about it since becoming principal of the elementary school.

The door popped open when I lifted my hand to pound once again, and I was grateful she gave me a minute to find my voice. My cat purred in delight, and all my muscles tightened. This morning's cold shower no longer held its sway over my dick, and I went rock hard in seconds. I closed my eyes, but the damage was already done.

Audrey's robe slid off one shoulder, revealing blushing, pale skin and a thin tank underneath. She didn't have any pants covering her legs, and her hair looked tousled from sleep. Her voice was rough, almost hoarse, when she spoke. "What do you want?"

I held out the flowers and took a breath, instantly wishing I hadn't. She smelled like sex and the toiletries I gave her. The cat immediately screamed his displeasure. She wasn't allowed to smell that way unless we were involved.

Her hand reached out for the bouquet, and the smell of sex strengthened. I couldn't stop myself from grabbing her wrist with my other hand and lifting her fingers to my nose. I kept my eyes on her face as my tongue darted out and licked her digits. She tasted fresh and sweet. A single sample wasn't anywhere close to enough to satisfy me.

She froze as I cleaned her essence off her hand. Her eyes half closed, her chest heaved, and her nipples poked through the thin robe. I could smell her fresh desire. She wasn't immune to me. That gave me hope.

"Did you think of me when you fingered yourself? Did you moan my name as you came?" I licked her again, wishing I could drop to my knees and drown in her juices. I nearly did just that, but Audrey surprised me.

She jerked away, and the door slammed in my face. I fought my instinct to break down the door and chase her down. I rested my head against the smooth wood and sighed. "Audrey. Audrey, this isn't easy."

A finger tapped my shoulder, and I turned my head to see a teenage girl looking at me—by the smell of her, a wolf—and I almost snarled. I was so focused on Audrey I hadn't noticed her creeping up on me.

She looked like she belonged on a farm somewhere with her cowboy boots and hat. She rolled her eyes and held out her phone so I could see what she wrote.

Your game sucks. Flowers aren't going to fix this.

She pulled her phone back and began typing away before turning it once more.

Try being a little more conscious of her feelings instead of yours. It's obvious what you want.

I rolled my eyes. "What does a teenage girl know?"

"So much for subtle." She lifted a brow and crossed her arms. "I'm not the one on the wrong side of the door with raging pheromones making the air difficult for others to breathe. Try being sensitive male instead of primitive male. It might work better."

"Iris." A college-aged male version of the teen, right down to the boots, stood at the top of the stairs. "I thought you wanted to see if the slopes were open yet."

"Coming, Theo." She shook her head at me. "You need work."

I watched her go down the stairs and the man, another unfamiliar wolf shifter, tipped his hat at me. "Sorry about her. She's a romantic at heart. Good luck with your girl." He disappeared down the stairs.

I was almost embarrassed by the altercation. I'd never expected getting my mate to like me would be so hard. As a rule, mates understood and accepted they belonged together, but Audrey was different.

"Audrey." I rested my hand on the door, and my words died on my tongue. That smart-ass kid's snark still echoed in the air. "Audrey, I'm sorry. You're beautiful, and . . . I lost my head. I can't promise control. I wish I could."

"What do you want?" She sounded like she leaned against the door from the other side.

"I thought we could go out. Like on a date. Get to know each other." My cat and dick both protested any form of delay, but Audrey needed to be handled with kid gloves. The teen, Iris, was right about that. If Audrey ran from the town, I would have no future.

"Shifters don't date." Curiosity tinged her voice.

I frowned. "How do you know?"

"I stayed in a commune for a while around Lake Tahoe. They tried to help me figure out why I couldn't shift. It was . . . educating, among other things."

The way she hesitated, I thought there might be more story behind the commune experience. "Well, if you change your mind and would like to skip the human ritual—" My cat agreed with that line of thinking.

The door popped open a second, and Audrey snatched the flowers out of my hand. "Come back in six hours." The door slammed again.

I rested a hand on the door and shook my head. I wanted to push the issue. I didn't want to wait, but . . . Audrey wanted me to come back later. Her agreement was progress, wasn't it?

Bemused, I conceded and made for the stairs. At least I had secured the date. If I could convince her our lives depended on our bond, the pain in my chest might be resolved by the time the moon rose.

"If you had asked," Sindi began when she spotted me on the stairs, "I'd have told you she didn't come in until around four. She went out to Silk last night."

That explained her request for six hours. Audrey was going back to bed. I wished my mind hadn't conjured the image of her in bed, touching herself, while thinking of me. I had no doubt she thought of me. I certainly did a lot of thinking about her. If we didn't come to terms soon, I might lose my damn mind before the end of the week.

"Good luck." Sindi's laughter followed me out.

Audrey was being a stubborn ass. I was going to need all the luck I could get.

~

AUDREY

I SIPPED my black coffee as Nicholas stirred sugar and cream in his. He sat across from me at a little table in front of the windows at Coffee Haven. After yesterday's vicious slap of agony when Nicholas left, I intended to keep my distance, yet here I was. A headache that bordered on migraine remained, and I had a feeling it would be with me until I did something about the man.

Nicholas wasn't hard to look at. I blamed his prettiness for my inability to fall right back to sleep after he left. Hours later, I could still feel his tongue on my hand, and imagine all the better ways it could be put to use. My panties soaked through at the very idea of his tongue on my clit, and I averted my gaze when his eyes landed on me. Damn the man's sense of smell. The damn flowers were at fault for my decision to go on a date. I should have stayed in bed with all my dirty thoughts and the privacy to release the tension they created.

With all the traveling I did, getting to know someone was impractical, and I missed out on the little nuances of certain rituals. Shifters didn't date, but they did show affection. The flowers—now in a place of honor on the little desk in my room—softened me more than I cared to admit. Before I could think of how to start the conversation we needed to have, an older woman stopped next to our table.

"Hello, Nicholas dear." The older lady set down a plate with two muffins on it.

"Hello, Ms. Half-Moon. What can I do for you?" Nicholas smiled and leaned back in his chair.

The old woman's eyes landed on me a moment before focusing on Nicholas. "Oh, nothing, sweetheart. I brought you some muffins. I wanted to thank you for all the hard work you put in for this community. It seems every time something happens, there you are, swooping in for the rescue. You and the sheriff, of course."

The woman placed her hand on Nicholas's shoulder. For some reason, that single action rubbed me wrong, and I was ready to tear into the old lady for touching him. I took a deep breath. Nicholas was his own person. Despite the pull to him, I had no claim.

"I am a licensed paramedic. It's kind of in the job description, Ms. Half-Moon." Nicholas sipped his coffee. When he glanced in my direction over the rim, he winked.

"Well, we're lucky to have you." Ms. Half-Moon squeezed Nicholas's shoulder, and I ground my teeth. She smiled at me. "Who is this lovely young lady?"

"Audrey." I forced a smile, trying hard not to bare my teeth at the woman. "I've only recently come to town."

"Well, welcome to Havenwood Falls, honey. Have you had a chance to wander around and take in our wonderfully eccentric town? You should show her around, Nicholas." She let go of Nicholas and turned to fully face me.

"Just between us—" Nicholas touched Ms. Half-Moon's arm to get her attention and lowered his voice— "someone mentioned an end-of-the-year fundraiser for the public services and I overheard it could be a bachelor auction. All the single public servants are supposed to be participating. I heard the sheriff complain, but promised to do his duty, if it does occur."

"Oh, my, well." Ms. Half-Moon fanned her reddening face. "That would be . . . swell." She glanced at the watch on her wrist. "Oh, look at that. I'm sorry to cut this short, dearies, but I've got a girls' date set up with Irene for this afternoon. I'm going to be late."

"Of course, Ms. Half-Moon. You have a good time. You tell Irene I said hello." His grin widened when she fluttered a wave at him and hurried out of the coffee shop.

I narrowed my eyes at him. "You said that on purpose."

Nicholas rolled his eyes. "She was only over here for you. I've bought you some time before she comes back to snoop some more. There's very little that goes on in Havenwood Falls that she doesn't know about."

"So, how did she not know about the auction?"

Nicholas reached for a muffin and sniffed it. "Banana nut. The auction isn't official yet. It's one of many ideas we're throwing around for fundraising this year. It may not even happen. Though, now that Biddie knows, it has a better chance."

I took the other muffin on the plate when he pushed it my way. "Aren't you worried?"

He lifted a brow. "No. If we don't mate, I'll be dead before then. So will you. And if we do mate, I won't be single."

I choked on the muffin and grabbed my coffee to wash it down. "You don't know that."

Nicholas tapped a finger against his temple. "The pain hasn't gone away. How long do you think we have until it drives one of us, or both of us, mad? What do you think happens to an out of control shifter?"

I opened my mouth to respond, but closed it.

The commune shifters called them ferals. Ferals were collared and caged. Lawbreakers were put in the cage with them. No one came out of a cage alive. Not even the feral. I didn't know what would happen in Havenwood Falls, but since I'd already met the sheriff, I could guess. He didn't take a threat to Havenwood Falls lightly.

"Come on. This is only one shop on the square. Havenwood Falls is actually a really nice little town." Nicholas stood and stretched.

"I saw a nail salon in the plaza. I wanted to get my nails painted before going back to work tonight." I followed him out, holding what remained of my coffee.

I debated stepping away when he placed a hand on the small of my back, but it felt like a petty move. Besides, a simple touch wouldn't hurt anything, would it? I pretended the ever present migraine didn't fade when he touched me.

"We can go that way." When Nicholas paused to put his sunglasses on, the hairs on the back of my neck stood up.

I scanned the area. Despite not having a shift, my senses were keen and had never let me down before. A few people walked on the sidewalk, but nothing seemed out of sorts. Across the street in the square, a couple of blond teens wrestled on the snow and a few others threw a football back and forth. The scene looked completely normal.

"Something wrong?" Nicholas gave a cursory glance over the area.

"It's silly. Felt like I was being watched." I tried pushing the feeling away, but I still couldn't get past the sensation. I stepped away from his hand, suddenly uncomfortable with the idea of him touching me in public. The immediate return of the mild headache made me almost regret the action.

"Probably are." Nicholas turned in the direction of the plaza and set off at a stroll without comment on my action. "You're a new face in town, and I haven't been seen with a woman since a close friend of mine died. I wouldn't take it seriously."

"I'm sorry about your friend." I couldn't think of anything else to say. Instead I reached out for his hand and squeezed his fingers. When I pulled my hand back, Nicholas held on.

"It's in the past." Nicholas's tone hardened. "It won't happen again."

We walked hand in hand, in silence for a moment. It almost felt normal, and my heart cracked. I couldn't have normal—*I* wasn't normal—but he deserved it.

"Why haven't you called me instead of walking to work?" Nicholas hit the crosswalk button on the street light.

"The walk is fine." I shrugged and wished the light would turn faster.

"You're injured."

"You're stubborn. Pick your battles, Nicholas. You're not going to win this one."

"I could walk with you if you insist on walking. You could catch a ride with one of the other employees." He canted his body to look down at me.

"We're walking now, and I'm fine." I resisted the urge to growl at him. The man was a nuisance at times.

"It's not as far as Silk."

I nearly ran forward when the light finally cleared us to walk. The sensation of being watched faded when we crossed the block and passed the apartment buildings. Despite being out on the public sidewalk, our stroll felt more intimate than it should have been.

"Thank you for Melaina's information." I changed the subject, hoping he would let the topic of my transportation go.

"Sure. I do little odds and ends stuff for her brother, Savage, and Liam, who's like a brother to her, works on a voluntary basis with me. She's always looking for good help, according to the guys." Nicholas waved when someone shouted his name but kept walking.

"You sure are popular." I sniffed and wished I hadn't.

With him this close, I got a nose full of his scent. He smelled delicious, like sin and smoke. The aroma went to my head like a drug. All the things we could do together raced through my mind and made the body aches I thought I had under control return full force.

Nicholas leaned over and whispered in my ear. "I don't know what you're thinking about, but unless you're trying to get me to fuck you in a back alley, you need to stop."

I blinked and took a calming breath through my suddenly dry mouth. I hadn't realized we had stopped walking or that my heart raced a mile a minute. I felt my cheeks heat under Nicholas's scrutiny, but didn't look at him as I began moving again. "Sorry."

"What were you thinking about?" He didn't miss a beat and grabbed my hand before I got too far from him.

"Doesn't matter. You said you wanted me to stop thinking about it." We turned into the plaza as I wiped my mind blank of all salacious thoughts.

"I changed my mind." He didn't let go when I tugged on my hand.

"Well, too late." I reached for the door to the salon, but Nicholas beat me to it.

"Ladies first." He let my hand go and followed to the reception desk.

The shop was relatively empty. I noted the woman getting a pedicure, and two others getting nails done. In Reno, the nail salons were never empty; it was a welcome change.

"Welcome. What service today?" The technician seemed a little annoyed, if the way she flipped her dark hair to reveal the neon red underneath was any indication. To my relief, her accent wasn't so heavy she couldn't be understood.

I held out my hand to show the grown out nails. "Just a manicure."

"One manicure. You get anything?" The technician looked over at Nicholas.

"Not today." Nicholas dug out some cash and handed the bills to the technician. "But I'm more than happy to pay for my lady."

I sputtered as the technician accepted the cash. "You can't just . . . I'm not your lady."

"Pick color, and come to table four." The technician waved a hand at the double-sided wall of nail polish bottles between the waiting area and the manicure tables before moving away.

"You are, and I can. Get over it." Nicholas walked over to the nail polishes.

"I don't think you understand." I grabbed his arm when Nicholas ignored me to pick up colors and compare them.

My breath caught when he turned his head and met my gaze. I felt butterflies in my stomach and couldn't move when he leaned over close enough to kiss me, if he wanted to.

"This isn't going away, kitten. No matter how much you want it to. Get used to it. You need to wrap your head around it? Fine, but there's a ticking clock on how long you can pretend you don't feel the draw." His breath tickled my face, and I couldn't stop myself from leaning in a little.

He stepped back and handed me a bottle of polish. "I like this one."

I shook off the haze of need he created, and accepted the bottle.

Instead of arguing with him, I studied the color. I wanted to argue, to tell him he was wrong, but . . . But the ache in my soul, the nagging headache, and my uncontrollable reaction when in proximity to him said otherwise.

The bronze was somewhere between metallic and glitter. A perfect, low key, autumn color. I hated that he knew what I wanted without me saying anything. Frustration, fear, and sorrow all mixed together, and tears welled in my eyes.

"I just don't understand." I sat down at the table where the technician waited.

"I am Dao. Hands in water. Real nails or acrylic?" Dao accepted the bottle of color and pulled out tools while my hands soaked.

"You said you stayed in a commune." Nicholas lowered his voice and tipped his chin at the women two tables over as he sat in the vacant chair next to me. "Non-supes."

"These are real." I focused on Dao instead of looking at Nicholas. I matched his lowered tone. "Yes, but there were a handful of . . . mixed couples—primarily ignored—but for the most part, like with like. And no one talked to me about mating. We talked about why I couldn't shift and how to fix that."

"We have the same soul animal, I'm sure of that." Nicholas shrugged. "I don't care whether you do or not, but for some reason you're fixated on the fact you can't shift."

"It's taboo. You need a strong mate that can provide strong children." I scowled at him.

"Out here anything goes, and if we met out there, it would be the same. Fate has spoken. You're swimming against the current, Audrey."

"I don't understand how you can just accept. How is it fair that we don't have a choice?" I shook my head. How could he be so accepting? We were strangers.

"We have a legend in China." Dao spoke softly and clearly, startling me. She reached up into her bob and pulled out a long red hair. "It is said the god Yue Lao ties the red string of fate to those that are destined." Dao made tiny slip knots in each end of the strand. She looped one end over the pinky finger of my right hand and the other end over Nicholas's left pinky when he set his hand on the table at her gesture. "The string can stretch and twist, but it will never break. You complain about choice, but the gods have chosen you for each other. No one knows you better then they. Some of us will never have what you do here. Not because it doesn't exist, but because we never get the chance to meet. The Americans call it something else—soul mates."

"Nothing is forever." I jerked my hand and was surprised when the thin hair held and didn't break.

Dao smiled. "It can stretch and twist, but you cannot break the gods' will. You are destined, and for your species, that is forever."

"We don't know each other," I growled and pulled on my hand again. Still the hair stubbornly remained whole. Did she have steel hair?

"You have forever to learn what the gods already know." Dao took my hand and unlooped the hair from my finger and Nicholas's.

Before I could sort my thoughts, a siren went off, making me jolt. Nicholas cursed and pulled out a cell phone. The noise stopped when he swiped the screen. He scanned the screen and sighed.

"I have to go. Duty calls. Be good for Dao." He leaned over and placed an innocent kiss on the top of my head as he stood.

I watched him walk away, and a vise clamped around my heart. He paused at the door before stepping out. The stabbing pain was instant. My eyes closed, and I focused on breathing through the invisible agony.

"The gods do not like to be ignored." Dao's voice penetrated through the fog.

"I suppose not." I kept my eyes closed as Dao worked. The pain wasn't as bad as last time. Maybe the fact that he hadn't really touched me kept the pain to a minimum.

I wished I had someone I could talk to about it. Even if I was in the commune, no one there would talk about it. They made it seem that without the shift, the mate bond would never happen. Never in my life did I feel more alone.

CHAPTER 7

NICHOLAS

*T*he call hadn't been a major one, but I left Audrey to stew in her thoughts for a while instead of returning to her side like I wanted. She had an inferiority complex she needed to get past. For both our sakes.

As I pulled into Silk's parking lot, I saw Audrey step off the gondola platform and walk along the edges of the pavement. My timing couldn't have been better, if she was on a break. I hurried to park and intercept her on her walk.

Audrey's unique smell drew me like a moth to a flame. I could find her blindfolded if I was so inclined. She could likely do the same for me if she wanted to. When her posture stiffened, I smiled. She *could* sniff me out if she wanted to.

"How's your night going?" I matched my stride to hers and was secretly delighted I didn't have to check my steps any.

Audrey sighed and rubbed her temples. She subtly shifted away and her musk filled the air. Her physical response to my proximity gave me hope for our future. In my experience, there was only so long lust could be ignored.

"It isn't going to go away that way." I stepped in front of her and held out my hand.

Audrey stared at my hand and shook her head. "It's not a good idea."

"It's the only idea, Audrey. We're running out of time. My cat's growing more and more impatient. I don't think I'll be in control by the end of the week." My voice dropped, mindful that not everyone in the area was supernatural.

I hated admitting I wasn't in full control, but mating was an act between two. Even if I broke the promise to myself and forced her hand, she had to be willing for the deal to seal.

Her eyes darted to my face, searching. I waited while she studied me. After a long moment of hesitation, she dropped her hand into my waiting one.

My eyes drifted closed, and some of the tension faded from my muscles. "I need you to make a decision. I need to know if I should be saying goodbye to my family and turning myself in to Ric. I don't want to put the town in danger because I'm out of control."

Her voice shook a little. "What if I left?"

My eyes snapped open. "Are you out of your fucking mind? The cat is difficult to control now. If you leave . . . there's no pretense of control."

Audrey flinched. "I just thought—"

I pinned her against the closest car, pressing my body against hers. My cock stood at attention, hard and aching against her pelvis. A startled gasp escaped her, allowing me to dip in and plunder her parted lips with my tongue. One of us moaned, and Audrey's free hand fisted the fabric of my shirt.

The parking lot was lit, but not well enough that I worried much about the bouncer at the gondola seeing us, nor did I worry about some random club-goer. Since the club still had several business hours remaining, I doubted anyone would come along and catch us in a publicly indecent position.

I pressed my entire body against hers, never releasing her mouth, needing more contact. I could feel the desperation in myself, and wanted her to feel just as out of control. I needed her to feel as needy as I did.

I nipped her bottom lip with my teeth as I ran kisses down the side of her neck. "I've changed my mind. I'm not going to let you kill us. You come to me within twenty-four hours. If not, I'm coming to you. No more running away, Audrey. And don't even fucking think about leaving."

"I don't— I can't—" The haze of lust blurred her eyes, and I kissed her again, because I could.

My hand drifted down along the tight black shirt she wore and teased the edges of the fabric where it rode up away from her pants. She shuddered when my fingers touched her bare flesh and automatically shifted, opening her stance a little more when my fingers teased under the waistband of her pants.

"Nicholas."

I wasn't sure if my name was a prayer or a curse when my hand dipped deeper into her pants and cupped her dripping pussy. A low growl rumbled in my chest as I ran a finger through slick folds. When I rubbed her clit in a hard circle, Audrey gasped, her head fell back, and her hands grabbed at my waist. I pressed the little button a little harder, and she moaned, thrusting her hips against my hand.

"You're not exactly fighting me off, kitten." My tongue traced the curve of her ear. "As much as I would love to drag you home and claim you right now, I think Melaina would skin me and use me for a rug if I tried. She's not a woman to cross."

As much as it hurt me to, I pulled away, stepping back far enough to release myself from her hold. Audrey's hand lifted to reach out, before she caught herself and pulled back. I watched her struggle to contain her desire.

When she finally found her voice, her tone was soft and unsteady. "You deserve better."

I shook my head. "I deserve you."

"You don't know me." She didn't push me away when I rested my forehead against hers.

"I trust my instincts. You should trust yours more. If you want, just think of it as an arranged marriage. I'll even get you a human ring if you want. Those kind of arrangements are still in practice today." My kiss was gentle, teasing . . . promising but no less potent. I consumed her, knowing she would taste me long after I left her for the night.

When I pulled away, I felt drugged and muddled. "Twenty-four hours, kitten. I will come find you. We can't keep doing this, and I have no intentions of dying this young."

I walked back to my truck, aching with need and demand. The cat pressed against my will, fighting for control. We'd go for a run, and hopefully that would soothe the beast enough for tonight. I couldn't look back at her as I left her behind.

~

AUDREY

I waved at my last customer as Emiko escorted him away from my bar. Other than the constant ache in my muscles, which was completely Nicholas's fault, I had a good night. My heavy pocket promised a good tip amount, and every little bit would be needed if Joshua found the decent vehicle he promised.

The to-do list ran through my head as I cleaned up and closed down the VIP bar. Maybe I could avoid Nicholas, somehow, and let all this fade and blow over. The thought of him made my entire body pulse and ache. The pounding in my head increased—a little more insistent. I closed my eyes and took a deep breath, focusing on the rest of my things to do instead of the man.

After I took the dirties to the kitchen, picked up some cleans, and came back to the bar, I found Melaina waiting on a stool. My boss made everyone work hard, but she was fair. Despite not knowing much about her, I liked the always gorgeous woman.

"Hey, boss. You need me?" I grinned as I put the tray of clean glasses on the bar and refilled the station. Despite my smile, being alone with her made me edgy, and I couldn't quite put my finger on why.

"The bouncers have noticed your habit of walking to and from work." Melaina crossed her arms, her gaze traveling over me as though drinking me in. Even without meaning to, the woman exuded sex, which didn't help the ache in my already needy body. "How long do you plan on being in Havenwood Falls?"

My brows drew together as I reset the alcohol bottles. "I'll be here a while. The insurance is being difficult. I have to pay for a new car and . . ." I didn't say his name, but I needed to figure out what to do about the driving need to be with Nicholas. Pretty soon, I'd be humping his leg instead of wetting my panties every time he was close.

"And you have a mate you're refusing to accept. You want to fuck him, but for some reason, you deny him and yourself." Melaina's nostrils flared, as though she could smell the desire on me, and she held up a hand before I could even begin to protest. "Nicholas Jordan is an asset to this community. Denying a mate ends in death for both parties. You do know that, right?"

I shrugged and winced at the throbbing reminder that my shoulder was still healing. A real shifter would have healed by now. It was another reminder I wasn't good enough for Nicholas. "I don't want to cause any trouble, Melaina. Nicholas is mistaken. Fate wouldn't bind him to an orphan mate with no shift. As the asset to the community you say he is, we both know he deserves better than me."

Melaina tilted her head. "Who are you to decide if fate is wrong or right? But I digress. You're walking, alone, which isn't smart by the way, back and forth to Whisper Falls Inn."

I looked away from my boss and went back to my work. Since she knew about the car accident, I didn't see a point in reminding her about the lack of transportation. "It's a nice walk. I don't know where the running paths are, so the walk is a good way to stay in shape."

Melaina's perfectly polished nails tapped on the wooden bar top, and her face was unreadable. Something about the seriousness of her expression set me on edge. The boss, while serious, wasn't usually difficult for me to read.

My stomach pitched, and I forced my hands to go still before Melaina could see them shaking. "Am I being fired?"

"I could. If I did, I'd ask Savage to go with you to the inn, pack your bags, and take you out to Durango." Melaina looked down at the phone in her hand and sent a couple of text messages while I digested the statement.

Icy fingers ran down my spine. "You're going to force me to leave?"

"I could . . . but that would be disastrous. Not just for Silk." She smiled in a way that made me shift from foot to foot. The woman was up to something, but what, she kept to herself. "You're done for the night, right?" Melaina glanced around the bar. "Good job. Come." The way she said it, with her always sultry voice and the seductive twist of her body, the word sounded like an order to orgasm, and I could easily imagine many people—regardless of gender—doing so on her simple command. She just had that way about her. Then she added more curtly, "With me."

With dread pitting in my stomach, I grabbed my purse from under the bar and followed. What would I do if Melaina did have me taken out of town? What *could* I do? Would the insurance still pay out? I hadn't asked if I had to stay in place; I only assumed I did. And it wasn't like I had anywhere to go anyway.

What about Nicholas? Would he follow and leave Havenwood Falls without his service? His control was already slipping. Would he survive long enough to find me again?

Melaina sighed and glanced over her shoulder. "You're not being fired, Audrey. Your anxiety is giving me a headache."

"If I'm not being fired, where are we going?" I climbed onto the gondola with Melaina and stood next to the window so I could see the town as we descended. The lights were as beautiful as they were the first time.

Melaina's brows rose. "You know, so many don't enjoy the view. Such a pity. I find it a turn-on."

"Most are drunk or easily sickened by the motion."

"Touché." Melaina typed away on her phone as we descended to the parking lot.

At the bottom, I jumped out as soon as the doors opened. The bouncer nodded when I passed him and waited at the bottom of the platform stairs for Melaina. Tension still coursed through my muscles; I didn't like surprises.

I turned toward the trees on the east side of the parking lot. Nicholas was there, just beyond the tree line. I didn't see him, but could feel his presence.

"He waits for you, does he?" Melaina tipped her chin toward the trees I stared at.

I began to deny it, but the subtle movement in the trees answered Melaina for me.

"I don't suppose you noticed your entire body automatically turned in his direction when you stepped off the gondola? This way." Melaina pulled out a set of keys, and the headlights of a chrome Navigator flashed. "Probably good I drove the truck. There was a mention of snow in the forecast, but the weather has been contrary."

I said nothing about the monstrous vehicle as I climbed up into it. There was nothing about the SUV I identified as a truck. I fidgeted as Melaina drove toward the inn. "Can I ask what's going on?"

"You're staying at the inn. Not an inexpensive choice of housing. You need to save money for a car."

I gazed out the window without answering. Melaina didn't need to know about the check-in debacle. "I didn't see any cheaper rentals in the paper. And with the ski season upon us, I'm likely not going to find anything else affordable."

"False. My girls are important to me. Happy girls make happy employees. Happy employees make for really good business. I'm a fair business owner and a shrewd enough woman to know what drives my market. There's a room for rent in one of the houses I own in town. It's closer to work in a way; you can cut through the forest without Jordan having to stalk you from its shadows. If you choose. You could also ignore him altogether by following the streets." Melaina pulled into the parking lot for Whisper Falls Inn. "Pack up, check out. Don't take all morning. I have other things to do."

I turned to my boss instead of climbing out of the car. "Melaina, I really appreciate the offer—"

Melaina's smile was predatory. "It's not up for discussion. If you want to stay in town, go get your bags. My brother isn't that difficult for me to get a hold of. Your decision, of course."

With the second ultimatum of the night hanging over my head, I couldn't do anything else but comply. I sighed as I got out and went into the inn. I didn't have much to pack up—the trunk was still mostly packed, and I always put away the electronics at the end of my day, so nothing was left out. Checking out took more time than carting my things down the stairs. I tucked the receipt in my purse to give to Nicholas when I saw him next.

Melaina said nothing about the light amount of luggage I piled into the backseat of the Navigator. She put the SUV in drive before I had my seat belt back on. She began talking when we were back on Main Street. "Rent is four hundred a month for your room. You don't share the room, and all the furnishings are provided. There's a jack-and-jill bathroom you'll share with Liberty, who's in the room next to yours. Rent includes all utilities and a cleaning service that cleans the main areas of the house twice a week. Your room is your responsibility. I expect you to respect my property in the same manner you respect the bar property."

My head whirled as Melaina navigated through the streets of Havenwood Falls.

"Of course." I couldn't think of anything else to say.

"You can choose to pay me from your tips in cash, or I can take it from your check. Check would be an after-tax deduction. The girls rotate cooking for each other. I expect you to be sociable and pull your weight. You'll do your own laundry—there's a washer and dryer off the kitchen. There is no fighting in my house. If I hear of it, you're out. If you have a situation that is tense—you are all girls, after all, so it's bound to happen—I expect you to address it like responsible adults." Melaina pulled into a driveway and threw the SUV in park.

"Makes sense. I guess just take it out of my check." I stared up at the house. The porch light illuminated enough of the house to notice it looked like a normal two-story home with a bright fire-engine-red door. I looked around, and the house looked typical of an off-downtown area. "Where are we? I'm not really familiar with town."

"We're on McFeeny. The schools are at the end of the street to the west. Work is also to the west, and the town square is at the end of the street to the east. You'll get used to it. I don't restrict guests—you are grown adults—but I expect you to be respectful of each other's space and business. I honestly don't expect you to live out here more than a few days, but we'll see. Any other questions?" Melaina turned in her seat to look at me.

"No. Not really." I gazed up at the house instead of at Melaina. She wouldn't care if I voiced distress over living with other people, so why bother? In the past, I never made any friends or stuck around long enough to be memorable. And the nightmares—what would happen the first time I woke up screaming?

"One of the private room managers has the master bedroom on the first floor. He's gayer than George Takei, so you don't have to worry about that. Even as a manager at work, he has no authority to overstep in my house. You let me know if he does, but the girls generally love him." Melaina pulled out her phone and rapid-fired a text.

"Okay." There was nothing else to say. I jumped out and grabbed my stuff from the back. Sometimes the sad stack of belongings made me angry I didn't have more. In the present moment, however, I was grateful I didn't have to ask for help.

When I was two steps from the front door, it swung open, and a bronze-skinned woman stood in its frame. Her pants were so tight, her ovaries should hold a protest. She cracked a piece of gum before smiling. "Welcome. I'm Liberty."

The Navigator tooted, and the woman waved around me. For the half second of motion, I caught a glimpse of a long curly ponytail. "Let's get you in and settled. Melaina sent a text. Come on in."

Liberty stepped back, holding the door. Her smile never wavered. I straightened my shoulders and stepped inside. I could learn to be a friend. How hard could it be to deal with people in the house day in and day out? I already missed the noisy room at the inn.

CHAPTER 8

AUDREY

*L*iberty took the suitcase before leading the way through the house. She waved at a couple of girls in the kitchen before they climbed the stairs. "They work in the private areas of Silk. You'll probably only ever see them at home."

"Okay." After the work night, and Nicholas's havoc, I was too tired to hold a conversation. Thankfully, Liberty kept moving, and I only had a moment to nod an acknowledgment.

"Here's your room." Liberty opened a door and waited for me to enter.

I glanced around before setting the trunk next to the dresser. The room was an almost identical copy to the inn—bed, dresser, nightstand. The colors were different, and the room itself might have been a little smaller, but it was homey.

"Bathroom's through here." Liberty opened a door next to the closet doors. "I've already cleaned up for the morning. You can use it."

"Thanks." I knelt next to the trunk and popped it open.

Liberty sat cross-legged on the bed and watched. "Girl, your pheromones are crazy high."

My hand fisted on the nightshirt I reached for. I gave Liberty a glance. "What?"

"Pheromones. No wonder Melaina has you up front. You'd drive a supe crazy inside five minutes. How can you stand being that horny? Why haven't you taken your mate? I mean, I assume that's why your pheromones are off the chart. That's the only reason a shifter's pheromones go crazy. That and the mating season. Oh my goddess, are you in heat?"

Fire burned in my cheeks, and I could only stare at her.

Liberty crossed her arms. "We're all some kind of supernatural in the house. Secrets are a bit harder to keep here."

"I can't be in heat. I don't have a shift. And I obviously don't have a mate, for that same reason."

Liberty tipped her head. "From my understanding, you don't have to be a shifter to be a shifter's mate. The right human can be a mate."

I shifted my gaze away. "Nicholas said nearly the same thing."

"Nicholas? As in Jordan, the sexy paramedic?"

"You know him?" I turned and faced Liberty.

"Of him. The MC guys know him, but he's not actually part of the MC. Around the time I arrived in town, he left for Denver to get his state certification. I don't know the rules inside and out, but I'm pretty sure he had to get special permission to leave and come back. He'll probably get the same permission when it comes time for renewal."

"Oh. MC? What's that?" I hated asking, but better to be in the know than in the dark.

"Motorcycle club. I dated one of the guys on-again, off-again for a bit. For beings of questionable morals, they still retain some virtues. Sort of." Liberty rubbed her arms and stood up. "Look at me. Jabbering away and you still haven't showered or changed yet. I'll leave you to it. See you in a few hours."

Liberty walked out through the bathroom, leaving me to wonder what just happened. I was by no means an expert in relationships, but I would swear on my savings Liberty had a relationship problem. I had my own relationship problems, and didn't need to borrow any more.

I stared at the door Liberty disappeared through, and then the bed. I was bone-tired and wondered if some silent goddess I didn't know about would be offended if I just climbed in and dropped to sleep. Or at least tried to drop to sleep. I almost prayed for nightmares, instead of the perpetual state of lust.

Sighing with a little regret, I climbed to my feet with my toiletries and entered the bathroom. I didn't marvel at the double sink, or deep porcelain tub. I wanted to wash and pass out.

Seconds into the shower, the bathroom door creaked. "How's the water?"

I rolled my eyes. "Wet?"

"Good. Hopefully hot, too. With five of us in the house, the hot water doesn't usually survive after the back-to-back showers." Through the frosted shower curtain, I watched Liberty sit down in her doorway.

"What are you doing?" I tried not to be embarrassed by the lack of privacy.

"Talking to you. I did some thinking."

"In the whole two minutes we've been apart?" I returned my attention to my shower, since Liberty was set on staying and talking. I was careful with the soap. As I learned yesterday morning, orgasm did not provide relief—it only made the desire worse.

"I'm like the mother hen here. All the girls will say it. I'm even called Mom on occasion. It doesn't bother me in the least, and honestly I think everyone's happy with me as the house mom figure. You seem like a nice person, and down to earth, but I gotta say, I'm confused why Melaina would let you stay here with us." Liberty propped her arms up on her knees.

I froze in the shower. "What do you mean?"

"You're deliberately ignoring a mate. The longer you're here, the more dangerous the situation gets. I mean, how long do you think it's going to take before primal instincts take over? You're shifters. You're as much animal as human, and sometimes the animal is more prominent."

"I don't have a shift." My voice shook.

"But he does. Nick's a nice guy, I guess, but do you think the mountain lion is going to care who it rips through to get to you?"

"We were going to talk tonight." The statement wasn't a complete lie. I did hope to talk to Nicholas tonight.

"Why wait? Put something sexy on. Only that, and I'll let you borrow my trench. And then I'll drive you over to Nick's."

I chewed my lip. "I said talk. I'm not at a point in my life where I'm ready for a long-term relationship, let alone a mate. Besides, I don't own anything sexy. And I don't know where he lives."

Liberty laughed and shook her head. "Do you think mates just pop up out of the blue? You're drawn to each other, like two magnets. You came to Havenwood Falls, which means, whether you consciously think you're ready or not, subconsciously, you were always heading in his direction anyway."

"Are you a shifter?"

"I'm an equal opportunist. And I've been around a while. You don't live in close quarters with a species without getting to know them. But a direct answer would be I went to school with shifters. I've dated a few, and I've buried a few." Her voice grew somber. "Life is short for most. I know it better than a lot of other supes. Take what fate has given you with both hands, Audrey. You won't get a second chance."

Something about the way she said it struck a chord in me. "You were mated to one, weren't you? And you buried him."

Liberty stood up. "Every woman has something sexy. And it's a small town. Someone is bound to know how to find Nicholas. I'll do some research while you're finishing up."

"What if I don't want him as a mate?" The words popped out before I could consider them, and I watched Liberty stop in her tracks and face the shower.

Liberty crossed her arms. "After everything I said, really? I'll humor you. Why do you even think that's an option?"

"I—" I didn't have an answer. All my life I'd been treated like an experiment by other shifters, or a freak by humans when I tried to blend in—and failed. I was never once given a chance to be normal— as normal as a shifter could be—by anyone.

"Listen, I'm going to go dig up an address. You think about it, and we'll talk some more when you're done." Liberty closed the door behind her, leaving me with my jumbled thoughts.

Three days summed up the total time I'd spent so far in Havenwood Falls. I wasn't sure why everyone expected me to make life-altering decisions in such a short amount of time. While I did travel a lot, I was more cautious than impulsive in my day-to-day actions. If I didn't come to terms sooner rather than later, Nicholas would pay the price for my hesitation.

I closed my eyes and lifted my face to the spray of water. The steady shower stream washed away the silent tears. My old life didn't belong in Havenwood Falls. There was really only one choice. I didn't have to like it, but it was the right thing to do.

I snapped off the water and reached for my towel. After wrapping up, I went in search of Liberty and found her on a laptop in her room. "Did you find an address?"

Liberty glanced up from the screen and smiled. "You'll need to get gussied up first. Let's find you something sexy to wear."

~

NICHOLAS

THE DRIVE HOME was usually the time I used to unwind from my day, and began to relax. When I pulled into the driveway, I sat for a while in the truck and studied the cabin of my ancestors. Never had it looked or felt empty before.

I climbed the stairs to my porch. My body ached, not from the hour at the gym or the five-mile run afterward. The tension and pain from my denied mate made my joints feel a hundred years old, not thirty.

My cat was beyond restless, but I didn't want to risk a shift. Giving the cat control, without being completely mated, wasn't a good idea anymore. This morning had been torturous, shifting back. I might not regain control if I tried that again. I scoffed at myself. That would be a perfect way to freak out Audrey.

Something was off. I paused with my hand on the door knob. My cat stood at attention.

The lack of mating was really messing with my head. I smelled Audrey, or at least thought I did. She wouldn't be out here, and she didn't know where I lived to come find me in a cabin in the woods.

I stepped into my home and stood silently in the doorway. No unnatural sounds came to my ears, but the furnace ran, creating enough noise to hide anything quieter. I closed the door and locked it. If someone tried to run, they wouldn't find the door as easily opened as when they entered.

The trench coat folded over the banister gave me pause. I fingered the material, and a familiar, feminine perfume rose. I closed my eyes and took a deep breath. Every muscle tensed, and the fatigue dropped away like icicles in the hot sun.

She was here. In my house.

I took the stairs two at a time. The master suite took up the entire loft area. The potency of her scent strengthened as I approached the sliding barn doors with butterflies in my stomach. When I caught sight of her, my legs froze, unable to move forward or run away.

Audrey sat on the edge of my bed wearing white thigh-high stockings, hooker heels to match, and nothing else. She locked eyes with me and with a saucy smile, leaned back on one arm, giving me an uncensored view of perky tits with nipples begging to be sucked on. Her other hand was busy playing between her spread legs.

"Do you know the problem with being mates with a stranger?" Her husky tone snapped me out of my stupor.

I couldn't find my voice, so I shook my head, my eyes never leaving the hand between her legs.

"That's just it. We're strangers. We know nothing about each other." Her head tipped, and her eyes closed.

"Audrey." My voice was rough, needy.

Her eyes snapped open, and her coy smile returned. "I'm no quaking virgin, Nicholas. If there's something you want . . ."

She didn't have to tell me twice. My clothes fell to the floor in the short distance between her and the door. I dropped to my knees in between her legs, shoving her hand away and burying my face in her dripping pussy.

Audrey gasped, and her hand fisted in my hair. Her hips flexed, and the long moan she emitted made my dick jump. "Not enough. Not enough."

She jerked on my hair hard enough to pull my face away and slide down the bed into my lap. My hands dropped to her hips, pulling her against me, rubbing all that sweet juice against my cock. She ran kisses over my shoulder and nipped my earlobe when she reached it.

"Fuck me, Nicholas. We can make love later. Fuck me now."

I didn't give her a chance to change her mind. Shifting slightly, I breached her tight cunt and thrust in to the hilt. We both groaned, and her arms came around me, nails digging into my back.

"Fuck, kitten. Fuck." My hands tightened on her hips, holding her still, and I buried my face against her neck, kissing and nipping the sensitive skin. I was closer than I wanted to be to finishing, and after days of denial and waiting, I wanted this to last.

"Nicholas." Audrey nipped at my ear and attempted to move. She whimpered when I held her still. Her nails dug harder into my back, and I could swear they felt like a cat's claws. "Move." She bit down on my ear lobe, all gentleness gone.

My control snapped, and I gave her exactly what she asked for. A hand slid up to cup her breast and toyed with the nipple as I pounded into her. Audrey met me thrust for thrust, whimpering and panting out her pleasure. She wrapped around me like ivy on a pole, her mouth everywhere she could reach at once.

Without warning, she fisted her hand in my hair, yanking my head to the side. "I'm going to . . ."

She didn't finish her sentence. Her body tensed, locking me against her as she reached her orgasm. Her teeth nibbled down my neck and blood rushed in my ears as she bit down with full force just above my collar bone.

I growled as my cock exploded, and bit her shoulder. Marking her, bonding to her, just as she had to me. Whether she knew that or not, her shifter instinct had taken over. We stayed locked together, shuddering through the post-orgasm spasms.

Audrey sighed and went limp in my arms. Her mouth pressed absent kisses to the spot she bit.

I nuzzled her jaw, pressing little kisses to her skin until I reached her mouth and could kiss her fully. I felt amazing, completed in a way I hadn't known was missing. I drew away to stare into her beautiful languid eyes. "We skipped a lot of steps."

Her mouth curved. "I have no complaints."

"Why did you change your mind?" I ran my hand through her tangled hair. I would never get tired of touching her.

Her fingers traced the green man tattoo on my pec and followed the tribal lines down my arm. "I missed this somehow."

"We were busy with other things." I cupped my hands around her butt and lifted us off the floor. She laughed, tightening her legs on my waist, and threw her arms around my neck.

"I feel like a weight's been removed. Like I was carrying an albatross I didn't know about." She stretched under me as I laid us down on the bed, like the cat I knew she was.

I wrapped around her, pulling her onto my chest, debating between a nap and slow lazy sex. She decided for us when she curled around me and pressed a light kiss to my pec. I smiled as her breathing evened out and she dropped into sleep.

As I followed her into dreamland, I realized she never answered my question. Not that it really mattered. She was mine, and I was hers. Anything else could be dealt with as needed.

AUDREY

I woke up in an empty bed. The sheets were still warm, so Nicholas couldn't have been out of bed long. My eyes found the clock, and I panicked to see it was almost eight. I had to be at work in an hour.

Something shivered under my skin when I jumped out of bed, and I paused to examine the feeling. My skin felt too tight, like it did when

I sunburned. There was no reason for the feeling, and I brushed it off, intent on finding Nicholas and hightailing it to work.

Two steps away from the bed, pain exploded in my head, and I dropped to my knees on the floor. My mouth opened to scream as pain like I'd never felt before erupted throughout my body and dropped me the rest of the way to the floor. My bones felt like they were shattering into pieces while my muscles ripped and shredded like paper.

"Breathe. Audrey, breathe." Nicholas came into my line of sight as I contorted on the floor. "Don't fight it, kitten. Breathe, let it wash over you."

He rested his hand against my cheek. "Come on, kitten, you can do it. Close your eyes. Don't fight it. Breathe and let go."

Easier said than done. I didn't know what was happening, and the pain brought me close to fainting. I reached out a hand to him, and was surprised to see claws where my fingernails were supposed to be.

"Breathe, Audrey. The first shift is always the hardest."

Shift? He said shift. I was shifting? How? Why now?

I closed my eyes as instructed and tried to "let go." But I didn't know exactly what I was supposed to be letting go of. I focused on my breathing. Maybe if I could reach a meditative state, it would help.

I don't know how long I lay on the floor, but at some point, I passed out. When I came to, Nicholas still sat next to me. I whimpered and tried to crawl over to him.

My movement caught his attention, and he smiled. "There's my pretty kitten. It might take a minute to adjust."

Adjust? I tried to stand and wobbled a moment . . . on four legs. Surprised, I turned and looked at myself, or attempted to.

Nicholas laughed. "Here, there's a full mirror in the walk-in, if you can manage it."

I shuffled and tripped on my own feet as I followed him to the walk-in closet. I huffed and shook my head before pushing back up to my feet and trying again. Was this what a child felt like learning to walk?

My ears twitched, as I could hear all sorts of things now. Nicholas's feet, while nearly silent to anyone else, were easy to discern. The birds nesting in the gutters. It was almost overwhelming, and I bumped his leg with my head.

He pointed to the mirror, and I studied the cougar staring back. The tips of my ears were darker than I remembered for a mountain lion. A different species maybe? What did Nicholas look like as a cat?

My eyes weren't all that different. The pupils had changed, but the golden coloring remained the same. I wondered if Nicholas was a blue-eyed cat. There was no way for me to ask at the moment.

The malachite pendant Addie gave me still rested against my breastbone. If I could shift now, did that mean my curse was broken and she could tattoo me now? The responsible thing to do was to call Addie.

"Okay, kitten. Time for the hard part." Nicholas stepped out of the closet, and I followed, curious as to what he could mean by "the hard part."

He sat on the floor and patted the spot next to him. "You need to shift back."

I balked. My ears lay flat, and I crouched against the floor. Shifting had been so painful the first time. I wasn't ready for that kind of pain again so soon.

Nicholas shook his head. "None of that. You've got to get used to shifting both ways. It gets easier each time. Come on. You can do it laying down as well. Focus on taking control back from the cat. For me, it's a box I put the cat into. Cats love boxes, you know. Set your cat in the box and take back your control."

I rested my weight on the cool wooden floors and did as asked. I didn't think a box would work, but I didn't want to think of it as a cage, either. Instead, I created a cat space in my mind, complete with cute cat tree and play toys.

Coaxing the cat into her play space was harder than I thought it would be. We'd never shifted before, and there was still so much to explore and do. Pain exploded a second time, but briefly, and I found myself shivering with sweat in Nicholas's arms.

"You did fabulous, kitten." He pressed kisses all over my face. "Let's get you washed and fed. Shifting takes a lot of energy."

I did feel weak and exhausted. "I'm supposed to work tonight."

"I've already called Melaina and explained. She didn't sound happy, but it's not like any of us could control your ability to shift." Nicholas picked me up off the floor and carried me into the bath. "We'll go for a run after you eat, and work on your shifting ability." He sat me on the toilet while he ran the water in the jacuzzi tub. "How do you feel?"

"Is it supposed to hurt?" I rubbed my hands up and down my still twinging arms.

Nicholas glanced over at me. "Shifters are stronger than humans for a reason. Yes, it does hurt, but the stronger your muscles are, the less painful the shift. I don't know why that is, probably has something to do with the way our bodies rearrange themselves for the animal. The shift won't ever truly be painless, but go to the gym, do some weight lifting, and you can lessen the pain."

I sighed. "I've always hated the gym."

He chuckled. "Not uncommon for a woman. Come on. Water's ready."

I stumbled when I stood, but Nicholas moved fast and grabbed my arm to steady me. He climbed into the tub with me, and I raised my brows at him. He only smiled and pressed a kiss to my temple.

"You're beautiful in both forms."

I turned and straddled his lap. "I want to see your cat."

Nicholas purred—not a sound I'd associate with a man, but it was sexy as hell—and pulled me closer. His erection rubbed against my thighs. "After."

I didn't ask him after what. Instead I lifted my hips and teased us both by rubbing the head of his cock against my entrance. His hands found my breasts and pinched my nipples.

"Tease." He groaned as I sank down only far enough to take the head of him in.

"Am I?"

"You're playing with fire, Audrey."

"No." I leaned forward and caught his bottom lip in my teeth. "I'm playing with what belongs to me."

Nicholas groaned as I sank down a little further. "Take what you want."

His words were strained, and I felt his muscles quiver under me. I loved that he fought himself to allow me to be in control, but I was done playing. I dropped down, pulling all of him into my heat. His hips thrust up before he stopped himself.

I ran my tongue over his lips and delighted when he tilted his head and let me have access to his mouth. I was done with teasing. I wanted his release. I wanted him to lose control, and I would have it.

CHAPTER 9

NICHOLAS

The woods around my house were the safest place for Audrey to run for the first time. I owned most of the area around the cabin—thanks to my ancestors—and other shifters were mindful of our territories. For the most part. In comparison to what McCabe, the bears, or any of the wolf packs had, it was a pitifully small slice of the pie, but I had never been dissatisfied with it.

Watching Audrey learn the other side of herself was a treat. She frolicked to and fro, taking in the night. I watched her attempt to catch a field mouse end in failure, but she didn't seem to mind, and I wasn't certain she intended on catching it to begin with. She might have just been playing with it.

If she wasn't so new in her form, I might have initiated more intimate actions as well, but we had time, plenty of it, for my dirty thoughts. I wondered if she would be repulsed by the idea. Shifters could and did have sex in either form, but some were prudes. My kitten, so far, was anything but a prude.

Audrey climbed a tree, and I lost sight and sound of her. She was excellent at stealth and needed very little coaching on the subject. I circled around, trying to figure out where she went. When I came back to the tree she originally climbed, I sat puzzled. Her scent circled around a couple of times, but there was no way I should have lost her so easily.

I heard a twig snap and had a split second to react as Audrey pounced from the trees above. She pinned me with mortifying ease and licked my nose. When she took off running, I followed, fully intending to pay her back. I huffed when she vanished again.

A rabbit's scent caught my attention, and mindful not to scare the animal, I hunted. The smell led me to a small clearing along the creek, where I found Audrey already on the trail. I hung back, waiting to see what she would do about the rabbit. We'd eaten before heading out, and while I could always eat again, I wanted to see if her instincts would allow her to eat the fresh rabbit, or if she'd simply play with it the way she had the mouse.

I didn't have a long wait. Catching her scent, the rabbit took off running down the creek bank. Audrey gave chase, and for the first time, I realized she was wicked fast. Cougars were fast sprinters on the whole, but she took it to another level.

She caught the little animal as it tried to cross the creek and audibly snapped its neck. With what could be called a happy trot, she brought the rabbit to me and dropped it at my feet.

I gave her a lick on the cheek for the successful kill. She pushed the rabbit with a foot toward me and tipped her head. She wanted me to have it.

Shrugging my shoulders, I stretched out and began my little feast. The rabbit was decently fat—no doubt ready for winter. Audrey sat nearby, cleaning between the toes of a front foot, seemingly satisfied with herself.

Without warning, she stood and growled. All the fur on her body stood on end. I paused my chomping and glanced in the direction of her attention. Two wolves stood down the creek a little, close enough to catch our attention but far enough not to be a threat yet. They were announcing themselves, politely, though Audrey didn't know that.

The Kasun wolves didn't often come onto my land without reason, and though Audrey had met the sheriff in person, I doubted she'd recognize him in wolf form. I chuffed at her and walked over to the wolves, sitting a few paces from them.

Ric, the bigger of the two, stomped a foot, and jerked his head toward my cabin. He wanted to talk, but I couldn't fathom why. I nodded to Ric and turned back to Audrey.

She stood over the partially eaten rabbit in a protective stance. I had no doubt if the wolves had tried to take her kill, there would have been a fight. I picked up the rabbit remains and headed toward home. I didn't hear Audrey follow, but I'd already gotten used to the fact I wouldn't hear my woman unless she wanted me to.

I carried the rabbit up to my porch and shifted. Audrey's kill went into the unlit grill to be dealt with later, and I grabbed my pants. As I pulled them on, I noticed the sheriff's black Chevy truck in my driveway. The wolves walked over to the vehicle before shifting, and put their clothes on.

Audrey sat on the other end of the porch and whined a little. I walked over to her with my shirt in hand and sat down next to her. I worried that shifting would always be hard for her. It wasn't a skill that usually had to be acquired as an adult. We learned how to shift from the onset of puberty. She didn't have that luxury.

She shied away as footsteps echoed on the porch. I glanced over at the sheriff and deputy. "Could you give us a minute? There's coffee and cake, if you want to wait inside."

Ric raised his brows and touched Conall's arm before the younger wolf could object. "Sure. You have cream and sugar?"

"Yes. Make yourselves at home." I waited for them to walk away before turning back to Audrey. "Come on, kitten. We have company."

She whined again and moved forward, dropping her head in my lap. Her breathing labored, and I watched her muscles ripple and shift. After what felt like an eternity, my naked mate lay quaking in my lap.

"I've got you." I pulled my shirt on over her head and carried her into the house. I stopped in surprise when I saw Addie sitting in one of the living room chairs.

"What's this about?" I asked no one in particular as I made Audrey comfortable on the couch.

"Best if Addie explains." Ric sipped from the coffee cup he held.

"A few hours ago, a magic bomb, for lack of a better term, exploded inside the wards. The only thing different after the bomb went off, besides the extra magic lingering in the air, is that Audrey's registry went dark." Addie tipped her head at my mate. "We've got a couple of witches collecting the excess before it does any damage, and I'm here to see why Audrey's registry suddenly stopped working when it was fine before the magical incident."

Audrey pulled the malachite necklace off and tossed it to Addie with minimal movement. She looked exhausted. I needed to talk to my parents about her shifting. I didn't want it to be a strain on her every time it happened. I didn't remember it being like that as a teen.

Addie studied the stone, held it up to the light, and cupped it in her hands. "That's so weird. The magic is gone. As if it was never there to begin with." She looked at Audrey. "May I?"

Audrey nodded, and Addie moved to sit next to my mate. I hovered nearby as Addie did nothing more than hold her hand. "The magic surrounding you is gone as well. Whatever curse kept me from registering you is broken somehow."

Audrey's cheeks went pink. "I'm Nicholas's mate. That's the only thing that's changed in the past few hours."

Addie puffed out a breath and sat back. She looked out the window at something none of us could see. "It's possible. I mean, it would be the most ass backwards protection spell I'd ever seen, but I suppose it's possible."

"What are you talking about?" I crossed my arms and stared down at the women.

"Audrey can explain. I'm going to go get my tools out of the sheriff's car. I can officially do her registry tattoo now." Addie stood, and both the sheriff and deputy followed her out.

I sat down in Addie's vacated spot. "So. What am I missing?"

Audrey reached out and linked our fingers together. "I'm not even sure where to start."

I squeezed her fingers. "Let's try the beginning."

She chewed her bottom lip before nodding slowly. There was

nothing she could tell me that would drive me away, but her nervousness came through our linked hands. After a moment she took a deep breath and sighed. "I think I was born in Virginia."

"Think?" I slid closer and pulled her into my lap. "There's nothing you can tell me that will change what is."

Audrey leaned against me and sighed. Her words tumbled out, and with each new fact, my heart hurt a little more. She had drifted from place to place; she had no one to call her own, no place to call home.

"You'll never be alone again, kitten." I placed a kiss on her cheek. "Tomorrow, we'll go get your stuff, and then I'll take you to meet my parents, and see if my sister can bring her son, Finn, over. You have my family now."

"They probably won't approve." Audrey tilted her head up to look at me.

"We're not snobs. Mom will love you. She got another son when Becca mated, and now she gets another daughter." I kissed the tip of her nose. "You have nothing to worry about."

Addie reappeared, carrying her worn bag. "Let's get this show started."

~

AUDREY

Meeting Nicholas's family wasn't as terrifying as mating with him. I played the scene at breakfast over again in my mind as we walked back to the cabin from Creekwood. His parents were loving and accepting—it was clear where Nicholas got it from.

"You're thinking awfully hard, Kitten." Nicholas jumped stones across the creek and waited for me to join him.

"I've never met shifters like your family. Even in the commune, shifters were . . . different." I accepted his offered hand.

"Things are different in Havenwood Falls. The rules are heavily enforced . . ." His voice trailed off.

"Have you ever broken the rules?" I didn't think so—Nicholas was a rule follower—but we were still learning each other.

"No. Mike McCabe's son—Braden, my best friend—he broke the rules to protect his sisters. He died, and the girls were banned from Havenwood Falls." Anger clipped his words.

"You don't agree with the ban?" I squeezed his hand, and he responded in kind.

Nicholas sighed. "The rules exist to keep us all safe. There are no exceptions, though I think the witches bend the rules as far as they can sometimes, and the fae think they're more guidelines than rules."

We exited the trees and walked into the yard. Nicholas turned and pulled me into his arms. I laughed as he rubbed his nose over my face and his fingers teased my sides.

"You want to go for a run?" He followed his nuzzling with kisses. "I think you can manage the lower trails up the side of the mountains."

He tensed suddenly and released me. Nicholas stepped around me to stand in front as two large wolves moved out of hiding in the trees. Both growled low, and their hackles stood tall on their backs. Hostile, and a clear threat.

Nicholas held his voice low as he took two steps forward. "Run, Audrey. Go back to my parents."

I couldn't move. Something about the wolves felt familiar, though I couldn't place why. They were shifters by their scent, and something about their smell nagged at memories that didn't exist.

"Run, Audrey!" Nicholas shifted as he lunged forward, and the first wolf moved to attack. His shout startled me into motion, and I pivoted, running full speed into the trees.

I couldn't shift as fast as Nicholas. My shift took time and meditation. All I could do was hope I could outrun whoever followed on my two legs. I didn't turn to look when leaves crunched behind as fast as they crunched under my own feet.

Something plowed into me as I jumped the creek. The water was frigid, but I barely felt it over the panic that seized my mind. I scrambled to my hands and knees as a cougar sailed over my head.

I pushed to my feet and ran for the trees. I grabbed a low hanging branch, and ignoring the rough wood, pulled myself up. I continued up until I found a secure spot to wedge myself in. It was all I could do without my shift.

Tears ran down my face as I tried to process what was going on. There was an angry bear below, which for reasons I didn't know, was fighting a cougar I didn't recognize by scent, and Nicholas fought two other wolves I was sure didn't belong in Havenwood Falls.

A cougar screamed, and I watched as a second one jumped down from a tree onto the bear's back. The two cats moved with a synchronicity that spoke of long-time familiarity. The bear made the cats look small, but they were faster.

Fear beat in my ears. I didn't know what was going on. Without knowing whom to trust, there was nothing I could do. I was useless.

The bear reared back, throwing off the cougar on his back. He went flying and struck a tree hard. However, the motion left an opening for the other cat to lunge and latch onto the bear's throat. The bear came down on the cat, but he didn't let go of his choke hold. Despite the wild thrashing, the cougar remained stubborn, and the bear slowed and dropped.

The second cougar shook himself and came over to my tree. He sat and waited while the other cat retained his chokehold. When it was clear the bear wasn't getting back up, the cougar released the bear's throat and limped over to the tree.

I leaned forward to get a better look as the cougar limped over to where his partner sat. Angry red furless scarring covered a shoulder, down a front leg and part of his torso. He flopped down, and I could feel his fatigue in the motion. The uninjured cat began bathing his partner. They seemed unthreatening and in no hurry to move along.

Where was Nicholas? Should I trust these cats? Were they shifters? Based on behavior alone, they certainly didn't act like wild animals, and they lounged at the bottom of my tree, waiting me out. I couldn't stay up here forever. Despite my better judgment, I slowly climbed down the tree.

The cougars stretched and rolled over to expose their bellies to me.

I realized one was a male and the other—the scarred one—was a female. Confused, I wrapped my arms around myself. "I don't know what that means."

The scarred cat rolled to her feet and bumped my legs. My hand automatically went out, and she licked it. The male rolled back up and sniffed my hand before licking it as well.

"Okay. I get it. You're friendly." I looked toward the cabin. Was Nicholas okay?

The female walked a few paces off in the direction of the cabin, and then stopped. She looked back at me. Her partner joined her and sat.

"There were wolves. Nicholas . . . he tried to stop them while I ran." I wasn't proud of the admission, but there was no way I could have helped him.

The female stretched and yawned before moving a few more feet toward the cabin and waiting. My plan was to wait for Nicholas to find me. I glanced back at the unmoving bear. If they could bring down a bear, there wasn't really anything to be afraid of. Was there?

CHAPTER 10

NICHOLAS

*D*umb fucking dogs. I rolled my shoulders and watched as
Conall slammed his cruiser door closed. The car was
enhanced to hold supes, so I didn't worry about the trespassers getting
out of it. I turned my attention to the wolves that had saved my ass.

Theo and Iris from the inn. Well, Theo had backed me up while
Iris held onto his clothes. She hadn't been happy about that role either.
She-wolves, in my mind, were more vicious than males. She'd have
likely killed the trespassers by accident.

Sheriff Ric shook his head as Conall climbed into the cruiser and
left. "Been chasing those wolves all over town. Like I was some damn
bill collector and not the sheriff. I have better damn things to do than
play hide and seek with a bunch of hardheads." Ric looked well
beyond angry, which was out of character for him. "And there's still
two missing unregistered. You see anybody else strange on your land?"

"Can you talk and run? Something took off after Audrey. I sent her
toward my parents, but I don't know if she made it." I edged toward
the trees.

"We came to talk to Audrey. We'll go with you." Iris stepped up
next to me before I could get too far away from them.

Theo finished pulling on his pants. "It's only right we talk to her
first."

Ric held up a hand. "No one is going anywhere. I've got to call the Luna Coven. We need to verify your Registry."

"I'm not waiting for the Court to appear to go after Audrey." I glared at Ric. "I'm not willing to risk a dead mate because you want to be official at a time like this."

"There's Audrey." Iris took two steps forward but stopped and growled.

I turned to see Audrey with two cougars—by size and coloring, juveniles—walking with her. I didn't recognize the cats, but seeing as Audrey was calm, I didn't add that to my list of worry just yet.

"What are they doing here?" Iris crossed her arms.

Theo placed a hand on her shoulder. "They have a right. More than we do."

Instead of commenting on their conversation, I opened my truck to pull out some track pants and a tee shirt. I crossed the yard to Audrey and the cougars and held out the clothes. "They're going to need these if we're going to talk about what just happened."

Audrey wrapped herself around me. "Are you okay?"

"I'm fine." I caught her mouth with mine. "No major injuries."

When the juveniles shifted and took the clothes, I put two and two together. The teens shared an uncanny resemblance to Audrey. Their eyes were as golden as hers. Unlike Audrey, they were filthy.

The girl had terrible scarring on her left side, and the boy had fire in his eyes. He reached for his sister's hand—with as close as they looked in age, I'd say they were twins—and she accepted.

"We're Roxanne and Remy MacKinnon." The girl's smile fluttered. "Half siblings to Audrey."

Audrey jolted and spun on a heel. "What?"

Remy lifted his chin. "It's a long story."

I jerked my head over to where Ric, Theo, and Iris waited. "We've got time."

Audrey nodded to the sheriff and tilted her head at Theo and Iris. She continued to stare as she spoke to the sheriff. "There's a dead bear by the creek. These two took him down as he attacked me."

"Probably one of the other fools I'm looking for. Are you two registered?" Ric pinned the kids with his stare.

"Yes, sir." Roxanne tried smiling again. "Two weeks ago."

There was no hesitation in her words, and I didn't doubt them. The timeline didn't add up, but I kept that information to myself. Audrey had only been in town for four days.

Ric looked over at Theo and Iris. "And you?"

Theo pulled up his shirt to show off the mark along his hip. "You can't see Iris's but we got ours at the same time."

"At least some people can still follow a basic fucking rule." Ric was truly pissed. "I'll call a Bishop over to verify the Registry anyway."

My nose wrinkled at the thought of Roman or Ronan in my cabin. "I'd rather poke a sleeping bear."

"Addie's got some Court things she's doing today. Bishop is a valid alternative to verify the Registry." Ric lifted a brow. "Problem?"

I rolled a shoulder. "I prefer Fairchilds to Bishops."

"As public servants, we're not allowed to take sides."

"As a person who obeys the laws without argument, I prefer Fairchilds to Bishops."

Ric chuckled and some of the anger drained from him. "I'll call Addie and see if she's done with her appointments for today. If not, I can see if Elsmed is busy, but Roman was interested in talking to the shifters that were deliberately avoiding the Registry, so he's going to be nearby anyway."

"My cabin isn't big enough for all these people as it is." The excuse was flimsy at best, but I would stick by it. I didn't want Roman's temper touching Audrey in any way.

Ric nodded. "I'm going to go check on the bear. All of you stay in the cabin until I get one of the Court members out here. No exceptions."

"I don't mean to be crass, but do you have something to eat?" Roxanne rolled her good shoulder. "It's been a long two weeks."

"Come on inside. I'm sure we can find something for you." I led the way into the cabin, wondering what in seven hells was happening.

Only last night, Audrey had no family that she knew of. I wasn't sure I'd like what we were about to hear.

~

AUDREY

THEY LOOKED LIKE ME. The thought wouldn't stop circling through my mind. Roxanne and Remy looked like me. We were half siblings. I wasn't sure if I should rejoice that I had family or weep that I'd been left thinking I was alone all these years.

"I don't even know where to start." Remy pulled out a stool for Roxanne at the bar, and another for Iris, before he set himself between the two girls.

"First things first." I pointed at Theo and Iris. "Who are you?"

"Cousins. On your mother's side. Our father is your uncle." Theo grinned. "Dad will be pleased you're doing well."

"Where is he?" I regretted the question when Iris's face fell.

"Short of the long story, there's a territory war going on. He stayed behind. You have wolf half-brothers, too. Dad worried what would happen to them if you weren't brought back to the valley. He plans to smuggle them out of the territory, if things take a turn for the worse."

"Audrey is cougar *and* wolf?" Nicholas turned from the food he pulled out of the fridge. "I didn't think that was possible."

Remy sighed. "From what we were told, there was some voodoo involved in it."

"That's what we were told, too." Theo nodded to Nicholas when he was handed a plate of food.

"The Shenandoah Valley isn't huge," Roxanne said. "Our pride has held control of the territory for a while. When the Drummond wolf pack from Suffolk, Virginia, came requesting asylum, there was an agreement made with the Shenandoah Pride. Our dad, Wyatt, married Audrey's mom, Marian, as part of the established peace, with a voodoo witch's blessing. It was peaceful at first, from all accounts. Everyone got along on the surface, anyway." She gulped down the water set on the bar.

"Theo and I are part of the Drummond Pack," Iris clarified. "But there was another pack—the Endicott pack—that came from Pennsylvania. I guess they were looking to expand. Archibald, Marian's father—ours and Audrey's grandfather—made an under-the-table arrangement with the Endicotts, and a territory war broke out with the pride. From what Dad found out, Granddad never intended on permanently sharing the land with the pride." She propped her elbows on the bar and rested her head on her hands. She looked wiped out.

Remy nodded at her before turning his eyes back to me. "We went to the voodoo witch in Port Royal, Virginia, for help when the wolves attacked our home and killed everyone. She told us to find the place where magic collects but cannot be found on any map. We've been looking for three years."

"The Endicott enforcers caught up to us in Denver. I took a bit of a beating." Roxy tapped her left shoulder.

"Voodoo doesn't work without a sacrifice of some kind." Theo looked over at the twins. "What did you give the voodoo woman?"

Roxanne's face flushed, and she choked on the food she was wolfing down.

Remy patted her back and rubbed small circles. "We always knew someone was going to ask."

Roxanne swallowed but wouldn't look up from her plate. "Innocence. She wanted our innocence for her help."

I stared, trying to find words as my stomach twisted. Witches could do a lot of things without physically touching, and the voodoo witch likely never touched them but still . . . In the end, I could barely manage a whisper. "Why?"

"We agreed. We needed to find you first," Remy shot back.

I held up my hands. "You've found me."

Had it been worth the price, though? That wasn't for me to decide, even as my heart broke for them. They'd made the choice, and there was no undoing it.

317

Nicholas looked at Theo. "How did you find Havenwood Falls? I saw you at the inn as well. Why didn't you talk to Audrey then?"

"And get in the middle of your weird mating dance?" Iris snorted. "Not likely. We meant to talk to her that day, but after your pheromones choked everyone within ten feet, we thought it was a better idea to wait until you mated. You'd both be easier to talk to when you weren't so high-strung."

"We were in Denver and saw the ski lodge bus. Iris likes to snowboard. We thought a day of rest wouldn't hurt anyone. We took the bus to Havenwood Falls." Theo shook his head. "It was a complete fluke that Audrey was already here."

Nicholas nodded. I could see he had other thoughts on the matter, but he didn't voice them.

Roxy leaned back in her chair and stared at the ceiling. "The pride matriarch wants you. The original symbol of the peace. She doesn't care about Remy or me. She told Remy he couldn't stay in the pride's territory. Because our father died to wolves, his lineage is weak and of no use to the pride. Where would my brother go? He was exiled for something out of his control."

"Roxy." Remy moved his arm to wrap her in a side hug. "They would have exiled me anyway. The pride only keeps so many men within the territory."

"You weren't even given the option to fight for rank." Tears ran down Roxanne's face.

Icy fingers danced up my spine, and I crossed my arms. "I'm not going anywhere. My mate is here. This is his home, and this is where I will stay."

"Endicott is desperate. The alpha underestimated the strength of the pride and their alliances. He doesn't want to lose any more of his pack to the pride." Theo sighed. "That's why Iris and I came looking. We wanted to talk you into coming home before anyone else died. Endicott sent some of the pack to find you as well, and bring you back, willing or not."

"You can't force anyone out of Havenwood Falls who doesn't want to leave," Nicholas said, coming to my side. "We protect our own. The ones who attacked us will likely have their memories erased and be dumped in Denver or Durango. We don't tolerate having our rules broken."

I turned in to him, closing my eyes and taking a deep breath. He was calm, and it calmed me.

I had just found everything I never knew I wanted in Nicholas and his family. I felt as if some force I didn't understand was trying to pull it all away from me. In a few short days, Havenwood Falls had become home, and I wasn't going to give that up without a fight.

The twins had nowhere they could go. In theory, if I returned, they would still be homeless. They were my father's children. Regardless of never having them in my life or me in theirs, they were here now, looking for help. How would I live with myself if I abandoned them the way I was abandoned?

"I am by your side, no matter your decision." Nicholas pressed a kiss to my head.

"Your brothers need you as much as your cougar family does," Iris growled. "Are you going to abandon half your family to death because you don't share their shift?"

"Iris." Theo whomped the back of her head. "That was uncalled for."

"I will not apologize." She clenched her jaw.

"They have my uncle, don't they?" I watched Iris's face darken. "They don't need me. The twins have no one, and my place is here."

Nicholas patted my butt. "I have a few calls to make. Holler if Ric returns before I come back down. Put the twins in the guest room after they're done eating. They could use a shower and some sleep."

"All right." I didn't know what he was up to, but I trusted him, so I didn't ask.

"Why aren't we good enough?" Iris deflated in her seat. "We're family, too."

I considered my words. "No one in Shenandoah wants me for who I am. They want me for what I can do for them. That's no way to live."

Theo sighed. "It really isn't, is it?"

"We should contact Dad. Let him know." Iris looked ready to cry. "We're going to lose everything."

"We'll be alive. And that's always a pretty good starting point." Theo rubbed a hand along the back of his neck. "We should head back to the inn and call Dad."

"Fine." Iris marched to the door and slammed it on her way out. Theo hesitated.

"No one is making you leave Havenwood Falls," I offered quietly.

"Iris is a dreamer at heart. I think she imagined some big reunion with tears and hugs and instant love for family. The rest of us are a little more of realists." Theo's smile didn't touch his eyes.

Her dream made me a little sad. "I don't remember any of you."

"Voodoo witch," Roxanne offered with a yawn. "She took your past for your spell's payment. We asked when we were trying to haggle our own payment. You'll never remember Virginia."

Theo nodded. "That actually fills in some of the blanks."

Roxanne pushed her plate away and laid her head on the bar. "I think I'm ready for that shower and bed."

I nodded. "All right. The guest room is at the end of the hall there. I'll run up and grab some clothes for you guys."

"Thanks, Audrey." A dimple I hadn't noticed appeared on Remy's tired face.

I walked with Theo to the door. Iris was on a cell phone, pacing the porch. Her face was contorted in anger.

Theo turned to me as he stepped out. "We'll likely be here for a while until Dad makes a plan. Havenwood Falls seems the safest place to be for the moment. Thanks for at least talking to us, and not throwing us out. We'll go down to the Police Department and wait on the sheriff there. Iris likely won't be coming back inside to wait."

"You know where I'm at if you need me."

He nodded. "See you around."

I closed the door behind him and watched as he approached Iris. She didn't look any more pleased at whatever he said to her, but together they walked down the drive. Sorrow stung my soul that I couldn't be who they needed me to be, but my place was here. With Nicholas. I shook off the dreary thoughts.

As I ran up the stairs, I hoped Nicholas had some idea what to do about the twins. The cabin was only so big, and they were of an age they shouldn't be sharing a room for any length of time. I wanted to help, but I had no idea where to even start. Scratch that. The starting point would be clean clothes. Everything else would hopefully fall in line.

CHAPTER 11

NICHOLAS

*M*y first call was to Mike McCabe. I wasn't alpha, and to make any form of pride decision without him was terms for him to call me out. I didn't want to be alpha, so avoiding the challenge was important.

"McCabe."

"It's Nicholas. I have a situation. I was wondering if you and Anne would mind coming out to the cabin. And would you mind calling my parents as well? I have another call to make after this one."

"What's going on, Nicholas?"

"It's best to explain everything at once. We have a dilemma, and it's not something Audrey or I can solve without help."

"Audrey?"

Shit. I forgot to introduce them. "My mate. That's another long story."

"Give me the cliff notes, son."

I sighed. "She totaled her car. I was the rescuer. She's my mate."

"All right. I'll bring some meat over. We'll light the grill."

Tension tightened the muscles between my shoulders. "Ask my mother to bring sides, then. I've already fed a houseful of shifters once today, and haven't had the chance to call the butcher."

"I'm going to want to hear this full story when I arrive."

"You'll get it. I promise." I smiled at Audrey as she came into the room and dug around in the closet. When she came out with clothes, I realized I didn't ask the twins where their belongings were. As filthy as they were, I doubted they even had anything. They likely spent most of their time in shifted form—risky, with the hunting season open in Colorado.

"All right. We'll see you in about an hour."

"Good enough." I hung up and wrapped my mate up in my arms when she came out of the closet. "Has Ric come back?"

"Not yet." She leaned in, and I groaned when she nibbled on my lip.

"We don't have time to finish what you start." But I still pulled her down onto my lap, making sure to grind my erection against her on the way down.

"If I didn't know any better, I would call you a horny dog." She wiggled deliberately, rubbing herself against me.

"I'm not the only one." I pressed a hard kiss to her mouth. "Shoo. I have another call to make, and I'm sure the kids would like to cover up and sleep."

"Thank you." She leaned back and cupped her hands around my face.

"For?" I raised a brow.

Audrey grinned. "For being you."

She leaned in and barely brushed her lips over mine before jumping up and taking the clothes down to the kids. That little kitten was going to be the death of me.

The next call was harder than the first to make. I never asked for favors, and favors generally had price tags attached to them.

"Liam speaking."

"It's Jordan."

"I've got my schedule already. I know I'm on call for the next week."

I hesitated.

"What is it?" Liam cut through bullshit faster than I ever could.

"There are some . . . issues . . . surrounding Audrey. This guy,

Endicott, is trying to forcefully take her from Havenwood Falls, as some kind of peace offering for the pride in Shenandoah Valley, Virginia."

"What are you asking for, Jordan?" Simple and straight to the chase. There was no judgment in his voice, or curiosity.

"I know you and Savage have connections around the country. Is there a way to make it clear to both parties that Audrey stays where she's at until she wants to leave?"

Liam snorted. "Your mate isn't going anywhere."

"I know."

There was a pause on the line. "I see."

I waited. There was nothing else for me to say. I asked, and Liam, president of the outlaw motorcycle club SIN, either accepted or denied.

"Those shifters trying to avoid the Registry wouldn't have anything to do with this, would they?"

Asking him how he knew about that was pointless. There was very little the MC didn't know about. "They're part of the problem, yes."

"How's your kitty cat feel about this?"

"I hadn't planned on sharing this with her. I want her happy, not stressed and anxious."

Liam snorted. "That's a bridge you don't want to be on when it's burning." He sighed. "Everything has a price."

"She's worth it."

"Lovesick fool." But Liam laughed again. "Let me do a little digging. I'll have to see if my arms stretch to Virginia, and I'll get back to you. I don't want to hear shit when you're called out to the club in the middle of the night to deal with some trauma."

"Make this problem go away, and I'll be in the clubhouse, whistling a merry tune."

"I'll call you back."

"Looking forward to it." Not really, but what else could I say. Being club bitch for their injuries was a small price to pay for Audrey's safety and happiness.

AUDREY

My first impression of Mike McCabe was one of strength. Not only because of his build, but his demeanor as well. He was a man you wanted on your side in a fight. His wife Anne was small in comparison, but there was nothing about her I'd call weak either.

They came in with Nicholas's parents as the sheriff and Addie were leaving. Mike carried what looked like half a dozen of ribs over one shoulder and a bucket of ice cream in his free hand, and the women carried in bowls of side dishes. Nicholas's father, Ronald, stopped the sheriff on the porch for a brief conversation before he came in with several bottles of spirits.

"What's going on?" I pinned Nicholas with a look.

He came over to my side and wrapped an arm around my waist. "Pride meeting. Sort of. Mike is pride leader in Havenwood Falls and you haven't met him yet. And we need to discuss the twins."

As if on cue, the twins came out of the guest room, rumpled but looking more rested. Remy yawned, and Roxanne automatically moved into the kitchen to help Anne and Elaine, Nicholas's mom, with the sides. Remy glanced around and decided on the path of least resistance. He walked over to the couch and stretched out.

"Nicholas, why don't you get the grill lit? These are going to need a few hours." Mike patted the pile of meat with something close to affection.

"I lit it when you said you were coming with a hog." Nicholas waved to the giant grill on the deck. "Go ahead and put that thing in. It'll be done in time for supper, I think."

"Good lad." Mike disappeared outside with his meat, and both Ronald and Nicholas followed.

"This fridge is a disgrace." Elaine's sigh could be heard through the entire first floor.

"We ate it all." Roxanne's soft voice contrasted with the women's.

"Well, at least there's room to put stuff away until it's time to heat it up. Why don't you go sit with your brother, dear? You look a bit dead on your feet." Anne phrased it as a suggestion, but it was clear she expected it to be carried out.

I sat on a chair as Roxanne practically lay on top of her brother on the couch. He shifted enough to let her slide behind him against the back of the couch, and they were both asleep in seconds.

"Aren't they cute?" Anne came out of the kitchen, carrying a drink tray. She studied the sleeping twins. Her eyes narrowed a moment. I watched as she set the tray on the coffee table and reached for Roxanne's left arm.

Remy's hand shot out and grabbed Anne's wrist before she could touch Roxanne. They both froze, and for a moment, I thought she would scold Remy. Anne's face softened, and she patted his hair. "You're safe here. I just want to see how bad the scarring is."

Remy released her hand and ducked his head. "I'm sorry. Caught me by surprise."

Anne ran light fingers down Roxanne's arm, over the scars, before she picked up the young girl's hand. "How long had you been taking turns on alert?"

Remy yawned and scooted farther into the couch. He looked like he was already mostly asleep again, but he answered her. "Couple years. Safer that way in strange territories."

I waited for Anne to finish her examination. "Something wrong with Roxanne's scars?"

"They're deep. Really deep. It's going to limit her mobility. Poor thing. She needs a skilled healer. Jasper may be able to heal the deeper part, leaving the surface scars." Anne poured lemonade as the men came back in from outside. "Lemonade?" She offered Mike the first glass.

"Thank you, dear." He sat in the other vacant chair.

Nicholas, to my surprise, sat at my feet and leaned back against me. I ran my hand through his hair, delighted when he purred.

"Here we are." Elaine came out of the kitchen carrying a cheese-and-fruit tray. "Something to hold us over."

"So. There are obviously a few new things to discuss." Mike gestured to me. "Nicholas is mated. What are your intentions, son?"

"I plan to continue as I have been with Audrey at my side." Nicholas wrapped an arm around my leg and kissed my knee.

"I hoped one day Braden would make the challenge for alpha and let this old man retire. Should I expect your challenge soon?"

Nicholas shook his head. "You'll have to wait for Finn to grow up for that. Unless Ethan wants to take the mantle from you. I'm content."

Mike sighed and sat back in the chair. His weathered face suddenly looked a hundred years old. "You have potential. You always did." His eyes traveled to where the twins snored together. "The kids?"

"My half siblings through my father." I sat up and met his gaze. "They're now orphans."

"I wanted to propose an adoption by the pride." Nicholas sat up. "That would, of course, leave their primary care to you with the rest of the pride filling in as needed."

Mike pursed his lips and looked at his wife. She wore a considering, pensive face. "That's a lot to ask of the pride."

I wanted to protest, but before I could put the words together, Nicholas spoke again.

"As much as I love my mate and want to give her anything she desires, Audrey and I don't have the knowledge or space to take care of growing shifters." Nicholas squeezed my leg. "And Audrey struggles with her own shift."

I twisted his ear, and he yelped. "You could be a little more abstruse about that. I can shift; it just takes time and focus."

"But it shouldn't." Elaine folded her hands together. "Shifting is as natural as breathing. You shouldn't struggle with it."

"I didn't come into it until about twentyish hours ago." I debated boxing his ears when all eyes fell on me. "It's complicated."

"She was cursed to be shiftless until she mated." Nicholas cupped his hand around his ear.

"We can work on it." Elaine's statement made that part of the discussion final, if the nod from Anne was any indication.

Anne waved a hand at the twins. "I don't agree with a pride adoption. It wouldn't sit well with the Court, and if something happens to their caretaker, the children are left floundering within the pride. Mike and I will adopt the children. We'll give them the choice to change their names to McCabe or retain the name of their birth." Anne lifted her chin, almost daring Mike to challenge her decision, but he smiled at her.

"That's sound. They'll have plenty of room in the house, and we certainly know how to handle a teenager or two." Mike nodded. "And of course, Audrey, Nicholas, you're welcome to check in on them, and they're welcome to visit you at any time."

Remy stretched without sitting up. "I think I'm supposed to complain about not being wanted, but that's really not the case, is it?"

Roxanne propped her chin on her brother's shoulder. "It's going to be weird, in a pride where the matriarchy doesn't rule, but I'm game."

"We've got a couple of backpacks of stuff in one of the abandoned mines nearby. Roxy and I can fetch them after dinner."

Anne paled. "One of the mines? They're dangerous."

"So is rolling over in a tree." Remy sat up and continued rolling his shoulders and stretching his muscles.

"We have rules." Mike sent him a pointed look.

Remy reached for the cheese on the tray. "Good parents do. It's the parents without rules you've got to worry about."

Ronald snorted and stood. "Thank you, my friend, for accepting this challenge. I'll get you a beer."

I stood next to Audrey on the porch as she hugged and kissed the twins goodbye. She was nervous for them, but they were smart kids, and I didn't think they'd have any problems with the McCabes. In the yard, the twins handed Anne their borrowed clothes and shifted next to the waiting Mike and Ronald. They took off into the trees with the men behind them. They were going to the mine to collect the twins' meager possessions, and the women would meet them at home.

We waved as Mom and Anne backed out of the drive. Call me selfish, but it was nice to finally have my house back to myself—and my mate—after the day we put in.

I wrapped around my mate and pressed kisses to all the bare skin I could reach. "Want to go inside and snuggle?"

Audrey laughed and pulled away. "I have to work tonight."

I groaned. "I make enough for both of us. You could quit, take care of the house. Be a kept woman."

"And pigs could fly." She twisted out of my reach when I grabbed for her. The grin on her face was full of mischief as she darted inside.

"We could snuggle naked before you go to work." I leapt at her, and she danced away, laughing.

"Maybe I don't want to snuggle." She took the stairs two at a time, pulling off her shirt as she went. "I have something more . . . adult in mind."

My cock jumped to attention, and I growled, stalking her up the stairs while weaving around her discarded clothing. "You're playing a dangerous game."

She glanced over her shoulder, naked as a jay in the center of the room. "Fortunately, it's a game we both win. But sadly, you're wearing too many clothes to play."

I grabbed her before she could evade me again and rubbed my erection into her ass. "You are a troublemaker."

She lifted her arms behind her and wrapped them around my neck. "You can't live without me."

"No. I can't." I turned her, rested my forehead against hers, and kissed her again, nibbling a little at the corner of her mouth. "You are every star in the sky, every song on the wind. There's no possible way for me to love you more, and yet I don't think there's any way to measure just how much I do love you."

Audrey's brows rose even as her lips curved. "Who wrote the poetry?"

I nipped her lip, hard. "We belong to each other. You have my mark; I have yours. But it's not enough. I want you to have more than that."

Confusion crinkled her face. "I don't understand, Nicholas."

"You have my heart and soul. I've given you my home. I want to give you something else." I stepped back and pulled a small black box out of my pocket. "I always thought it a pointless human tradition. We're shifters. We have mates or we don't. And yet, the other day I found myself wondering if you would accept being more than just mates. I had planned this to go a different way, but this is as good a time as any. Will you take my name, Audrey? Will you let me give you this last thing I have to give?"

Her mouth fell open. I hadn't opened the box. By the look on her face, I didn't need to.

Audrey leapt up, wrapping arms and legs around me and fusing her mouth to mine. "I'll take everything you wish to give me and give back everything in my power to give you, I promise. I love you."

I carried her over to the bed and pinned her underneath me. I gave her a wicked grin. I ground my quickly hardening cock against her cleft.

Her eyes half closed, and she arched up against me, creating mind-numbing friction. "Tease."

"Should I collect on your promise now, then?"

"I insist." With mischief on her face, Audrey flipped our position so she straddled me.

She leaned back enough to slide her hands under my shirt as she gyrated her hips over my stiff cock. There was a wicked gleam in her eyes when she leaned forward and nipped my bottom lip between her teeth.

Her nails scraped lightly over my stomach and continued up to run over my nipples. She let go of my mouth and dipped back again. "Take the shirt off, or you're going to lose it."

I didn't waste time pulling it over my head. With my eyes on hers, I grabbed the tee by the collar and ripped it down the center for her. Her pupils expanded, and she pounced on my bared flesh.

My hands fisted in her hair when she bit down on my left nipple.

"No." She straightened, linking her hands with mine and pushing them to the headboard. "You don't touch. Let me love on you."

I groaned. "You're going to kill me."

"I have a funny feeling you'll survive." Audrey's hands explored my exposed torso, and where her hands weren't, her mouth seemed to be.

When her tongue dipped under the waistband of my jeans, my dick throbbed, and I twitched in anticipation.

"Audrey." I wasn't sure if I was begging or making a demand, but it didn't matter.

She opened my pants, and I fisted my hands above my head to keep from touching her when her hands closed around my cock. Audrey's purr made my length twitch between her palms, and the little minx tightened her hands as she stroked from base to tip.

331

Audrey stroked a second time, and I watched her lean down to place a kiss on the tip of my cock as her hands stroked back up.

"Now who's the tease?" I forced the words out as her mouth sealed around the tip of my cock and sucked hard. My hips bucked up of their own volition.

Audrey's mouth was almost as hot and wet as her pussy. The feeling of her gliding up and down, playing with my balls, was almost too much to handle. My hands abandoned their post to tangle in her hair and pull her away from my dick before I exploded.

She chuckled and crawled up my body to give me a kiss. "Something wrong?"

I pulled her in for another kiss, and with my right hand, guided her hips so I could rub my cock all through her wet pussy lips. She groaned into my mouth and shifted enough to allow me to press into her heat. I broke the kiss and rolled us over so I was on top, sinking further into her.

Audrey rolled her hips. Pleasure flickered across her face. "Fuck me, Nicholas."

How was a man to resist the demands of his beautiful mate? I would make sure she never questioned being my mate. For the rest of my life.

CHAPTER 13

AUDREY

*C*offee Haven bustled with activity. I stirred my coffee, waiting. Apprehension twisted my stomach into knots as I considered how this morning could go. Theo and Iris asked me to meet. I was so anxious about the conversation, I hadn't slept yet.

Iris plopped into the chair across from me while Theo set down a couple of muffins and their coffees. Iris's eyes were puffy, and while I didn't know her well, I knew enough not to ask her about her crying jag.

Theo sat between us, his appearance no less worn than Iris's. He at least attempted a smile in my direction before staring into his coffee. The air felt too heavy to breathe.

"I'm sorry." The words left my mouth before I could consider them.

Iris sighed and picked up her coffee. "You don't have any reason to be sorry. You made the best choice for you." She sounded like she parroted words.

I cupped my icy hands around the warm coffee cup. "What's the plan now? Can I ask?"

"I've gone to the sheriff to ask what would have to be done to become residents of Havenwood Falls, since he seemed like the best source of knowledge. At Dad's request." Theo cut his muffin in half and then in quarters. He picked up a wedge and dipped it into his coffee before taking a bite.

"He's got Milo and Felix, your brothers. They were in Illinois when we spoke. Some place called Peoria. He's taking precautions as they head this way." Iris stole a piece of Theo's muffin and ate it in one bite, without dipping it into the coffee.

My heart fluttered. "You want to stay?"

"There's nothing left in Virginia. Without you, the pack and the pride are in an all-out war, and it's not the best place for any kind of shifter to be at the moment, as it will require declaring loyalty to one or the other." Theo sliced up the second muffin.

Iris propped her elbow on the table and rested her chin in her hand. "I do like it here. The slopes are killer. I homeschooled in Virginia, since I was ahead of my class in nearly everything. I don't know if I can continue that here."

I rolled over the information in my mind. My fingers tapped against my cup as I calculated the options. "I can't make any promises —I'm new here, too—but I can talk to Nicholas and his parents. They're not huge, prominent figures in Havenwood Falls, from what I've seen, but their family's been here for generations. I think we might be able to work it out for you all to stay."

"We appreciate any help you want to offer. Dad won't be in the area for about another week. We wanted to make sure we had everything in order for when he got here." Theo pushed the muffin plate toward Iris.

"What do you plan on doing in Havenwood Falls?" I sipped from my cup.

Iris shrugged. "Live, I guess. Go to school, flirt with boys. See if I can get a job on the slopes."

Theo rolled his eyes. "You're too young for a job. Let's not let Dad hear you talk about flirting with boys. Dad's a surgeon. I haven't checked out the employment offerings yet, to see if Dad could find work in a town this small."

"A surgeon?" I tipped my head.

Iris nodded. "Trauma surgeon. He started his residency as an ER doctor, but after a couple of years, redirected to trauma surgery. I never asked why."

"I haven't either." Theo shrugged. "Just a calling, likely. Dad does stuff on impulse a lot of the time. Remember when he thought it was a good idea to breed rabbits?"

The thought didn't process. "Rabbits? But you're . . ."

Iris snorted. "We know. The plus side? We didn't have to go very far for fresh meat that winter."

I shook my head. "But why?"

Theo shrugged. "Who knows?"

Talking about the past brought up a question I hadn't really considered before. "The twins said the pack killed our dad, but what happened to my mom?"

Both Theo and Iris sobered.

Theo ran a hand through his hair. "She died. A couple of months after Granddad's announcement to support Endicott. She seemed a little crazed, and I think it might have been the voodoo witch's blessing turning in or something."

"Oh." I didn't know what else to say.

"Did you want to come house hunting with us?" Iris gestured out the window. "We originally thought the apartments looked nice. But they're not really big enough for all of us."

Before I could answer, Theo held up a hand. "No pressure. You can tell us no."

Iris sniffed. "You can even bring along the twins. Since we're all family in some kind of way, it's only logical we try to get to know each other before we settle on mutual distaste."

"I can see what the plan is with the twins. Maybe we can try to have dinner or something." I didn't think either family would mind sharing a meal. The white elk that the twins, Mike, and Ronald caught on their jaunt to the mines was certainly large enough to feed us all.

The situation couldn't get any more awkward. How did I explain I had wolf shifters and cougar shifters as blood-related family to others?

Nicholas didn't care, but he was the best example of open-mindedness not prejudices.

"Great. You should get home and sleep. You look a little dead." Iris stood. "And I want to hit the slopes before Dad cuts me off."

"We can walk with you if you like." Theo copied his sister.

I shook my head. "I'm going to text Nicholas. He'll come pick me up. He dropped me off on the way in to the station."

"All right. We're still at the inn. You're welcome to come talk to us anytime." Theo pointed to the muffin remaining. "Eat that."

I watched them disappear up the block before texting Nicholas. All my life I'd lived as a nomad, never daring to dream for more than an escape from my present. For the first time since waking up memory-less in a hospital in Virginia, I looked forward to my future. I still had no memories of my childhood, but I didn't need them to enjoy today or my new family.

We hope you enjoyed these stories in the Havenwood Falls series featuring a variety of supernatural creatures. The series is a collaborative effort by multiple authors.
Books in the Havenwood Falls Sin & Silk series:

More books releasing on a monthly basis

Also try the signature line, Havenwood Falls, and the historical paranormal line, Legends of Havenwood Falls

Stay up to date at www.HavenwoodFalls.com

Subscribe to our reader group and receive free stories and more!

ABOUT THE AUTHOR

ONCE UPON A time, long, long ago, Victoria was born in sunny Florida, except it wasn't sunny; it was the middle of the night. Midnight actually, well, two minutes past, but she tried really hard for midnight.

Victoria has attended twenty-one schools in her lifetime. With all the continual switching around, she's relied on her imagination for friends and books for close companions. In high school she remained apart from the crowd and spent most of her time in the library, either reading or writing.

Currently, Victoria has set down roots in New York with her family. She still reads and writes every day. She finished her debut novel *Of Gaea* in the spring of 2013, its sequel *Of Sparta* in the winter of 2014, and has many other projects planned. Look forward to seeing more.

Social Media:

Facebook: facebook.com/V.Escobar.Writes
Website: vesccobarwrites.com
Tumblr: authorvescobar.tumblr.com
Pinterest: pinterest.com/vescobarwrites/

ACKNOWLEDGMENTS

I hate writing these things. I always forget someone.

Thank you, readers, for enjoying Audrey and Nicholas's story, and of course thank you, EJ, for allowing me the honor of writing Nicholas.

I have to say the Havenwood Falls group is one of the tightest cliques of people I've ever had the privilege of working with, and one of the friendliest. Thanks for letting me into your club and humoring the seven million questions.

Thank you, Kristie, for all your hard work, and making my words legible.

Until next time,

VE

AN EXCERPT

Stolen Wishes (A Havenwood Falls Sin & Silk Novella) by Victoria Flynn

After being gone for several decades, Gabriel Doyle feels drawn to his former hometown in Colorado. His memories are vague and blurry, but he can't resist the urge to go, especially when the woman in his dreams begins to appear in real life. What he's not so sure about is what he faces on his return—leading the Lilith Nest vampires.

Needing a fresh start, Alina Anand takes a nanny job for a mage family in Havenwood Falls. At first, life is great. She loves her charges and finds the town quaint and welcoming, but everything changes when her employers steal her amulet—and take control of her wish-granting powers. Bound to them by tradition, she has no choice but to serve them.

When their destinies collide, Gabriel and Alina discover a connection that goes beyond their undeniable passion. But to save Alina, Gabriel must decide whether to pick up the dark life of bloodshed and revenge he left behind, or to ask for help from those who demand sacrifice. Nothing in life is free. The star-crossed lovers must fight for what they desire most—to be who they are, love who they want, and escape the bonds of their pasts in a town that forgives little and forgets nothing.

STOLEN WISHES

BY VICTORIA FLYNN

GABRIEL

Her skin was smooth and flawless like Chinese porcelain, and the way her heart drummed excitedly in her chest when I touched her drove me wild. She was a drug I was hopelessly addicted to.

"I've missed you," she whispered, dropping the sheet she had wrapped around herself.

The scent of her arousal invaded my senses and blurred any clear thoughts. All-consuming, that was what the vixen was to me.

Tugging my shirt over my head and throwing it to the ground, I strode toward my prize. Her nipples were drawn up into tight buds as I crossed the expanse of my hotel suite to her. Oh yes, she wanted me. She rubbed her thighs together as if it could relieve the pressure of her desire.

"You're all I can think about. Even when I'm awake, I feel like I'm just passing the time until you're in my arms again," I confessed.

My nameless beauty closed the gap between us, nipping the tender flesh over my collar bone and sliding down me, sinking to her knees. Her hands worked quickly to free me from my slacks. My cock sprung free and her eyes devoured every inch. Her pink tongue swept over her lips, and her eyes dared me to deny her what she wanted.

"Hungry?" I teased, stepping out of my pants and fisting my throbbing cock.

She nodded slowly, leaning forward until her breath fanned over me, making me damn near lose control on the spot. Her fingers skimmed over my sensitive skin before wrapping around me securely. Her hand slid up and down my length lazily, and I let my eyes fall closed, relishing every second. Her hot, slick tongue traced the thick shaft from the bottom up, and her lips enveloped me as she reached the top.

"Fuck," I groaned, my hips flexing instinctively and driving me deeper into her mouth.

I could feel the muscles of her mouth stretch into a coy smile just before she set about her task, taking me in as deeply as she could. Pressure was growing low in my belly, and every nerve was firing like a Fourth of July display. Picking up the pace, her head bobbed up and down as she pushed me faster toward my peak. Her deft fingers worked furiously between her legs. It was a sight that would drive a lesser man to his knees with need, but she was mine, only mine, to savor.

She repeated the same pattern, taking me in deep and then flicking her succulent tongue over the head of my dick. The woman was driving me wild and playing me like a well-loved instrument. Her free hand snaked down, cupping my balls and dragging her nails over them, bringing me to my tipping point.

"Christ, you need to stop, or I'm going to come," I warned her, holding back and giving her plenty of time to release her hold, but she didn't.

Her devious eyes darted to my own, dancing with mirth as she sucked harder. I was a goner under her skilled touch. Not two minutes later, thick ropes of cum erupted from me, coating her throat as I roared in ecstasy. The vixen swallowed down every drop like she was starved for it, drawing it out until my last spasm faded.

She licked her lips with satisfaction, her heavy-lidded eyes betraying her arousal.

"I want more."

Drained of energy, I crossed to the bed and held my hand out to her. Just before she came close enough, the room faded to black, and she was torn away from me.

My eyes cracked open before I could reach her. The room was dark, but I could tell the sun was beginning to set. It was another dream.

Every day for months, the bronzed goddess had visited me and drawn me into her thrall. Women had thrown themselves at me, yet the nameless woman from my dreams had been all I could think about. Hell, my dick wouldn't even respond to another anymore, not of its own volition anyway. My cock was painfully hard, and my fangs dug into my lower lip with my desire, despite the exotic woman's absence.

I could still see her stunning figure standing before me as vividly as though it had just happened, begging me to come for her. Her sensuous voice called to me, telling me she was waiting for me in Havenwood Falls, and I couldn't live on dreams anymore. I had to know if she was real, no matter what.

∼

GABRIEL

There it was again. The relentless pull to leave. This time was different, though. This time, it whispered a name I'd heard before . . . in my dreams. My recurring vision came back to me. An exotic beauty and somewhere called Havenwood Falls. The name had been repeated until it was all I could think about. When I'd done a search, nothing had shown up. I decided to make some calls. Eventually, I'd been able to narrow it down to the mountains of Colorado. No one could remember the town, nor its location, but I'd been told at least twice that I should check out the majestic mountains of the western state. With the red-eye tickets booked, I gave my thoughts back to the beauty who'd been haunting me. I could still picture her sensual form standing before me in my Paris hotel room, whispering for me to come to her in the mysterious town. She was waiting for me.

In the many nights we'd shared, never had I learned her name. It tormented me incessantly. When I ventured out into the city, it never failed that I'd catch a glimpse of a woman who shared some feature with the woman I'd come to care for—long black hair like a raven's feather, a rich tan, eyes like a smooth cognac. Those women were never her.

I pushed the thoughts away, not wanting to obsess over the identity of the mystery woman more than I already had. Swirling my whiskey around the tumbler, I stood on my suite's balcony overlooking Montmartre.

Paris had grown gray with the late autumn season. Rain drizzled down on the city, and I found I wasn't sad to be leaving. When you lived as long as I had, cities like London, Rome, Paris, and Prague lost their luster.

Home.

It was an odd thought. The closest thing I'd ever had to a home had been with my closest friend and sire, Viktor. He'd settled somewhere in Colorado and started a small empire for himself.

He was gone now, which had been a large part of why I'd stayed away from America as long as I had. Would home still be home if the person who made it special was no longer there? That was still to be seen.

"Lorenzo!" I called out, striding into the parlor and abandoning the balcony overlooking the narrow streets of France.

"What can I do for you, sir?" the small Italian man chirped, appearing almost out of nowhere.

"You may let the staff know we will be departing for America in the coming week. Have you ever been to Colorado, Enzo?" I asked, loosening my tie.

"No, sir. This will be my first trip." His thick Italian accent was barely comprehensible. "I hope you'll let me know what to expect and what I should pack for."

"It's late autumn. The Colorado mountains are cold, damp, and could be snow-covered. Layers, my friend."

"*Grazie*, sir. I will make the necessary arrangements. May I ask why the sudden change in plans? I was under the impression we'd be staying in Paris until the end of January before continuing on to Amsterdam."

Lorenzo was good people and the only person I fully trusted. He was nearly forty and had been in my service since he'd reached adulthood. As a blood servant went, he was top notch, and as a friend, he was one of my closest. His family had served me since Viktor had raised me out of the gutter and turned me into a proper gentleman over three centuries earlier. Blend in, watch, find a weakness, and exploit it—those had been my first lessons. I'd done that when I'd stumbled across Alessio De Luca, Lorenzo's seventh great grandfather. He'd been able to do something I'd thought was lost to me since becoming a vampire: he could make me laugh. Instead of killing the poor bastard, I'd offered him a job. The rest, as they say, was history.

"It's hard to explain. I've always been a nomad. However, there's something different about Colorado. It's the closest thing I've ever had to a home, even more than Ireland," I joked, letting my natural brogue slip back into my words.

"How long?" Enzo asked, concern written in the shallow creases beginning to form from age.

Despite being a few hundred years younger than me, Lorenzo looked older than my frozen twenty-eight years.

"I haven't been home in more than forty years. Not since before Viktor passed," I answered, ignoring the pangs of loss that could still send me reeling, if I let them.

"Understandable, sir. He was a father to you, and that sort of grief is felt for a lifetime," he replied.

He was right. I knew Viktor was gone, but going home without his warm welcome would be difficult. That was the thing about vampires —we'd grieve a loss for centuries, because time no longer mattered. Things were felt on a deeper level because such things are fleeting.

"I suppose you're right, but there are other matters to tackle while on this trip," I answered, and there were.

Being a vampire came with its constraints, like not being able to walk in the daylight, but it also gave those like me ample time to grow a fortune. Unlike some, I'd grown with the times, seeing no point in dwelling on the inventions and ideals of the past. When the internet had come along, I'd invested, knowing that it would somehow change the future of the modern world. Then had come the capability to conduct such investments online, and I never needed to work again. When you've been around longer than the stock market itself, you pick up a thing or two about money, stock trends, and good investments. Having spent the better part of two centuries building a fortune, I was now in a position to make moves and flex my muscles. Everyone, regardless of species, could recognize that money was power, and whoever had the most made the rules of how the rest played the game.

"I'm sorry, Gabriel. I don't follow," Enzo said.

I frowned slightly, realizing I hadn't mentioned the dreams or the side trip.

"I apologize, old friend. Things have been difficult. These dreams I've been having . . . I've never experienced anything like them. Actually, I don't believe I remember ever dreaming until a few months ago."

"Would you like me to search the archives? Perhaps there could be an answer there as to what this means?"

I nodded. "Sure. Thank you, Lorenzo. That would be helpful, though my point was that in these dreams, a voice keeps saying *Havenwood Falls*. I think it's in Colorado, near Viktor's old home. I need to know if there's something to all of this there."

"I understand. I'll make the necessary preparations. In the meantime, you haven't fed in a few days," he stated, undoing the button holding his sleeve together.

"I've already booked our flights, but other transportation will need to be arranged."

Enzo pushed his sleeve up, exposing his arm to me. He sat on the sofa, leaving room for me to join him. A pinch in my gums was all I needed to know my fangs had extended, ready to feed. The tight hold I kept on the monster inside me slipped a little, and I pounced on Lorenzo's offering. My fangs tore through his flesh like a hot knife through butter. His blood was like cinnamon and cloves, spicy and aromatic. I drank until the beast inside me was sated and released before I'd taken too much. Like the professional he was, Enzo produced a small hanky and wiped the crimson smear at the edge of my mouth before wrapping his wound tightly. He rose a little unsteadily, my only indication that I'd gotten a little carried away this time. With a quick bow, Lorenzo turned and exited the room.

Shame coursed through me.

There was a time I wouldn't have felt anything for those I'd fed from. Anyone who was unlucky enough to cross my path was lower than me on the food chain; it was natural. That's what I'd told myself for years. Hell, I'd lived for the hunt. The feeling when life finally left someone and the light faded from their eyes had been a drug to me. Viktor and I had even gone to war on several occasions, making a game of killing our foes in the most imaginative way possible. Grown men had fallen in shreds at my feet. Then one day, all of that changed.

I couldn't put a finger on what had been the turning point for me, but after almost a century of living in a constant bloodbath, I'd found myself wanting more. Viktor was calculating. One always had to be on their toes around him. He'd taught me a lot, yet there no longer seemed to be a point to life without someone to share it with, on a different level. I wanted to watch art be born from a beautiful mind and bright thinkers rise to the famed pages of history. I wanted to experience it all as a free man.

As a mortal, I'd been nothing more than a slave. Despite the practice being considered illegal, I'd been taken after the soldiers slaughtered my mother at the Siege of Galway, when King Charles II's men came to topple Catholicism in Ireland. My father had succumbed to the pox a year earlier, along with my little sister, Mary. In my twenty-eight years as a human, I'd never known what it was to do as I pleased. As a vampire, I was desperate for a taste of freedom.

My change of heart had driven a wedge between Viktor and me, but eventually, he came to understand that I needed more than he could give me. Like a baby bird, I had reached the time to leave the nest and spread my wings. So, I did.

In my arrogance and stubbornness, I'd lost almost thirty years with my sire. He'd been gone more than ten years now, lost to the insanity that came with drinking drug-tainted blood. I couldn't help feeling responsible for it. If I had been there, would things have gone differently for him? I'd spent far too long running away from my past, and it was time to go home. It was time to say my final goodbyes to Viktor Azimov, my father and sire, and it was time to look to the future and the mysteries that Havenwood Falls would offer.

Purchase *Stolen Wishes* wherever books are sold.

www.ingramcontent.com/pod-product-compliance
Lightning Source LLC
Chambersburg PA
CBHW021526250626
47154CB00006BA/1994